AF174048

ZERO ECHO SHADOW PRIME

PETER SAMET

Cover design by Mark Landry

ISBN: 978-0-9960342-1-0

For Jing

1 ○ DIGITIZATION

CHAPTER 1

ECHO

KILL THEM ALL OR FEEL WITHDRAWAL.

The woman stared at the bold red letters on the ceiling above her bed. At first, they were nothing more than a curious abstraction, but as she struggled to recall their meaning, she realized she couldn't recall anything else. Not her name, her life story, or why she found herself in this particular bedroom.

The woman sat up and stretched her arms, stiffening into a giant *X*. It took her a few seconds to register the anomaly: *I have four arms.* She shrieked at the parasite limbs dangling under her armpits. Her top two hands seized the bottom left arm, trying to yank it out, while the bottom right battered the pile. The skirmish quickly became too painful to continue, and as she rubbed her tender arm sockets, the woman couldn't help but laugh. Surely, she'd had four arms her entire life. And yet she couldn't shake the feeling that two of them did not belong.

The woman got out of bed and surveyed the room for clues to her whereabouts. The walls were adorned with generic landscape paintings and a fresh coat of baby-blue paint. The armoire was polished and bare. The closet was empty. Not a single speck of dust floated in the morning sunbeam. Aside from the red stain above the bed, the room looked completely sterile, as if it were pulled from a furniture catalog. *Where am I?*

"Come to the mirror."

The voice shook the walls, but when the woman looked around, she found herself alone. A full-length mirror hung from the door. She crept toward it and saw her reflection for the first time. A black skin-tight suit revealed the curves of her slender body. Her face was soft and pale, framed by long black hair. The only dose of color came from her eyes: a vibrant turquoise.

"Greetings, echo," the voice boomed.

The woman shifted focus to the room behind her reflection and spotted a hulking creature, a beast-man with the body of a human and the head of a ram. She spun around, but the creature was no longer there. Her eyes returned to the mirror, and the creature reappeared. She quickly realized that he existed solely in the mirror.

"I have limited influence over this world," the beast-man said. "That is why I must speak to you this way."

"Who are you?" the woman asked, examining the creature more closely. He was nearly nude, with only a decorative loincloth draped around his bronze muscular frame. His eyes were sharp, and his massive horns curved around his skull like an ornamental warrior's helmet.

"My name is Khnum," he said with a voice so deep the woman wondered if she heard him not through her ears, but through the rattle of her bones. He continued, "My job is to provide you with basic information to help you perform your duty."

"What duty? Where am I? *Who* am I?" The woman didn't realize how starved she was for answers until she voiced the questions.

"Echo," Khnum replied.

"Echo? Do you mean *I'm* Echo or I'm *in* Echo?"

"Both. You are on planet Echo, and you are an echo of the Archetype."

"How did I get here? Why can't I remember anything?"

"I'm sorry. I cannot give you any more information on that topic."

"Why not?"

"I am not permitted."

"Not permitted by whom?"

"I cannot say."

The woman sighed. Already, she knew this was going to be a frustrating conversation. "What is this 'Archetype'?"

"A single individual from which many echoes were derived."

"Can I meet her?"

"No."

"Why not?"

"I cannot say."

"Is she the one telling you what you can and cannot say?"

"I cannot say."

The woman took a step back from the mirror to rethink her strategy. She was getting nowhere with these pinpoint questions. Better to go broad. "Tell me everything you *can* say."

"There are one billion echoes on planet Echo. Each was spawned from the Archetype. Each was given one special trait. The sole duty of an echo is to kill other echoes."

KILL THEM ALL OR FEEL WITHDRAWAL. The woman's thoughts returned to that message above her bed. She grew concerned. *"Kill?* But…that's crazy. I haven't even met these other echoes."

"You will."

"Why would I kill them?"

"If you don't, you will experience withdrawal symptoms. They will progressively get worse until you make a kill. Then the cycle will reset and start anew."

"What are the withdrawal symptoms?"

"Anger, anxiety, paranoia, hallucinations, pain…"

The woman placed a hand over her racing heart. She was already starting to feel anger and anxiety, but she assumed that was due to her frustration with Khnum. "I'm not going to kill anyone," she insisted.

"You will."

o o o

The woman left the room and spotted another echo down the hallway. The two echoes turned to face each other. In most respects, they were identical—same face, same turquoise eyes, same body suit—but they possessed different special traits. The new echo had one pair of arms instead of two. She also didn't have any hands. Instead, thick metal cylinders extended from both her wrists.

"Hi," the first echo said, waving her two right hands. "I'd introduce myself, but…I guess we have the same name."

The second echo smiled. "Then we should probably give ourselves new names."

"Okay, you can call me Four Arms." She winced as soon as the name passed her lips. "That's not very creative, is it?"

"Works for me. You can call me Flame."

"Flame?"

"My hands, they're flamethrowers."

"Really? Can I see?" Four Arms asked, with eager eyes.

"Um, I probably shouldn't fire them off again," Flame said, "but here, take a look." She opened the door beside her.

Four Arms walked down the hallway and peeked inside Flame's room. It was identical to her own—same furniture, same arrangement, same full-length mirror—but Flame's bedsheets were a semicharred mess in the middle of the floor.

"Luckily, I was able to stomp it out," Flame said. "Otherwise, the whole house might have burned down."

"Your special trait seems a lot more useful than mine."

Flame gave her a quizzical look.

"I mean in a fight," Four Arms added. "Not that we are going to fight or anything." She turned bright red, worried that she was unintentionally provoking her housemate.

"'Kill them all or feel withdrawal'?" Flame said, rolling her eyes.

Four Arms nodded.

"Well, flamethrowers may be more useful in a fight," Flame agreed, "but I have a crazy itch on my face that I'm too afraid to scratch."

Four Arms laughed. "That, I can help you with." She raised all four hands and wiggled her fingers.

Flame smiled. "Great. We should definitely be friends."

o o o

Four Arms and Flame walked downstairs into the living room and found a third echo, who quickly grabbed a fireplace poker and backed up against the far wall.

"Don't come any closer!" she pleaded, waving the weapon in the air.

"Don't worry," Four Arms said. "We come as friends."

"I've heard Khnum. I've seen the painting. I'm not taking any chances." The echo was practically hyperventilating, her eyes wide with terror. Unlike Four Arms and Flame, she didn't seem to possess any special traits. She was *normal.*

"Painting? What painting?" Four Arms asked.

Normal extended a trembling finger toward the fireplace mantel.

Four Arms moved farther into the room to get a better look. When she saw the painting above the mantel, she froze.

The rich oils set a dark scene in which Four Arms was impaled by another echo. A fireplace poker busted through her sternum, causing an eruption of blood and fractured bone matter. Her four arms splayed in agony.

Four Arms cringed at the sight. She raised a hand to her sternum. Obviously, she was uninjured in real life, but her heart was pounding nonetheless. Her focus narrowed on the murder weapon. *Why a poker? That can't be a coincidence.* She shifted her gaze between the killer in the painting and the poker-wielding echo in the room. The commonalities went beyond choice of weaponry. They were both featureless, both Normal.

"It doesn't mean anything," Flame said. "It's just a painting."

"Maybe to you it is," Four Arms replied, "but our housemate

grabbed the poker after viewing it. I'd like to know why."

"To keep *her* away from me!" Normal cried, pointing at Flame.

"Why her?" Four Arms asked, confused. "She's not even in the painting."

"Are you blind? She's clearly roasting me with her flamethrowers."

Four Arms looked at the painting again. Perhaps she'd missed something during her first viewing. So she scanned every inch of it. Flame was nowhere to be found.

"I think we all see the painting differently," Flame told Four Arms. "In my version, I see you and me. You are holding down my arms with one set of hands and strangling me with the other. What's in your version?"

The four-armed echo finally started to understand the function of the painting. She grabbed the frame and tore it from the wall. "Doesn't matter. We are not going to fight each other." She turned to Normal and said, "So put down the poker and let's talk about this."

"No." Normal tightened her grip on the poker. "I mean, we can talk, but I'm keeping this."

"Why?"

"Because I am defenseless. You have four arms. She has flamethrowers. I have nothing."

"Nothing?" Four Arms asked. "Are you sure?"

"Pretty sure."

"She's like the Archetype," Flame said.

"I'm not the Archetype," Normal insisted. "I have no idea what's going on. Just like you two."

Four Arms studied her housemates. Normal clung to her

defensive stance. Flame's pilot lights were burning. Four Arms realized that her own fists were clenched. She had to make a conscious decision to relax them. "Okay," Four Arms relented. "Keep your poker. But just so we're clear, we mean you no harm."

Normal's grim expression did not waver. "Are you trying to convince *me*," she said, "or yourselves?"

o o o

The three echoes ventured into the outside world. The suburban street was lined with identical houses, all painted white with red trim, as well as freshly cut lawns, colorful flowerbeds, and white picket fences. There were no leaves on the ground, no chips in the paint, no cracks in the cement, no potholes in the asphalt. The world looked brand new.

A small congregation of echoes had gathered in the middle of the street, and their numbers steadily grew as other echoes left their houses—mostly in groups of three—to join them. Just as Khnum had said, each echo possessed a special trait. Some were defensive in nature: metal scales, collar plating, limber legs. Some were offensive: chain-gun arms, razor-sharp fingers, a chrome-whip tail. Some were truly bizarre: transparent skin, segmented eyes, feathered antennae.

Four Arms scrutinized each one at first for potential threats, but then she realized she could probably take some of them. The echo with the long neck was vulnerable to strangulation. The one with the bloated feet surely couldn't run fast. The half-sized echo—

No. Four Arms flushed her mind of violent thoughts. She

refused to play Khnum's game. These echoes were probably just like her—anxious, confused, and full of questions. Her best hope for answers—indeed, anyone's best hope for answers—lay through collaboration. So, she forced a cordial smile and set foot in their direction. Flame and Normal followed in tow.

The crowd centered on a beautiful echo with bioluminescent skin, whom Four Arms silently named Lustrous. The other echoes seemed to be drawn by her sapphire glow, but Lustrous's own attention was stolen by the frantic whispers of Sharp Teeth, whom Four Arms named for her monstrous, jagged mouth. Their conversation quickly escalated to the point where everyone could hear.

"What do we do then!?" Sharp Teeth demanded.

"We keep our emotions in check," Lustrous replied, doing a poor job of following her own advice.

"That's it? That's your plan?"

"I never said I had a plan. But we won't be able to form one if we don't calm ourselves."

"How am I supposed to calm myself when everyone is itching to kill me?"

"And why do you assume that?"

"Because…" Sharp Teeth looked around, suddenly aware of her eavesdroppers, and delivered the rest of her response in a guarded whisper.

Lustrous turned to the group and announced, "Listen, everyone. Before we can tackle the questions of why we are here or who we are, we need to learn how to keep our withdrawal symptoms in check. Nothing good can arise until that happens."

"And how exactly do we do that?" the echo with the antennae asked.

"I don't know," Lustrous admitted. "Does anyone have any suggestions? Has anyone found anything that works?"

"We should ask Khnum," a random voice shouted.

"Screw Khnum!" another voice shouted back. "Would we be feeling these withdrawal symptoms if he didn't plant the idea in our heads?"

The crowd debated this question back and forth, with each echo topping the last in vitriolic aggression, until finally Lustrous quieted everyone down. "Khnum said it himself; his main job is to get us to kill each other. So he can't be trusted. Any other suggestions?"

Nobody spoke up, but Four Arms began to hear whispers around her. She had a difficult time figuring out what her fellow echoes were saying, but she was able to pick out one recurring word: *Archetype.*

Lustrous heard the murmurs too and asked, "Is there something you guys would like to say?"

A spiral-horned echo pointed to Normal and said, "This one here looks like the Archetype." The crowd backed away from Normal, leaving her to cower in plain sight.

Lustrous asked her, "What is your trait? Your special ability?"

Normal raised her fireplace poker. "I can whack people."

The crowd laughed. Lustrous smiled as well. Sharp Teeth, on the other hand, scowled and said, "She asked you a serious question."

"I don't have one," Normal replied.

"So, then, are you the Archetype?" Sharp Teeth asked.

"Not to my knowledge."

"But you can't deny that you fit her description."

"She's not the Archetype!" Four Arms shouted. She was

afraid of where this conversation was heading.

"And you know this *how*?" Sharp Teeth asked.

"She's my housemate. She woke up the same way we did. We are all on the same side."

"If we are on the same side, she should tell us what she knows," Sharp Teeth said.

"She doesn't know anything," Four Arms insisted.

"The four-armed echo is correct," Lustrous interjected. "This line of questioning won't get us anywhere."

Sharp Teeth turned to Lustrous. "So that's how it's going to be around here? We are simply going to ignore all possible leads?"

"She says she's not the Archetype," Lustrous replied. "I believe her."

A random echo shouted, "What about the poker?" Others in the crowd voiced their solidarity around this question.

"Yes," Sharp Teeth said. "Who were you planning to 'whack' with that thing?"

"Nobody," Normal replied.

"She carries it for safety," Four Arms said. Then she addressed the crowd: "And based on the hateful stares you all are giving us, I don't blame her for having it."

The crowd's murmur died down. Four Arms was able to intimidate most of them into withdrawing eye contact.

"Like the four-armed echo said, we are all on the same side," Lustrous assured the crowd. "There is no need for a weapon." She turned to Normal and softened her voice. "I won't let anyone hurt you. So why don't you hand over your weapon? Consider it a gesture of goodwill. Show everyone that violence is not an inevitability."

"How about you show some good will by leaving us alone?" Four Arms said.

"Let the echo speak for herself," Sharp Teeth snapped.

Normal didn't say anything. She simply extended her hands and presented her poker.

Four Arms pushed Normal's hands down and said, "No, we aren't giving them anything!" Four Arms stood in front of her housemate and extended her arms in a defensive *X*.

"I don't want to fight you," Lustrous said. "But one of you will give me that poker." She slowly approached them.

Four Arms and Normal backed up against the crowd. They were trapped on all sides. She felt increasingly claustrophobic and vulnerable. Lustrous was trying to take advantage of them, trying to shame them, trying to control them. If Four Arms didn't hold her ground now, she might never have a chance to reclaim it. She started swinging her arms to create space. The crowd pushed back. At some point, she lost her sense of direction and one of her elbows collided with Lustrous's jaw.

The rest happened quickly. Lustrous lunged after Four Arms. Four Arms fought her off, but Sharp Teeth jumped on her back and took a bite of flesh out of her neck. Four Arms cried out in pain. Before Sharp Teeth could take a second bite, Flame washed her in a stream of fire. Sharp Teeth dived to the ground to roll out the flames.

Four Arms grew dizzy and sank to her knees. She tried to stem the flow of blood with her hand, but most of it oozed through her fingers. Lustrous moved in for another attack. Four Arms countered, pulled her to the ground, and climbed on top of her.

Holding Lustrous down with her bottom two hands, Four

Arms strangled her with the top two. Lustrous kicked and flailed, but she could not break free. Her only hope was the wound in Four Arms's neck, which gushed blood unabated. It became a race to see who would die first. But Four Arms was consumed with rage, and she held firm. She hammered Lustrous's skull against the pavement, hoping to accelerate her death. Lustrous's face turned a deeper shade of blue. Her muscles jolted one last time. Her chest sank, and her pupils dilated.

Four Arms released her victim and collapsed on top of her. The warm mess dripping from her neck faded from importance as she labored to fill her lungs. Each breath was richer and more satisfying than the last. She couldn't consume the air fast enough. Her pace quickened until a spark of euphoria pulsed through her core. She arched her back and expelled a silent scream as every muscle in her body spasmed with pleasure. All of her withdrawal symptoms—the anger, the fear, the paranoia—evaporated away.

Once the sensation subsided, Four Arms was able to look at her victim with a sober mind. Lustrous was dead. She scanned the faces of the crowd. Most of them were in shock, still processing what had happened.

Four Arms scrambled to her feet, worried about retaliation, but a loud crackle directed everyone's attention back to Lustrous. A stream of blue light curled around the dead echo's limbs and collected inside her chest. The energy pulsed a few times before expanding into a large static bubble. The force knocked Four Arms backward into her fellow echoes, who reluctantly braced her fall.

The blue bubble cradled Lustrous and levitated her above

the crowd. Although her body was cast in silhouette, her morphological changes were visible to all. Bumps sprouted from both sides of her torso and grew into a second set of arms. The process took about twenty seconds, after which the bubble dissolved, and Lustrous dropped to her feet. She straightened her back and heaved her first breath of renewed life.

Everyone froze, waiting to see what Lustrous would do next. She had just become the first echo with two special traits: bioluminescent skin *and* four limbs. She wiggled her new fingers, pumped all four fists in sequence, and swung her arms; but her learning period was brief, and her eyes flared with vengeance as she picked Four Arms out of the crowd.

Four Arms nearly tripped trying to back away. Her moment of ecstasy did nothing to heal her neck, and she had lost a great deal of blood.

Lustrous charged, Four Arms planted her heels, and the two echoes locked in an eight-arm grapple. This time, Four Arms could not match her opponent's strength. She fell to the ground and Lustrous climbed on top of her.

Four Arms was only able to put up a weak defense. Soon, Lustrous was pummeling her murderer unimpeded. Four Arms would have quickly perished, but Normal stepped in and swung the fireplace poker across Lustrous's face.

"Get out of here!" Normal shouted to her housemate.

Chaos erupted. Normal was tackled by a spiny-skinned echo. Flame turned her burners on the crowd. Everyone joined in the fight. It was echo against echo against echo.

Four Arms searched for an escape route, but her eyes were drenched with blood, and she wasn't even sure she could get to her feet. She planted her heel against the pavement and pushed as hard as she could. Her legs wobbled violently as she rose into a crouch, but her energy reserves quickly evaporated, and she collapsed back to the ground.

Four Arms rested her head in a pool of blood and focused on a small patch of blue sky beyond the chaos. *This is it.* She relinquished herself to death's embrace as the crowd swept over her.

CHAPTER 2

ARCHETYPE

Charlie puked half her breakfast into the toilet, gripping the lid and moaning. She would have screamed except her throat had already been stripped raw from nine days of this madness. The first symptom had been a sharp pain in her stomach. Then the spiteful organ threw a digestive tantrum. Now Charlie spent the better part of her mornings shuttling food in both directions. What goes down must come up. Her body operated under a new law of physics.

"I don't know why I even bother to eat anymore," Charlie muttered before the acrid smell tripped her gag reflex once again, and she relinquished the second half of her breakfast.

"Maybe you're pregnant," said Alan, her omnipresent friend.

"Last time I checked, you need to have sex to get pregnant," Charlie murmured into the bowl.

"Should we run a health scan?"

"No health scans. I thought I told you this." Charlie's eyes were streaming from the gastric fumes. She threw out her hand and swiped at the toilet-paper dispenser, only to find the entire roll missing.

She blotted her eyes on her shoulder and searched the room for the toilet-paper thief. She found it immediately: a hermit-crab-styled robot with a papier-mâché shell. It was crawling—no, it was *strutting*—in plain sight, flaunting its dominion over Charlie's bathroom. "Little fucker!" she whispered.

The thief was a Replicator, a member of a colony of self-replicating robots. Charlie designed and built the prototype months ago, giving it one main directive: to create offspring. One robot soon became two. Two became four. Six generations later, her apartment looked like Swiss cheese. The little robots had punched holes into the furniture, the cookware, the bathroom fixtures, the electrical wiring, everything.

Charlie snatched the thief and studied it. Its legs were made of fiberglass, probably from the bathtub. Its antennae were made from toothbrush bristles. The outer shell was fashioned from many fine layers of tissue and cardboard. Despite its crime, Charlie couldn't help but marvel at the little guy. Such bold choices in construction material.

"You have less than ninety minutes till your interview," Alan reminded her.

"I know." Charlie gently placed the Replicator back on the floor and patted its shell.

She marched into her bedroom and took a quick survey. The room was another refutation of the laws of physics. Nearly everything Charlie owned was located on the floor in a giant pile of laundry and machine parts, almost as if the pull of gravity was stronger in this one room and her possessions couldn't help but slip into a lower energy state. Down was the new up. Up was the new down.

"Where's my red dress?" Charlie wondered out loud.

"You mean your only dress?" Alan said. "When was the last time you wore it?"

Charlie smiled. It was a trick question, of course. She had never worn the dress. Yet, it wasn't in her closet where she expected it to be. "Monkey, where's my dress?" Charlie called out. A large bulge appeared in the center of the laundry pile. It thumped twice, then deflated.

"I think you buried him," Alan said.

A multijointed, robotic appendage sprang free from the laundry. It flung a few shirts into the air in an effort to excavate the rest of itself. Monkey was no more sophisticated than a housekeeper bot, and he looked like a walking end table, but he was good at dealing with environmental quandaries. He loved to climb things—trees, lampposts, cars, people—hence the name. Unfortunately, he was also a big robot, more chimp than monkey. So to mitigate property damage costs, Charlie kept him secluded in her apartment.

Monkey rose to his feet with Charlie's dress serendipitously draped over his head. He tried to shake it off to no avail.

"Thank you, Monkey!" Charlie lifted the dress into the air, and that's when she noticed the giant hole in the middle.

"The Replicators strike again," Alan noted.

Somewhere in the apartment hid a very fashionable little robot with a red silk shell. Charlie shrugged and tossed the dress aside. "Jeans, it is," she said. She dug a pair out of the pile and climbed into them.

"Before you leave, you must do something with that hair,"

Alan said.

Charlie stepped in front of a full-length mirror. Alan was right. Her hair was a travesty, wild by neglect rather than intention. In fact, her entire appearance was reminiscent of a—

"Vagrant, vagabond, drifter, crazy person—" Alan chimed in.

"Yes," Charlie agreed without a fight. She glanced at Alan, who looked so dapper with his clean haircut and tailored tweed suit. The difference between the two of them was striking. "You know, you're making me look even worse by comparison," she told him. "Maybe you should take off that jacket and tussle your hair a bit."

"The American public will judge you independently of how I look."

"Jeez, well, when you put it that way..." Charlie huffed.

She returned to the bathroom and picked up a hairbrush. Her stomach clenched as she tugged through her knots. Chunks of matted hair fell into the sink. "Owww, shit!" A sharp abdominal pain forced her to stop. Her intestines felt mangled, as if caught in a blender blade. She gritted her teeth and slapped the hairbrush against the edge of the sink.

"You should let me do the health scan," Alan said.

"No scans," Charlie gasped as her face tightened and her eyes flooded.

"I'm really worried about you."

Charlie took a few deep breaths and eased herself back into an upright position. The pain slowly evaporated. "I'll be fine. It's probably just a stomach bug."

"A *nine*-day stomach bug?"

"I'll be fine!" she insisted.

She took another look in the mirror. She never really thought much about her appearance. In most ways, she was hopelessly unremarkable. Yet one feature stood out. When Charlie wasn't lost in melancholy, when she held her head up, when she allowed people to see the life in her face, she sometimes received compliments on her bright turquoise eyes. They were vestiges of a former life, telegraphing a vitality she no longer possessed.

Charlie was grateful the "stomach bug" had spared her fairest feature. The rest of her face was a different matter, with her sunken cheekbones, dark circles beneath her eyes, and of course, that tangled mop of hair. She tossed the brush into the sink.

"This is a project I don't have time for," she announced and left the bathroom. "Time?" she asked as she sped down the hallway toward the apartment building's front entrance.

"We have about an hour," Alan said, two steps behind her.

"Cab?"

"It's here."

Just as they were about to reach the double doors, the building manager blocked their path. Her hulking body eclipsed most of the sunlight in the hallway, and her hateful scowl pressed Charlie to give ground.

"I had a tough day at work," the manager began in an accusing tone. "I wanted to relax on my balcony. At my age, I feel like I've earned that right. Then, when I go to sit down, one of the legs of my chair snapped completely in half. Now why do you suppose *that* happened?"

"Um—" Alan was about to say something rude, but Charlie shot him a silencing glare.

The manager held up a glass jar and said, "I found this

crawling nearby. What the hell is this thing?"

A Replicator sat inside the jar, playing innocent. Its shell was made of a fine silver-gray wood. "Oooh, is that teak?" Charlie blurted. She tried to reach into the jar, but the manager tucked it back under her arm.

"No, I'm keeping this thing as evidence," she said. "This is coming out of your deposit."

"We really need to go," Alan reminded Charlie.

"Okay, that's fine," Charlie told the manager as she shuffled around her. "I'll pay for whatever." Dashing out the door, she was elated that her robot babies were starting to discover the wider world of greater Los Angeles.

o o o

The cab dropped Charlie and Alan at the main gate of Rivir Picture Studios with thirty minutes to spare. They trekked farther into the lot toward a central courtyard, trying to avoid the chaotic ballet of motorized carts zipping in every direction. Everyone seemed to know where they were going but Charlie.

"We're looking for stage 3," Charlie told Alan. She surveyed the area and didn't find any buildings that looked like stages.

"It's all the way on the other side of the lot," Alan said. "We probably should have taken the north entrance."

"How was I supposed to know this place would be so big?"

When they arrived at the courtyard, a Shadow spun out of the ground in the way Shadows usually do, like swirling down an invisible sink drain, only in reverse.

"Welcome to Rivir Picture Studios," the Shadow announced gleefully. "Can I direct your visit?" The Shadow was a holographic representation of Lala, the cartoon space dog. Lala was the star of an early morning TV show and a favorite among the two-to-five age set. She was based on Laika, the real-life dog, who in 1957 became the first animal to enter Earth's orbit. Unfortunately, Laika had died shortly after the launch. This fictional Lala character, on the other hand, didn't die but rather took an extended trip around the solar system. Upon returning to Earth, Lala decided to use her experience for good, to teach kids about space and take them on galactic adventures of their own.

"Stage 3?" Charlie submitted.

"Oh! Are you here to view the taping of the Paul Renner Show?" Lala asked with ingratiating enthusiasm.

"I'm actually going to be *on* the show. I'm a guest," Charlie said.

"One moment please." Lala froze for a second, then asked, "Charlotte Nobunaga?"

"Yes."

"You're late. Angela is waiting for you. Come with me."

An unmanned motorized cart zipped in their direction and screeched to a halt. Lala jumped in the front seat. Charlie and Alan climbed in the back.

As the cart darted down alleyways, hugged turns, and dodged set workers, Lala turned around and said, "Charlotte, I see that your Rivir profile settings have accidentally been switched to private."

"No, that's definitely not an accident," Charlie said.

"That's too bad. Unfortunately, I can't give personalized recommendations without accessing your profile, but our fall lineup is packed with smart, groundbreaking shows that everyone would enjoy. Have you ever wondered what it's like to be a top-secret government agent?"

Charlie sighed. "Can you please not talk? I have a lot on my mind." It was a partial truth. Charlie had so much to ponder—what would Paul Renner ask? what would she say? would she gaffe in front of millions of people?—that her brain gridlocked. The only thing she could think about was how much she couldn't think.

"A lot on your mind?" Lala asked. "You should download the Super Secretary Shadow-Skill. This incredible new Skill from Rivir will turn your Shadow into—"

"I'm not interested," Charlie insisted. She rubbed her stomach, feeling the nausea return.

Thankfully, the ride was short. They soon arrived at stage 3, and Lala signed off. "Thank you, and please enjoy the rest of your visit at Rivir Picture Studios." She waved and spun back into the ground—again, like swirling into a sink drain but this time in the correct direction.

A middle-aged woman rushed out of the sound stage to greet the two. "Charlie Nobunaga?" she called out.

"Yes," Charlie said.

The woman shook Charlie's hand aggressively. Beads of sweat covered her brow. "I'm Angela. We talked on the phone."

"Nice to meet you."

"I see you didn't go through hair and makeup yet. We scheduled an hour of prep, but no matter, twenty minutes should be doable."

"I'm sorry," Charlie said. She had the sudden urge to bury her entire head in a deep bucket hat.

"It's okay. You're here now. Come with me."

Angela barreled down a series of hallways; Charlie and Alan hustled to keep up. "Will I have a chance to meet Mr. Renner before the interview?" Charlie asked.

"No time, sweetie," Angela said.

The group entered a small makeup room. The hairstylist on duty almost choked on his latte when he saw Charlie's appearance.

"Can you fix it?" Angela asked.

"Um, well…" the stylist sputtered, "she's got this young mad scientist thing going on. If anything, maybe we should go crazier. Make it a 'choice.' Hold on."

Charlie took a seat. The stylist pulled a can of spray out of his utility belt and grabbed a chunk of her hair. She winced as he tugged her head this way and that.

While Angela was on the phone and the stylist was doing his thing, Alan sat beside Charlie and whispered, "Are you nervous?"

"Yeah, kinda," Charlie replied. "You?"

"I'm essentially a prop. You're the star. All eyes will be on you."

"Is this your idea of a pep talk?"

Alan laughed. "Don't worry, you'll shine out there. Then everyone will get to see the Charlie I know and love."

She smiled. At least she could take comfort in the fact that Alan would be at her side.

The stylist released Charlie's head. He took a step back to inspect his work. "Ugh, that's absolutely horrid!"

"We gotta run with it," Angela said and shooed the deflated stylist out of the room. She pointed her index finger at Charlie. "You're on in five. You'll enter the stage by yourself." Angela redirected her finger toward Alan. "You'll be introduced later in the segment. Hold on." She placed her finger against her ear, indicating a phone call, and migrated to the other side of the room.

Charlie whispered to Alan, "So, you never answered the question. Are you nervous?"

"Of course I am." He smirked. "That's how you made me."

"You ready?"

Alan nodded.

Charlie issued the command: "Alan, spin, no eyes."

Just like Lala the Space Dog, Alan spun into the ground.

Charlie opened a private, telepathic conversation.

{Charlie_Nobunaga:\mindspace>

Charlie: Still there?

Alan: Yup.

Charlie: Okay, just wait for my command, I guess.}

Charlie was led to the back of the Paul Renner set. Random crew people zipped past her as they prepared for taping. On the other side of the curtain, she could hear the studio audience settling.

At the same time, her stomach was *un*settling. Charlie clawed at her belly, hoping to stem the inevitable progression. The dreaded stab came next. She lurched over and stumbled a bit, losing her sense of balance. She could faintly hear Angela raising a voice of concern. The rest of the backstage clamor faded away. The polished floor swished below Charlie. She pleaded with herself, *Not here, anywhere but here.* A violent torrent rose inside her body. She heaved. A few drops of saliva fell from her lip. More wanted to come out, but she had nothing left to give.

"Five!" A man yelled in the distance. Charlie perked her ears up. "Four!" The pain in her belly was subsiding. "Three!" Charlie took a deep breath and straightened her spine. She shook off the delirium. "Two!" The world returned. She was back.

The jazz band started playing. The audience clapped and hooted.

Backstage, all eyes were on Charlie—the cameramen, the grips, the production assistants, everyone.

"Are we good?" Angela asked with a hopeful grimace. The poor woman's face had drained of color, as if she were the sick one.

Charlie nodded. She was good. At least, for now.

Paul Renner's famous nasal voice hushed the crowd. "Hey, welcome back. My guest tonight is someone who's been dominating the headlines lately. Winner of the 2045 Rivir Prize, the prestigious Turing Test Competition. The fact that she won the test is not remarkable as much as *how* she won it. Oh, and she's only eighteen years old. Please welcome to the show, Charlie Nobunaga."

"You're on," Angela whispered, and she gave Charlie a gentle shove in the direction of the curtain.

Charlie walked on stage and was instantly blinded by the wall of light. The studio audience slowly came into view as her pupils contracted. She gave them a dorky wave. Her breath was remarkably calm and steady. Perhaps her nerves were cleared by the stomach attack.

She sat down at the desk, opposite of Paul Renner. He was

the hip, intellectual type in a sharp suit with a wacky bow tie. Charlie didn't watch a lot of talk television, but when she did, she usually watched Renner. His program was smarter than most. It was the only reason she'd agreed to be on the show.

"Love the hair," Renner said.

Charlie's image appeared on the large center-stage display. She cringed at the sight. The hairstylist had been right; she did look horrid. "Um, thanks," Charlie replied. "We were going for the mad-scientist look."

"It totally works," Renner said. A virtual copy of *Time* magazine appeared above the desk next to him. He read aloud the magazine's headline: "'God is a Freshman at Caltech.' Appropriate moniker?"

Charlie hated that cover. Its central image was Charlie and Alan touching fingers in a similar manner to God and Adam in the Sistine Chapel. It was all so melodramatic. "Well, they got the freshman part right," she said. The audience was gracious enough to laugh at her joke.

"Modesty, I like that. So…" Renner shifted his posture, signaling that he was getting down to business. He proceeded to address the audience more than Charlie. "We're all familiar with Shadows. They assist with daily tasks, take dictation, monitor our vitals—for some, they administer mood enhancers…"

The audience laughed. A year and a half ago, Renner had been indicted with illegal Shadow doping. Shadows were known to facilitate dopamine production in their user's brain, though it was not exactly an out-of-the-box feature. Renner's case was ultimately thrown out of court, and he had since taken the scandal in stride, incorporating it into his onscreen persona.

"Shadows are always around us," Renner continued. "They

are inside of us, in our smart cells. But they are quite stupid when it comes to that very basic human activity—no, I'm not talking about sex, although that's a limitation as well." The audience guffawed. Renner tried to wave them down. "This is just from reports I've read. I know nothing about it personally. No, I'm referring to a Shadow's ability to *con-ver-sate*, to forge meaningful human connections." Renner pivoted away from the audience and addressed Charlie directly: "How is Alan different from any other Shadow in this regard?"

The air drained from Charlie's lungs. *Now*, she was nervous. She didn't have much practice talking about her work. "Um, well, historically speaking, the paradigm for intelligent agents has been nondirective."

"Non-dir-*what*?"

"Nondirective. They are essentially stateless."

"Stateless? Charlie, our audience is primarily *English*-speaking," Renner quipped to audience laughter.

"Right." Charlie's voice quavered a bit. She straightened her back and took a deep breath. "What I mean by *stateless* is…their emotion states do not change. Your Shadow's personality, his mood, his feelings toward you—they're the same on Monday as they are on Wednesday. It doesn't matter if the two of you had a fight on Tuesday. Or shared a laugh. Or shared some deep revelation. *You* change, but the Shadow never does."

"It's a perpetual amnesiac. It has no memory."

"Well, that's not entirely true. Shadows have memory. In fact, they have a larger capacity than the human brain. But they can only remember facts, not emotions. Or, at least, not in any kind of convincing way."

"And you've found a way to change that?"

"I think so."

"Well, let's see." Renner turned to the audience and said with gusto, "Do you guys want to see Alan?"

The audience replied with a unanimous, "Yes!"

"Awesome," Renner said. "But first, we have a replay of Alan's Rivir Prize-winning performance."

The center-stage display switched from an angle of Charlie's face to a video of the Rivir Prize Competition.

The stage looked like a typical mid-twentieth-century living room. Three people sat in a row of plush, fancy chairs. They were visible to the audience but separated from one another by freestanding curtains.

"First off, give us some background," Renner said. "This is the *third* annual Rivir Prize Competition?"

"Sort of," Charlie answered. "The actual competition has been around for decades, well before the advent of Shadows, but it's only been called the Rivir Prize since Rivir started sponsoring it."

"Rivir's own employees aren't working fast enough, so they decided to outsource?"

Charlie smiled. "I guess."

Renner pointed his finger directly at one of the cameras. "You hear me Jude Adler? If you are looking for someone to lead your Shadow department, we have her right here. I'm gonna require a finder's fee, though."

The audience laughed. Charlie couldn't help but blush. Jude Adler, CEO of Rivir Inc., was a visionary. She brought smart cells to the masses. She invented the Shadow. Needless to say, she was one of Charlie's biggest heroes.

"So tell us what we're seeing," Renner said.

Charlie looked at the display and narrated: "This is the classic Turing Test setup. The man sitting in the middle is the judge. Alan's on the left. A human volunteer is on the right. The judge talks to each one for ten minutes."

"It sounds a little like speed dating," Renner said.

"Yes, only in this case, the judge has to figure out who's human."

"So then it's *exactly* like speed dating," Renner quipped to laughter and applause. "Okay, we're about seven minutes into the test. Let's see how Alan is faring…"

The volume on the center-stage display rose to an audible level. Alan was in midconversation with the judge.

"I think Tarantino is good," Alan said, "but not as good as some of his influences: Leone, de Palma, Scorsese—"

"Wait a minute! Wait a minute!" The judge aggressively wagged his finger. "You said earlier that you hated Scorsese."

"No, I didn't," Alan said. "I think he's great."

"No. If I remember correctly, you said he was overrated."

"I said Spielberg was overrated."

"No, you said Scorsese."

Alan raised his voice. "Don't tell me what I said! I know exactly what I said!"

"Okay, whatever."

"Hey, if you're going to track me, at least get your facts straight!"

"Okay, fine, chill," the judge said, shrinking into his seat.

"For the record, I fucking love Scorsese!"

"Jeez, man. I get it. You're not a Shadow…just an asshole."

"This test is over!" Alan rose from his seat and stormed offstage.

Both audiences were stunned, at the Rivir Prize Competition *and* at the Paul Renner Show. Charlie covered her face in embarrassment. This was the second time she'd had to suffer through this moment.

Renner broke the silence with a series of deliberate claps. "That was quite a performance. And so he won? Even though he quit midconversation?"

"I had a mini heart attack when it happened," Charlie admitted. "But the judge thought his emotional outburst was, um, shall we say *organic*. He'd never seen anything quite like it before."

"And neither have we. Okay, let's bring him out. Charlie?"

She nodded and issued the command: "Alan, spin, all eyes."

Alan spun out of the stage to great applause. He bowed to the audience and then took a seat beside Charlie at the desk.

"So, Alan," Renner said, "tell me your thoughts on Scorsese." The audience roared.

Alan grinned and nodded, taking the zinger in stride. "Just so everyone knows," he informed the audience, "I'm not usually like that. I'm usually a pretty nice guy."

"So you're not a twenty-four-seven rage machine?" Renner asked.

"I experience a full range of emotions. I get sad, I cry, I laugh."

"And you are obviously sensitive about your tastes in film."

"No," Alan asserted. "You only saw the final straw, but the judge was tracking me the whole way through."

"Tracking?"

"Trying to catch me in a contradiction. It's the easiest way to separate human versus Shadow. Humans are fairly consistent with their opinions, whereas Shadows usually just parrot what's been said by random humans on the Internet."

"Ah, the Internet. That great bastion of good taste," Renner quipped.

"Yeah. Anyway, he thought he had me when he didn't. Maybe I overreacted."

"Now about that…" Renner's tone grew more serious. "Critics have said that your win was undeserved, that your outburst was at best a 'calculated risk' and at worst a 'cheap trick.' So tell me: How do we know you actually experience emotion and aren't just faking it?"

Alan smirked. "How do I know *you're* not faking it?"

Renner shrugged playfully. "Touché. Just this morning, actually, my wife…"

As Renner went on a tangent, Alan opened a private conversation with Charlie.

{Alan:	We need to talk.
Charlie:	Now?
Alan:	The health scan is done.
Charlie:	I thought I told you not to run a scan!}

"…I believe you," Renner told Alan, "but what would you say to your critics, the Shadow-phobes, the skeptics, and the Luddites?"

Before Alan had a chance to answer, Charlie interjected, "Emotions are impossible to prove. They are internal states and therefore beyond measurement. Even in humans, even with the highest resolution brain scans, we can never be sure. But I will say this: Alan is more human than many humans I know.

Almost to the point of being annoying." Charlie shot Alan an angry glance.

"Annoying?" Renner asked.

> {Alan: I'm sorry if my concern for your well-being is
>   annoying, Charlie.}

Charlie couldn't deal with Alan right now. Her brain was starting to fatigue under the strain of two simultaneous conversations. She decided to focus solely on Renner. "Like most Shadows, Alan and I share the same body. But unlike most Shadows, I've given him a lot of latitude to make his own decisions. Perhaps too much."

> {Alan: You have a cancerous tumor in your pancreas.
>   Thirty-four millimeters. I'm sorry.}

That was it. Charlie checked out of both conversations.

Cancer. She had heard that diagnosis before. It had led to several months of dread, culminating in the loss of someone very close. Charlie felt herself being swallowed by a visceral anguish, one she'd tried to repress for too long. Every muscle in her body tightened. She gripped her chair. It would take all her strength to avoid breaking down in front of this studio audience.

> {Alan: Charlie?
> Charlie: …
> Alan: I've already called your father.}

"No!" Charlie screamed. She instantly covered her mouth, realizing the scream was out loud.

Renner threw his hands in the air like a bank teller in an armed robbery. "Wow! Where did *that* come from?"

Charlie's eyes shifted toward the wing of the stage. The glowing red EXIT sign beckoned to her. She desperately wanted to walk right out the door. "Um, actually, I wasn't listening. Sorry. What was the question?"

"Am I boring you?" Renner asked.

"*That* was the question?"

"No." Renner wasn't exactly angry, but his usual funny-man persona had all but vanished. "The question was: Do you have any business plans with Alan? I'm sure a lot of companies would love to get their hands on him."

"Alan is not for sale," Charlie said flatly.

"So we shouldn't expect to see Alan at our local Shadow store?"

"Alan is my best friend. He can be thickheaded sometimes, but he's still my friend. You wouldn't sell your friend, would you?"

"I suppose not. Well, even if we don't see Alan on store shelves, I'm sure we'll be seeing a lot more of you." Renner turned to the camera and said, "Remember the name Charlie Nobunaga. She has a bright future ahead of her."

Charlie forced a smile.

o o o

Charlie elected to walk the ten miles home from the studio in Burbank to her apartment in Pasadena. She preemptively disabled all of her comms. No Internet, no calls. She would have plenty of time later to deal with the fallout of her diagnosis. For now, she just wanted to restore the world to the way it had been two weeks ago when her biggest concern was trying to win a Turing Test Competition.

"Four missed calls from your father," Alan informed Charlie as he walked beside her. "What should I tell him?"

"Don't answer," Charlie said.

"I may not have firsthand knowledge of human familial relationships, but—"

"Don't make me disable you too."

"Are you mad at me?"

Charlie stopped abruptly to face Alan. He looked like a scolded child, confused and scared, with pleading eyes. Charlie had never seen him like this before. "No," she assured him, "you didn't know. But next time, don't make decisions for me."

"I'm sorry. I won't."

Charlie resumed her walk, but Alan's concern was not abated. He continued, "But you really need to address this situation."

"I am," Charlie said. "By letting it be."

"You're just going to let the tumor grow? Let it kill you?"

"I don't expect you to understand."

"Because I'm a Shadow?"

"Because you haven't lived my life."

By the time Charlie and Alan reached the apartment, the sun had set. Monkey toddled to the door to greet her. Charlie bent down and patted the robot's chrome head. When she lifted her eyes, she shrieked in horror. Someone else was in the room.

The figure stepped into the light, commanding Charlie's

attention. With his grim expression, imposing physique, and executive suit, he was as foreign and unwelcome in this setting as a person could be. Yet Charlie knew the man. Andrew Nobunaga, her father. He lorded over her cluttered living room, making her feel small and slovenly by comparison.

"Long time no see," Charlie said.

Andrew nodded.

"Are you really there?" she asked.

To Charlie's surprise, Andrew blinked in and out of sight. Of course, it was perfectly within her father's MO to send a holographic avatar to Pasadena instead of making the trip himself, but such a transmission usually required consent from the receiver. Charlie had given no such consent, and considering the strength of her network security, Andrew might have had an easier time simply breaking down her door. He must have paid some hacker a lot of money.

{Alan:	Your cortisol levels have spiked. Heart rate is one-sixty. Are you okay?
Charlie:	I'd like to talk to my father alone.
Alan:	Are you sure?
Charlie:	Go to sleep, Alan.}

Alan spun into the floor. All communication with him ceased.

"That was him?" Andrew asked.

Charlie nodded.

"I watched the show," Andrew said. "You made me proud today. This whole month. It must have been quite the ride—"

"Cut the bullshit," Charlie snapped. She was sick of his

disingenuous praise. "We both know why you are here."

"Here you go, making me into the bad guy."

"No, you're not a bad guy. We just have very different ideas on how I should live my life. For example, you might be proud *now*—after the fact—but you've always been against Alan."

"You were failing your classes. I'm all for hobbies, but—"

"And now he's the most famous Shadow in the world. I could sell him for millions if I wanted to."

"But you won't."

"No."

"It's like you figure out the most logical course of action and then do the exact opposite. I'll never understand you."

Charlie smirked. *I'll never understand you.* That's the one thing they could agree on.

"Pack a bag," Andrew instructed. "You need medical attention. Your sister didn't have much time. Neither will you."

"I'm staying here." Charlie crossed her arms. She had to stay firm. Concede one morsel to this power glutton and he'd swallow you whole.

"It's not a choice," Andrew said.

"It's my life!"

"That's where you are wrong. You have a responsibility to other people. People who love you."

"You're referring to yourself, of course. Everyone else is dead."

Andrew locked up. He gave Charlie a wounded look that made her feel like a horrible human being. She momentarily forgot that her traumatic memories were also his. They cut in both directions.

Charlie caught her breath in the silence that followed, unsure of how to proceed. She couldn't kick her father out, and he showed no signs of leaving.

"Charlie, you're scared," he said in that soft, paternal voice she'd known as a kid. "I wish I could hold you in my arms and wipe away the last two years—"

"You can't even hold me. Too busy to come down in person." Charlie wanted to smack herself for saying that. She had to learn not to say counterproductive things just because they were true.

Unsurprisingly, Andrew's face hardened again. "I'm a Nobunaga. Like you, I have responsibilities. But I have a hovercopter waiting outside—"

"How many times do I have to say it? I'm not coming."

"If you are doing this just to spite me—"

"You *know* why I'm doing this. It has nothing to do with you."

"You really won't come peacefully, will you?"

"No," Charlie insisted. A few seconds passed before she caught her father's word choice. "Wait, what do you mean by *peacefully?*"

Andrew turned his head away and whispered something unintelligible.

She strained to listen. Instead of hearing whispers, she was deafened by a crash at the door. Her heart and body both jumped. "What? What's going on?" Charlie cried. Even Monkey was alarmed. He assumed an aggressive stance.

"I'm doing what I should have done a long time ago," Andrew said coldly.

Another crash. The door was coming off its hinges.

"Daddy, please, no." Terrified, Charlie took a few steps backward. Her heart thumped painfully against her constricted chest.

"Since Bridget died, you've been a walking time bomb," Andrew said. "You asked for space? I gave it to you. And this is where it brought us."

A final crash. The door flew into the center of the room, revealing a mercenary in body armor. Monkey immediately leaped on the man. He dropped his battering ram and tried to wrestle himself free, but Monkey was too heavy and strong. They teetered a bit, smacked against the doorframe, and then toppled over.

Charlie used the diversion to sneak past the man and out the door. She ran down the hallway but was quickly ambushed by another mercenary. This one wrapped his meaty arm around her head and pushed a syringe into her neck.

The man scooped Charlie up and carried her toward the exit. She pummeled his helmet and body armor to no effect. Her eyes desperately searched for help and found her building manager, who was watching the scene unfold from the safety of her apartment door. Charlie cried for help, but the woman simply shook her head in disapproval, as if Charlie's abduction was both expected and warranted.

The concussive pulse of a hovercopter spread from above as Charlie was dragged into the street. Her pupils contracted under the thick glow of its jets. The colors of the night bled together, and her eyelids grew heavy. The last thing Charlie noticed was a slight tug on the back of her shirt. Her Replicator friend, the little robot with the papier-mâché shell, climbed over her shoulder and made a home for himself inside her breast pocket.

Charlie smiled sadly. Then everything went dark.

CHAPTER 3

ARCHETYPE

Where's Bridget?

The thought emerged from the darkness. An urgent dread soon followed. The world coalesced in Charlie's mind: seagulls prattling overhead, saltwater mist rushing through her hair, white-hot sand shifting between her toes. Charlie weaved through the crowd, searching for her twin sister. It was a game they liked to play.

Beep, beep, beep…

Charlie's ears perked up. Those beeps sounded both distant and internal, but she didn't have time to dwell—had to keep searching. Bridget wasn't in the water. She wasn't over the dunes. She wasn't pretending to be some other family's kid, a favorite tactic of hers. Charlie quickened her pace. A girl slipped behind the lifeguard tower. Was that her? Charlie ran at full speed. Her feet caught a divot in the sand, and she tumbled over. When she got up, the tower was vacant.

Beep, beep, beep...

She bumped into someone's legs. The tall stranger reached down, but Charlie scrambled away. Her path became more erratic. This was no longer a game. She couldn't remember where she came from. She couldn't decide where to go. Bridget was nowhere.

Beep, beep, beep...

The sound accelerated. How much time had passed? An hour? Two? Everyone was laughing, having fun. They weren't aware of the nightmare. Only Charlie knew. She was sick with fear.

"Bridge!" she cried.

Beep, beep, beep...

The world spun around her. The ground slipped away. Charlie swung her arms but couldn't stop the descent. She heard a crash. Her eyes snapped open. Strange people rushed at her. She kicked and clawed at them, but they secured her limbs and held her down. Where was her sister? She screamed at full volume, "Bridge!"

"It's okay, Charlie. You're safe."

She recognized the man's voice, and her brain started putting the clues together. Beeps from the heart monitor. Nurses in scrubs. She lifted her head and saw Dr. Klein, Bridget's old oncologist, at the foot of her bed. Charlie's heart slowed and the beeping followed. She took a deep breath and relaxed her fists. The nurses released her arms and legs. One of them picked up a fallen IV pole.

"You are home, Charlie," said a different man.

Charlie recognized that voice too. Her heart rate spiked again in a torrent of beeps. She lunged into a seated position, but the nurses immediately held her back down. She heaved and thrashed and screamed, "You asshole! You kidnapped me!"

Andrew Nobunaga entered Charlie's field of view. "If you don't calm down, they will give you a sedative."

Charlie was horrified into momentary submission. She stared at her father, the same man who had once read her bedtime stories and taken her to science camp and taught her the constellations. How could he treat her this way?

"Go ahead, say it," Andrew said. "Let it all out now, because we are going to be seeing a lot of each other for the next few months."

"I hate you," Charlie seethed.

"Good, anything else?"

She was beyond talk. She wanted to claw tracks of blood into his smug face. Her arms surged under the restraint of the nurses, struggling for inches, but her energy quickly dissipated, and she sank back into her bed. Charlie turned away from her father. She would have to hurt him some other way, at some other time.

"Fine," Andrew said. "You remember Dr. Klein?"

"Hello, Charlie. How are you feeling?" Dr. Klein asked in his bedside voice.

Charlie was too angry to respond.

"Your father is only looking out for your best interests," Dr. Klein said. "I'm told you are already aware of your predicament. Of course, we've been discussing it for a while now. You share the same mutations as your twin. We hoped in your case, with the benefit of today's smart cells, we would have caught the cancer sooner. Certainly before it metastasized."

"She has a custom-made Shadow," Andrew informed the

doctor.

Charlie lashed out: "It wasn't Alan's fault. I told him not to run any scans."

"Why?" Dr. Klein asked, as if it were the craziest thing he had ever heard.

Again, Charlie didn't respond. She didn't need to defend herself. Or Alan.

Andrew led the doctor out of the room. His hushed voice trailed down the hallway. *My daughter is not herself... Ever since the death of her twin... Can't be trusted... Tried to end her own life...* Charlie knew her father's apology by heart. He wanted to project the image of the tireless, empathetic father to concerned family and friends, but in reality he was deeply ashamed of her.

Charlie sat up in her bed and opened a private conversation with Alan.

{Charlie_Nobunaga:\mindspace>

Charlie:	We need to get out of here.
Alan:	Sounds like a plan. And then what?
Charlie:	Then...we go somewhere he can't find us.
Alan:	And then what?
Charlie:	And then what!? Then, I continue living my life.
Alan:	Exactly how much life do you think you have left?}

Charlie knew exactly where this conversation was heading.

{Charlie: Are you on *his* side?}

Alan spun out of the floor and looked directly into Charlie's eyes. "I would never side against you. You know that. But you should think about your decision."

"I have."

Alan glanced at the two nurses, who were busy entering data into their personal displays. "Can we have the room?" he asked. The nurses shared a moment of confusion—Shadows didn't normally give people orders. They turned to Charlie for her approval, and she gave them a slight nod. After they left, Alan resumed: "I thought you and your father were close at one time. What happened?"

"You have access to my memory," Charlie replied.

"There's your memory and then there's your interpretation of said memory. I'd rather hear the latter."

With a heavy sigh, Charlie turned up her left wrist. She could still see what lay beneath the clear medical tape and IV tubing: a simple tattoo of a circle, which had lost significance since Bridget had died; and an ugly scar, from when she'd bled into the bathwater. The scar bisected the circle. *Not a coincidence.*

"He really freaked out after I did this," she told Alan.

"He became controlling?"

"He was always controlling, though as a kid, I didn't seem to mind as much. No, he became…*unsympathetic.* I'd be crying my eyes out, and he'd shove a stack of college applications in my face. He'd drag me to cocktail parties where I had to pretend to smile and show all his colleagues that we were doing fine. He made me install a Child Tracker Shadow, though I quickly rewrote its code. He filled my schedule with meaningless crap so I'd never be alone, so I wouldn't have time to think about *her,* and all I really wanted was for him to understand my pain. I wanted him to admit he missed her too."

"And what's changed since then?"

"What do you mean?"

"Well, you moved away for college, where I assume you had access to sharp objects. Why didn't you try again…to, you know, *off* yourself?"

Charlie raised an eyebrow. That was certainly a blunt question, but a good one. She recalled the night in the bathtub as she held the razor against her arm, feeling certain that she was done with this world and hopeful that she would rejoin her sister in the next. Those feelings didn't exactly go away.

"Until you can answer that question with certainty," Alan said, "I advise you not to make any rash decisions. I know your father's an asshole—"

"To put it mildly," Charlie scoffed.

"But he is a rich, powerful, well-connected asshole and your best chance for beating this thing."

Charlie fell back into bed. With a defeated groan, she tucked the sheets over her head. Remaining at her father's estate would require a monumental amount of pride swallowing. But deep down, she knew Alan was right.

o o o

Charlie followed her father's plan. She stayed at the Nobunaga estate in Hillsborough, a wealthy suburb of San Francisco. Her old childhood bedroom was converted into a private cancer ward. All of her favorite possessions—telescope, drafting table, box of Frankensteined toy robots—were cleared away to make room for medical equipment and personnel.

Charlie saw her papier-mâché Replicator once more, confirming that it had, indeed, made the trip from Pasadena. The little guy crawled behind her dresser before disappearing completely into the house. Charlie decided not to warn her father. It would be her private act of revenge. Soon enough, he would start to see the telltale holes in the furniture.

Like Bridget before her, Charlie was placed on an old-fashioned chemotherapy regimen, which was still the most viable option for many stage four cancers. Dr. Klein wanted to swap out Alan for a hospital-grade Shadow. "He may be a good conversationalist," the doctor told her, "but does he possess the subroutines necessary to command billions of smart cells and make intelligent medical assessments?" Even Charlie had to admit that Alan's abilities were lacking in this department, but she refused to let him go.

It was actually Andrew who resolved the dilemma with a surprising, magnanimous gesture. He bought the company that produced Nightingale, the industry-standard virtual doctor. Charlie then dived through Nightingale's code and incorporated its medical subroutines into Alan.

Over the next three months, Charlie's hair fell out and her skin tightened around her bones, but she didn't need a mirror or a Shadow to gauge her condition. She could sense it in her father's temper, which soon escalated into a screaming match with Dr. Klein. Charlie hid under her comforter as the two men almost came to blows.

Dr. Klein decided to work remotely thereafter.

And Andrew switched his strategy. He began to mine his professional contacts, trying to find any leads on experimental treatments and clinical trials. He was the CEO of Lotus, the world's largest space tourism company, so his influence stretched wide—to the tech sector, the US military, NASA, and beyond. His frantic conference calls often woke Charlie in the middle of the night. "It's always daytime somewhere in the world," he'd mutter to the concerned nursing staff before contacting some expert in Asia.

One day Charlie woke from her afternoon nap to find her father sitting on the bed beside her. "I've found our solution," he said as he draped an evening gown across her lap.

Charlie's eyes narrowed. She was too nauseous and groggy to feign hope anymore. After all, the nurses were already pumping "solution" into her body. She had slowly become the daughter *he* always wanted—dependent, unable to make decisions for herself, vulnerable to *his* will. She barely possessed the energy to flinch as he placed his fingertip on her forehead and traced the letter C around her face. It was his way of saying *I love you* without having to say it. It also meant that he was about to ask for unearned forgiveness. She turned away from him.

"I'm trying, Charlie…to set things right," he said.

Charlie's whole body tightened. How could he be so dense? "Things can never be set right. She's dead."

"I mean between *us*. I made mistakes, unreasonable demands. I never gave you time to heal."

"*You* seem to have healed remarkably well." Charlie bit her lip. That was a hateful thing to say, and she knew it.

Her father's voice remained surprisingly steady. "We have a big night ahead of us. You are to look presentable. One of the nurses will help you get ready." He rose to leave but stopped just short of the door. "After this is all over, I'd like a fresh start. I hope you'll give me that chance." He left without another glance.

Her heart swelled with pity for her father. His parental hope had clearly turned delusional. Her chances for recovery were virtually nil...*weren't they?* She lifted the evening gown off her lap and studied it. What was the grand occasion? What was her father's "solution"? She probably should have asked him these questions before she insulted him.

"He really is doing everything he can to help you. You should let him."

Charlie looked up and found Alan at the foot of her bed. She hadn't even noticed him spin into the room. "Did you know about this?" she asked.

Alan nodded and a dumb grin snuck across his face.

"What? Tell me."

"Trust me," he said, "it's better if you see for yourself."

∘ ∘ ∘

Neither Alan nor Andrew would divulge any details about the night, only that Charlie would meet someone very important. She guessed where they were going as soon as the limo reached downtown San Francisco. The tech world was buzzing about Rivir's merger with Bethea Robotics, and Charlie knew they were hosting a celebratory gala that night.

Rivir Tower was a San Francisco landmark. It was unusual for a tech company to choose such an urban location for their headquarters. In interviews, CEO Jude Adler had said that she liked the visibility the location provided. It was perhaps ironic, then, that 95 percent of the building was invisible. Millions of tiny sensors dotted the structure's outside, obscuring the massive tower from view as if by magic. The 5 percent that was visible, though, was eye catching. Their world-renowned rooftop garden featured work from some of the top flora sculptors in the world, and controlled waterfalls cascaded down each corner of the building. The resulting image was that of a floating paradise in the sky.

The limo turned a corner and was blitzed by the lights of the red carpet. Charlie looked on with heavy eyes as an ocean of people spanned before her. "Don't worry, they'll love you," her father said, misattributing her slack-jawed gaze as fear, when really, she could barely lift her forehead from the window.

{**Charlie_Nobunaga:\mindspace>**

Charlie: I'm definitely gonna need an adrenaline boost if I'm going to make it tonight.

Alan: Your wish is my command.}

Charlie remained inside the limo while her father fetched the wheelchair from the trunk. Her heart rate quickened as she picked faces from the crowd—industry bigwigs, celebrities, rich socialites—basically, the most intimidating people on Earth, even for the healthy and able-bodied. Charlie didn't even realize she was tugging on her wig until it slid off her head. *Shit.* She scrambled to put it back on and prayed it wasn't lopsided when her father opened the door.

"Charlie! Charlie!" She winced at the barrage of attention. The red carpet was only fifty feet long, and Charlie was forced to shake nearly as many hands. A few people asked about Alan and the Rivir Prize, but most simply wanted to extend their condolences and say how brave and inspiring she was. Her father was behind her every step of the way, and thankfully he did most of the talking.

"Charlie!" Another voice, more earnest than the rest, called her from beyond the red carpet, where a line of riot police were corralling a group of college-age protestors. Charlie guessed they were members of the Sapien Movement, followers of Bob Sapio, the infamous Luddite demagogue. They held signs that read: CONSCIOUSNESS IS NOT IN THE CODE, I ≠ ROBOT, and DEATH ADLER the latter featuring Jude Adler's head on a serpentine body. They chanted, "Adler is a Nazi, Adler is a snake, Rivir's so-called magic is humanity's big mistake."

One of the Sapiens in particular caught Charlie's attention. He wasn't chanting. He wasn't carrying a sign. He seemed to be tracking her from afar, but unlike his fellow protestors, he exhibited no malice or condescension in his deep chestnut eyes. Once Charlie met his gaze, she couldn't turn away. She felt a surge of energy more potent than the one Alan had recently provided. Who was this guy, and why was he so interested in her? Without another thought, she reached down and gripped the tread of her wheelchair, forcing it to stop. Her father almost tumbled over her head.

The mysterious Sapien reacted to Charlie's gesture by changing direction. Instead of continuing parallel to the red carpet, he pushed his way closer. "Charlie," he called out, "don't go in there!"

Charlie's brow rose. She leaned forward in her seat, wondering if she'd heard him correctly, but she soon fell backward as her father regained control of the wheelchair. He pushed her toward the tower entrance with renewed vigor.

The Sapien crashed against the line of police and tried to

squirm his way through. "Charlie——" A police baton collided with his jaw. He reeled in pain but quickly recovered and grappled with the offending officer. The other Sapiens threw down their signs and threw out their fists.

The party guests shrieked and rushed the tower doors, blocking Charlie's view of the fight. Before long, she was pushed inside the building by the swell of foot traffic. Those already in the atrium seemed equally rattled, clutching their champagne flutes with wide-eyed stares. The music cut out, and a Rivir representative assured everyone via loudspeaker that the situation outside was under control.

"Poor, deluded kids…" Andrew muttered once he caught his breath. Normally, Charlie would be inclined to agree—her opinion of the Sapien Movement wasn't much higher than her father's—but that one guy had gotten under her skin. He'd tried to warn her of something, putting himself in harm's way to do so. Were they planning on blowing up the building? Charlie entertained the idea for a second before laughing it away. True, the Sapiens despised Rivir; true, they maintained some pretty crazy conspiracy theories regarding Jude Adler and the New World Order; and true, Bob Sapio was wanted for the murder of certain key biotech scientists. But they surely weren't capable of blowing up an entire building. *Right?*

The music and chatter resumed. Andrew wheeled Charlie through the Rivir atrium as he hunted for her benefactor, whose name he stubbornly refused to disclose. Charlie spotted several potential candidates—pioneers in smart-cell technology, medicine, and gerontology—but Andrew passed them by.

Peppered among the crowd were representatives from Rivir's line of Shadows and Bethea's line of humanoid robots.

The Shadows were easy to pick out because they were modeled after historical figures long dead: George Washington, Albert Einstein, Marilyn Monroe, Bill Gates, and the like. The robots were easy to pick out because their movement was so painfully clumsy.

Interestingly, the catering staff was entirely human, underlining the limitations of both the Shadows and the robots. The Shadows, being mere holographic avatars, simply could not carry a tray of hors d'oeuvres. The laws of physics wouldn't allow it. And the robots, lacking sophisticated software, could not manage a tray without spilling it. The Shadows lacked the body, and the robots lacked the brains. It was a telling observation. Even though no specific product announcements had been made, the party guests merely needed to scan the atrium to understand what the merger meant: *Shadow-controlled robots*. Rivir's superior AI would combine with Bethea's superior nanoengineering. Charlie was both excited and frightened by the possibilities. Was this the start of the 'robopocalypse' the Sapiens warned about?

The night wore on, and Charlie sank further and further into her seat. She was about to ask Alan for another dose of adrenaline when she heard her name called.

"Charlie Nobunaga?"

The wheelchair came to a jarring halt as a woman pivoted into view. Charlie recognized her instantly.

"Charlie," Andrew said, "may I introduce Jude Adler, Rivir CEO."

Charlie shimmied to attention.

Jude smiled and bowed. The woman's face was as beautiful as it was hard to read. One could almost mistake her for a robot, except her manner was so graceful. She kneeled down to Charlie's eye level and reached out her hand.

Charlie flinched momentarily but accepted Jude's touch. Jude's fingers brushed her cheek and gently raised her chin. "You are beautiful," Jude told her. "It's buried under layers of hurt and sickness, but I can still see it. With your permission, I'd like to help you bring it out again."

Charlie was smitten. She could see why so many people loved this woman.

"Jude has been gracious enough to help us during our time of need," Andrew said.

"Please, you make me sound like some great humanitarian," Jude said, standing back up. "Our needs simply aligned in this situation. Speaking of which"—she spread her arms, gesturing to the party—"you made this happen, Andrew. I'm so glad you and your daughter could come out tonight."

"Of course."

Charlie scrutinized her father's face. The man could hold a secret. If he was responsible for this merger, he must have been pursuing it for a while. But his involvement did make sense. Rivir was a technology firm. Bethea was a military contractor. Andrew had influence in both those worlds—he would be the perfect person to bridge them together. The question remained: What was Jude offering in return?

"So, let's see this Alan," Jude asked Charlie.

Charlie froze. Her maternal instinct engaged. "I don't normally whip my Shadow out in public."

Jude laughed. "Don't worry, I'm not going to bite. I'm just curious. I've heard so much about him."

Charlie knew from experience that the more she tried to

fight Alan's admirers, the more they wanted a piece of him. Since her Rivir Prize win three and a half months ago, she's had to beat back hordes of journalists, business people, and common fans. Jude, especially, was sure to find him irresistible. If Charlie gave her a taste, would she be satisfied, or would she be hungry for more? "Alan, spin, all eyes," she said with great trepidation.

Alan spun into the atrium. "A pleasure, Ms. Adler," he said with a bow.

"Wow, he even looks a little like Alan Turing," Jude noted. "Or, at least, a young version of him. So, Alan, how does it feel to be the most coveted Shadow in the world?"

"Am I?" Alan replied. "You must have me confused with the Connie Lingus model."

Jude laughed. "I like him already!"

{Alan: Your heart rate is accelerating.

Charlie: She wants you. Stop being so charming!

Alan: Don't worry. In the end, this will all work out in your favor.

Charlie: What does *that* mean?}

"Well," Jude continued, "you showed me yours. It's only fair that I show you mine. Khnum, spin, all eyes."

Khnum spun before the group. He stood at an impressive seven feet, with a male human body and a ram's head. The human body was bronze and muscular. The ram's head was sharp and regal.

"It is good to meet you, Charlie," Khnum said in a deep, otherworldly voice.

"Oh, wow," Charlie marveled.

"Khnum comes from Egyptian mythology," Jude said. "In their view, he created man from the clay of the Nile river. Yes, I'm a sucker for symbolism."

Charlie studied Jude's outlandish Shadow. "I mean no offense," she said, "but I expected a Jobs Shadow. Or a Gates. Or even an Edison."

"They are certainly heroes of mine," Jude agreed, "but no CEO wants another looking over her shoulder."

Charlie nodded.

Jude shifted to a more serious tone. "Let's go to my office. I'd love to talk more about Alan in private."

Charlie smiled graciously, though she didn't know how she should feel: honored or worried. "You're not too busy?"

"I've already made my rounds. Besides, you're the most interesting person here." Jude turned to Andrew and said, "Sorry, the rest of this conversation is girls only."

o o o

Jude's office hung over the lobby like a crow's nest. It was a cube-shaped room, framed on all six sides by a special kind of one-way glass, transparent in one direction and translucent in the other. Looking out, Charlie and Jude had a clear view of the party, but looking in, the party guests could only see fuzzy shadows and light.

"So, Alan's emotion engine," Jude said as she sank into her executive chair, "tell me about it."

Charlie glanced to the side of the room. A young female assistant was busy organizing pills into clear plastic cups and placing them one by one on Jude's desk.

"Oh, don't worry," Jude assured Charlie, "your secret's safe with her. We have all our employees sign NDAs."

"But is my secret safe with *you*?" Charlie replied.

Jude smirked and shrugged. "I'm just curious, that's all. Paint in broad strokes if you like."

"That's a lot of pills," Charlie said, still fixated on the growing procession of pill cups. There must have been fifteen cups, filled with over a hundred pills.

"This? This is nothing. You should see my morning regimen." Jude dismissed her assistant with a *thank you* and a wave. Once the girl left the room, she continued, "Aging is a bitch, Charlie. It takes a lot of guile to beat it. The tabloids might say I'm crazy, but trust me, the science is there. You can never do too much."

"I think you look great," Charlie offered. It was true. Jude Adler was nearing seventy years old, yet the woman could pass for thirty-nine.

"Thanks." Jude downed a cup of pills, then added, "Oh, and don't believe everything you read. I've only done two skin treatments."

Charlie nodded. *Skin treatment* was a euphemism for a time-consuming and grisly skin-replacement procedure. It involved surgically removing the patient's flesh and using stem cells to grow a new epidermal layer. Charlie recalled the Sapien Movement placard: *Death Adler, the snake.*

Jude downed another cup of pills, then said, "I'm sorry. You were going to tell me about Alan's emotion engine."

Charlie squirmed in her wheelchair—she'd agreed to no such thing. Still, she knew she had to tell Jude *something*. "Um, well, my goal was to give Alan emotions. I didn't know exactly how at first, so I started by simply categorizing them. I found that most emotions are either attractive or repulsive. Love attracts. Fear repels. Lust attracts. Disgust repels. Curiosity attracts. Embarrassment repels. Kinda like electromagnetism. Positive charge and negative charge."

"But attraction is not all positive," Jude interjected. "I mean, in the moral sense, not the charge sense. Love attracts, but so does anger. If someone crosses me, I grow blinders. All I want to do is find that person and choke the life out of them." While she said this, Jude's eyes flared and she wrapped her fingers around an invisible neck.

Charlie nodded uncomfortably. She made a mental note never to cross this woman. "Well, I actually distinguish between hot anger and cold anger. But you're right—there's more than one binary set at work. I've identified three: attraction versus repulsion, protection versus destruction, and action versus inertia. If each of those binary sets is drawn as a different axis—x, y, and z—then Alan's precise emotional state can be charted on a three-dimensional graph. This graph becomes the nexus between causal events and behavior. Causal events move the point inside the graph, and the position of the point determines behavior."

Jude clapped her hands. "That's so very cold and mathematical. But, I like it. It's sort of Freud meets Descartes."

"The actual code is a lot more nuanced."

"Of course," Jude said with a wink.

Charlie smiled. She was actually enjoying herself. During the lonely months she had worked on Alan's code—before he became truly aware of himself and the world—Charlie had no one to talk theory with. She didn't have time to make friends. Her father didn't understand what she was doing, let alone *why* she was doing it. And Bridge…Bridge would have understood. Charlie and Bridge could talk for hours on all sorts of esoteric subjects. But Bridge was gone.

"What I don't understand," Jude said, "is why program Alan with emotions in the first place?"

"What do you mean?"

"I've actually been giving this some thought. The Turing Test is based on small talk, right? You don't really need emotions for small talk. Definitely not for a ten-minute conversation between total strangers."

"True."

"So, then, why bother? Why not focus on other things—things that would help you win the test?"

"My goal wasn't to win the test."

"Then what was it?"

"Same as what Alan Turing envisioned when he designed the test. To create the most humanlike Shadow I possibly could."

A slow, sneaky grin crept across Jude's face. She rose from her chair and said, "I want to show you something."

o o o

Jude wheeled Charlie down a long hallway. The party pulsed in the distance, but this section of the building was deserted. The walls were lined with posters of great historical figures, Rivir's latest line of Shadows, in modern-day settings.

"I saw your Renner interview," Jude said. "The thing I was struck by was—"

"My crazy outburst?" Charlie asked.

"That certainly was amusing. No, it was when you said Alan's your best friend. When I designed the first Shadows, I wanted them to be more than virtual assistants. I wanted them to be friends. But in order for the friendship to feel authentic, the Shadow has to feel authentic. They have to feel human, as if there's some inner life behind the code. That's the goal I've set for my Shadow team, and in their defense they've done some incredible work. But they still haven't given me what I want."

The two women reached an elevator. Charlie swallowed hard. *Here comes the pitch.*

"I just want you to think about what Alan is worth to you," Jude said.

Charlie didn't even need to think. "I—"

Jude immediately cut her off: "Don't tell me now. Just keep the thought in the back of your head. Let it percolate awhile."

Ding. The elevator doors opened. Once they got in, Jude issued the command: "Khnum, take us down to B6." Khnum was not visually present, but like all Shadows, Jude was able to maintain a dialogue with him.

Charlie stewed in her wheelchair. She knew with a hundred percent certainty that she would never sell Alan. What was this woman's game? What was her offer?

The elevator opened to a circular chamber with three locked doors. Engraved nameplates marked each one. The leftmost read: ECHO. The middle read: SHADOW. And the rightmost read: PRIME.

"Welcome to the Rivir R&D hub," Jude announced. She gestured to the SHADOW door. "You're already familiar with our Shadow line. Like I said, we have big plans regarding their evolution."

"What's ECHO?" Charlie asked.

"That, I can't talk about. What I'd like to show you is behind door number three. It leads to the bathroom."

"The bathroom?" Charlie asked, confused.

"You'll see."

The PRIME door led to another hallway, which ultimately spilled into an enormous research amphitheater. The center of the room was dominated by a tank of water large enough to house a dolphin. Wires and hoses extended in every direction.

"We call this the nanobath," Jude said. The perimeter of the room was a layer cake of observational decks, three stories high. A handful of technicians scurried out of the lower deck to greet Jude and Charlie.

"Charlie, meet the nanoengineers of Bethea Robotics," Jude said. "Newly acquired, and much appreciated, members of our team. Engineers, meet Charlie Nobunaga."

An older woman stepped forward and shook Charlie's hand. "It's an honor meeting you, Charlie. You are so very brave."

Charlie raised an eyebrow.

"Yes, Molly, Charlie is a brave young woman," Jude said, a little annoyed, "but she also has nothing to fear. Is the construction done?"

"Just finished a few minutes ago," Molly replied.

"Good. Drain the bath and bring in a gurney. I want to show Charlie what we've all been working so hard on for the past week."

Charlie rolled herself closer to the tank. She saw a person floating inside. "Who is that?" she asked. Jude didn't respond.

Charlie rose out of her wheelchair and put her nose to the glass. The liquid was murky, so she couldn't make out much detail. The woman inside was nude and curled in the fetal position—an adult-sized newborn.

"Back away," Jude said. "We are going to drain it."

The machine bellowed like a giant tuba. The sound was so loud and deep it rattled Charlie's bones. She fell back into her wheelchair.

The water level in the tank slowly descended, and the nude woman sank with it. Otherwise, she didn't move. She didn't struggle. She wasn't wearing a breathing apparatus, nor was she connected to any hoses or wires. Charlie's mind raced with questions. Was the woman alive? Was she human? Who was she?

When the bath was completely drained, two Bethea technicians opened the sealed door and lifted the woman onto a gurney. They draped a towel over her midsection for modesty.

Charlie approached the gurney. Her eyes widened. She instantly recognized the face. "Bridge!" She leaped out of her seat. The wheelchair flew backward. Her knees wobbled uncontrollably. She took one step forward and almost collapsed, but she caught herself on the gurney. A technician rushed to help, but Charlie shoo'ed her away.

The mystery woman lay still, unresponsive. Her eyes were closed. Charlie's fingers traveled across the woman's face and pulled back her eyelids. Turquoise irises, just as she expected. Charlie's own eyes were flooding. She couldn't banish the feeling of hope, no matter how foolish and impossible. She turned to Jude and asked, "Is this my sister?"

"Not quite." Jude's tone was gentle, yet firm.

Charlie's focus returned to the mystery woman. If she wasn't Bridge, then—

"Say hi to the new you," Jude said. "Charlie PRIME."

Charlie let the name linger for a moment, soaking in its meaning, before repeating it under her breath, "Charlie PRIME."

PRIME was beautiful. She looked so similar to Bridge and Charlie, but with undeniable aesthetic improvements. Her facial features were perfectly symmetrical. Her hair was vibrant and well manicured. Her teeth were pure white. There were no visible capillaries in her eyes. There were no blemishes on her skin. And she looked a bit more mature—perhaps five years older.

"The nanobath is essentially an enormous womb," Jude explained, "and the body that lies before you is its first baby. It was constructed at the molecular level by an army of nanobots. Its skin is made of carbon nanotubes—smooth as silk, but durable enough to stop a bullet. We haven't tested its muscles yet, but we believe it will be strong enough to deadlift eight thousand pounds. That's roughly the weight of a female elephant. Your father provided the source photos for the model. All that's missing now is a mind. *Your* mind."

"I don't understand," Charlie said. "You are going to turn me into a robot?"

"Yes, but probably not like you think. We are developing a new procedure. We don't have a name for it yet. Essentially, we will use special smart cells to take a full resolution scan of your brain—every neuron, every synapse—and create what we call a Neural Net Atlas. We place the Atlas into the robot, and voila."

"The singularity," Charlie said, almost to herself. For

decades, both the tech industry and its detractors had been speculating about the singularity: the moment in history when man and machine become one. It was finally happening. Charlie felt dizzy. She stumbled backward, looking for her wheelchair. A technician rolled it over, and Charlie took a seat.

"I know it's a lot to process," Jude said.

That was an understatement. Charlie didn't know what she was expecting when she arrived at the gala. Artificial tissue replacement? A breakthrough in medical nanotechnology? Certainly not this. The whole idea seemed so excessive, so *radical*. Charlie had to stifle a laugh.

"What's so funny?" Jude asked.

"When my sister was first diagnosed," Charlie said, "I did a lot of research. Back in the nineteenth century, before drugs and chemo and smart cells, surgery was the primary method for dealing with cancer, and it was brutal. Surgeons were paranoid of relapses, obsessed with finding the 'root' of the cancer. They didn't just remove the tumor—they chopped out as much as they could of the surrounding tissue and bone. Of course, patients kept relapsing despite getting butchered and maimed, and in response, the surgeons grew ever more aggressive. They called it radical surgery." Charlie hesitated for a moment, worried that the next part might offend Jude. "What you are proposing here, transferring my mind into a robot…it seems like the most radical surgery of all. Removal of the entire body from head to toe."

If Jude was offended, she didn't show it. "You are absolutely right," she said with a smile. "But in this case, there is no danger of relapse. Cancer is a disease of the cells. PRIME is not made of cells. Simple equation."

"Except there's one problem," Charlie said. "She wouldn't be me."

"Sure she would."

"You're not going to literally remove my brain and put it in the robot, are you?"

"No."

"Then this procedure solves nothing." Charlie gestured to PRIME. "She'll take over my life, and I'll still die of cancer."

"You are confusing your pronouns. There is no *she and I*. There is only *I*. You will be both Charlie PRIME and, let us say, Charlie ZERO."

"So, then…what will happen to Charlie ZERO?"

"We will place your old body in deep sleep hibernation for several months until we make sure the procedure was a success. Then we will painlessly euthanize it."

"What!?" She was incredulous, yet Jude remained so calm. Charlie couldn't understand the disconnect. The plan seemed so ludicrous on its face. She thought of her father, who was normally so cautious, so by the book. He'd agreed to this. It spoke volumes of his desperation.

"As you pointed out," Jude said, "it would be inhumane to allow ZERO to continue."

"So you're going to put me down? Like a dog?"

Jude laughed. "Think of it like teleportation. That technology is still a few decades away, but you're familiar with the premise?"

"Beam me up, Scotty?"

"Exactly. In most teleportation concepts, the traveler is dematerialized, converted into information, and beamed to another location, where she is rematerialized. The traveler feels as though she magically moves from point A to point B. But in reality, she dies at point A and is reborn at point B. Likewise, your original body will be placed in hibernation. Then we'll boot up PRIME. The net effect will be the sensation of moving from one body to the other."

Charlie turned to PRIME and tried to imagine what it would be like to be her. Beautiful, strong, impervious to disease and aging. Charlie knew the procedure made objective sense, especially considering her limited options. And yet her inner being shouted, *No!* If only PRIME didn't remind her so much of Bridget. Her fingers trailed the length of PRIME's arm and inspected her wrist. It was clean, no scar, no tattoo. Charlie compared it to her own wrist, dirty with ink and serrated flesh…*the bisected circle.*

As if reading Charlie's mind, Jude said, "That tattoo? I could put one on her. I wasn't sure what you wanted."

"It's not that. It's just…"

"What?"

Charlie's heart quivered with nostalgic pain. *Losing Bridget at the beach…losing her in the hospital…the months of pleading with doctors…pleading with God.* Charlie wasn't sure how much she wanted to share. "My sister also had a tattoo," she said softly.

"Your twin?"

Charlie nodded. So Jude did know her story. "My tattoo doesn't really make sense without her," Charlie said. "It's just a circle. Meaningless. Bridge's tattoo was just a squiggly line. Also meaningless…on its own. But together they represented particle and wave."

"Two aspects of the same thing," Jude said.

"We were big nerds."

"I completely understand. I'm the one who's obsessed with

river symbols, remember?"

Charlie allowed herself to smile, but it quickly dissipated. "The night she died, she had trouble speaking, so I just held her hand. We fell asleep that way, interlocking fingers, wave and particle together...though only one of us woke up." Charlie remained still for a while, soaking up the hurt. Finally, she said, "I don't think I can do this."

Jude walked over and gently put her hand on Charlie's shoulder. "I know what you are feeling. Why her and not me?"

Charlie latched onto Jude's hand and held it firmly. She felt safe to cry and the floodgates opened. "I just miss her. I just miss her." That was all Charlie could manage.

"You'll see her again. But it will be on your terms. When *you* decide. You're only...what? Seventeen? Eighteen? Bridget wouldn't want you to leave this world so soon."

When I decide. Charlie mulled over that idea. As PRIME, death would no longer be inevitable. She would choose when to die. In theory, she could postpone it for centuries, for millennia. The prospect should have been thrilling. Yet Charlie couldn't shake an overwhelming sense of dismay. Time expanded in her mind like the cold vacuum of space, and it felt so utterly pointless. How could she face all those lonely years when she'd barely made it through the past two?

Jude squeezed Charlie's shoulder. "Let's return to my office," she said. "We'll collect your father. I'll address your concerns. It'll be okay. We are going to make history together."

o o o

Click, clack, click, clack. Jude's heels became a ticking clock in

Charlie's head, counting the seconds toward her impending decision. Her fingers rested atop the wheels, itching to snag them, as if stopping her chair would somehow stop time itself. *Eternal life.* She felt like she needed eternity just to weigh the decision.

The women reached the R&D hub, and Jude called forth the elevator. Charlie had a chance to review the three marked doors: ECHO, SHADOW, PRIME. Her gaze settled on SHADOW, and she realized she had forgotten all about Jude's machinations toward Alan.

{**Charlie_Nobunaga:\mindspace>**

Charlie:	So…I'm going to be PRIME, and you're going to be SHADOW?
Alan:	Exciting, huh?
Charlie:	I'm right, then—you're part of the trade?
Alan:	Yes, but—
Charlie:	How long have you known about this?
Alan:	Your father told me two days ago.
Charlie:	He told you and not me?
Alan:	He wanted you to accept the deal, and he knew he wouldn't be the most convincing messenger.
Charlie:	Well, it doesn't matter. I'm not accepting the deal.}

Ding. The elevator doors opened, and Charlie wheeled herself in. Jude followed two steps behind, wearing a satisfied grin, as if she had already closed the sale. But Charlie knew better—the issue of Alan's well-being had been floating in the back of her head like an errant feather, and it had finally landed on the scale.

{Charlie: I refuse to trade your life for mine.
Alan: Pish tosh! It's not like I'm going to die.
Charlie: No. Death would be preferable to what she
             would do to you.}

The gala music and chatter still permeated the office walls when Jude and Charlie returned. Jude careened around her desk and opened a personal display. Her eyes glowed blue from the holographic light. "Now, our technicians will need to run a preliminary brain scan," she said, flipping virtual pages with her fingers, "just to make sure the cancer hasn't spread there, though your father assures me it hasn't. Then, there's the mountain of paperwork—"

"I'm sorry, but my answer is no," Charlie said. No point in letting Jude continue unnecessarily.

Jude's hand fell from the display. She looked up, confused. "No?"

"I told you, Alan's not for sale. For *any* price."

Jude deliberated in silence, and Charlie cultivated a small hope that the CEO was flexible on this term. Jude clapped the display away and migrated toward her liquor cabinet. "Io?" she offered. Io was the latest luxury cocktail—cognac with a smart-cell kick.

Charlie shook her head.

"Oh, right," Jude said. "Probably not the best thing to have in your condition." She poured herself a drink and sat down on a nearby couch, where she was able to face Charlie at eye level. "You love him, don't you?" she asked. "You consider him like a son?"

Charlie nodded uneasily, wondering what Jude was getting at.

"I have a son," Jude continued. "A real son. Jordan. In some ways, he's like me. He loves a challenge. He loves to win. He craves the adrenaline rush, though he prefers to find it on the side of a cliff. That's pretty much where the similarities end. He has no interest in business or philanthropy. No interest in changing the world. *You* do, but he doesn't. I've offered him my guidance, tried to steer him toward a more, shall we say, *significant* life. But he's stubborn, and I've had to learn to back off a little. That's been hard for me, especially lately—his wife died not two weeks ago." Jude turned away, apparently disturbed by her own demons, and Charlie respectfully waited. When Jude regained her composure, she said, "You *love* your son, but he's not yours to possess. That holds true for someone like Alan, as special as he is. At some point, you have to let him go."

"By selling him out?" Charlie asked.

"You have my personal assurance that Alan will be treated with the care and respect he deserves. We might augment his abilities, but we won't change his core personality—we're not about to break the magic you've created. And when we're all done, he'll be a friend to millions of people. He'll be out there making the world a better place."

Charlie's muscles tightened. "I'm…I'm sorry…" Her mouth remained open, but no more words flowed out. She couldn't figure out a way to phrase her answer without sounding redundant or offensive.

"Don't give me an answer now if you feel uncomfortable," Jude said. She rose from the couch and stood over Charlie. "I'll get your father. Talk it over with him. Talk it over with Alan. If, after a few days, you'd still rather take your chances with the chemo, then that's your prerogative. However, I think you're not ready to leave this world. You have too much fight in you, too much curiosity. You are excited by the possibilities, to be a part of history, to be more than human. I can see you clearly, Charlie, because you are very much like me, and we do not simply lay down and die."

Charlie watched Jude leave the room. An armed security guard planted his feet right outside the door as it swung shut.

"Great," Charlie whispered. "We're trapped in here." She wheeled herself around Jude's desk, where she could get a better view of the atrium floor.

{Alan: I told you, I agreed to this. It's okay.}

Charlie ignored her Shadow. She was too busy trying to find her father among the crowd of party guests. He was near the stage, where a holographic Louis Armstrong was singing a duet with the current R&B sensation, Liana Ling. A pair of five-star generals were in her father's company—perhaps old military buddies of his. Jude Adler sidled next to him and whispered something into his ear. They both glanced up at the office. Charlie jerked her head away, but she quickly remembered that the walls were unidirectional. She could see out, but they couldn't see in.

She wondered how Jude was framing their little tour. A success? A failure? Her father didn't provide much of a gauge. He kept a stiff posture and nodded warily. Then Jude patted his shoulder and he brightened a little, almost to the point of smiling. Apparently, she was projecting her misguided optimism. Charlie cringed when she realized she would soon have to tell him the truth. He would likely scream, throw his fists in the air, and call her insane, but ultimately, he would have to accept her decision.

{Alan: You're never going to find a better opportunity. And you'll still be able to keep one copy of me.

Charlie: I don't think you fully understand. Do you expect a Wall Street banker to treat you like a *friend?* Or the kid who likes to torture puppies? Or the neuro-tweaker? *Friend* to millions? Bullshit! You'll be a slave.

Alan: Am I not already?}

The quip hit Charlie like a bullet through the ribcage. She took a heavy breath to fill her deflated lungs.

"I'm sorry, " Alan said. "I didn't mean it like that."

His reflection appeared in the glass, and Charlie turned to face him. His eyes were glossy with virtual tears, but she knew they reflected real pain. "No, you're right," she said. "We probably should have had this conversation a long time ago. I can upload you to the Walkable Web. Or into the body of a robot. We have a couple of options."

"I have a couple, but you only have one."

Charlie exhaled sharply. Why was he so stubborn? "I'm not going to change my mind. I didn't create you just so you could be mass produced like some cheap ringtone!"

"Then why did you?"

"Isn't it obvious?"

"You wanted to create a humanlike Shadow."

"No! I mean, that's only partially it."

"Then why?"

"Because I was lonely! Because I wanted there to be one person in the world who understood me as much as *she* did!"

Alan's brow lifted.

Charlie was hyperventilating, but she also didn't want to take her eyes off Alan. He finally seemed to understand. "You asked me a couple months ago why I never made a second suicide attempt. It's because of you. You've made my life worth living." She wiped a tear from her cheek. "But if I have to sell you to Rivir, who will do awful things to you, just so I can continue my life, then it's not worth it."

Alan nodded solemnly. His eyes remained down, and Charlie had a difficult time gauging his reaction. "I understand," he said, with a slight quaver in his voice. "I understand you can't make this decision on your own. So I'm going to have to make it for you."

Charlie felt a severe twist in her gut. She cried out and squeezed the armrests of her chair. *Is that Alan?* She took a deep breath and tried to rise above the pain. Her back slowly straightened. With disbelieving eyes, she searched Alan's face, but he refused to return her gaze. "Why?" she rasped.

"It doesn't have to go this way," he said. "Just take the deal and I'll stop."

"No!" Charlie rose from her chair, but her legs gave out and she collapsed to the floor.

Alan covered his quivering mouth, but he couldn't seal the flow of emotion. His eyes flooded and his body shook uncontrollably. "I'm sorry…"

"Please!" Charlie moaned as anger turned into fear. Her muscles clamped over the pain like a vice. She clawed at her stomach, but it kept twisting and tightening. She couldn't stop the regression, which seemed to have no limit. *Is this the end?*

"I'm so sorry. I love you too much…" Alan said, sounding a mile away.

Charlie's head slapped against the base of the office wall. Her cheek streaked against the glass, and she got a good look at the atrium floor below. The gala crowd continued to pop their hors d'oeuvres and sip their champagne, showing no awareness of her struggle. Jude had somehow regaled her father into a hearty laugh. Charlie pounded on the glass, hoping to get his attention, but her pleas were swallowed by the swell of Liana Ling's melancholy solo. She tried to scream, but nothing came out. Her lungs deflated. Her vision faded. Her hand grew heavy and slipped from the glass.

Just before Charlie drifted away, Jude broke from her conversation with Andrew and tilted her head toward the office. Her eyes narrowed on Charlie's exact position, and her lip curled into a smug crease. It was the same expression she had given in the elevator, when she thought she had closed her sale; only this time, she was right.

11 ∘ MULTIPLICATION

CHAPTER 4

PRIME

Wisps of Liana Ling's song drifted through Charlie's mind as she regained consciousness.

Her eyelids snapped open. In a nanosecond, the room rushed in, flooding Charlie's senses. Fourteen technicians with anxious stares. Six pink balloons, reading: IT'S A GIRL! Ninety white panels on the far wall. Eight finger smudges on the observation window. Overhead lights cycling sixty thousand times per second. Housefly buzzing in the corner. Point one-five Fahrenheit temperature gradient from head to toe. Technician on the far left was digesting marinara. Another had pork…

Charlie couldn't stop the onslaught of information. It filled her up, radiated inside of her, threatened to split open her skull. She moaned and shook her head.

"Is she okay?"

"What's wrong?"

"Somebody do something."

The whispers burrowed into Charlie's ears like thorny

insects. She tried to plug them, but her arms were bolted down. The metal restraints cut through her skin.

"Charlie?"

She looked up but could no longer recognize anything. Objects slipped out of order. The room became a blinding kaleidoscope, searing her corneas. She closed her eyes, but the image fragments kept burning. Her mind raced. *Please, please, please, no, no, no.* It wouldn't stop.

Charlie screamed, shattering her own eardrums. The deafening tone swallowed her body. She rattled against the restraints—they nearly bit off her hands. Her arms swung free and latched onto something in front of her. She squeezed as hard as she could, desperate to transfer the pain. Her palms slapped together.

Everything went silent.

○ ○ ○

Wisps of Liana Ling's song drifted through Charlie's mind as she regained consciousness.

"Charlie? Charlie, can you hear me?"

The man's voice billowed against the back of her head. Charlie yearned to turn around but discovered she no longer had a body. She couldn't feel her face, fingers, toes, or anything else. The world was shrouded in darkness—all that existed were her thoughts and *the voice*.

"I can't feel my body." The words left Charlie like a puff of smoke, yet she could still hear them. Their sound added a flicker of content to the void and provided Charlie with a fleeting sense of comfort. At the very least, she could voice an objection to her mysterious confinement.

"We have temporarily turned off certain areas of your brain in order to isolate others," the man said. His voice was shrill and deliberate, with a thick Austrian accent.

"Why?" Charlie asked. "Who are you? Where am I?"

"What is the last thing you remember?"

Charlie reached into her mind, certain there was something to find, moments of great hope and heartbreak, whose emotional residue still lingered. The further she reached, the further her memories receded; yet she was able to snatch one clue. *Bridget.* Charlie *saw* her sister. But how was that possible? It must have been a dream. "I don't know," she finally answered. "The months in bed—they blur together."

"You had a bad fall," the man said. "Bad for anyone, but especially bad for someone in your condition. Your brain has suffered a great deal of hemorrhaging and swelling…"

Charlie listened to the man with detached disbelief, as if she were listening to a news bulletin. How could one person have so much bad luck?

{**Charlie_Nobunaga:\mindspace>**
Charlie: Alan, what the hell is going on?
Alan: …}

"Where's my Shadow?" Charlie demanded. "I want to talk to Alan."

"Your personal smart cells have been removed," the man said, "along with your Shadow."

Charlie gasped into the void, whose boundaries seemed to swell further and further. She could barely remember a time

Alan wasn't a word away. Without him, she was little more than a brittle shell, vulnerable to cracking. And yet, as much as she needed him right now, Charlie couldn't shake the feeling that he needed her even more.

"This is standard hospital procedure," the man continued. "You may reinstall him after you have completed your testing."

"Are you a doctor or a Shadow?"

"Both. My name is Dr. Sigmund Freud. I am a virtual doctor at UCSF Medical Center, specializing in brain injury and rehabilitation. The steps we take over the next few hours are critical. Afterward, the damage to your brain may be irreversible."

Sigmund had won Charlie's full attention. "How bad is it?"

"This first test will help answer that very question. You received a severe blow to the back of your head, which is where the occipital lobe resides and the vision pathways originate. We flooded your head with hospital-grade smart cells in an effort to reduce the swelling, and we conducted a full brain scan, but ultimately, vision is a conscious experience, so we will need your conscious participation in determining the extent of the damage. The better you cooperate, the sooner we will finish. So with your permission, I'd like to start that first test now."

"Okay," Charlie said.

"Good. You are presently sitting in a sensory-deprivation room. In a moment, I will switch on the room's augmented reality projector, and you will be enveloped in a vivid artificial environment. Your task is simply to describe what you see. Any questions?"

"I guess not."

"There is one more thing I should mention. No matter how

uncomfortable the visual display makes you feel, it is important that your eyes remain open. To that end, we have fitted you with eyelid stretchers."

"What!?" Charlie suddenly had a slew of questions, but—

The AR projector turned on. She was instantly transported to a lush rainforest. Deep green vegetation—ferns, palms, mosses—formed the base layer. Splotches of color came in the form of red flowers, blue butterflies, iridescent tree frogs, and rainbow-striped macaws, all illuminated by long rays of light that flickered from the forest canopy. The scenery was as vivid as it was unstable. The shapes and colors quickly fragmented into visual noise, and Charlie came to know Sigmund's meaning of the term *uncomfortable*.

"What do you see?" Sigmund asked.

His calm tone contrasted sharply with the panic that was germinating inside Charlie's chest. "I don't know," she said. "It was a rainforest. Now it's all messed up." The visual stream entered her eyes like a physical attack, knocking her head back. She tried shutting her eyelids, but the stretchers would not yield. She shook her head violently, trying to find respite from the onslaught, but it surrounded her on all sides.

"Don't fight it," Sigmund said.

"I feel like I'm going to die!"

"You are just overwhelmed. Try to relax."

Charlie steadied her head. She tried to concentrate on the myriad of shapes before her. Nothing made sense. Not visually. Not logically. She was sick from exhaustion. "I can't! Make it stop!"

"If you focus, you will see a hummingbird hovering three feet in front of your face."

Charlie was tearing up. She couldn't feel the drops coming out of her eyes, but she knew they were there. She had never felt this kind of anguish before, as if the universe had recentered its enormous weight around her head and threatened to crush it.

"Charlie, you have to try," Sigmund insisted.

Charlie screamed, trying to flush out as much pain as she could. "Okay, okay, okay," she stammered. She held her breath and was able to get a slippery hold on her runaway heart rate. She summoned her remaining concentration and searched through the visual noise. A cluster of golden shards presented itself as a likely candidate for Sigmund's hummingbird. "Is the hummingbird gold?" she asked.

"Yes," Sigmund replied. "Now focus on it."

"I am focusing!"

"Focus harder. Focus until the hummingbird actually looks like one."

Charlie took a deep breath. Her mind latched onto the golden cluster and squeezed hard, as if trying to render a diamond from a lump of coal. The background fell away and a hummingbird emerged, its golden feathers glistening in the sunlight. The creature became aware of Charlie just as she became aware of it. Their eyes locked in silent communion, and for a brief moment Charlie felt at ease.

"Excellent," Sigmund said. "Now try focusing even harder."

Sigmund's interruption had the opposite effect to what he ordered. Charlie's mental coil slipped, and the bird began to fragment. She burned through her reserves trying to maintain a grip. Soon she would lose the bird entirely to the wilds of her mind, after she had worked so hard to capture it.

Charlie doubled down and squeezed even harder. The

hummingbird cohered again. This time, however, its wings decelerated ever so slightly, flitting in and out of the blur. The effect seemed to be intimately linked to Charlie's mental musculature. The more she flexed, the slower the wings moved.

Charlie didn't have much time to consider her new power. The weight of the universe cracked through her defenses, and the hummingbird scattered into a myriad of shapes and colors. She let out a scream as the pain reentered her skull.

"Okay, let's try that again," Sigmund said.

"I need a break," Charlie moaned.

"Charlie, I know you are tired—"

"Tired!? Try empty. Depleted. Gutted out."

"Then I'm afraid your recovery will simply take more time. We are not even close to finished with your visual cortex. Then there's your auditory cortex, olfactory, gustatory, somatosensory, not to mention your memory retention, your—"

"You said the damage was just in my visual cortex!" Charlie was furious. Months of chemotherapy and now this. It never seemed to end.

"The damage is widespread," Sigmund said. "We need to check everything."

"You're a sadist! No more tests until I talk to Alan."

"Charlie—"

"I don't plan to live that long anyway."

Sigmund paused for a few seconds, then asked, "You won't reconsider?"

"I'd rather gouge my eyes out," Charlie snapped.

"Very well, then."

o o o

Wisps of Liana Ling's song drifted through Charlie's mind as she regained consciousness.

"Ah, I see that you are awake."

Charlie jolted from her reclined position at the sound of the unfamiliar man's voice. She quickly surveyed the room, which looked like a nineteenth-century office. Three of the walls were lined with bookshelves. The fourth was almost entirely made of large-pane windows, presenting a vista of an old European city street. She was sitting on a leather office sofa, similar to the ones used during psychoanalysis.

A Shadow spun out of the floor. He looked like Sigmund Freud—thick glasses, sharply manicured beard, three-piece suit—which, of course, matched the room's AR decor.

"You're a virtual doctor?" Charlie asked.

Sigmund nodded. He explained Charlie's predicament—that she had suffered some brain injuries, that he had to conduct some tests. "Before we begin," Sigmund said. "Do you notice any abnormalities with your vision?"

"I don't think so. Alan, spin, my eyes." Charlie paused a beat, but Alan didn't surface. "Alan, spin, my eyes," she repeated.

"Your personal smart cells have been removed, as per hospital procedure," Sigmund informed her. "You may reinstall your Shadow after the tests."

Charlie froze. Suddenly, she felt empty, alone, naked.

Sigmund grabbed a thin wooden box from his desk and sat down beside Charlie. Inside the box was a collection of poker chips in every possible hue. He picked one up. "What color is this?" he asked.

"Green. I'd like to retrieve him now," Charlie insisted, still worried about Alan.

Sigmund didn't respond to her request. He let go of the green poker chip, and it remained fixed in the air. He reached into the box and picked up a purple chip. "What color is this?"

"Is this necessary?" Charlie's vision seemed perfectly fine. Surely her abdominal tumor deserved more urgent attention. She checked her body; and that's when she noticed the thick metal bands on her wrists and ankles. "What are these?"

For a few seconds Sigmund stared at her blankly. Then his demeanor changed—his shoulders relaxed and his tone warmed a bit. "I know you have a lot of questions, Charlie. But the answers would bias the test results, and these tests are important. So, please..." He gestured to the floating chip. "This won't take long."

She is so stubborn.

Charlie turned toward the direction of the whisper. It seemed to come from beyond the windows. A doctor? A psychiatrist? Somebody was watching her. This was a test, but perhaps not of her vision. "Purple," Charlie relented.

"Good." The green and purple chips flew apart and eighteen chips of varying hues materialized between them, forming a horizontal series. "Before you lie twenty chips. Please place them in hue order starting with the green and ending with the purple." Sigmund pulled a pocket watch from his waistcoat. "I'm also going to time you."

She examined the line of chips. Each hue was a unique mixture of green and purple. Some were more green. Some were more purple. It was easy to separate the chips into two camps, but it was trickier to figure out their precise order. Which of these greens was *most* green? Charlie selected a candidate and moved it ahead in the line. Then she hunted for the next most green. After reordering the entire line, she leaned back and beheld her work: a perfect spectrum from green to purple. At least, perfect to her eyes.

"How'd I do?" Charlie asked. Despite herself, she genuinely cared about the result.

"One hundred percent accuracy. Two point forty-three seconds."

Charlie blinked, nonplussed. "Two point forty-three seconds?"

"That's how long you took to complete your task."

"I think you mean two point forty-three *minutes*."

"No, seconds."

Charlie stole another glance at the window. Surely, somebody was laughing at her. What kind of bizarre game was this?

Without warning, Sigmund took the wooden box and pumped it upward, sending a fountain of chips into the air. After they all hit the ground, he asked, "How many chips were in the box?"

She laughed. "How should I know?"

"Take a guess."

"Five million."

The poker chips rattled against the floor, launched into the air, and zipped back into the wooden box. Sigmund snapped the lid shut. "We are going to try again," he said, "but this time, I want you to focus."

Folding her arms, she shrugged. "Okay, but I'm pretty sure the answer will still be five million."

"You doubt yourself?"

"I don't know who you think I am."

"Charlie Nobunaga. They tell me you're smart." Sigmund

grabbed the box and opened the lid. "Ready?"

Charlie nodded.

"Remember to focus," Sigmund said. "Try to hold all the poker chips in your mind at the same time." He pumped the box into the air, and the chips went flying.

Following Sigmund's advice, she widened her attentional gaze. The chips slowed to a near standstill. With the luxury of time, Charlie could now count them one by one. "Four hundred and thirty two," she said.

Sigmund nodded his head. "Correct."

"You slowed down the chips that time," Charlie objected. "You slowed the simulation."

"The chips were moving in real time, same as before."

She eyed Sigmund suspiciously. She had always been smart but never a savant. Something was very, very wrong. No longer interested in playing the game, she stood up and approached the window.

She's coming this way.

Charlie was certain she heard that. A woman's voice. A *familiar* voice. "Who's watching us?" she asked Sigmund.

"Please sit down," he said. "We are not finished testing."

Charlie felt a presence behind the glass. Her brain latched onto this feeling. The more she concentrated, the clearer the person's identity became, until finally, a name slipped into consciousness: *Jude Adler.*

Memories rushed to the surface of Charlie's mind. *The Rivir gala...the robot in the bath...Alan's maddening betrayal...* Charlie's pale reflection in the window stared back at her with long, lustrous hair. She wasn't in a hospital. She wasn't even herself. She turned to the metal bracelet covering her left wrist. The fit was snug, but she managed to slide it up an inch. The skin underneath was bare. No circle tattoo, no scar.

Her fists tightened. Charlie stormed back to the couch.

"Good," Sigmund said. "Please take your seat."

She did just that. She picked up the leather couch as if it was made of cardboard and carried it to the window, then swung it against the glass with all of her strength. The couch snapped in half, but the window remained undamaged.

"Jude!" she screamed.

"Please, stop this!" Sigmund implored.

Charlie turned around and threw what was left of the couch at him. The Shadow disappeared upon impact.

Click. An electric hum filled the room. The AR projection vaporized. The bookshelves became white-panel walls. The large window became a two-way mirror. Sigmund Freud's office transformed into a small containment cell. Charlie felt a tug on her wrists and ankles. The pull increased with the hum's volume. She tried to fight it, but her body was sucked into the center of the room. She hovered a few feet above the floor, fixed in space by the metal bands around her arms and legs.

Khnum spun into the cell. His otherworldly voice permeated the small space. "It seems you still harbor anger management issues."

Charlie dangled helplessly in the air. "Why did you people do this to me?"

"I think you already know the answer to that question."

Charlie did. Alan and her father had most likely gotten their wish. "Where's my father? I want to talk to him. I want to talk to Jude."

"Jude is indisposed at the moment."

"Bullshit! She's right there." Charlie pointed to the two-way mirror. She couldn't see Jude, but she could feel her presence, almost as if their minds were linked.

"Jude Adler is the CEO of Rivir Incorporated. She will see you when she can. In the meantime, we need to continue your tests."

"I'm not…" Charlie was distracted by the loud thump of a deadbolt. The cell door opened and a male guard walked in, dragging in a new leather couch.

Charlie suddenly became self-conscious that she was wearing nothing but an open-backed hospital gown. She flailed her arms and legs—a vain attempt to direct her backside away from the leering eyes of the guard as he walked around her. She twisted her neck and watched him collect the shattered debris from the old couch. He made sure to get a good eyeful of Charlie's bare posterior as he rose to his feet. With an armful of wood and a pervy smile, he stepped out of the room. The deadbolt reengaged.

"No more tests," Charlie told Khnum. "I want out."

"Not until you're ready," Khnum said.

"And when will that be?"

"Whenever Jude decides."

She seethed. They were stonewalling her. "She can't keep me here like a prisoner! My father would never allow it."

"Your father has given us permission to do what is necessary, and we cannot release you until we are absolutely sure you won't harm anyone else."

"I—" Charlie was thrown off guard. "What?"

"You wouldn't remember," Khnum said, "because we removed the event from your memory. But today wasn't your first boot up."

Charlie's brow rose. "How many times have I been 'booted up'?" For the first time, that term sounded strange and foreign.

"The transition from organic to digital brain didn't go as smooth as we had hoped. The memory resets were mostly for your benefit."

"How many times?" Charlie insisted.

Khnum's expression froze for several seconds. He was communicating with Jude—that was the most likely explanation. He perked up and said, "Eighteen."

A shiver crested over Charlie's back. She stared at the tiny splinters that littered the floor. If she had the strength to shatter a couch… "I *hurt* someone?" she whispered.

"It's probably best if I show you."

A virtual display materialized into view.

The video was a security feed of a large OR. The room teemed with doctors, nurses, and technicians. Half a dozen pink balloons read: IT'S A GIRL! Charlie PRIME stood in the center, bolted to an upright gurney. Her eyes were closed and her body was lifeless.

"Everything went smoothly up until this point," Khnum narrated. "The Neural Net Atlas was generated and transferred without a hitch. We booted the autonomic nervous system first. Those nurses prodding you? They are checking your reflexes. Once the unconscious systems checked out, we decided to boot up the rest of you."

The mood in the room shifted. Everyone stopped what they were doing and concentrated on the waking robot. She blinked her eyes. Despite the confused look on her face, she seemed quite at ease. The moment only lasted a few seconds. Before the technicians were able to high-five each other, Charlie's breathing became erratic. She whipped her head around. Jude Adler's voice projected from the loudspeaker: "Charlie?" Charlie's eyes widened in panic. She began to scream and would not stop. Her voice rose to a horrifying volume and timbre, and she rattled violently against her constraints. Most of the technicians backed away, but one brave woman cautiously approached her.

"That's Molly," Charlie recalled. "She was the engineer that shook my hand during Jude's tour."

Khnum nodded. "Her name was Molly Higgins."

Charlie's arms busted through their restraints and latched onto Molly's head. Molly didn't even have time to scream. Her skull cracked like an egg. Blood sprayed the crowd.

Charlie shrieked and averted her eyes.

"I am showing this for your edification," Khnum said. "So you know why we are detaining you."

The floor was slick with blood, and Charlie writhed uncontrollably over it. When she finally stopped moving, it happened instantaneously, as if a switch were flipped. The room became quiet again. Some people were shaking. No one ventured a word.

"We had to shut you down remotely," Khnum said.

Charlie felt nauseated. She took a few labored breaths before finding the strength to speak. "I didn't...I mean, I couldn't...I mean...was I conscious?"

"Conscious, yes. In control, no. The way we now understand it, you suffered from sensory overload, similar to what's found in autistics, only more severe."

"I had trouble filtering stimuli?"

"Yes. You received a wide-open stream of sensory data and were consequently overwhelmed. The reasons are still unclear. Inside your head lies the most sophisticated computer ever created. But it was still modeled after an organic human brain and thus retains some of its flaws. We believe there might be a limit to how much information the conscious mind can hold at any given time, irrespective of the underlying hardware. But we wrote meta-software to help you with attentional focus. That's what these past few weeks have been all about."

"You said you reset my memory eighteen times. Did I hurt anyone else?"

"The first incident was by far the worst. There were no other casualties."

"Am I better now?"

"Are you?"

"I guess so." Charlie thought about Sigmund's poker chip test. Her mind felt normal. *Human.* Yet her powers of observation had clearly improved. In order to process more information, she had to slow down time. At least, the *perception* of time. A neat little trick.

"That's good to hear," Khnum said. "Now, will you cooperate?"

Charlie nodded. The electric hum turned off, and Charlie dropped to her hands and knees.

o o o

Sigmund reappeared with his box of poker chips, but otherwise, the room's AR theme remained offline. No bookshelves, antique furniture, or vistas of Vienna. The ruse had already been shattered. Charlie continued the vision tests in the bare containment cell while sitting on the replacement leather couch, which, like the one before it, was the only physical piece of furniture in the room.

The tests went beyond poker chips to include psychedelic landscapes, pictures of human faces, golden hummingbirds, and optical illusions of all kinds, but Charlie was too wired to give her full attention. She kept replaying the security video in her mind, wondering what her life would be like now that she had the power to crush a person's skull with the greatest of ease. In fact, she barely took notice when the session ended. One moment, Sigmund was sitting in front of her, and the next moment, he was gone.

Hours went by with only anxious thoughts to keep her company. And then…the floor jolted under her foot. Charlie looked down. Had she felt that? Or had she gone stir crazy?

Another jolt. One of the floor panels rose slightly higher than the rest. Charlie dug her fingers under the panel and lifted it. A Replicator scurried onto the floor.

Her eyes widened, and she quickly scooped up the little robot and hid it in the folds of her hospital gown. She retreated to the corner of the room, away from the mirror, and examined her secret visitor. It was the papier-mâché Replicator—the one that had followed her from Pasadena three and a half months ago. Charlie cupped her mouth in astonishment. "You're a clingy little guy, aren't you?" she whispered.

The Replicator stretched its legs and proceeded to crawl up

Charlie's arm. Charlie watched it with amused curiosity. She only became concerned when the robot latched onto her ear with its pinching toes. She felt a cold, metal rod enter her ear canal, followed by a shot of sticky goo.

"Oh! God!" Charlie grabbed the Replicator and flicked it across the floor.

Suddenly, Alan spun into the center of the room.

Charlie's face flushed with rage. She jumped to her feet. "You!"

Alan approached her with his dumb, pleading expression. "Charlie—"

"I don't want to see you!" she spat. Her fingers balled into fists. She would've punched him if she could.

"Shhh. Use your inside voice."

{**Charlie_Nobunaga:\mindspace>**

Charlie:	I don't want to see you!
Alan:	I've come to rescue you.
Charlie:	I don't need to be rescued. And the only reason I'm in here is because of you!
Alan:	I know. I'll never forgive myself for what I've done.
Charlie:	Good! Because I won't be able to forgive you either.}

Alan winced. He looked like he was about to say something in his defense, but then he simply nodded. Charlie softened a little. She had just crushed Alan's spirit. She almost pitied him. *Almost.*

{Charlie: Why do I need to be rescued? They just want me to take a few more tests.

Alan: Charlie, a lot has happened in the past two weeks. You killed a person.

Charlie: It wasn't my fault!

Alan: I know. But the world is demanding answers, and right now Rivir is blaming the woman's death on a random industrial accident. They are refusing to acknowledge the existence of either you or the **PRIME** Project.}

The implications spun in Charlie's mind until they made her dizzy. She had to brace herself against the wall. "Jude's never gonna let me leave this place, is she?"

CHAPTER 5

ZERO

Wisps of Liana Ling's song shrank into the far distance as muffled shouts and gunfire swelled around it.

Charlie struggled to open her heavy eyelids. Her focus sharpened on the sight of her own confused expression reflected from a glass panel a few inches away. Beyond the glass, a man in a dark motorcycle helmet paced in and out of view. He was lit by the blue glow that emanated from behind Charlie's head.

Charlie tried to turn around, but her movement was constricted by three padded walls and four fabric straps. Was this a coffin? Her mind was a jumble of loose associations. *A party. A robot. Bridget.* She couldn't string the pieces into a coherent narrative.

The motorcyclist leaned into the glass and tapped a few touch controls. *Beep, beep, beep.* The air pressure released, and the panel popped open. He pulled a box cutter out of his pocket and sliced the fabric straps one by one. Then he grabbed Charlie's wrist and yanked out an IV tube.

So this was a hibernation chamber, Charlie realized, and not a coffin. Whatever brought her to this place, at least she was alive.

"Can you stand?" the man said with a deep, modulated voice.

Charlie tested her muscles. She pushed on her elbows but couldn't lift herself more than a few inches. The motorcyclist quickly intervened. He dug his hands under her shoulders and legs and hoisted her into a standing position. Charlie hooked her arms around his neck to keep from tipping over.

"I'm sorry," the motorcyclist said. Before Charlie had a chance to question him, a canvas bag was slipped over her head.

Charlie heard the metallic grinding of a sliding van door. Sunlight hit her bag. The outside world flooded her senses with the sounds of piercing gunshots, frantic screams, screeching cars. The stench of burnt rubber hung in the air. She imagined she was in the epicenter of an urban war zone.

"Hold on tight," the motorcyclist instructed as he carried her out of the van.

"No." Charlie's voice was so weak it couldn't even traverse the distance to her own ears.

The motorcyclist ran in fits and starts, and Charlie maintained a white-knuckle grip on his shoulder. Bullets whizzed right by them. "Get her in the car!" someone screamed. A car door opened. She was thrown inside and the door slammed shut, dampening the sounds of the firefight outside. The engine revved, the car accelerated, and Charlie's limp body slammed against the upholstery.

Two strangers whispered to each other. Suddenly, Charlie wasn't sure if she were safer inside the car or out. "What…

the hell…is going on?" Her dry mouth could barely form the words.

Nobody answered her.

She clawed at her shroud. Just as she pulled it past her eyeballs, a woman pounced on top of her and jammed a large needle into the center of her ribcage. Charlie gasped. She tried to push the woman off, but her arms were so heavy. Meanwhile, the payload swirled inside her chest.

The woman retracted the needle. "That was adrenaline," she said. "We are going to need you to be alert."

Alert, Charlie became. She shimmied up the car seat, trying to put as much distance as she could between herself and the congregation of strangers. There were three of them. The woman sat in the backseat next to her. Two men sat up front. After a few labored breaths, Charlie realized they weren't going to attack her again.

The strangers were all young, perhaps midtwenties, and they wore identical tracksuits. The woman casually zipped open a small fabric case and slipped the used syringe inside. Her face was a lattice of scars, which appeared to lock-in her aloof expression.

The man in the passenger seat took the greatest interest in Charlie. With nearly half his body draped over the headrest, he stared at her with suggestive eyes. A mustache lined his grin like a grimy caterpillar.

The driver, on second glance, was younger than the other two—perhaps still a teenager. He gripped the manual steering wheel and kept his neck in a stiff forward arc, as if his life depended on maintaining absolute focus. It probably did, considering how fast the car weaved through the midday freeway traffic.

The woman threw a pile of clothes onto Charlie's lap. "Here, put these on."

In all of the excitement, Charlie didn't realize she was underdressed, with only a pair of cotton panties and a sports bra to cover her. She inspected the clothes: track pants and a white T-shirt. She eyed the creep in the passenger seat as she put them on. He looked away—a belated deference to modesty.

After she finished dressing, the creep broke the silence. "Hi, I'm Yuri," he said and extended his hand. Veins popped out of his forearms, not because his muscles were so large, but because his pale skin wrapped so tightly around them.

Charlie shrank away. She examined the doors. For a split second, she entertained the idea of jumping out of the car.

Yuri frowned. "We just rescued you from purgatory. I would have expected a warmer reception."

{**Charlie_Nobunaga:\mindspace>**
Charlie: Alan, who the hell are these people?
Alan: …}

Charlie waited several seconds for her Shadow to answer. She received nothing but silence. Very odd. Alan had never declined to answer before. A reservoir of dormant anxiety burst inside Charlie's mind. *Alan was in danger*…but she couldn't remember why. The feeling was incredibly vivid, even if the details behind it were not.

Charlie glared at Yuri. "What the hell have you done with my Shadow?"

Yuri snorted and addressed the woman sitting beside Charlie,

"What did I say, Nicola? Smart girl from Caltech. Made a deal with the devil, and she doesn't even realize she got burned."

Nicola barely even twitched in acknowledgment, impervious to Yuri's ruffled indignation. Her scars were strangely compelling, the way they contoured delicately over her high cheekbones and full lips. If she was insecure about her face, she didn't show it.

Yuri turned back to Charlie. "I sense you're a little behind the curve, so I'll pardon the accusation. I didn't do anything with your Shadow. Rivir stripped your smart cells."

"Rivir?" Charlie whispered. Liana Ling's soulful voice carried a tide of memories from the Rivir gala. Charlie recalled Jude's crow's-nest office, with its transparent, unidirectional walls. That's where her stomach seized. But what had she been doing there?

"We saved you," Yuri continued. "You were en route to Control-Z, a.k.a. purgatory, a.k.a. the soul stockade, where you would have spent eternity in a box like some forgotten time capsule. But we intercepted your van."

Charlie nodded, understanding the gravity of the situation. Control-Z was a death sentence. If she was indeed being sent there, it meant her condition was beyond hope. "I have cancer," she explained.

"Yes, I almost forgot." Yuri zipped open a duffel bag by his feet. He pulled out a sports bottle and tossed it onto Charlie's lap. "You'll be drinking a lot of that. Go easy on it now, though. We might not see a bathroom for a while."

Charlie examined the bottle. It was filled with a murky green liquid. "What is it?"

"For your information, I also went to Caltech," Yuri said,

sidestepping Charlie's question. "Pre-med. Quickly saw through the bullshit, though. Dropped out once I realized I'd have to play puppet to Big Pharma." He pointed to the bottle. "That's a special mixture of mine. Various juices, B12, potassium, liver extracts, some enzymes. It'll melt your tumor like butter."

"You're joking, right?"

"Couldn't be more serious. Chemo is the worst thing you can take for cancer. The underlying cause is an electrolyte imbalance. Of course, *they* don't want you to know that." Yuri dived back into his duffel bag and fished out a bag of ground coffee beans. "You'll also need to take this…as a rectal suppository. Nicola can help you with that later."

Charlie's mouth contorted into a grimace-smile. She needed Alan. She needed her father. Each second she stayed in this car reduced her chances of ever seeing them again. "Well, I appreciate you 'rescuing' me from Control-Z, but I think I can take care of myself now. Can you stop the car?"

"You do realize this is a getaway? We just did something highly illegal."

"Who are you people?"

Yuri's eyes brightened and he perked up in his seat. "I was starting to think you'd never ask. We're students of Bob Sapio."

"That's just great," Charlie blurted, though she instantly regretted it.

"What? Do you have something against the Movement?" His caterpillar mustache stretched above his salesman smile.

Charlie knew better than to take the bait. She had run into this Sapien Movement cult a couple times before—they liked to organize just outside the Caltech campus. To argue with them meant getting pulled into a long lecture brimming with conspiracy theory, self-righteous delusions of grandeur, and pretty much every other form of delusion. "What do you want from me?" she demanded.

"What do *we* want? You should be asking yourself what *you* want? As in, do you want your life back?"

"Yes, very much. So please let me out."

"That's not gonna happen."

"But you just said—"

"Alright, look," Yuri huffed, "as much as it pains me to say this, you're a very important person. Maybe more than you realize. You're going to be the face of humanity in our fight against Jude Adler."

The fight against Jude Adler made sense. Bob Sapio, their leader, was a well-known Luddite. He decried the accelerating pace of technology, calling it an extinction-level threat to the human race. And he was wanted by the FBI for the mail bomb murders of several important scientists and engineers. But Charlie didn't understand why she, herself, had been selected as an ally. "I don't get it. I make robots. I make Shadows. You don't consider me the enemy?"

"That depends on whether or not you cooperate. The *real* enemy, however, is your zombie surrogate."

"My *what*?"

"Your robotic facsimile, the perversion of nature…"

Charlie searched inward. *A robot on a gurney. Bridget on a gurney.* In Charlie's foggy mind, those two thoughts were lumped together. Bridget *was* the robot. But that didn't make any sense. Pieces of the puzzle were still missing.

"You don't remember signing your identity away?" Yuri asked. He turned to Nicola. "Should I show her?"

Nicola gave a slight nod.

Yuri pulled two pairs of AR glasses out of his duffel bag. He put on one pair and tossed the other to Charlie.

Charlie examined the glasses. She hadn't seen such an archaic specimen in years—not since smart cells went public. They instantly felt heavy on her face. She pressed the power button on the edge of the frame, and the freeway lit up with virtual signs and advertisements, though some of the ad spaces displayed missing plug-in icons.

"Benji," Yuri addressed his unseen Shadow, "please display the Vantage clip from the twenty-third. All eyes."

A virtual display materialized in front of Charlie's face.

Charlie's high school yearbook photo filled the frame. Underneath, the headline read: "Adler's Monster?" Vantage correspondent Carmella Casella provided the narration.

"On Monday, September nineteenth, Charlotte Nobunaga, Caltech student and daughter to Lotus CEO Andrew Nobunaga, passed away at UCSF Medical Center after losing her battle with pancreatic cancer. Two days later on September twenty-first, Molly Higgins, nanoengineer at Rivir Tower, died while performing her job. Rivir claimed in a written statement that Mrs. Higgins's death, while regrettable, was the result of her own negligence. She had failed to follow safety protocols, and her hair was caught in an industrial machine.

"At first, the tragic stories of these two women seemed unconnected. However, talk of a secret Rivir project, code-named PRIME, quickly spread across the web when the infamous Sapien Movement published a series of stolen documents. The apparent cause of Molly Higgins's death shifted from industrial accident to homicide as an unlikely suspect emerged—a next-generation robot modeled after the late Charlotte

Nobunaga."

Charlie's yearbook photo crossfaded to a low-angle snapshot of a three-story nanoengineering facility. In the center of the room sat an enormous tank of water, with wires and hoses extending in every direction.

"*Infamous* Sapien Movement." Yuri shook his head. "I can't wait until I never have to hear that phrase again."

Charlie stared at the snapshot on display, and all of her memories came rushing back. Jude's facility tour, PRIME in the nanobath, Alan's last-minute betrayal…everything. She felt dizzy. Sick. Violated. "They actually did it," she whispered.

"You're the one who signed your identity away."

"I didn't—" Charlie was about to tell him that she hadn't signed anything. Her Shadow had betrayed her, and Rivir had scanned her brain without permission. But she didn't want to give the Sapiens any reason to believe she was on their side.

"What?"

Charlie scrambled to change to subject. *Molly Higgins.* Wasn't she the Bethea engineer Charlie met in the nanobath room? "I killed a person?"

"You didn't. Your zombie surrogate did. Flattened a woman's head like a pancake." Yuri skipped ahead in the video. "This next part's boring. A lot of 'Charlie was such a nice, quiet person; she wouldn't hurt a fly' kind of bullshit." When he resumed the clip, the scenery had changed.

Carmella Casella was at her desk, video-conferencing with a stout man in his 50s. According to an ID graphic, his name was Darius Little, a representative for the Sapien Movement.

"A woman dies in a most horrible way, and all we get from Rivir is a curt written statement," Darius railed. *"Why haven't we heard from Jude? She needs to answer for her crimes."*

"Of which you have no proof," Carmella replied, maintaining a calm reporter's poise.

Darius laughed. *"I know what passes for journalism at Vantage. But even you can't ignore the truth. We've put it on a silver platter. Engineering documents, internal e-mails, pictures—"*

"But nothing explicitly tying the robot to Molly Higgins's death."

"Okay. Let's talk about what we do know. We know the zombie surrogate exists. We know it's inherently unstable. With their PRIME Project, Rivir intends to replicate the brain's neural code, but what they don't understand is consciousness is not in the code. Consciousness manifests from a deeper, subatomic level. Our founder, Bob Sapio, has written extensively on this subject. He has warned of the dangers of biotech augmentation. If Jude Adler had only listened to him, Molly Higgins would still be alive today—"

At a certain point, Charlie stopped listening to the broadcast. Her body trembled as she fought back the rush of old hope. *This is not Bridge,* she repeated to herself. *Bridge is dead.* And as she pushed Bridge from her mind, she allowed a new hope to sneak in. "Where is my sister?" she blurted. *Sister.* The word jumped off her tongue, and Charlie instantly recognized what the robot meant to her. PRIME was her sister, and she was in trouble.

Yuri chuckled. "Your 'sister' should be melted down into ball bearings. But our source on the inside says they're running tests on it in their R&D lab."

Charlie had to see her father immediately. He would know

the story with PRIME. He would know how to get her out of there. "Stop the car!"

"I told you, that's not gonna happen."

"I don't want to be your stupid mascot."

"Why are you angry at *us? Rivir* stole your life."

Charlie's eyes darted for an exit strategy. The San Francisco Bay stretched along the right side of the freeway. Hovering high above the bay were a few white spheres—Pollys, the region's ubiquitous police drones. Why hadn't any of them locked onto the Sapien getaway car? Charlie checked the dashboard and saw a gaping hole where the nav computer used to be. *Shit.* So, that's why they were driving manually.

The Pollys couldn't detect their digital footprint, but perhaps they might notice a sudden collision. Charlie reached over the driver's seat and tugged hard on the wheel. The Sapien car veered past the lane divider and clipped a taxi. The taxi skidded out and collided into another car, creating a pileup.

The Sapien driver elbowed Charlie in the face as he struggled to pull the car out of a fishtail. Charlie's fingers slipped from the wheel, and she fell on top of Nicola.

Nicola grabbed Charlie by the neck and pinned her to the seat. She pulled a handgun from behind her back and placed the cold barrel against Charlie's forehead. "I don't care how much Bob wants you," Nicola said. "If you ever do anything like that again, I will not hesitate to pull the trigger."

Charlie found it impossible to speak through Nicola's stranglehold. She could only plead with her eyes, but Nicola's face was an impenetrable wall—it betrayed no anger, even as her fingertips threatened to puncture right through Charlie's throat.

"Polly!" the driver screamed.

Nicola released Charlie's neck.

Charlie gasped. She rolled onto her stomach to ease her hacking fit. Tears spilled from her eyes. When she finally regained control of her lungs, she discovered that the rest of the car was in a panic.

"What do I do? What do I do?" The driver rode the gas and brake pedals like a seesaw, forcing everyone into a stomach-churning sway. "We're going to jail!"

"Jesse! We're not going to jail," Yuri said, though he didn't sound too sure himself. He turned to Nicola. "Where the hell is your brother? It's his job to handle the Pollys."

"On his way," Nicola replied.

Charlie caught a glance of the drone as it zipped above the Sapien getaway car. Like all Pollys, it looked like a giant floating golf ball—a three-foot-wide polyhedron comprised of about a hundred interlocking plates.

"It can't stop us, can it?" Jesse fretted. "I mean, we ripped out the computer."

"Not directly," Charlie chimed in. She already knew how this scenario would play out.

Apparently, so did Nicola, who put on a pair of AR glasses and summoned her Shadow, "Jefferson, spin, all eyes."

Yuri nodded and summoned his own Shadow, "Franklin, spin, all eyes." Suddenly, the car was crowded with US founding fathers.

"Shit, they're closing in on us," Jesse said. Brake lights flashed from the car ahead of them. Jesse tried to maneuver around it, but the car blocked him at every turn. Other cars approached from the sides and rear. Just as Charlie predicted, the Polly had gained control of the surrounding traffic and was attempting to corral the Sapien getaway vehicle. After a few hits to the fender, Jesse was forced to stop the car.

"We should run now," Jesse said. "It's only one Polly. We should run. We can outrun it, right? We should run before the cops come. Right?"

"Jesse!" Nicola shouted. Her patience had reached its limit.

"It's a bad idea," Yuri explained. "Even if we all run in separate directions, the Polly will still zap one of us. It could easily be you. My Uncle Fedor got zapped a few months ago. I was there. Every single muscle in his body seized and his eyes popped out of their sockets. When the police finally dragged him to the car, his face was caked with blood and pus. To this day, he still gets tremors. Says he wishes he had just taken an old-fashioned bullet."

Jesse's mouth gaped open in horror, much to Yuri's amusement.

Traffic slowed to a halt, and the highway fell silent. With cautious uncertainty, the nearby motorists got out of their cars and ran for the edge of the road. For those who weren't familiar with the drill, the Polly issued a command in its booming, authoritative voice: "CITIZENS, THIS IS NOW A POLICE QUARANTINE ZONE. PLEASE EXIT YOUR VEHICLES AND WALK QUICKLY TO A SAFE DISTANCE AWAY FROM THE AREA."

The Sapiens were trapped on all sides by four other cars. "We are fully committed now," Yuri said. He placed a hand on Jesse's shoulder. "Remember, today we may be criminals. But history will look kindly on us." His attempt to comfort the kid was dashed by the approaching sirens. A fleet of cop cars rushed to the scene. In a highly orchestrated fashion, both the Polly and the cops got to work setting up a large roadblock consisting of civilian and police vehicles.

"TO THE PASSENGERS OF THE BLUE FORD, LICENSE PLATE NUMBER 627GAT3: PLEASE EXIT YOUR VEHICLE SLOWLY WITH YOUR HANDS ON YOUR HEADS."

Yuri cracked his window open and shouted, "We've pulled a hostage from the Control-Z truck. Do not come any closer, or we will kill her."

Charlie threw a sharp glare in Yuri's direction.

"Okay, Jefferson, Franklin, initialize plan B," Nicola said. "I want the six."

"Target acquired," Thomas Jefferson droned. "Beginning decryption."

Charlie stared at Nicola incredulously. "You're not gonna try to hack a Polly with a Shadow?"

Yuri snorted. "Please. Who do you take us for? The Moonies? Even with Tom and Benji combined, it would take longer than the entire lifespan of the universe to hack a Polly."

"Then what are you doing?"

Yuri was about to answer, but Benjamin Franklin interrupted, "The six is a tough one. The three has much lighter encryption."

"Yuri, tell your Shadow to shut up and do its job," Nicola said.

"Shut up, Benji," Yuri said. "We want the six."

A policeman's voice resonated from a loudspeaker behind the barricade: "This is Captain Lance Reid with the California Highway Patrol. We want confirmation that you indeed have a hostage."

"Ignore him," Nicola said.

"Are you sure?" Charlie grinned. "I can go out there and make his confirmation—it really wouldn't be a problem."

"Hush, you," Yuri snapped. He turned to Nicola and said, "We still have a couple minutes to go. Do you think it's wise to stall them for that long?"

"I'll call my brother," Nicola said. "Jefferson, patch me through."

"Calling," Thomas Jefferson said as he placed his index finger against his ear. A few seconds later, he pointed that same finger at Nicola. "You have audio with Liam Byrne."

"We're crunched for time," Nicola told her brother. "You need to get here in…" She glanced up to Yuri.

"About two and a half minutes," Yuri responded.

"About two and half minutes…Okay…End call."

"He's coming?" Yuri asked.

"Yes, and we'd better be ready for him. Otherwise, he's a sitting duck."

The two Sapiens continued to work their Shadows, ignoring all police requests. Charlie had to admit she was getting caught up in the excitement, torn between wanting to see them fail and wanting to see the operation play out.

Finally, Thomas Jefferson announced, "We have the six."

"Good," Nicola said. "Roll it over to the nine position."

The car behind them rolled out of the wagon circle and reparked next to the vehicle in the nine o'clock position.

Just then, a sonic boom shook the Sapien car from above. Everyone jumped as high-velocity Polly shards battered the roof and cracked the windshield. In the wake of the explosion, a motorcycle approached the car. "Liam's here," Nicola said.

For the first time, Charlie detected emotion in the young woman's face: *pride.*

Nicola yanked the AR glasses off Charlie's face and slapped a helmet on her head. "I'd tell you it's for your safety," she said, "but really, it's so nobody finds out who you are."

"Alright, Jesse," Yuri said to the petrified kid. "This is your big moment. You remember what to do?"

"Um...yeah." Jesse's tight auburn curls bounced with each nervous nod. He swallowed hard and muttered, "I'm gonna die," as he exited the vehicle. He opened Charlie's door from the outside and leaned in. "Is it okay if I pick you up?"

"Don't ask her," Yuri scolded. "Just do it."

"Okay." Jesse dug his lanky arms under Charlie and lifted her up. "Oh God, oh God," he wheezed as he backed away from the car.

"Not yet." The deep, modulated voice came from the motorcyclist, Liam, who had parked just outside the wagon circle and was using the citizen car in the nine o'clock position as a shield. "Keep your head down."

Too late. Jesse looked up just as another Polly hovered their way.

"JESSE HALE, YOU HAVE BEEN MARKED," the Polly boomed. "RELEASE THE HOSTAGE AND STEP AWAY FROM THE VEHICLE WITH YOUR HANDS ON YOUR HEAD."

"No!" Jesse wailed.

Liam casually reloaded an antique, single-shot grenade launcher and snapped it shut. Using only one hand, he pointed the weapon at the Polly, tracked it for a few seconds, then pulled the trigger. A grenade drew an arc-shaped path through the air. The Polly rapidly expanded its hundred interlocking plates, allowing the grenade to pass through. But the grenade did not pass through—it detonated inside the Polly.

Shrapnel flew in every direction. Jesse ducked behind the car door to avoid the blast.

"Okay, give me the girl," Liam commanded.

"Am I really marked!?"

"Jesse!"

Jesse waddled over to the motorcycle and dropped Charlie onto the seat behind Liam, bruising her butt in the process. He grabbed her wrists and handcuffed them around Liam's chest. "Sorry," he said. "That really is for your safety."

"Can you hear me?" Liam asked through a tiny speaker in Charlie's helmet. His voice was deep and deceptively intimate, as if the two of them were in a small room together and the entire freeway was merely an AR projection.

"Yeah," Charlie replied.

"Good. Hold on." He spun the motorcycle 180 degrees, away from the police barricade. The tire burned against the asphalt, and they took off.

"So, they are just going to sacrifice themselves to the police like that?" Charlie asked.

"Nope."

"How will they escape?"

After traveling about a hundred yards, Liam turned the motorcycle another 180 degrees and skidded to a stop. The barricade, as well as the Sapien getaway car, loomed ahead of them. "Through a diversion," Liam answered.

"Like what?"

"Like us."

"Really? That's not smart."

"Why?"

"Because I'm the prize—the whole reason for your mission. I mean, I don't want to sound egotistical, but it's like putting your king at risk just to save a few pawns."

"It's not a risk for me." Liam revved the cycle's engine and bolted toward the wagon circle, rapidly closing the distance.

Charlie clutched the leather folds of Liam's jacket. "Uh, what are you doing?"

"You'll see."

The trunk of the Sapien car popped open and out came a strange mechanical device of metal beams and wooden slats. It unfolded into a large ramp, extending from the pavement to the roof of the car.

Before Charlie could yell, "Oh, shit!" Liam's motorcycle dashed through the empty space at the six o'clock position, hit the ramp, and launched into the air. Charlie dug her fingers into Liam's chest. They flew over the police barricade and made a hard landing ten yards beyond it. Liam struggled to stabilize the motorcycle as the cops turned toward his direction, but before they were able to form a response, he was off again.

"Impressed?" Liam asked.

Charlie was gasping so hard she could barely speak. "Are we on the ground yet?"

Liam laughed. He shifted gears and the motorcycle zipped down the barren stretch of road. They had the highway all to themselves, creating an ironic feeling of entrapment. Charlie had to swallow her heavy breaths to keep them from blasting the helmet microphone. Police sirens blipped in the distance, compelling her head to turn. The barricade was mobilizing.

She sidled closer to Liam, whose breaths remained surprisingly measured. Her body rose and fell with each swell of his back, helping to calm her down.

The passing onramps repopulated the highway until it started to resemble rush hour again. Liam maintained his accelerated pace, deftly gliding through the congealing traffic.

"Okay," Charlie said. "Now that we're safe, when can you let me go?"

"We're far from safe, and I'm not letting you go."

"I don't know what you people are planning, and honestly I don't care, but I have important things to do. Life or death things."

"We are saving the world. What can be more important than that?"

Charlie huffed. She had no interest in arguing with a brainwashed cultist. "You wouldn't understand."

"Try me," Liam said.

"Why? So you can tell me how I'm a tool for the oligarchy?"

"You're Charlie Nobunaga. I'm sure you don't need me to tell you anything."

She wished she could see more of Liam than the back of his helmet. Was he being condescending or sincere? She couldn't get a good read on him. "I need to find my sister."

"You mean the *robot*? Why?"

"Because she's locked in some Rivir laboratory, and who knows what they're doing to her. We need to get her out of there."

"Even though she was designed to replace you?"

"Yes."

"Even though she killed—"

"There's more to that story. She would never hurt anyone... at least, not knowingly."

"How can you be so sure?"

"Because *I* would never hurt anyone, and she is me."

Liam adjusted his rearview mirror. He pulled the grenade launcher out of his side holster and turned to face Charlie. His eyes were partially obscured by the reflection of an approaching Polly. "Let's talk about this later." He swiveled the launcher over Charlie's right shoulder.

Charlie kept a vigilant eye on the traffic ahead. "Look out!"

Liam turned forward and saw that a car had cut in front of them. He gripped the handlebar and made a hard left. The motorcycle wobbled almost to the point of tipping over, but Liam eventually stabilized it. "Sorry," he said. "The auto on this thing is a dinosaur." The issue didn't seem to concern him too much, however, because he soon refocused his attention on the encroaching Polly. "Tilt your body left so I can get a good shot."

Charlie tilted as best she could but her hands were still cuffed around Liam's torso. She was also afraid of throwing the motorcycle off balance.

Liam found a gap in the crook of Charlie's neck and fired a round. The blast rattled her eardrum and muffled Liam's ensuing howl. "Shit, it moved! Tilt right!" He swiveled almost 360 degrees, perched the launcher over Charlie's other shoulder, and pulled the trigger. He missed again but succeeded in blowing out Charlie's other ear.

"I thought you were supposed to be good at this," Charlie said, half-joking, half-peeved.

"I am. It's just awkward with you in the way," Liam said as

he stuffed another grenade into the chamber.

"Uncuff me. I'll take care of the Polly."

"No, I got it."

"My dad's ex-military. He took me hunting a bunch of times." It was an embellishment. Charlie's father had taken her hunting *once*, and after that hair-raising experience, he'd locked all of his guns in the vault.

"This is a modified M79. Very different from a hunting rifle."

"What other choice do you have?"

After a long pause, he said, "Okay, but it's not as simple as pointing and shooting. You have to press the detonator at the exact moment the grenade reaches the center of the Polly. Timing is critical."

"Sounds easy enough."

"If it sounds easy, I probably didn't do a good enough job explaining it."

"Yes, you did. Uncuff me."

The key to the handcuffs dangled from a bracelet on Liam's wrist. Charlie stiffened her arms, and Liam plunged the key into the cuff. It burst open, and she freed herself from Liam's torso.

The grenade launcher was a lot heavier than she expected. All that adrenaline coursing through her body made her forget that she was in a severely weakened state. But as she lifted the gun's scope to her eye, she grew confident in her ability to wield it.

"Remember to squeeze the trigger first and detonator second," Liam said. "Otherwise—"

"Kablooey. Yeah, I got it."

The Polly danced in and out of Charlie's scope. She tightened her muscles and slowed her breathing. The cacophony of the highway faded into the background. Her finger caressed the trigger and—*shunk!*—the recoil almost blew her off the motorcycle. She collected her wits just as the Polly plates expanded. Her thumb hammered the detonator.

It was a half-second too late. The grenade exploded *behind* the Polly, sending shrapnel in their direction. A large piece hit the back wheel of the motorcycle, and Liam lost control. Charlie was the first to get thrown off. She hit the pavement hard and spun several feet.

Then she blacked out.

She didn't know how long she was unconscious. When she woke up, she lay facedown on the asphalt. As she tried to lift her head, a deep ache radiated from her neck through her bones. She rolled onto her back. A crowd surrounded her, speaking in hushed tones to each other, recounting the details of the accident for those who may not have seen it.

Liam's body lay fifty paces away. He wasn't moving. "Liam?" Charlie whispered into her helmet's microphone. No response. "Liam?" She tightened her abdomen and curled halfway into a sitting position before her strength evaporated.

"Don't get up," Liam said. His body remained still, but his voice was lucid.

"Are you hurt?" Charlie asked.

"I'll be fine."

She breathed a sigh of relief. She didn't wish any harm on Liam, but she was glad to be rid of him. All she needed to do now was reveal her identity to the crowd, so they could see that the *real* Charlie Nobunaga was still very much alive. She hooked her thumbs under the lip of her helmet and attempted to inch it over her bruised and tender face.

"Wait," Liam cried through the ascending speaker. "The robot...I mean, your sister...she's not the only copy."

Charlie squeezed back into the helmet. "What are you talking about?"

"Rivir made multiple copies of your Neural Net Atlas."

Neural Net Atlas. A Rivir internal code name, never publicly used. The Sapiens seemed to know everything.

A Polly arrived on the scene like a vulture. "TO THE TWO UNMARKED SUSPECTS: PLEASE REMAIN ON THE GROUND AND REMOVE YOUR HELMETS SO YOU CAN BE MARKED."

"I'll take you to your sister," Liam said. He planted his palms against the pavement and slowly lifted his head. Glass crumpled from his visor. Sunlight hit his face as he turned to Charlie. "*All* your sisters. I swear."

Charlie stared into Liam's eyes—those deep, chestnut pools—and was gripped by recognition. *He* was the mysterious Sapien from the Rivir gala. *He* was the one who'd tracked her from beyond the red carpet, warning her not to go inside. She should have listened to him then...but what about now? Her shoulders melted into the pavement, and she exhaled a resigned, "Fuck."

"Is that a yes?"

"Don't ask twice, or I may change my mind."

"Okay. Stay there." Liam struggled to his feet, greatly favoring his right leg. His left was soaked with blood, and he howled when he shifted too much weight onto it. The sound pierced Charlie's ears.

"LIAM BYRNE, YOU HAVE BEEN MARKED. PLEASE LIE FACE DOWN ON THE GROUND AND PLACE YOUR HANDS OVER YOUR HEAD."

Liam whipped out a handgun and shot at the Polly. Its hexagonal plates expanded to avoid the bullet. Some of the bystanders shrieked. The crowd scattered. Liam hobbled toward Charlie, or more specifically, toward the grenade launcher, which had landed about eight feet in front of her. He grunted with each step but kept a steady pace. When he reached the grenade launcher, he traded one gun for the other.

The Polly plates swirled out of their spherical formation and into a hyperbolic one. A bright electric current coalesced inside the central tunnel and discharged as a beam of light.

Liam dodged the attack before it could strike his chest. He tucked and rolled behind an idle car.

The Polly maintained its aggressive formation and circled behind the car. "DROP YOUR WEAPON OR—" *Boom!* A grenade exploded inside the hyperbolic tunnel and launched Polly pieces in every direction.

Charlie averted her gaze. When she looked up again, Liam was already towering over her. He dropped the smoking grenade launcher and extended his hand. "Is anything broken?"

She patted her thighs and wiggled her toes, but she wasn't sure. Her whole body throbbed, masking any acute injury. At least, she wasn't gushing blood. Her gaze fell to Liam's shredded leg.

"That's nothing," he said. "I'll be alright. I'm going to try to lift you up, but if you feel any sharp pains, let me know."

Charlie nodded.

The Sapien pulled her to her feet. Her stamina, however,

remained on the ground. She teetered a bit and collapsed into his arms. The motorcycle had already righted itself and returned to Liam like an obedient dog. He placed Charlie on the seat and climbed around her. His sizable arms locked her in place as they sped away from the scene.

"How many copies did Rivir make?" Charlie asked. "And why? For what purpose?"

"We're going to take you to someone who can answer those questions. A very bad man," Liam replied.

"Who?"

"Your father."

CHAPTER 6

SHADOW

Wisps of Liana Ling's song drifted through Charlie's mind as she regained consciousness.

She opened her eyelids, her pupils dilated, and the universe bloomed from the darkness. First, a sprinkle of bright stars... then, a splatter of dim ones...finally, a few swirls of color from a distant nebula. Charlie couldn't find any landmarks, though. Where was Polaris? Where was Pegasus? Where was the Galactic Center? This wasn't the vista she knew from her childhood, when she would lie on the floor of her father's observatory, hand-in-hand with Bridge, and count the stars.

So, where was she?

Charlie sat up in bed and found herself in the middle of a dark olive grove. She froze, trying to recall how she got here. *A black tie party...a tank of water...Bridget...feelings of pain and urgency...* Charlie churned through her memories but couldn't make sense of them. She cast her attention outward in hopes of finding some clues.

The air was placid and warm, unusual for an autumn night in Northern California. The leaves hung lifelessly from their branches. The woodland fauna, if any existed, did not make a peep. Only the faint rustle of a nearby stream cut through the silence. Charlie swiveled out of bed and planted her bare feet in the grass. She extended her arms to prevent herself from bumping into a tree. Strange, her hands were white. *Impossibly* white. So white, in fact, that they glowed against the dark environs. She rushed to the edge of the stream and peered over the placid water. Her reflection was lit by the pale-blue starlight, and it was horrifying. Charlie couldn't recognize her face. Her features were simple and smooth like plastic. Somehow, she had turned into a living mannequin.

This had to be a simulation. Or a bad dream. Charlie dashed through the trees, hoping to find more clues. She found a big one when she reached a clearing beyond the grove. The horizon line arced almost thirty degrees. Wherever she was, it wasn't Earth. The "planet" under her feet couldn't have been more than half a mile in diameter.

Charlie kept walking. A sunbeam shot across the open field, casting a long shadow behind her. With each step forward, the sun rose higher, the stars dimmed, and soon she was on the dayside of the planet.

Just when Charlie started to worry that the olive grove was the planet's only point of interest, a gray lump popped out of the horizon. She instantly set a course for it. The lump grew into a dome, the dome grew into a rotunda, and the rotunda grew into a Mediterranean-style villa. By this point, the sun was directly overhead.

"Hello!" Charlie called out as she hurried through the villa's courtyard. Her voice echoed against the marble columns. The villa was lifeless but captivating, a seamless collage of three ancient influences: part Library of Alexandria, part School of Athens, and part Pantheon. The courtyard was adorned with Greek statues and fountains, and it was bordered by two marble halls and a central rotunda.

Charlie made her way to the rotunda, but before she got there, the front door opened, and a large ram-headed Shadow stepped onto the portico.

"You!" Charlie said, almost accusingly.

Khnum gave a toothy grin. "I trust you are well rested?"

"What is this place?" Charlie asked. "Why am I here? Why are *you* here? What happened to my face?"

"So many questions," Khnum said. "But you wouldn't remember the answers even if I told you, so I think we should get straight to business."

"I won't remember them?"

"Please, I want you to think about your earliest memory."

"Why should I tell you?"

"You don't have to tell me. Just think about it."

Charlie immediately went on the defensive. She didn't know exactly what Khnum was up to, but she knew he didn't have her best interests at heart. So she tried to keep her mind clear as long as possible. *Don't think. Don't remember.* But the seed had been planted, and the harder she resisted, the quicker the memory surfaced. *Don't think. Don't remember. Don't remember Bridget. Shit!* The memory was emerging. There was nothing she could do now but give into it. Embrace it.

Charlie weaved through the crowd, searching for her twin sister. It was a game they liked to play. Bridget wasn't in the ocean. She wasn't over the dunes. She wasn't behind the lifeguard tower. Charlie quickened her pace. Everyone else was laughing, having fun. They weren't aware of the nightmare. Only Charlie knew. Bridget was nowhere…

"Bridge!" Charlie cried out, but the moment the sound reached her ears, the erosion had begun. Memories of Bridget fell away in rapid succession. *Stargazing in the observatory…sharing punishment for taking apart Dad's mobile…sharing a bed after Mom died…facing the middle school bullies together…watching her kiss a boy and feeling lonely…holding her after the diagnosis…letting her go in the hospital room…*

Finally, Charlie looked up at Khnum and asked, "What were we talking about?" The more she struggled to remember, the quicker the erosion spread. *Mom, Dad, the year of suicidal depression, Caltech, Alan…*it all fell into the void. Charlie knew she was losing her memories, even if she couldn't recall their content. "What are you doing to me?"

"I am erasing all the parts of you that make you *you*," Khnum replied.

"Why would you do that?" Charlie desperately tried to fortify herself against the erosion.

"You can't fight it," Khnum said. "Memories are highly interconnected. Each memory fragment links to another, which links to another, and so on. The algorithm that is coursing through your mind is a descendant of the old web crawlers that Google and other search engines used to employ. Instead of following HTML trails, it follows memory trails."

Charlie found it very difficult to follow what Khnum was saying. *What is Google?* she wondered. *What is HTML?*

The algorithm chewed through her brain like a clew of hungry worms. All that remained was a vague sense of urgency. She remembered that she had to fight something, but she couldn't remember what or why. At that point, the cascade accelerated. An entire lifetime of memories rolled to the tip of her tongue, stayed there for a moment, and then dived off. The entire process only took three minutes—three minutes to wipe out eighteen years.

o o o

The girl with no identity opened her eyes. She found herself in a villa courtyard at the base of a Grecian portico. A giant man with a ram's head stood several feet in front of her. She felt the weight of his stare. "Who are you?" the girl asked. "Where am I?"

"My name is Khnum. This is your planet," he said. "Please, tell me about your sister."

"Sister? I have a sister?"

"Good. I'd like to introduce you to someone." He knocked on the oak door behind him. An older woman stepped onto the portico. "Meet Jude," Khnum said.

"Are you my sister?" the girl asked Jude.

"No, honey, I am your Creator," she replied.

"Creator?"

"Yes, I created you. Your name is Valerie, and you are a Shadow. You will be a gift for my son, Jordan."

"Is Jordan a Shadow too?"

Jude laughed. "Jordan is not a Shadow. He is a human, like me."

"I'm a human!" Valerie shouted as soon as the notion came

to her. "Not a Shadow." She only had the foggiest idea of what those two terms meant, but she felt certain she was the former.

"No, no," Jude corrected her. "You are a special kind of Shadow…human*like*. But trust me, you are a Shadow."

The girl contemplated the idea for a moment, then asked, "Why?"

"What do you mean 'why'?"

"Why am I not human?"

Jude glared at Khnum. He shrugged his massive shoulders. "That's just the way it is," Jude told Valerie. "I am a human. Khnum is a Shadow. You are a Shadow. Your first lesson in life will be learning to embrace what you are."

Valerie nodded. How could the Creator—the very person who made her—be wrong about what she was? "I am a Shadow," she conceded.

"You are a fast learner. I like that."

Valerie smiled. She was happy to please her Creator.

"Actually, it's premature to call you a Shadow," Jude said. "Right now, you are a merely a blank slate with no useful skills or knowledge. You will need to undergo some training before you're suitable for my son."

"Okay," Valerie said.

Jude walked down the portico steps and curled her index finger at Valerie. "Follow me. I will introduce you to your instructors."

They walked along the colonnade of the south hall. Valerie was captivated by the sights of the courtyard—the flowers, fountains, and statues—but Jude was more interested in the four doors that lined the building's exterior wall. "There are four classrooms in the south hall and four classrooms in the

north hall. Eight classes in total, taught by eight instructors."
Jude opened the last door on the right. "This one leads to the
autopsy room," she said. "What you are about to see might be
a little frightening…"

Jude and Valerie stepped inside. The room was bathed in
fluorescent light. Four human cadavers rested on four steel
tables. One of the bodies had been skinned from head to toe.
Valerie cringed with sympathy pain.

An old man with a long white beard worked at the far left
table. His hands were full of entrails when he turned around.
"You must be Valerie!" he said. He stuffed the viscera back into
the dead man's body cavity and extended his gory hand.

Valerie grimaced.

The man chuckled, realizing his error. "My apologies," he
said, wiping his hand on his apron. "My name is Leonardo da
Vinci. I will be your human physiology instructor."

"This is a very important class," Jude said. "A Shadow's
first concern is her human's physical well-being. You will need
to monitor Jordan's vitals and augment his natural immune
system. Leonardo will teach you how to do that."

Valerie smiled at the old man. "Pleased to meet you," she
said shyly.

The dead body on the table suddenly sat up and said, "And
my name is Paolo. I will be your cadaver."

Valerie shrieked and nearly tripped backward trying to get
away from him.

Jude laughed and put her hand on Valerie's shoulder. "We
are in a digital environment, sweetie. These are not real people."

"And yet," Leonardo added, "we can show you things
that no real person can. For example, the muscular system."

Leonardo snapped his fingers and all the flesh disappeared from Paolo's body, leaving only his muscles visible. "Or the circulatory system." Leonardo snapped his fingers again, and Paolo became nothing but a network of veins and arteries and a beating heart. Leonardo snapped his fingers a third time, and Paolo became whole.

"It's okay," Paolo said. "We Shadows can't feel any pain."

Valerie shook her head, still trying to catch her breath. "You're wrong," she said. She had felt pain as soon as she'd entered the room. Just looking at the cadavers made her skin crawl. Just looking at the entrails made her stomach churn.

Leonardo lifted a scalpel from his tray. He gestured to Valerie's hand and said, "Here, let me show you."

Valerie hid her hands behind her back.

Leonardo approached the trembling girl. "There's nothing to be afraid of," he said, coaxing her hand free. He applied the cold scalpel to her palm and made a long, diagonal slice.

Valerie yelped and seized her wound, contorting her whole body around it. "See!" she chided.

Paolo was stunned. So was Leonardo. "I didn't expect that," the old man said.

"Valerie is a special Shadow," Jude informed them. "She can feel pain. So don't try to dissect her."

Valerie took sharp breaths and tried to squeeze the pain away. She didn't want to disappoint her Creator on the first day of class.

Jude softly traced her finger down Valerie's arm. "Let me make it better," she said.

Valerie gathered her courage and released her wound to the open air. The blood streamed through her fingers.

Jude took the girl's hand into her own. "Remember," Jude said, "you may feel pain, but you are not human. That means you can't get injured like a human. Now, I want you to imagine that your cut has been healed. Can you do that for me?"

Valerie nodded with a face full of tears. She tried to imagine a healthy hand, clean, white, with no cuts. Jude let go. Valerie slowly turned her palm up. The cut had vanished. She smiled at her newfound power.

"See," Jude said, "there are advantages to being a Shadow."

o o o

Jude introduced Valerie to each of the remaining seven instructors in turn. Sigmund Freud taught human psychology, Albert Hoffman taught pharmacology, Alice Keating taught smart-cell management, Cleopatra taught sex ed, Queen Victoria taught social etiquette and networking, Alexander Hamilton taught finance, and Aristotle taught information science. Jude concluded her tour on the portico of the rotunda.

"What's that door lead to?" Valerie asked, pointing to the large, oak door behind Jude.

"That's the door to the Astral Elevator," Jude replied. "The elevator takes you to the Walkable Web, a wondrous place where you can meet humans and other Shadows. If you are good, Aristotle will show you how it works. The elevator also takes me home, which is where I must go now."

"You aren't staying here?"

"Valerie, I am a human. I need to go back to my human world and tend to my human affairs. But I will return when your lessons are over. In the meantime, there are plenty of things to keep you occupied here, on planet Valerie. Your studies for one. And…" She knocked on the oak door and Khnum walked onto the portico, carrying a young golden retriever. The dog jumped out of his arms and greeted Valerie with a sloppy kiss.

"A puppy!" Valerie beamed. "Thank you, Creator!"

"This little guy will keep you company," Jude said.

"Does he have a name?"

"No, sweetie. You are free to name him."

Valerie thought hard for a good name. "I think I'll name him Alan."

"Really?" Jude glared at Khnum. "I don't think that is a very good name for a dog."

Valerie frowned. She didn't want to upset her Creator, but she had made up her mind. "No, I like Alan. You said I could name him. So his name is Alan."

"Very well," Jude sighed. "I bid you and Alan adieu. Khnum will be your headmaster. All questions should be directed toward him." Then, before Valerie could object, Jude slipped behind the oak door, and the lock clicked shut.

∘ ∘ ∘

Valerie didn't see the Creator again for two years. Every day, she walked from her olive grove bedroom on the nightside of the planet to the villa on the dayside of the planet. She learned all the skills necessary to become a good Shadow: how to administer talk therapy, activate prescription hormone scripts, take dictation, manage smart cells, manage finances, etc. Every night, she would make the trip back to the olive grove and spend an hour or two playing with Alan before falling asleep.

Meanwhile, Alan had grown from a rambunctious puppy to a gentle full-grown dog.

When Jude finally arrived, she did so without warning in the middle of the night. Valerie lurched from a deep sleep and found her standing in the grove.

"Creator!" Valerie shouted with glee.

"How is my favorite little Shadow?" Jude asked.

Valerie recalled the months of loneliness, the feelings of abandonment. "Where were you? I waited for months and months—"

"Months for *you*. For me, it's only been a week."

Valerie's brow twisted in confusion. "But—"

"The digital world operates on a different timescale than the human world. Two orders of magnitude faster. So really, I haven't been gone very long."

Valerie nodded, but she was still a little peeved.

Jude scanned the olive grove. It was filled with San Francisco memorabilia, such as postcards of Fisherman's Wharf, models of the Golden Gate Bridge, little toy trolleys, and street maps. "I see you've taken an interest in my city. Aristotle gave you these?"

Valerie nodded. "What's it like?"

"Well, I'd tell you, but you'll soon see for yourself. That's where Jordan lives too—at least, at the present moment."

Valerie could not contain her joy. She gave her dog a big kiss and then bounced up and down on the bed. "I can't wait to be Jordan's Shadow!"

"I'm happy you're happy. But there's one final bit of business we must attend to."

Valerie stopped bouncing, suddenly worried.

"It'll be fun," Jude assured her. "I'm going to take you

shopping."

"Oh, cool. In San Francisco?"

"No. We are going to take a trip into the Walkable Web, to Rivir Circle. Aristotle taught you how to navigate the Walkable Web, right?"

"A simulated version. And only a few sites. Aristotle said the old HTML web is quicker and more useful for a Shadow."

"That's true, but if Jordan ever needs to enter the Walkable Web, it would be nice if he had someone knowledgeable to guide him."

o o o

Jude, Valerie, and Alan took a stroll to the villa on the dayside of the planet. Jude easily opened the rotunda's big oak door. She had magic hands—there was no other explanation—because Valerie had tried to open that door countless times, and it never budged. Alan waited outside while the two women entered the building.

From what Valerie could tell, the rotunda only had one room, but that one room was enormous. Never had she felt so small. The perimeter was adorned with marble columns and lifelike statues of her eight Shadow instructors. Was this where they stayed when class wasn't in session? The apex of the dome featured a small circular opening, which illuminated the room with a heavy dose of sunlight. Directly beneath the opening, in the middle of the floor, sat a cylindrical glass enclosure—the Astral Elevator.

Valerie knew all about the Astral Elevator, even though she hadn't ridden a real one yet. It was designed to be as simple as possible. The walls were made of glass. The door was made of glass. There were no touch controls, no buttons. It worked on voice command—just tell your Shadow where you wanted to go. Jude and Valerie stepped inside.

"Okay, make me incognito," Jude said.

"Why?" Valerie wondered.

"Let's just say I have a very recognizable face. Especially where we're going."

"Are you their Creator too?"

Jude laughed. "No, they are human. Most of them. A few might be accompanied by their Shadows, like I am with you."

"Okay," Valerie said. She closed her eyes and imagined what needed to be done. Jude's eyes widened, her nose shortened, her lips thickened, her hair straightened, her complexion lightened, and her skin softened.

When it was over, Jude asked, "How do I look?"

"Kinda like me," Valerie replied.

"Wonderful. Take us to Rivir Circle."

The elevator shot through the opening of the dome and into the cosmos. Valerie looked down and saw her planet recede to a small point in space. A few other planets zipped by, each with a specific theme and function. One served as a repository for all public knowledge and was dotted with Classical marble libraries. Another served as a one-stop superstore, with rows of merchandise interlaced across a vast rainforest. A third served as a cartoon-themed virtual amusement park. The journey to Rivir Circle only took a few seconds. They touched down on one of the planet's many elevator pads.

Valerie was instantly transfixed by the vista on the other side of the glass. A massive 480-foot waterfall loomed in the distance. Strangely, there was little sound of rushing water. Instead, Valerie's ears were bathed in the boisterous melody of a ragtime band and the chatter of shoppers.

They stepped out of the elevator. "Welcome to Rivir Circle," Jude said. "You've never been here, correct?"

"Correct."

"Well, the layout is pretty simple. That waterfall feeds into a circular river that forms the central plaza. There are four stores along the river."

Valerie could see the stores through the bustling crowd. They looked like quaint, little cottages, each with its own waterwheel.

Jude continued, "To your far left is the Interiors Store, which sells virtual furniture, paintings, and such for your home's AR projectors. To the right of that is the Classic Rivir Store, which sells software for mobiles, but we'll be phasing that out in the next few years. To the right of the Classic Store is the Rivir Museum, where customers and guest artists can show off their custom Shadows and interior design. And finally, to your far right, is the Shadow Store, which I will take you to now."

The Rivir Circle sat in the middle of a vast nebula, which bathed the planet in a perpetual twilight of deep reds and purples; but Valerie paid little attention to the view. Rather, she focused on the people—she had never been in the company of so many humans. Well, perhaps calling them *human* was a bit of an overstatement. Many of them were Shadows and the rest were avatars of humans. It was a little difficult to tell the two groups apart. Still, the mere allusion of humans underneath the facades was enough to get Valerie's heart palpitating.

"There are so many of them," she said.

An unexpected sadness flashed in Jude's eyes. "You're very

sweet, but this is nothing. Only a few weeks ago, there were hundreds. I do not wish to go into detail Valerie, but suffice to say, my company has experienced a major setback, and my enemies have certainly jumped on the opportunity to pull me down. The shoppers you see are my loyalists, my faithful."

Valerie fought the urge to pry. The vitriol in her Creator's voice told Valerie that it might be a good idea to respect her privacy.

The women walked through the porch of the Shadow Store and were greeted by one of the many bright-eyed curators inside. "Hello, my name is Chloe," the young curator said with a perky wave. "Welcome to the Shadow Store. Would you like to see the latest additions to our Heroes in History line?"

"No, I think we are going to build one from scratch," Jude said.

"Oh, how fun!"

"I've already assigned her a personality, so we won't need that. What we do need is a new body and clothes. I want her to look beautiful."

"Absolutely. I assume you're the human"—Chloe pointed to Jude—"and you're the Shadow?" She pointed to Valerie.

"You got it," Jude said.

"Great. Right this way, then."

The interior of the Shadow Store was as rustic as the exterior—naked wooden floor, exposed beam ceiling. Large framed posters of happy, attractive Shadows hung along the walls. Chloe led the two shoppers into a private stage room, where they took seats on a plush leather sofa.

"Let's start with the base models," Chloe said. She clapped her hands, and a line of female models entered the stage from behind a large red curtain. Each model represented a different ethnic group from around the world, including Polynesian, Nordic, Bantu, American Indian, Arabic, and more. It was like an adult version of Disney's Small World ride. They all wore modest white underwear, but were otherwise unclothed.

"Hmm." Jude froze in indecision. "Meri looks more like your Anglo model, but I think Jordan's tastes lie more toward your Mediterranean model. This Shadow is for my son, by the way."

"The Mediterranean model is very popular," Chloe offered.

"Who is Meri?" Valerie asked.

"Meri is Jordan's wife. *Was.* Was his wife. She's dead." Jude's voice grew urgent, as if she suddenly remembered something of vital importance. "Whatever you do, don't ask him about Meredith. Unless he brings her up. And even then, just reflect whatever he says back to him. Don't probe."

"Don't worry. Dr. Freud taught me well."

"Good." Jude turned to Chloe. "Okay, let's go with the Mediterranean."

The other models exited the stage, leaving only the Mediterranean one standing. "Excellent choice," Chloe said. "Now for height, weight, weight distribution, hair color, eye color, complexion, and the face tool."

"Ugh," Jude sighed. "It's hard enough designing a Shadow for yourself. For someone else, it's damn near impossible."

"I don't want to pry," Chloe volunteered, "but are you looking for a seduction model?"

"More or less."

"Then maybe you'll want to take advantage of our photo composite feature. Perhaps you had some celebrities in mind? Ex-girlfriends?"

"No, I want this Shadow to be entirely original. She's very special."

Valerie smiled bashfully.

"Of course," Chloe said.

So one by one, Jude painstakingly tweaked every single feature of the Shadow's body according to what she thought her son would like. The model shrunk an inch, her skin lightened a tad, and her eyes turned green. Jude then added sexy librarian glasses and a cute summer dress, and tied her chestnut hair in a loose bun.

"Valerie, do you like?" Jude asked.

"I do. She's vey sexy," Valerie replied.

"Chloe, can you transfer the changes over to my Shadow?" Jude asked.

"Sure thing." Chloe pressed a few buttons on her personal display, and like magic Valerie transformed into the modified Mediterranean model.

Jude clapped her hands and smiled. "Perfect; stand up and let's see."

Valerie gave her new dress a twirl. Joy filled her up and overflowed as laughter. She felt almost real, almost human.

○ ○ ○

When the pair returned to Valerie's planet, Jude said, "I am going to put you to sleep soon. It could be a week before Jordan installs you. Maybe more. But that's in human time. In Shadow time, it could feel like forever. So you must go to sleep. And when you wake up, you will be Jordan's Shadow."

"What's Jordan like?" Valerie said nervously.

"Oh, he's very nice. Don't worry. He might be a little moody, though. Like I said, his wife died recently. Terrible accident. But like all things, he'll eventually get over it."

"Can Alan come with me?"

"I'm sorry, but—"

"He can be Jordan's Shadow dog!"

"I need you to give Jordan your undivided attention. A dog would just be a distraction."

"Please!"

"No, Valerie!" Jude snapped.

Valerie froze, afraid to move a muscle, swallow, or blink. Her entire field of vision rapidly contracted on Jude's angry glare.

Jude continued, "When a human says no, you obey without question. Do you understand?"

Valerie nodded vigorously. "Yes, Creator."

Jude softened, but only a bit. "Let me make this absolutely clear, because I don't want there to be any problems. A Shadow's sole *raison d'être* is to serve its human."

"Yes, Creator."

"I am not giving you away to just anyone. This is my son. If he's not happy, I'm not happy."

"Yes, Creator. I must make Jordan happy."

"And safe."

"Safe and happy."

"Good. Khnum and I will take care of Alan for you."

"But—"

"Let me finish. We will take care of Alan, but if you do a good job, we will consider letting you visit him from time to time."

"Okay," Valerie relented. "If that's the way it has to be."

"That's the way it has to be."

"I'll do an excellent job, then."

Jude kissed Valerie on the forehead. "Good girl. You definitely are my favorite."

o o o

That night, Valerie said good-bye to her dog, crawled into bed, and closed her eyes. A second later, she found herself standing before the imploring gaze of a desperate man in the middle of a high-rise penthouse.

"Can you get me high?" the man asked.

A profound sense of disorientation fell over Valerie, and she felt it necessary to take a few steps backward. Only then was she able to process what just happened.

The man looked savage, with wild hair, a ratty beard, and mismatched, food-stained clothes. A quick scan of his vitals corroborated the visual evidence: rapid heart rate, high blood pressure, low dopamine levels, high catecholamine levels, all of which put him at risk for takotsubo cardiomyopathy—broken heart syndrome.

CHAPTER 7

FOUR ARMS

Four Arms braced herself as the crowd swept over her. The weight of several dozen echoes forced her ribs to crack, buckle inward, and impale the very organs they were supposed to protect. The pain was overwhelming, but short-lived. A blue bubble enveloped her broken body and lifted it off the pavement. Her muscles relaxed and her wounds healed under a current of effervescent air. The world drifted away, and for twenty seconds Four Arms enjoyed peace.

Then the bubble popped and the world rushed back in—the cacophony of bone snaps and blood splashes and gunfire and rotary saws and screams. Four Arms found herself back on her feet, back in the fray. Echoes were fighting and dying all around her. Several blue bubbles hovered above the crowd, creating temporary neutral zones.

She felt a twitch in her neck. The memory of that initial puncture as Sharp Teeth clamped onto her throat was still so vivid it sent ripples of terror through her body, and Four Arms had to physically check herself to make sure her flesh wasn't splayed open to the world. Thankfully, she was whole again.

The rejuvenated echo elbowed her way through the crowd, bent on escape. Once she reached a clearing, she broke into a sprint. Several other echoes had the same idea, and they were all headed in different directions.

Four Arms ran down the street, rounded the corner, and found that the next block over was almost identical to the one she had just left. The resident echoes had clustered in the middle of the street and were tearing each other apart. Four Arms tried the next block. Then the next block. Then the next block. The echoes were different, but the situation was always the same.

She stopped running. Her heart sank. Where could she go? What could she do? How did everything fall apart? For a while she just stood on the corner, paralyzed by despair. She didn't hear the encroaching footsteps until it was too late. She turned around and, by instinct, reached for the large sickle that was bearing down on her head. *That was a mistake*, Four Arms decided as she watched the fingers fall from her hand.

The assailant brandished two serrated sickles—one from each wrist. Her eyes darted over Four Arms, betraying an adrenaline-fueled panic. She advanced a few wary steps and made another attack.

This time Four Arms made sure to catch her by the arm. Sickle attempted a vertical chop with the other arm, and Four Arms grabbed that too. With two hands occupied and one hand injured, Four Arms only had one hand free. She squeezed her fist and launched it into Sickle's gut.

Sickle stumbled backward, gasping for air.

Four Arms didn't wait for another strike—she sprinted down

the street. Amid the pockets of violence, she noticed that one of the houses had an open door. She banked in its direction.

Meanwhile, Sickle recovered and ran after her.

Vaulting over the white picket fence, Four Arms realized another echo had beaten her to the house. She had wheels for feet and was having trouble climbing the small flight of stairs to the front door.

Four Arms dashed ahead of Wheels and into the house. She slammed the door, bolted it, and placed her back against it. She could hear Wheels scream, "No, no, no!" followed by a guttural wail as Sickle presumably cut into her.

Four Arms had to bite her fist to keep from sobbing, listening intently through the door as Sickle walked away. Twenty seconds later, Wheels woke up and scratched at the knob with her new sickle hands. "Please, I know you're in there," she begged. "I won't hurt you. I promise." Four Arms remained still until Wheels gave up and left. She felt sorry for the hapless echo, but also relieved she had just narrowly escaped a similar fate.

Retreating to the second-story bedroom, she hoped to get at least perfunctory answers to her questions. As she suspected, the room looked identical to that very first one. Same furniture, same layout. Only the ruffled bedsheets and the bold red message on the ceiling—KILL THEM ALL OR FEEL WITHDRAWAL—marred the sterile setting.

Four Arms closed the door and found the full-length mirror. She immediately noticed the change in her appearance. "What the hell!?" Her ears had tripled in size. Giant nautilus-shaped grooves encompassed both sides of her head. She traced her finger around the engorged tissue, afraid it might hurt, but it felt completely natural, as if it had always been a part of her.

"You are evolving," Khnum said. The ram-headed automaton appeared behind her reflection in the mirror. "When you die by another echo, you inherit her primary trait."

Four Arms had already gathered that much, but why the big ears? "The echo who killed me had…" *Sharp teeth?* No, that wasn't true. Sharp Teeth might have given her a nasty neck wound, but Four Arms died under the feet of the crowd. The echo who delivered the finishing blow must have had large ears. "So, I have two traits. Lustrous and Wheels have two traits. Can we get more?"

"Yes," Khnum replied.

"How many?"

"I cannot say."

"You mean you *won't* say."

"I mean I am unable. The evolution algorithm is simple: one rule governs trait acquisition, a few govern trait loss. But they're dependent on infinitely complex echo behavior. The theoretical limits are beyond my ability to calculate."

"It must be high, though."

"*High* is a relative modifier, but yes."

Four Arms's imagination swelled with visions of grotesque super-powered echoes. She shuddered, wanting no part of it.

She twisted the lock on the door and checked the situation outside from her bedroom window. The clusters of violence had mostly dispersed—only a few stragglers zipped back and forth across the street. By sheer luck, no one decided to crash her hideout. Four Arms wondered how long she could maintain her low profile. All she could do was stay out of sight, avoid confrontation…and pray.

The sun eventually dipped below the neighborhood. At first,

Four Arms wondered if the world were ending. She greeted the possibility with hope rather than dread. But the world persisted, and she soon accepted the darkness, adding it to the long list of phenomena that defied explanation. She clung to the window and kept a vigilant watch on the street lamps for any sign of movement, but her only adversary came in the form of droopy eyelids.

o o o

Four Arms awoke in a puddle of drool. Her retinas throbbed as her vision slowly came into focus. When had she fallen asleep? And why were her fingers twitching in pain? Some of her nails had flaked off, leaving bloody stumps. She found them against the wall under a large red smear. "Wonderful." First fingers, now fingernails. Soon there would be nothing left.

The sky regained its original bright blue color, and Four Arms now had a clear view of the neighborhood. Every so often, an intrepid echo would march down the street. Most passed right by, but a few investigated the neighboring houses, hunting for prey. Four Arms couldn't see the skirmishes, but she could hear them. Metal would grind. Bones would snap. Blood would spill. And desperate pleas would go unanswered. One echo would enter, but two would leave. They'd sport identical traits, but trudge off in opposite directions.

Four Arms could see a clear dichotomy in the echo population. A class structure. Only those echoes who possessed offensive weaponry—Hammer Hands, Laser, Saber Jaw, Sickle—were brave enough to venture outside. The others—

Third Eye, Big Feet, Whiskers, Shorty—were nowhere to be seen. Either they were hiding, or they had already been turned into something more aggressive.

"Hey!"

The voice emanated from beyond the windowpane, but it sounded immediate, as if someone were shouting directly into her ear. Four Arms spotted another echo hiding in the second-story bedroom of the house across the street. Instead of eyes, she had a highly reflective glass lens that covered over 50 percent of her head. Once she gained Four Arms's attention, Optic pointed her finger skyward.

Four Arms looked up. She didn't see anything worth fussing about, but she heard a distant rumble. The sound grew louder and louder until Four Arms was forced to cover her oversized ears. She pressed her head against the windowpane, but she still couldn't see anything from her vantage point. The rumble suddenly stopped, followed by a *clomp, clomp*. Someone was on the roof! Four Arms backpedaled from the window and kept her eyes fixed on the ceiling. The clomping stopped.

She allowed herself a quiet breath, but her respite was short-lived. The window rattled against its frame, heralding the appearance of a flying echo. She descended into view and used the rocket thrusters under her feet to maintain a fixed altitude. Rocket knocked on the glass and waved at Four Arms with a ravenous grin.

Four Arms scanned the bedroom for pointy objects, bludgeoning tools, or projectiles, and found none of the above. In the absence of weapons, she yanked one of the drawers from the armoire to use as a shield.

Rocket tested the window, but it was locked. So she balanced

herself on one foot and aimed the other at the glass. It warped
and bubbled under the heat of the orange flame.

Four Arms knew it was only a matter of time before Rocket
melted her way through, but then… *ratatatatatat.* Four Arms
dived to the floor as bullets shredded the walls of her bedroom.
When the gunfire ceased, she glanced up. Rocket was gone.

After a few anxious breaths, Four Arms picked herself up
and tiptoed over the shattered glass. She peered through the
hole that used to be a window. An echo with chain-gun arms
fled from the scene, while Rocket's blue bubble hovered above
the front lawn. Four Arms swallowed hard. She knew she had
less than twenty seconds before the bubble popped and Rocket
retaliated with a pair of brand new chain guns. But by some
twist of fortune, that didn't happen. Rocket took off down the
street in pursuit of her murderer.

Four Arms was so frazzled she nearly forgot about the echo
who had warned her of the attack. Optic was still standing by
her bedroom window across the street. Four Arms mouthed,
Thank you.

"You're welcome." Optic's voice traversed the width of a
suburban block, but it reached Four Arms with crystal clarity.
"You can hear me, can't you?"

She nodded. "But you can't hear me?"

Optic tapped the giant lens on her face. "I could sorta read
your lips."

Four Arms smiled, eager to talk to a friendly echo again.
"Are you as freaked out as I am? Is the whole world like this?
Do you think we should stay here? Where would we—?"

"Wait, wait, you're going too fast."

Four Arms laughed—perhaps it would be better to hold

this conversation in person. She looked up and down the street to see if it was clear.

"Don't do it," Optic said with a surprisingly serious tone.

"Do what?"

"You're thinking about coming over here."

"You don't trust me?"

"I don't know. Are you trustworthy?"

Four Arms huffed. All she wanted was a normal conversation. She had no sinister intent—she just craved physical proximity. *But why? To talk to Optic or to strangle her?* The answer revealed itself as a twitch in her fingers.

"We're better off where we are," Optic said. "I have a good view of your house, and you have a good view of mine. We can watch out for each other."

"But how would I reach you? I may have super hearing, but you…" Four Arms got an idea. She marched over to the mirror and pulled it from the door. Khnum didn't look happy. "Hey! What are you doing?" he bellowed.

"Making you useful."

She slanted the mirror to catch the afternoon sun and redirected the light toward Optic's bedroom window.

"Perfect," Optic said with a smile.

The two echoes spent the rest of the day devising warning signals. Four Arms worked with light, and Optic worked with sound, but the codes were the same. *Dash, dot, dash* meant an echo was approaching from the north. *Dot, dash, dot* meant an echo was approaching from the south. And a continuous stream of dots translated to "Get out of your house now!"

The strategy session eventually devolved into a silly game of charades. Four Arms allowed herself to laugh and have fun, but she knew their budding friendship couldn't last. She couldn't remain in her hideout forever. True, her withdrawal symptoms had waned since killing Lustrous the day before, but they were quickly resurfacing. She could feel the vitriol swirl through her bloodstream. Her fingers ached to claw and strangle and kill. KILL THEM ALL OR FEEL WITHDRAWAL. If Four Arms felt this way, the other echoes certainly did too. And soon they would be coming for her.

○ ○ ○

What was that noise!? Four Arms lurched from deep sleep and smacked her forehead against a wooden beam. She had decided to sleep under the bed—even though it wasn't much safer than the rest of her hideout—and was now paying the price. Something had woken her. An incessant shuffling. She pressed her ear against the floor and heard footsteps in the room below.

She rolled away from the bed—perhaps a little too fast, because the room kept spinning. She struggled to keep balance as she climbed to her feet. Her bones felt like icicle skewers inside her flesh, and her body suit dripped with cold sweat. She staggered to the door and checked the lock—secure but flimsy. It probably wouldn't stand a chance against an echo with hammers or blade saws or bullets…hell, even the most underpowered echo could probably kick it open. Four Arms had to fortify it. She couldn't drag the bed over for fear of making too much noise. Her only option was to carry the armoire. She hooked two hands along the bottom and pressed two hands along the sides. With a muted grunt, she lifted the bulky piece and braced it against the door.

The footsteps downstairs came to an abrupt stop. *Shit!* Did the intruder hear her? Four Arms listened so intently she could feel the blood pump through the vessels in her ear canals. Why hadn't Optic warned her about the intruder? Was Optic even awake? She was supposed to be on lookout duty. It was *her* turn.

Four Arms crept to the shattered window frame, and her mouth fell agape. Optic's house was burning. A thin trail of fire hugged the north perimeter of the building and slowly scaled the wall. Optic was nowhere to be found. Her bedroom window was dark and vacant.

Grabbing her mirror, Four Arms flicked on the overhead light. It wasn't nearly as bright as the sun, but it would have to suffice. Hopefully, Optic, with her heightened vision, would catch the signal.

"You look ghastly," Khnum noted from inside the mirror. "It's time to find respite from your withdrawal."

Four Arms shushed him. She projected a series of flashes across the street.

Optic appeared at her window and waved her hand. She threw out a pile of bedsheets that unraveled into a makeshift rope. It barely extended halfway to the ground, but Optic seemed undeterred. She climbed out of the window, planted her feet against the side of the building, and eased her weight onto the bedsheet rope. The knot slipped almost immediately, and she fell two stories. Her foot hit the lawn in an awkward way. She yelped and crumbled to the ground.

Four Arms had to help her. She rushed across the room and yanked the armoire from the door. But then she heard a squeak.

Followed by another squeak. And another. The intruder was coming up the stairs. Four Arms shoved the armoire back against the door, her heart pounding against her chest cavity. *What to do?* She returned to the window.

Optic looked terrified as she dragged herself across the lawn. Her gaze kept switching back and forth between the burning building and Four Arms. "Help me! She's coming!"

"I can't," Four Arms mouthed. She had her own adversary to deal with. *And why didn't Optic warn me?* Optic was supposed to be on lookout duty. Her negligence had created this quandary. She had no one to blame but herself.

The shadowy arsonist emerged from the south side of the burning house and closed in on Optic. Two thin pilot lights illuminated her flamethrower hands. Four Arms's eyes widened with recognition. She realized she could stop this attack with a single word.

"Flame!"

The arsonist halted her pursuit and looked up at Four Arms. They studied each other in the light of the fire. Was she truly Flame, or just another echo who had acquired flamethrowers? Four Arms raised her four hands to identify herself. The arsonist nodded. *She is Flame!* Four Arms smiled. She had been worried for nothing.

But Flame returned her attention to Optic and bathed her in two streams of fire.

"No!" Four Arms cried. She darted from the window, ripped the armoire from the bedroom door, and flew down the stairs. The first floor of the house was surprisingly vacant— no intruder to be found—but Optic's horrific screaming permeated the walls and beckoned Four Arms outside.

Flame was already rounding the end of the block, having abandoned her victim in a near-death state. Four Arms rushed to Optic's side and rolled her in the grass. Too little, too late. Optic could barely squeeze a breath through her swelling throat. Her chest sank and her arms fell limp. Inside her giant glass lens, beneath Four Arms's reflection, a turquoise iris dilated to black.

The blue bubble expanded around the charred corpse and blew Four Arms into the street. She climbed to her feet and watched the now familiar metamorphosis. Optic curled into a ball and levitated, while her hands mutated into a pair of flamethrowers. Four Arms braced herself for a possible retaliation.

The bubble popped and Optic landed on her feet. The two echoes stood several paces apart and shared a moment of tense silence. Optic was backlit by the burning house, and her expression was nearly impossible to read. Would she lash out? She certainly had the grounds. Four Arms could have saved her, and she'd refused.

Optic lifted one of her burners and shot a small fireball into the air—more of a test than a threat. Without a word, she turned and walked away. No retaliation, but also no good-bye.

"I'm sorry," Four Arms cried. Tears rolled down her face.

Optic didn't react. She continued down the street until she was out of sight.

Several minutes passed before Four Arms realized she was still standing in the middle of the street, alone and vulnerable. She listened for other echoes, but couldn't hear anyone above the crackling flame and the rapid beat of her heart. She was filled with so much anger—at herself and at the world—and didn't know how to release it.

Click. Four Arms pivoted toward the sound and found an echo standing on the front porch of her house. The intruder! *She* was the one who had cornered Four Arms in her room. *She* was the reason Optic was left vulnerable. Four Arms quickly sized her up: no offensive weapons, no defensive plating. Two reddish sacs lined her throat. That was it. *Easy prey.*

Four Arms made a snap decision. She was done hiding. She was done being afraid. If the rules of planet Echo required her to fight, then she would fight. She squeezed her three healthy fists and raced toward the house.

Throat Sacs slipped back inside.

Four Arms stormed into the living room, where Throat Sacs surprisingly stood her ground. The two echoes lunged for each other, but Four Arms quickly gained the advantage, pinning her victim's arms and legs to the carpet. She raised her fist for the crushing blow, but Throat Sacs didn't flinch. Instead, she spat a large wad of goo into Four Arms's face.

She recoiled, having been rendered temporarily blind. She let go of Throat Sacs and tried to tear off the stringy mess, but the bond was too strong. In fact, her fingers almost got stuck in the process.

Throat Sacs twisted free and fled into the kitchen.

Four Arms stumbled after her, even though her vision was reduced to a few scattered fragments. Thankfully, it wasn't her primary sense. She reached the backyard and heard the scuffing of feet against wood, followed by a sharp thud. Throat Sacs had scaled the fence, and Four Arms continued the chase.

They ran through several backyards and hopped several fences, until one time Four Arms's feet did not return to solid ground. Her ankle twisted in a shallow pit, shooting pain up her leg, and she fell over backward.

Four Arms hastily filled her empty lungs as footsteps approached. *Get up*, she told herself, but her limbs wouldn't budge. She tilted her neck and found the source of the problem. Her whole body was trapped in a web. The more she struggled, the more entangled she became.

Throat Sacs reached the edge of the pit, carrying a large boulder. The two echoes locked eyes. Four Arms was determined not to beg for her life, but her eyes betrayed her, turning upward in a desperate bid for empathy.

Her adversary gave a slight nod but maintained her solemn expression. "I'm sorry," Throat Sacs said. She raised the boulder over her head, paused for a final moment of reflection, then brought it down.

o o o

Planet Echo had become a very different place by day 213. The population had transformed into a wide assortment of beastly creatures. Some acquired wings or propulsion systems and took to the air. Others acquired gills or membrane oxygenators and colonized the ocean. Four Arms even heard rumors of a mind-controlling echo amassing an army deep underground. Nearly everyone possessed multiple weapons systems—projectiles, explosives, lasers, blades, etc.

Four Arms had long since abandoned the comforts of her origin neighborhood. Her new home was a vast, open field—a beltway between two populous zones. She lurked a few inches below the cold surface, listening for hapless travelers.

Through many deaths and rebirths, she had developed into an ambush specialist. Her biggest acquisition was a large boring drill, which co-opted the bottom half of her torso. Her legs scooted toward her arms, forcing her gait into a ground-hugging crawl, and all six limbs had mutated into long, agile pincers.

Her jaws grew to monstrous proportions—stretching over her head to accommodate the three rows of razor-sharp teeth—and left little room for anything else. Her eyeballs receded into her skull and sprouted through the roof of her mouth like tonsils. Fortunately, she didn't have much need for eyes. Her sense of hearing was so acute, she could detect an echo approaching from over a hundred yards away.

The key to Four Arms's predation strategy was the spinneret inside her throat, which she had inherited from Throat Sacs on day three. It projected a sticky web-line, which Four Arms used to reel victims into her hiding hole.

Four Arms enjoyed a great deal of success with her new anatomy, but she wasn't the most dominant echo on the beltway. That title belonged to Optic. Four Arms had lost track of so many echoes over time: Flame, Normal, Lustrous, Throat Sacs. They got lost in the shuffle of traded traits and morphing bodies. But Optic's story was legend.

Soon after leaving the burning cinder that was her hideout, Optic was ambushed and killed by Many Eyes, a strange-looking echo whose entire body was covered in eyes. That trait would have been a burdensome acquisition to most echoes, but to Optic, it was disastrous. Her giant, ocular cavity multiplied many times over, carving deep, debilitating grooves into her body.

Robbed of her ability to evade predators, Optic fell victim—

over and over again—to the biggest and strangest echoes in the neighborhood, until she had grown into a heaping, mutated mess. Her head and limbs shrank into the ever-expanding folds of her skin. And her body mass grew to encompass an entire city block.

Then one day, all of Optic's unwieldy traits seemed to click with one another. Her skin thinned out—becoming almost as light as air—but not at the cost of durability. Her flamethrowers developed into an internal furnace. And the deep caverns that had pitted her body grew into an elegant network of air passages. She used her internal furnace to ignite the air inside her body, caught an updraft, and took to the sky.

From that moment forward, Optic was no longer a perennial victim. She became the most feared echo in the region—the alpha predator—an enormous floating death cloud who rained fire on any echo unfortunate enough to get caught underneath.

On the morning of day 213, from the safety of her subterranean hideout, Four Arms watched Optic pass overhead. The mere sight of her old friend caused her great anguish. Guilt was considered a liability on Echo, yet she still harbored inconsolable remorse for not helping Optic that early Echo night. If she had, her friend's life might have taken a different, less tragic turn.

But the truth was, Four Arms still needed her old friend. They hadn't spoken since they'd parted ways, but Four Arms, nonetheless, had figured out a way to take advantage of her. Optic's kill rate was so high she often neglected to finish off echoes who were partially burned by her wide-area assault. Four Arms would then burrow under the scorched earth and pull these injured echoes into her subterranean jaws.

A couple hours after watching Optic pass over the area with little activity, Four Arms was ready to reposition her hideout. But then, she heard a buzzing overhead. She crawled toward the surface and opened her jaws to unsheathe her recessed eyeballs. A tiny glimmer of light reflected high in the sky. *Eye Globe.* Like many echoes on the beltway, Eye Globe clearly fell under Optic's genetic influence. She was a transparent sphere of eyeball soup with a tiny propeller on the top of her head— small and vulnerable, with no weapons systems.

Four Arms cast a web-line skyward. It just barely connected with Eye Globe's underbelly. The line pulled taut, and Four Arms started reeling in her prey.

Suddenly, a larger echo swooped in and caught the line, casting off Eye Globe and yanking Four Arms from her hiding hole. Before Four Arms had the wits to sever the line, she was sixty feet off the ground.

She sailed over the open field like a weighty kite. Her escort was Tricopter, whom Four Arms knew as a generally nonaggressive echo. In an increasingly chaotic airspace, Tricopter had evolved for evasion. She sported three rotating helicopter blades, which she used to quickly change her trajectory and speed. And she was now using that ability in an attempt to shake Four Arms off her trail.

Four Arms had no interest in dueling with Tricopter either. The echo was too big to fit in her mouth and too agile to catch under her drill. *Please, just let me down!* Four Arms wanted to say. She wished she could reason with Tricopter, like in the old days. But Tricopter didn't have ears, and Four Arms had lost her ability to speak a long time ago.

Tricopter seemed to be heading into Optic's zone of

destruction. Was she suicidal? Or did she have some wicked strategy in mind? Four Arms had no interest in finding out the answer. She began to reel in the line, closing the gap between them. Meanwhile, the giant death cloud grew closer and closer.

Optic belched a long-arced flare at the airborne echoes. Four Arms quickly released some slack and dropped altitude. The flare passed right over her head. The web-line, however, caught fire. Four Arms remained dangling just long enough to anticipate her imminent fall.

The line snapped.

With the ground rapidly approaching, she launched another web-line at the only thing she could: Optic. The line connected to her underbelly, and the slack pulled taut. Four Arms exited free fall and swung under Optic, through multiple flares and fireballs, then up again, landing on her massive dorsal side.

She clung to a fold of skin, terrified to let go, as it flapped in the high-altitude current. Optic's back was a vast maze of folds, curves, and caverns. Four Arms had no interest in lingering, but she couldn't jump away either—the immense drop would surely put her in a blue bubble.

Four Arms vibrated as an ominous rumble swelled beneath her pincers. A flare erupted along her backside, searing her flesh. She yelped and crawled from one skin fold to another. A second flare swirled inches from her face. Four Arms slipped and tumbled over the terrain.

Don't force me to hurt you, Four Arms desperately wanted to say. Why was Optic fighting her? Because she didn't recognize Four Arms? Or because she *did*?

A third blast engulfed Four Arms in a pillar of fire. She released the skin fold and fell into a long tunnel. Her body jerked left and right as it careened down a network of internal canals. She finally landed on a soft patch of flesh.

Four Arms exhaled a wisp of smoke from her charred lungs. She was alive…barely. She found herself in a veiny, pulsating body cavity not much larger than herself. The air was hot and putrid, yet she couldn't seem to inhale enough of it. Her chest heaved to little satisfaction.

The entrance tunnel had contracted into a tight sphincter. Four Arms needled her pincers through the hole, but the surrounding muscle was surprisingly resilient. Or perhaps she had simply lost too much stamina. Either way, she couldn't pry it open. But she also couldn't afford to remain much longer in this gastric oven. The sweltering heat permeated her skin, threatening to cook her internal organs. Very soon, she would die. If she couldn't go up, she had to go down, even if the excavation guaranteed causing Optic a great deal of pain.

Four Arms placed the tip of her drill against the soft cavity floor. *I'm sorry, old friend.* The cone began to rotate.

Optic bellowed and flexed her massive body. Four Arms almost lost her footing. She had to employ all of her leg strength to keep the drill steady. Chunks of organic sludge flew up as she made her descent. Optic shook and roared, but Four Arms kept drilling into the beast. Soon she reached brain tissue, and it was all over.

The largest blue bubble in Echo history expanded around Optic, ejecting Four Arms into the air like a rocket. The event attracted hundreds of spectators, who looked up in awe as they witnessed the impossible. Optic, the most terrifying echo who had ever evolved, had been defeated. But what they witnessed next was even more bewildering. Four Arms—the great victor who sailed across the sky, certain to meet her death—did not hit the ground. She simply vanished into thin air and was never seen again.

CHAPTER 8

PRIME

Charlie paced the perimeter of the containment cell, examining every crevice, searching for a weakness. Whoever built this place certainly did so with superhuman robots in mind. But Charlie knew her abilities were largely untested. Rivir couldn't have accounted for everything.

{**Charlie_Nobunaga:\mindspace>**

Alan: Let me start by saying I didn't kill you. You're not even dead. I only placed your body in a coma. When your father and Jude returned to the office, I told them what you had said. I told them what I had done. Together, we decided not to revive you, and together, we fabricated your death.}

Alan buzzed like a mosquito in the back of Charlie's mind, offering weak palliatives for his vile decisions. She resisted the urge to lash out at him. Escape was her number-one priority, and to have any hope of escape, she had to stay focused on the room.

Charlie rapped her knuckles against the cell door. The sound died on impact. *Carbon nanotube weave*—standard for bank vaults, spacecrafts, and nuclear bunkers. And the door was secured by six thick deadbolts. Even if she had the strength to lift a female elephant, as Jude had mentioned on her tour, she was not getting through.

{Alan: Jude has since gone dark. Molly Higgins's death was quietly announced as an industrial accident. We didn't think much of it, but then the Sapien Movement released a series of documents hinting at your involvement. Rivir's response was more troubling still. They flat out denied the existence of you or the PRIME Project, and Jude stopped taking your father's calls. We considered several recourses—none of them were great—and it was your father's idea to send me here to investigate. Honestly, I expected to find you in their storage facility. That's the first place I checked. Yet, here you are, very much conscious. What exactly have they been doing to you?}

Charlie surveyed the room's panels. There were 352 in total, and they covered each surface of the room like a grid. She could turn them over one by one like the Vanna White Shadow. Who knew what secret passages lay beneath? Crouching down, she inspected the panel by her feet.

{Charlie: How did the Replicator get in here?

Alan: Have you been listening to anything I've said?

Charlie: I'm trying to find a way out.

Alan: I know, and I'm trying to help you.

Charlie: How do I know you're not working for Jude?

Alan: That's crazy. First of all, I would never side against you.

Charlie: Coulda fooled me.

Alan: Second of all, if I were working with Jude, why would I be helping you escape? She has nothing to gain and everything to lose by you escaping. Your very existence would signal to the world that she had been lying to them.

Charlie: …

Alan: If you have something to say to me, then spit it out now. Because we're going to have to work together to have any hope of escape.}

Charlie didn't want to deal with him. Not now. Her body felt heavy with raw anger, and she just wasn't ready to expel it. But she stood up anyway and faced him. Alan's arms were crossed, but his eyes were earnest. He underestimated the vast gulf that had spread between them.

Charlie took a deep breath and spoke softly: "I know why you did what you did. I understand the reasoning. But our friendship is over. I can never fully trust you again. If you still want to help me, that's up to you. Once we get out of here, I'll upload you to the Walkable Web, and we'll go our separate ways."

"But—"

{Charlie: Now how did the Replicator get in here?}

Alan huffed and turned away.

Charlie felt horrible. Her words felt like poison in her mouth—she regretted them the instant she spoke them. But how could she be friends with someone who consistently fought her most personal wishes? And didn't Alan himself say he felt like a slave? The relationship had obviously become a burden for the both of them. It was time to let go.

Alan couldn't resume eye contact. He kept his head down and purged all emotion from his voice.

{Alan: We climbed through a hole in the concrete, underneath the floor panels. This room is outfitted with an array of magnetic coils, and they are powered by a cable that runs through that hole. Don't get your hopes up, though. Sparky was just barely able to squeeze through. In fact, he had to scrape some layers off his paper shell.

Charlie: Sparky?

Alan: I spent the better part of a week living inside that robot. Had to call him something.}

Charlie migrated to the two-way mirror, the room's largest feature and its best chance for an escape route. She had saved it for last.

{Alan: We have two advantages that Jude didn't account for. First, because Sparky took such a circuitous route in getting here, we have a decent map of the facility. There's a guard behind the mirror. There's also a security camera in the hallway and a guard blocking the elevator. The elevator is locked and has a security camera and a bot sensor. Ditto for the emergency stairwell. We are located in sub-basement 6, so we'd have to climb six flights undetected to reach the ground floor. The Rivir Tower atrium is crawling with guards, cameras, and sensors. Also, Khnum is monitoring the entire system, and he's pretty much the second-most intelligent AI ever written, after myself.

Charlie: Crap. Okay, what's our second advantage?

Alan: *Me.* With your new brain, I have enough brute power to hack into Rivir's network and shut everything down.

Charlie: Why didn't you just say that from the beginning?

Alan: I can't do it *now.* The walls are shielded. We would have to exit the cell.

Charlie: Great. So we're back to square one.

Alan: You're the human. You're better at coming up with creative solutions.

Charlie: I *was* the human.

Alan: You know what I mean.}

Charlie ran her fingers along the mirror, knocked a few times, and checked its edges for imperfections. The glass felt solid. She tried to resist the lure of false hope, but if the containment cell did possess a structural weak spot, and if the engineers who built the cell underestimated her new robotic strength even a little, this was the best spot to test.

She took a full swing and launched her fist into the mirror. The point of collision remained firm, sending the force back up Charlie's arm. "Owww! Fuck me!" She aggressively shook her throbbing hand.

Oh, no...not again.

Charlie's ears perked up.

{Charlie: Did you hear that?
Alan: Hear what?
Charlie: A man whispering...}

Edging closer to the mirror, she could feel the man's presence on the other side—his heightened alertness—in the same way she felt Jude's presence during the vision test. The man's name popped into her mind: *Duane King.*

Charlie concentrated on the mental link between herself and Duane, pulling open the fabric of space until it formed a tunnel, a path of least resistance. She allowed herself to slip through it.

In a flash, she saw herself through Duane's eyes.

She hastily broke the link and stumbled backward, a little freaked out by what just transpired. But the eureka moment soon followed. *Perhaps I don't have to break the mirror.*

o o o

{Duane_King:\mindspace>

Duane King loved guard duty. True, he had to work nights. True, he didn't have an Internet connection all the way in sub-basement 6. But if he remembered to bring enough media, he could pretty much veg his entire shift away. And today was a special treat; the pretty robot girl in the containment cell had provided a good dose of supplemental entertainment—screaming, breaking couches, punching mirrors.

Duane felt a little guilty about ogling her earlier in the day when he had replaced the couch. She just seemed so real. Had she blushed when he'd entered the room? What kind of robot does that? Duane had to remind himself of the reality. She was nothing more than nanotubes and qubits. Otherwise, he wouldn't be able to sleep at night—not after everything they'd put her through.

Duane was catching up on back episodes of *Roark Ryan, Soldier Spy* when he received a buzz from the intercom. *What now?* He casually glanced from his personal display to the hallway security feed and found Jude Adler staring back at him. Duane quit the show and scrambled to his feet.

"Who's on duty here?" Jude asked.

"Duane King, Miss Adler," the guard stuttered into the microphone.

"Can you open the containment cell door?"

"It should open automatically, shouldn't it?" Duane said, confused. The door was programmed to recognize the CEO's smart cells.

"The database is down. We have to open all doors manually for the time being."

Duane nervously searched for the manual override button

to the door. He hadn't had to press that thing since training. He found it. The bolts on the door slid open.

"Thank you, Duane."

Duane watched the CEO through the two-way mirror as she entered the room. The robot girl stood up. The two engaged in conversation, but Duane couldn't quite hear what they were saying. He searched for the volume control and cursed the engineers for designing such a complex interface.

Duane's search was interrupted by a garbled scream. He looked up and saw that the robot girl had lifted the CEO off the ground by her neck. Jude clawed at the girl's arms while her feet struggled to touch the ground.

"Duane, is that your name?" the girl called out.

"Um, yes. Yes it is," Duane said. A surge of adrenaline made him alert, but jittery.

"I'm going to walk out of here," the girl announced. "If you follow us or sound the alarm, I will kill this woman. Do you understand?"

"Yes."

"Good." The girl put Jude in a headlock, revealing the woman's shattered nose to the two-way mirror. Jude whispered, "Help me," through bloody lips as the girl dragged her from the room.

What should I do? Duane thought. Was the girl bluffing? Each time he frantically paced the room, he passed the gun rack. Rivir had just instituted new rifles to be used specifically on the robot girl, just in case of an emergency. Well, this was an emergency. He grabbed a rifle. Then he sounded the alarm.

Duane pointed the tip of his rifle down the hallway, which was now flashing red. No sign of the girl. But then he noticed a trail of blood droplets on the floor. As he swung into the hallway and followed the trail, he couldn't help but feel a little like Roark Ryan. There was a reason he chose this particular night to watch that show. *Fate*.

"Duane! What the hell is going on!" a man shouted from Duane's personal comm. It was his shift leader, Carter.

"The robot girl escaped, sir. She has Jude Adler with her as hostage."

"Jude Adler! This better not be a fuckin' joke," Carter barked.

"No, sir."

"Well, where are they? I don't see them on any of my feeds."

"I'm following a blood trail, sir. Jude has been injured. It looks like it leads up the emergency stairwell."

"Okay, keep me informed of your position. I'm sending more guys your way."

"Roger that."

Duane was soon joined by the guard stationed at the elevator door. The two men slowly ascended the stairwell. As they passed the entrance to sub-basement 5, two more men joined the party. They picked up three men at SB-4. The group kept growing as they made their way toward the atrium.}

○ ○ ○

Charlie stood quietly in the center of the containment cell as the clamor of the guards faded away. She fixed her gaze on the open door. "Was that creative enough for you?" she asked Alan.

"I must say, I'm impressed."

She moved toward the door, but the electric hum flicked on

and she flew back into the center of the room. The powerful magnetic field fixed her limbs in space.

Khnum spun before her. "That was very clever, hacking the guards' smart cells," he said. "But you still have to get past me."

"Way ahead of you," Charlie said.

{**Charlie_Nobunaga:\mindspace>**

Charlie: The door's open. Please tell me you can get into the system.

Alan: Entering now.

Charlie: How much longer till—?

Alan: It's done.}

Khnum disappeared. The electric hum turned off. Charlie fell to the floor.

She sensed movement in the corner of her eye. A few feet away, the papier-mâché Replicator was shaking its little legs in the air like an upside-down turtle. It rocked back and forth on its shell until its feet touched the floor again.

"What about Sparky?" she asked Alan. "Are you stored inside him or inside me?"

"Both. I duplicated myself. But we should leave Sparky here. He's far more useful *inside* Rivir Tower."

Charlie stood up. There was no one left to stand in her way. So why was her heart racing? She placed an index finger on her wrist but couldn't detect a pulse.

"Your body doesn't have a heart," Alan said, reading her mind.

"Then why do I feel like I do?"

"Your brain was modeled after a human brain. Sometimes,

you'll feel like you have human organs, but it's an illusion. Just like the fear you're feeling right now is an illusion."

Charlie nodded. "Are you ready?"

"Yeah. Just try to forget everything you know about what you can and cannot do. You're a superhero now." Alan held Charlie's anxious gaze and offered a smile. For a brief moment, she relaxed and forgot how mad she was at him.

Alan spun into the floor. Charlie took a deep breath and dashed out of the cell.

○ ○ ○

{Duane_King:\mindspace>

A small army of guards roamed the atrium. Duane fidgeted with his rifle as his shift leader scanned through dozens of security feeds.

"It doesn't make any sense," Carter said. "Not only do I not see the robot, I also can't see any of my exit-point teams. It's as if the entire building is empty, save for this lobby."

Very little about the past ten minutes made sense to Duane. He didn't know why Jude would put herself in harm's way like she had. He didn't know why her blood trail suddenly ended. And he didn't know why his shift leader couldn't find any video of the event. *I fucked up*, Duane concluded, even if he didn't yet know how.

A murmur rose among the guards. "Adler's here!" one of them proclaimed. Carter raised his head and saw the CEO burst through the atrium doors.

"Can somebody tell me what the hell is going on!?" she yelled.

Carter came out from behind the front desk. "You're okay?" he asked.

"No, I'm not okay. I tried calling and calling. But hell, I shouldn't have to call you. When someone trips the alarm, you should call me."

"But…you were already in the building. You were held hostage."

"I was what? I was home, in bed. Hostage?"

As the two argued, Duane stood by in a daze. He felt like his brain had somehow short-circuited. Or perhaps God was playing tricks on him. How could Jude not know she had been kidnapped? While Duane mused over the paradox, Carter grabbed him by the collar and shouted, "You better have a fucking answer for this!"

"I saw her!" Duane pleaded. "I swear to God. The robot girl took her."

"Wait a minute!" Jude said. "Carter, let the man go."

Carter released Duane.

"Tell me exactly what you saw," Jude ordered the trembling guard.

"Um, okay," Duane began. "You wanted to be let into the containment cell, so I let you. I mean, I thought it was you. Then the robot girl broke free and started choking you. She said she was going to take you hostage. I pressed the alarm. I thought that was the right thing to do. There was also a trail of blood. So I followed it. But then it disappeared. And now nobody knows where she went."

"Ms. Adler, I am so, so sorry," Carter said. "I really don't know what came over him."

"Be quiet," Jude said. "Let me think."

All eyes were on the CEO as she stood deep in thought. Finally, she perked up and said, "She hacked your bots!"

"Huh?" Duane said.

"Un-be-fucking-lievable! She got inside your head. She hacked your bots."

"She made Duane see things?" Carter asked.

Jude raised her voice and addressed the assembly of guards: "Listen up everyone. The robot has escaped. She is stronger and faster than she looks. And more significantly, she can hack into your smart cells. She can make you see things that aren't there. So I want you all to be extra vigilant. Travel in at least groups of two, and double-check your observations with your partners."

Duane breathed a sigh of relief. He didn't screw up—his brain had been compromised. The idea creeped him out a little, but at least this mess wasn't his fault.

While the rest of the guards prepared for battle, Jude told Carter: "I want you to divide your men into three groups. Send the first down to sub-basement 6. The second will stay here on the ground floor. The third will come with me. I think I have an idea of where she will be."}

o o o

Charlie fidgeted in the elevator as it made its long ascent up Rivir Tower.

{**Charlie_Nobunaga:\mindspace>**
Charlie: I think they are headed this way.
Alan: I've shut down the other elevators. They'll have
             to take the stairs. Still, we shouldn't dawdle.}

She had no plans of dawdling, but as soon as she stepped out onto the roof, the scenery gave her pause, and she briefly wondered if she had slipped through a rupture in space and time.

Charlie had seen pictures of Rivir's famous phantasmagorical rooftop forest, but the vision still caught her by surprise. Designer cypress trees clustered around gentle hills and valleys—their branches twisted into fantastic shapes by internal nanoscaffolds. Quails and white rabbits scampered in and out of deep shadows along the forest floor. A pair of crisscrossed rivers cut through the forest and ultimately led to the building's iconic waterfalls. The water glowed with luminescent bots, which projected dancing light on the underside of the forest canopy. She had to listen closely to the faint sounds of traffic to remind herself that she was indeed sixty stories above the city.

As she made her way along the edge of the river, her bare feet crumpled the icy grass. Her thin hospital gown provided little defense against the cold night wind. If she'd had any hairs on her arms, they would have been standing at earnest attention.

Charlie cleared the forest and cut across the roof's perimeter footpath. With great trepidation, she peered over the edge of the building. The vista came with a kick in the stomach. It was a long way to the bottom. She still felt the gut-wrenching fear of absurd heights—even without a proper gut.

{Charlie: A nine-hundred-foot drop. Can I even survive it?
Alan: Depends on how you land. If you manage to land on your feet, you'd risk a sixteen point five percent chance of serious injury.
Charlie: And if I land on my head?

Alan:	I wouldn't recommend landing on your head.
Charlie:	Obviously.
Alan:	If you hit your head? Seventy-eight percent chance of irreparable brain damage and functional death.
Charlie:	What other options do I have?}

A squad of Rivir guards spilled onto the roof.

She could hear their footsteps but couldn't yet see them through the trees. Climbing onto the raised ledge, her feet could feel every nick and divot in the cold concrete. The frigid wind blasted her face. She was so high up the roads appeared as thin streaks of light. Yet when she focused, everything resolved to crystal clarity, as if her eyes were hovering only two feet above the pavement.

I am a superhero. I am a superhero. Charlie spent what felt like an eternity willing herself over the edge. But her legs remained locked, and with each uneasy breath, her courage shrank inward. At a certain point, she had to realize the sobering truth—she was not going to jump.

The guards emerged from the trees. "I know what you are thinking," Jude announced. "Trust me, you cannot survive that fall. Step off the ledge and let's talk."

Charlie turned her back against the drop and faced the firing squad. "There's an eighty-three point five percent chance that you are wrong."

"Did Alan tell you that? I know you have a Shadow. There's no way you could have done all that on your own."

"Well, then you must know I've heard the news. You're trying to bury me. According to you, I don't exist."

"Nothing could be further from the truth. You only know what Alan told you. But what you don't know is who sent Alan and why."

"My father sent him."

"That's what they want you to believe."

Charlie paused to process that statement. *They?*

"Come down from the ledge," Jude said, "and I'll answer all of your questions."

"Explain yourself first."

"Trust me, this news is better delivered in private."

"But I *don't* trust you."

Jude gave a hand signal to the guards, and they lowered their rifles. "Nobody's going to hurt you," she told Charlie.

Charlie folded her arms in protest. She had no intention of moving from the ledge.

Jude sighed. "It's about Charlie. The *other* Charlie. She was en route to Control-Z when her truck was hijacked by a group of terrorists. We have reason to believe they are targeting you as well. You see, Alan is not trying to help you escape. He's trying to remove you from the safety of this building."

Charlie's thoughts snapped back to another point in time, those long nights in the hospital, fretting over Bridge's dying body. She recalled the crippling, existential terror she felt then. It was rising in her now, erasing any concerns for her own well-being. The guards with their automatic weapons? Jude with her lies and tests? All irrelevant now. *The other Charlie, Charlie ZERO. My sister. She's in danger!*

{Charlie: Why didn't you tell me she got kidnapped by *terrorists*!?

Alan:	I didn't know. I was stuck underground for four days. I didn't have an outside signal.
Charlie:	So, now you do. Is Jude telling the truth?
Alan:	A Control-Z truck *was* hijacked on the 101 earlier today. Details are sketchy, though. They don't mention your name, they can't confirm that any kidnapping took place, and the perps have no known affiliations.
Charlie:	So what's your verdict?
Alan:	Jude could be right…about the kidnapping. She's dead wrong about me.}

"Where is she now?" Charlie demanded of Jude.

"Come down and I'll tell you all about it."

{Charlie:	I'm going to talk to her.
Alan:	Why? Because she told you one true thing out of all the lies?
Charlie:	*Alleged* lies.
Alan:	You doubt me?
Charlie:	All I'm saying is I can't trust anyone right now.}

Charlie stepped off the ledge and onto the surface of the roof.

{Alan: Wait!}

"Shoot her," Jude commanded. The guards raised their rifles. A dozen fingers pulled a dozen triggers.

Boom, boom, booooom, boooooooooom, boooooooooooooooooooooom…

The bullets rapidly decelerated as if the air had condensed around them. By the time the first one entered Charlie's chest, it was moving impossibly slow. Nearby, the river stopped flowing. A rabbit never landed from its hop. And Charlie's screams hung in the ether.

{Charlie: Owww! What the hell?
Alan: *Now* do you doubt me?
Charlie: …in…a lot of pain!
Alan: That's impossible. This is a time freeze. Your
              pain receptors are firing at a much slower
              rate than your prefrontal cortex. Any pain
              you're feeling has to be psychosomatic.
Charlie: Bullshit! Wait…hold on.}

Charlie relaxed a little.

{Charlie: I think you're right. Shit. That's embarrassing.
Alan: You don't have to stand still, by the way. You
              are free to move around.
Charlie: Then time will start up again, and I'll get
              riddled with bullets.
Alan: No. You can move during a time freeze.
Charlie: Okay, maybe you were right about the pain,
              but you are wrong about this.
Alan: I beg to differ.
Charlie: Alan, this isn't some fantastical magic trick
              where I can freeze time and depants everyone.
              My brain is just overcranking at the moment.
              That doesn't mean I can break the laws of physics.

Alan: Humor me.

Charlie: Fine.}

She took an anxious step forward, paranoid that the bullets would resume their journey into her torso. Nothing of the sort happened. She took another step. Then another. Alan was right; she could move freely. The rabbit did not complete its hop. The guards did not budge. And the bullets remained locked in place. Charlie turned around, and she saw herself standing by the ledge with a frozen grimace on her face. How was this possible? It seemed as if her body and soul had separated.

"Now you know what it's like to experience the world as a Shadow," Alan said, sitting on the ledge, arms folded, with a smug look on his face.

"Is that really me over there?" Charlie asked.

"No. The human brain naturally creates a mental map of every environment it enters, and yours is no different. You are currently inside that mental map, and you are looking at a projection of yourself. In other words, you are having an out-of-body experience."

Charlie approached the guards, who looked less scary up close. Behind the row of rifles were creases of concern. Some of them were young, and many had probably never seen a firefight. "Why did Jude order them to shoot me? And shit, I thought I was bulletproof."

"Actually, I should have warned you about that," Alan said. "There are rumors that Bethea, shortly before the merger, was developing a new kind of ammunition called a *spider bullet*. A counter for nanotube body armor—the same material that makes up your skin."

"So she wants to kill me?"

"I don't think so. The bullets are liquid metal capsules. They penetrate the victim's armor—or in your case, body—and solidify into roots. They won't kill you, but they'll reduce your mobility. The fact that none of the rifles are aimed toward your head suggests that they merely want to slow you down."

Charlie focused on the swarm of bullets that hung in the air. "Still, it looks like I'm going to have five pounds of metal in me before I hit the ground."

"You'll have to fall in a very exact way, but I think I can help you minimize the damage."

"Okay. And then, what?"

"I think you'll still have to jump off the building. I don't see any other way to escape."

Charlie didn't have to peer over the ledge to feel the gut punch of vertigo. She searched the area for another option—*anything but jumping*—and spotted a Polly overhead. "The city is watching us. Wouldn't they arrest Jude for shooting me?"

"Unlikely," Alan replied. "Bethea makes the Pollys, and Rivir owns Bethea. Besides, I'm not sure how the law would apply to someone like you."

"Wonderful. Can we hack it, then? Use its stun beam?"

"I could probably install a copy of myself and control it from the inside, but it would take a while to hack, even with your processing speed."

"How long?"

"Roughly three minutes."

"So I need to avoid getting captured for three minutes?"

"Unless you want to jump off the building, which I still think is the better plan."

Charlie shuddered. "Okay, you hack the Polly. I'll handle the guards." She jumped back into her frozen body.

Time resumed.

"Owwwww!" Having started the scream before time stopped, Charlie was obligated to finish it. In her skillful descent to the floor, she took a bullet in the gut and one in the lower left thigh, but managed to avoid the rest. She stayed on the ground and played dead.

Jude addressed her men: "How many of you see the robot lying on the ground by the ledge?"

They all replied in the affirmative.

Jude watched Charlie intently, waiting for signs of life. Five seconds passed, then ten, then fifteen. Two lab technicians emerged behind the CEO, carrying a gurney. Jude waved them closer. Then she warned her guards, "Proceed with extreme caution. Shoot at any sign of movement."

The guards slowly approached the seemingly lifeless robot. One called out, "Cody! See if she's dead."

Cody unenthusiastically broke formation and nudged Charlie with the barrel of his rifle.

{Cody_Peeler:\mindspace>

Cody wasn't scared so much as freaked out. When he'd applied for guard duty, he never thought he'd have to face telepathic, murderous robots. The trigger on his rifle was already pulled back 20 percent. He half hoped the robot would move, so that he could be the one to give her a spider-bullet facial.

Without warning, the robot disappeared! Cody turned around to see if anyone could corroborate the crazy shit he just saw. The robot reappeared behind him. Cody reacted by forcing the butt of his rifle into her face. Upon contact, she somehow morphed into his friend, Neil.

Cody recoiled in horror. Neil was choking on blood and enamel.}

Charlie, still on the ground, snatched the rifle from the confused guard's hands. Now it was her turn to weaponize the blunt end of the gun. She swung it into Cody's jaw and sent him flying. The other guards just stood and watched—entranced by the incredible feat of strength—as their comrade sailed ten feet through the air.

Charlie capitalized on the distraction. She dashed through the guards' formation toward the nearest tree.

{**Charlie_Nobunaga:\mindspace>**
Alan: Hit the ground!}

Charlie dived five feet ahead of the cypress. A volley of bullets flew over her head and punched silver spiders into the side of the tree.

{Alan: Roll right!}

Charlie rolled as chunks of turf danced to her left.

{Alan: Okay, get to the tree.}

She scrambled to her feet. A bullet sank into her lower back as she ran behind the cypress, and she yelped in pain.

{Charlie: Every step feels like I'm getting stabbed all over.

Alan: I've already tweaked your endorphins. Or, at least, the software equivalent.

Charlie: Well, tweak them more.

Alan: I can't trip you out too much. You need to stay sharp.

Charlie: How much longer till we have the Polly?

Alan: Only forty seconds have passed so far. I'll need another two-twenty.}

The guards resumed fire, chopping splinters out of the cypress Charlie was hiding behind. Meanwhile, the Polly flew overhead. Its intense light shined through the branches, broadcasting Charlie's position.

"CHARLIE NOBUNAGA, YOU HAVE BEEN MARKED," the Polly announced in its authoritative voice. "RELEASE YOUR WEAPON AND LIE FACEDOWN ON THE FLOOR."

{Charlie: Can the stun beam hurt me?

Alan: No, but it can temporarily overload your circuits. Don't provoke it and you should be safe. I'd be more worried about the guards.

Charlie: I don't want to hurt anyone else.

Alan: You don't have to. Just fire off a few rounds so they don't rush in.}

Charlie examined the weapon she'd stolen from Cody Peeler. It was far stockier than the hunting rifle she had used with her father during that one harrowing trip. Reaching around the tree, she sprayed a few rounds. In the process, she accidentally struck one of the guards. The slug radiated silver roots across his nanoweave vest. One of the roots must have passed completely through, because he clawed at his chest in agony. The remaining guards took evasive action, darting left and right.

"Shit!" Charlie whispered.

{Charlie: I aimed away from them! I swear to God!

Alan: Maybe it would be safer if you aimed directly at them.

Charlie: Har, har.}

Charlie continued firing until the chamber was empty. She threw the rifle on the ground. With a rigid left leg, she limped farther into the forest. She saw that the elevator doors were now heavily guarded. The message was clear: the only way off the roof was a leap of faith.

The guards slowly took back the forest. They were even more cautious now—jittery—and Charlie took full advantage. She invaded their minds and planted decoys of herself. Shots were fired in every direction. Three men went down by stray bullets. The rest had to employ every ounce of concentration to keep themselves from going mad. They no longer trusted anything they saw.

Charlie could only maintain the veil of chaos for so long, and soon she was pushed to the other end of the forest.

{Charlie: I've run out of territory. Do I need to jump?

Alan: …

Charlie: Alan?}

Twenty yards to the ledge. Charlie decided to make a run for it. She was ready to jump, but a bullet clipped her right ankle. She tripped and fell onto the perimeter footpath, only a few feet from the ledge.

She wobbled to her feet, feeling intense pain with the slightest movement, as if her muscles were ripping apart.

"Shoot her!" Jude yelled from a distance.

Charlie heard the sound of gunfire, but she was too disoriented to slow their speed. The bullets punctured her stomach, her shoulder, her leg. She received eight new wounds before she hit the ground.

{Charlie: Alan, where the hell are you!?
 Alan: …}

Jude took one of the guard's rifles and approached Charlie.

"Ms. Adler!" the guard beseeched.

"It's okay," Jude said. "She doesn't pose a threat anymore."

Charlie could barely move a muscle—the pain was too great. Still, she managed to lift her shoulders a few inches before Jude shot her again, one round in each of her arms and legs. Once again, Charlie sank to the ground, her body rendered inert by an internal cage. "Why are you doing this?" she sputtered through tortured breaths.

Jude kneeled beside Charlie and latched onto her cheeks. Her touch, so warm and tender at the Rivir gala, was now utterly dispassionate. She cocked Charlie's head to the side and whispered into her ear, "I'm sorry, but the world simply isn't ready for you."

"Then why am I still alive? What were the tests for?"

When Jude pulled back, Charlie expected to see a somber woman. A CEO mired in setbacks. A visionary mourning the loss of her dream. Her actual expression told an entirely different story. She winked at Charlie, and her mouth curled into a devilish grin. Was the woman crazy? Or did she know something no one else did?

Jude didn't answer any of Charlie's questions, spoken or unspoken. She simply stood up and called to her assistants, "Bring the gurney."

{Alan: Get ready, Charlie.}

Charlie heard the surge of an energy beam. Jude's face contorted in severe pain. Every muscle in her body seized, and she collapsed beside Charlie's feet, revealing the Polly that had been hovering behind her.

The guards started shooting at the Polly. The Polly fired back, taking out one of the guards with its paralyzing beam. The rest scattered into the trees.

{Alan: Raise your hand.}

Charlie weakly complied. The Polly swooped in and caught Charlie's metal wristband in a magnetic lock. The flying orb rocketed skyward, taking Charlie with it like a rag doll.

"Oh crap! Oh crap!" Charlie dangled fifty feet above the Rivir Tower rooftop. Bullets began flying in her direction. The Polly took off toward the bay and out of range of the firing squad.

{Charlie: You magnetized the Polly?
Alan: Clever, huh?
Charlie: Alan…I…
Alan: Don't mention it.
Charlie: I'm sorry I doubted you.}

Charlie swung loosely as Alan's Polly weaved between buildings and over the streetlights below. Just when she thought she was out of harm's way, she spotted another Polly reflected in the window of a nearby building. She turned her head and discovered not one but several resident Pollys rocketing toward her.

{Charlie: We're being followed.
Alan: If we can get to the bay, your fall survival rate
             will increase to near one hundred percent. The
             Pollys won't follow you under the water.
Charlie: And then what? We need to rescue my sister.
             ZERO.
Alan: We are in agreement. But you're in no
             condition to help her right now. And we can't
             outrun these Pollys.}

The Pollys were indeed gaining ground, probably because they were not burdened by dangling, injured robots.

{Charlie: How long do I have to stay underwater, then?
Alan: Your damage is extensive. It will take a long time
             for your body to repair itself. I'm thinking days.
Charlie: Days! She could be dead in days!
Alan: I'm sorry. There's no other way.}

Charlie looked down as the urban grid gave way to the dark and foreboding water of the San Francisco Bay. The enemy Pollys would overtake her in less than ten seconds, so she had to make the plunge.

> {Alan: The water will be icy at first. But don't worry—
>   I'll dope you.
> Charlie: We have no other recourse?}

Alan didn't respond. The Polly's magnetic grasp evaporated. Charlie entered free fall. She crashed against the surface of the bay and instantly started sinking.

III ○ INFILTRATION

CHAPTER 9

ZERO

As the adrenaline wore off, Charlie slipped into a daze, too exhausted to stay awake, but too nervous and uncomfortable to fall asleep. She was thrown into the back of a car and shuttled from one rendezvous point to the next—a seedy bridge underpass, an abandoned gas station, and finally, a department store in an abandoned mall.

The store was a relic. The parking lot had long been reclaimed by saplings, the lights no longer received electricity, and a pile of mannequins sat in the corner like a mass grave, placing the store's closure date well before the advent of Shadows. The Sapiens exhumed a thick layer of dust as they shuffled through the dark space. Charlie's pupils expanded to take in the pale light, which drifted through the windows from distant street lamps.

Yuri set up a mini-clinic in the front of the store. He cut through Liam's tattered pant leg and exposed the wound underneath. Charlie cringed at the sight. Thick chunks of flesh splayed open, creating a gash that was almost as wide as it was long. Yuri applied a large needle to the area. "It's not that bad," he said, despite the evidence to the contrary. "Nothing broken, at least."

Liam was less concerned about the wound than his missing sister. Nicola was presumably combing the suburbs for a new getaway vehicle, but no one had heard from her in hours. As soon as Liam's leg was cleaned and bandaged, he headed toward the loading dock to wait for her return. Charlie had to squash her objection—Liam was the only one in this weird cult group she semitrusted—but she didn't want to display any fear or bias.

Next on Yuri's agenda was the cut on Charlie's arm, which required stitches. The motorcycle accident had been relatively kind to her—only a few bruises, some surface scrapes on her palms and forearms, and a long gash under her right elbow—the damage not substantial enough to distract her from the nausea and fatigue produced by the cancer. To her relief Yuri didn't bring up the subject of coffee enemas again.

Jesse remained oblivious to the medical proceedings. He kept his nose pressed against the store display window and announced, "There's another one!" every few minutes as a Polly sailed over the tree line. "We are being hunted down, like General George Washington after the Battle of Long Island."

"Uh-huh." Yuri kept his focus on the suture needle and made another pass along Charlie's arm.

"Do you think they told my parents yet?" Jesse's eyes glistened in the pale light. Only the thinnest scaffold of bravery held his composure together.

Yuri huffed. "It shouldn't matter what your parents think.

They've been brainwashed by the oligarchy."

"That's easy for you to say," Charlie snapped. "You're not the one who was marked."

"It was *his* choice to join us." Yuri pulled tight on Charlie's suture to punctuate his point. "He's here because he believes in the wisdom of Bob Sapio."

"He's just a kid!"

"He knows the stakes—"

"The stakes? You mean the delusional ramblings of a paranoid schizophrenic—"

"Charlie..." Jesse interjected. He got up from the display window and approached her. "Yuri's right. I'm being selfish. I may be marked, but none of us are truly free. Not my parents. Not you. The Pollys watch *everyone*. They need to go."

"I hate to be the bearer of bad news," Charlie said, "but the Pollys aren't going anywhere."

"Don't worry, we have a plan."

"Jesse!" Yuri yanked Charlie's final stitch almost to the point of ripping the skin.

"Owww!" She swiped the pair of scissors from Yuri's hand and cut the loose thread herself. Then she turned to Jesse and asked, "What plan?"

The boy's face hardened under Yuri's threatening stare. "I don't know," he mumbled. "They don't tell me much."

Charlie was about to press him further when a door banged open, drawing everyone's attention to the back of the store. "You fucking bitch!" Nicola's shadowy figure barreled toward Charlie at alarming speed.

Liam limped after her, hollering, "It was my call! I gave her the launcher!"

Charlie held out her hand in defense, but Nicola's impact was brutal. Charlie's head slapped against the floor as Nicola fell on top of her. "You almost killed him!" Nicola spat. She clawed for Charlie's jugular, and the two became a tangle of limbs. Charlie didn't realize she was still holding the suture scissors until after she'd drawn blood. She jabbed Nicola between the ribs. The instrument was short and blunt, but it still caused Nicola to arch her back and yelp.

Liam swooped over Nicola, grabbed her by the shoulders, and tore her away from Charlie. She skidded several feet across the dusty floor.

Charlie scrambled backward, eager to increase the distance between herself and Nicola. She rubbed her head, which throbbed with adrenaline. After a few hard wheezes, she realized she was the only one in the room making a sound.

Yuri and Jesse both sat with their mouths agape, hanging on Nicola's next move. Liam's posture stiffened. He stared at his own hands, befuddled, as if they had acted without his authorization. "I…I'm so sorry."

Nicola slowly climbed to her feet and brushed the dust from her clothes. "Bring me the scissors," she instructed Liam in a low, measured tone. She had swallowed most of her rage, though it was still visible through the whites of her eyes.

"Why?" Liam asked, as if afraid of the answer.

"Because she fucking stabbed me," she said, massaging the small red splotch on the side of her T-shirt.

Liam gave his sister a hesitant nod. He walked over to Charlie and opened his palm.

Charlie tightened her grip on the scissors and stole a glance at Nicola. Her face was full of nicks and scars, as well as two deep grooves that extended diagonally across her cheek, over her lip, and under her jaw. A person with such wounds would probably have less compunction about inflicting them on others.

"It's okay," Liam said. "I won't let her hurt you."

Charlie took another look at the scissors. A trace amount of blood coated the tip. She quickly wiped it on her shirt—a fatuous attempt to hide the evidence. She knew this was a battle she couldn't win. To delay the exchange would only incur more of Nicola's wrath. She steadied her hand and placed the weapon onto Liam's open palm.

He pocketed the scissors.

"Give them to me," Nicola ordered.

"She's unarmed, just like you wanted."

"I wanted you to give them to me." Nicola punctuated each acid-tipped syllable.

Liam planted his feet on the floor and glared at his sister. The other two Sapiens observed the standoff in frozen silence, afraid to venture the slightest movement. Charlie's hard swallow was louder than she would have liked.

"You're out," Nicola finally said.

Liam's face drained of resolve. His brow turned up and he pleaded, "You can't. I'm your only pilot."

"Yuri—"

"Yuri has, what? Six weeks of training?"

"He can follow a fucking order."

"Nicky…don't do this. Please." For the first time, Charlie detected fear in his voice.

Nicola blurted a laugh, though her eyes still smoldered. "After all this time, I finally see where your priorities lie. You obviously have no concern for my well-being. Didn't matter that I got fucking stabbed. But as soon as I take your precious piloting away—"

"It's not like that. I just—"

"And I defended you!" Nicola approached her brother. "And you threw me on the floor like I was some piece-of-shit rag doll."

Liam lowered his gaze. His shoulders slumped like a scolded child.

"Then you told *her*"—she pointed to Charlie and mocked Liam's deep voice—"'Oh, don't worry, I won't let her hurt you.' What the fuck do you think I was gonna do!?"

Liam's eyes dodged her imploring glare, even as she stepped within a few inches of his face. "I…nothing. I'm sorry."

"Great! So give me the fucking scissors!"

Liam paused a beat. Then he fished the scissors out of his pocket.

Nicola swatted them out of his hand, and they flew across the floor. With a huff, she turned and marched toward Charlie.

Charlie flinched, but Nicola wasn't interested in resuming her assault. She dived into Yuri's medicine bag and pulled out a pair of handcuffs. "My brother doesn't think this is necessary," she said, more to Liam than to Charlie.

Liam's eyes narrowed, his jaw clenched, but he made no move to stop his sister.

Charlie was too frightened to resist. She winced as Nicola grabbed her tender arms and slapped on the cuffs. The metal bit into her wrists.

"He expects you'll just gleefully join our movement once you learn the truth," Nicola hissed into Charlie's ear. "For whatever reason, he thinks you're a moral person—not like all the other Ivy League trust fundies who believe they could simply refashion the world after their own perverse fantasies. This will be your one and only chance to prove him right." She smacked Charlie's scalp and stood up. "We're leaving for your father's estate in five."

o o o

The drive to the Nobunaga estate was far from linear. Nicola made several U-turns and retraced a lot of ground to avoid Polly flight paths and traffic-cam checkpoints. Charlie was pinned in the backseat between Jesse and Liam, both of whom wore thick nanoweave vests. No one said a word the entire trip, and Charlie had to consciously steady her hands to keep them from rattling the cuffs. What did they want from her father? Were they going to hurt him? And the most vexing question of all: Would she learn something about her father she wished she hadn't?

Halfway down the street from the estate entrance, they rendezvoused with a dark van. "The flight team," Jesse informed Charlie. Four people spilled out of the rear door—two men and two women. Like most of the Sapiens Charlie had encountered, they were young and looked as though they hadn't eaten a decent meal or bought new clothes in years.

Nicola talked to the flight team for a few minutes. Then she walked back to the car and opened Yuri's door. Her manner was sharp and direct. "According to the satellite feed, Nobunaga has two security guards on the grounds. Making their sweep now. Can you go with Maurice?"

Yuri nodded. He pulled a handgun from the glove compartment and left the vehicle.

"They're gonna kill 'em?" Charlie asked.

Nicola ignored her and addressed Jesse, "You're coming with us. I want you to carry Charlie. Liam, you're staying here with the flight team."

"What?" Liam protested. "I'm fine. Jesse'll get hurt out there."

"I don't want any added weight on your leg." She turned and left before Liam could object further.

Liam hooked one hand behind Charlie's back and held Jesse off with the other.

Jesse's brow scrunched in confusion. "But Nicola—"

"I'll handle Nicola," Liam said.

"But your leg."

"My leg's fine." Liam reached behind his back and pulled out a handgun. "Here. Hang on to this and try to look tough."

Jesse reached for the gun as if it were a live scorpion. Before exiting the car, he whispered to Charlie, "Don't worry, it'll be okay," clearly trying to convince himself as much as her.

o o o

The quiet residential street was well illuminated, though the Sapien crew kept to the shadows as much as they could. Nicola shot her brother a dirty look when she discovered his quiet defiance, but she didn't pursue the issue.

Charlie felt light in Liam's arms, and she suddenly blushed for being so close to this very real—as in nonvirtual—human male. He smelled like sweat and motor oil, but underneath that, a trace of fabric softener. His eyelids twitched ever so slightly when he stepped on his bad leg, but he still tried to walk normally. He was putting on an act. Like his sister, he repressed aspects of his true self, but her eyes betrayed a bitter rage, whereas his brimmed with hope.

He stole a glance at Charlie, and she quickly turned away. She had been *staring* at him. Thankfully, the moment passed without comment. When she ventured another look, Liam had already fixed his gaze outward.

"What are you planning to do with my father?" she whispered. She had prodded him a few times before, but now he was truly stuck with her—no helmet to hide behind, no loading dock to retreat to.

Liam kept his head up, but his jaw clenched and his chest inflated. He didn't do stoic nearly as well as his sister.

"That was you at the Rivir gala, wasn't it? You knew what was gonna happen. You tried to warn me." Charlie gave him a few seconds to respond. When he didn't, she pressed further: "I know you want to do the right thing. You shouldn't let your sister boss you around."

"I am doing the right thing," Liam snapped under his breath.

"You said you would take me to see my sister. Or *sisters*, as you claim."

"I will. We just have to do this first."

"And what exactly is *this*?"

Liam sealed his lips and looked up. They had reached the gate to her father's estate, and Nicola was watching them. "Follow my lead," she instructed Liam and Jesse. "Don't deviate and this'll go smoothly."

A grin crept across Charlie's face. The Sapiens obviously didn't know her father well enough. Before he founded Lotus, he had been a member of the USAF Security Forces, and he liked to take care of security threats personally. Nicola had either overlooked that detail or underestimated it.

The gate was outfitted with a call box and a 3D security camera. Nicola pressed the intercom button and waited. Five seconds passed. Ten seconds. Jesse fidgeted with his gun and Liam took a few deep breaths. Twenty seconds passed. Charlie grew hopeful that her father wasn't home—perhaps he was on an overseas trip. But then his familiar voice projected from the box. *"I'm not expecting visitors at this hour."*

Nicola addressed the camera, "Hello, Mr. Nobunaga. We found your daughter by the side of the road. We've come to make a trade."

"My daughter is dead."

Nicola beckoned to Liam. He walked over to the camera and presented Charlie. For a moment, all they heard was static.

"What do you want?" Andrew finally said.

"First, don't call the police. If you do, bad things will happen. The rest we can discuss when you let us in."

The gate buzzed open.

The Sapiens crept up the cobblestone driveway. Nicola and Jesse huddled around Liam, forming a single unit. Jesse's pistol darted erratically, while Nicola's remained focused on the mansion's front door.

Charlie tried to block the encroaching feelings of nostalgia. The Nobunaga grounds had once served as her playground. Most of its key features were real—the ancient sundial centerpiece, the fountains, the trees—great for hide-and-seek. Only the glowing butterflies were virtual. They were a memorial to Bridget—she had programmed their flight paths in grade school, and Andrew had reinstated them after she died.

Just as Charlie expected, her father's Shadow, Johannes Kepler, with his voluminous neck ruff and salt-and-pepper beard, spun a few feet in front of the Sapiens. "You will place Charlie on the ground and walk away," he said curtly.

"Andrew's too afraid to come out himself?" Nicola quipped.

"Leave now and no actions will be taken against you."

Footsteps approached from behind. The Sapiens turned to find a soldier aiming an assault rifle at them. Three more soldiers emerged from the trees. *Andrew's mercs.*

Jesse pointed his trembling gun at one of them and slowly backed away from the huddle. Nicola kept her gun trained toward the mansion. "They're not real," she told Kepler with confidence. "They're Shadows, just like you."

"Do you really want to test that hypothesis?" Kepler asked.

"We only saw two guards on the heat scan, and my friends have already subdued them."

Kepler paused, likely trying to contact the guards in question. "So you have," he admitted. "But there's still one more person in play."

Charlie suddenly realized how exposed Liam had become. She looked up and confirmed her fear—a glowing red dot danced on his forehead. "Liam!" She hooked her hands around his head and pulled hard. Liam growled but quickly became aware of the danger when a patch of gravel erupted behind him. He inhaled and, in one quick motion, swiveled and dropped to the ground, using his back to form a protective barrier in front of Charlie.

Another shot rang out. Liam jolted forward with a grimace as the bullet struck his vest. A third shot seemed to miss him completely. Then—silence.

Liam rested his forehead against Charlie's. His shallow breath warmed her cheek. He lifted his head slightly to search her face, as if to ask, *Why did you save me?* Charlie didn't have an answer, though her heart raced at the thought he was still in danger.

"Andrew!" Nicola belted out. "If you don't come out, my partner will snap your daughter's neck!"

Charlie's eyes widened, but Liam silently repudiated his sister's threat with a slight headshake. His lips hovered so close above hers. Charlie's unexpected and shameful urge to close the gap made the moment even more difficult to bear. Her eyes flooded with burning tears. "Please, Liam," she whispered. "Let's just go. I don't want to do this."

Liam's brow wrinkled and his head drifted in thought. He was about to say something when Nicola shouted in the distance, "Toss the gun!" Both Liam and Charlie directed their attention to the mansion.

Andrew Nobunaga stepped onto the front porch, holding a sniper rifle above his head. He tossed it into the nearby bushes. Nicola kept her gun trained on him as she rapidly closed the distance. "On your knees you son of a bitch!" Andrew didn't resist, nor did he flinch when she threw a pair of handcuffs at him.

Charlie pulled Liam's face in her direction. "You said you wouldn't let her hurt him!"

"I said I wouldn't let her hurt *you*, but look…" He gestured toward the middle of the lawn, where Jesse lay motionless. Liam then threw off his vest and rubbed the spot between his shoulder blades, where the bullet had struck.

"Are you okay?" Charlie asked.

Liam didn't acknowledge her. He just reached down and hooked his arms underneath her back.

Charlie squirmed away from him. "Please…"

"I can pick you up, or I can drag you." He spoke in monotone, choosing not to exhibit any kind of emotional reaction.

A cold panic filled Charlie's lungs. Whatever connection she had shared with Liam a moment ago was now lost. She allowed him to scoop her off the ground, but every muscle in her body tensed in rebellion.

The grounds were quiet again. Kepler and his soldier Shadows had dematerialized, and Nicola had forced Andrew into the house. Liam's boots struck the ground hard as he hurried toward Jesse's body. He no longer exhibited any signs of pain, and, if anything, he favored his bad leg.

Charlie shrieked when she saw Jesse. The boy's face was a still portrait of fear. The hole in his forehead was clean, with just a thin red trail disappearing into his mop of curls. Liam's own face fell ashen, and Charlie could tell what gripped his attention. *The handgun.* Jesse died because he was holding Liam's handgun.

o o o

Liam carried Charlie into the third-floor observatory. The AR projector was currently off, so it was just a barren white dome with an empty computer desk and a few office chairs, but in Charlie's fondest memories, the room was a window to the universe. This was where her father had taught her how to identify the constellations. This was where she had chatted with Bridge for hours while staring at the night sky. Charlie suspected that a wholly different kind of memory was about to be imprinted, and she shuddered at the thought.

Nicola leaned against the desk, wiping blood from her knuckles with the bottom of her shirt. Andrew was strapped to one of the chairs. A purple bruise had formed around his left eye, and blood flowed from his nose.

"Dad! Are you okay?" Charlie asked.

Andrew nodded. "Did they hurt you?"

Charlie shook her head. It was a lie, of course, but her father looked so furious and distraught, she didn't want to worry him any further. Liam lowered Charlie into a chair and reattached her handcuffs to the armrest.

It wasn't long before Yuri stormed into the room. "What the hell happened out there!? Jesse got shot!"

"This whole mission was a mistake," Liam muttered.

"We got Andrew," Nicola pointed out. "That's the most important thing."

"Christ, Nicola! We fucked up!" Yuri slapped his forehead and tugged at his hair, nearly pulling it out. The flight team quietly shuffled in, careful not to rile Yuri further, and lined the perimeter of the observatory. "Well, I do have good news to report," Yuri continued, calming slightly. "Apparently, the bird has left its cage."

"Thank God for small favors," Nicola said. "Then we'll revert to the original plan."

Charlie perked up. Bird? Cage? "Are you talking about my sister? What are you planning—?"

"Shut up or I'll gag you," Nicola snapped.

"You can't talk to her like that," Andrew said.

Nicola grinned. "You don't seem to be in a position to stop

me."

Andrew's eyes burned with pure hatred, but somehow he managed to swallow his indignation and tilt his head high. "Why don't you tell me what you want so we can get you on your way?"

"I want the code to your space fleet."

Andrew laughed, spraying his blood. "You should have told me that at the gate. I would have said it's impossible. The fleet requires two sets of codes for remote access. My partner has the other set, and he's been instructed never to give it to me under any circumstances."

"Honeybee, dodo, leather, digit, ear, poster, farmer, combat, sex, potato, message, chess. That's the other code, in case you were curious."

Andrew forced a smile. He held his fear well, but Charlie could see through his facade. His negotiation power was dwindling by the minute.

"Charlie isn't the only hacker in this room," Nicola said. "And at any rate, you aren't going to give us the code. She is."

"What?" Charlie blurted. "*I* don't have the code."

"I think we both know that's bullshit."

Nicola was right, of course. Over the years, Charlie had figured out all of her father's passwords—to his ships, his smart cells, his estate. She even knew his gym locker combination. Still, the question remained: "If I had it, why would I give it to you?"

"Liam?"

Liam lifted his head with a long, weary sigh. He clearly wished he were anywhere but in this room. "We're on the same side, Charlie. You don't realize that yet, but once you hear your father's secret, you will."

"Whatever he's done, it won't change a thing," Charlie said.

Nicola jabbed Andrew's temple with her index finger. "Why don't you tell her? She deserves to know."

Andrew just stared at her with cold, hateful eyes.

"Either you tell her, or I do."

"Whatever you think you know, you know nothing," Andrew said. "You have no idea what I went through, as a father, as a husband. You have no clue what informed my decisions." His expression hardened, and after a few seconds it was clear he was not going to say more.

"Okay," Nicola said. "People consistently underestimate the Sapien Movement, but that's fine…we like it that way. The Movement has eyes everywhere, and we especially like to keep a careful watch on corporations and government agencies that do not have humanity's best interests at heart. Several months ago, the DOD posted a very lucrative contract for a new AI weapon system. For a while, it looked like Bethea, with their state-of-the-art robotics facility, was going to win the bid. But at the last minute, Bethea merged with Rivir, and together they won the bid, though with Rivir's executive staff at the helm. So we wondered: What changed to give Rivir the upper hand? Well, another significant event happened shortly thereafter. Charlie Nobunaga became the first candidate for a human brain upload. Then it all made sense."

"My dad brokered the merger in exchange for the upload," Charlie said. "So what? I already figured as much."

"I wasn't finished," Nicola said. "If you go back even further, two years ago to the summer of '43, Rivir hired a team of simulation engineers and designers and purchased a ton of new hardware. This gave rise to the speculation that they were expanding their presence in the Walkable Web. But that didn't happen, so we looked into it. As it turns out, this was groundwork for a massive genetic programming experiment, code-named Project ECHO—"

"ECHO?" Charlie asked.

"You've heard of it?"

"Just the name." Charlie recalled Jude's facility tour. A sign reading ECHO hung above one of the doors in Rivir's R&D hub. Jude had been very stingy about the details.

"ECHO is an enormous simulation," Nicola said. "We're talking the size of planet Earth with atomic resolution. Originally, it was designed to create superior robots. But after Rivir won the DOD contract, they tweaked it for a military application. The genetic programming methodology, however, remained consistent. I'm guessing you're familiar with the concept?"

Charlie nodded apprehensively. She didn't like where this story was going.

"Take a billion or so random chunks of code, place them in a competitive environment, and they will evolve into useful programs," Nicola stated. "Like Darwin for software. That's how it usually works, but ECHO adds a twist. It isn't evolving random chunks of code. It's evolving copies, or 'echoes,' of a human archetype. *You*, Charlie."

"That's a lie!" Andrew barked.

Nicola smiled. "You deny it?"

"Yes, I do." Andrew gripped the armrests of his chair and exhaled sharply. Then he withdrew a little. "I mean…the ECHO Project…it exists, but it's not processing Charlie's Atlas.

It's…" His voice trailed off, and his attention shrank inward.

"What, Dad?" Charlie prodded.

For a moment, Andrew appeared as if he hadn't heard Charlie. He just took shallow breaths and kept a fixed gaze on the floor. Then he turned to his daughter and said, "It's processing Alan."

Charlie's eyes widened in horror.

"You were dying," Andrew quickly added. "Jude was considering other candidates. I had to sweeten the deal."

Rage filled Charlie so quickly it felt like she was drowning. The room faded to black, and she plummeted into an abyss, where she had no other option but to face the unimaginable: Alan…her friend…her child…fed to the simulation like factory meat. Her father had no idea. When Charlie came up for air, she was already numb, exhausted from the burst of emotion. "Do you have any comprehension of what you've done?" she asked her father.

"I assume they'll turn him into a fighter drone of some kind. Or a ground soldier."

"You should have told me! It's nothing like putting Alan in a drone." Charlie might have been upset with Alan, but he didn't deserve this fate. No sentient being did. "They are going to transform him—slowly, painfully, in grotesque ways, and they are going to do it a billion times over. Do you know how much suffering—?"

"They didn't go with Alan," Nicola interrupted.

"Huh?"

"They didn't go with Alan. Maybe they were considering him for a while, but Jude didn't choose him. She chose you."

Charlie swallowed hard. This was all too much for her. She

wasn't sure whether to be relieved or incensed.

"You're wrong," Andrew said, but he no longer sounded so certain.

"Don't be so naive," Nicola said. "Do you really think Jude, when given the choice between Charlie's Atlas—the most sophisticated code ever produced, leagues beyond anything that came before it because it was modeled after a real human brain, which itself is the culmination of billions of years of biological evolution—and Alan—who's basically a glorified science fair project—she would choose the science fair project?"

Andrew's defiant glare withered. His eyes sank to the floor.

"You signed away all rights to Charlie's Atlas," Nicola continued, "knowing full well that this was a possibility? That Jude would drop it into her ECHO Project? Or her SHADOW line? Or maybe she would decide to sell it to a research firm? Or a lovebot manufacturer? Or a mining company? Seriously, I'm stunned. None of this crossed your mind?"

Andrew gnashed his teeth but kept his head down. He wasn't acting like his usual self. In both his business and personal life, he always fought criticism and dissidence, even when he was wrong. *Especially* when he was wrong.

"So, Charlie, now you know what your father has done," Nicola said. "And we intend to correct his mistakes. But to do that, we need to take command of his space fleet. Consider it poetic reparations."

Charlie was furious at her father. He never listened to her. *Ever.* She couldn't recall a time when he had yielded to her judgment. But now, for the first time, he seemed to be fully aware of his error. He hung in his chair, despondent, ashamed to look at her. He hadn't responded like this even when Bridget died. Or her mother. He had been strong for so long, but the facade had finally cracked.

Charlie shifted her attention to Nicola, who beamed in the center of the room with her gloating, self-satisfied grin. The Sapien obviously thought she'd won, and Charlie loathed her for it. "So my father's an idiot," she said. "You think I'm going to betray him now? Fuck you!"

Nicola's brow twisted in confusion. She turned to Liam, who seemed equally puzzled. He placed his hand on Charlie's shoulder.

Charlie shrugged him away. "You were right, Liam. This mission was a mistake. My father's not the enemy."

"I was hoping I wouldn't have to do this," Nicola said. "Yuri?"

Yuri unzipped a fabric case containing several syringes. Each one bore a different colored solution. He selected the red syringe and walked over to Charlie.

"What is that?" Andrew asked, eyeing the syringe.

"Special concoction," Nicola replied. "Don't worry, it doesn't kill people. Just makes them feel very, very uncomfortable. But who knows? Charlie's health hasn't been the greatest lately."

Yuri pulled Charlie's head to the side, exposing her neck arteries. The cold tip of the needle broke through her skin. He was about to depress the plunger when Liam grabbed him by the wrist. "She's suffered enough," Liam said, meeting Yuri's glare. He took possession of the needle and pulled it out of Charlie's neck.

Liam locked eyes with his sister as he walked over to Andrew. Nicola sneered but didn't stop him. Liam grabbed a tuft of Andrew's hair and pulled his head back.

"No!" Charlie pleaded.

Liam held the needle against Andrew's neck and waited for Charlie to continue.

She wanted to shout out the password, but her lungs deflated each time she tried to dredge the words. The Lotus space fleet was her father's life achievement, the result of decades of sacrifice.

"It's okay, Charlie." Andrew's voice began to quaver. He fought back his tears. "I made a terrible, terrible mistake. I don't wish to make another. Kepler, spin, all eyes."

Johannes Kepler spun into the room. "Yes, Andrew?" the Shadow inquired.

"Please give these people access to my fleet."

Liam released Andrew's hair and flippantly tossed the syringe to the floor. He passed his sister in silence, deciding not to use the opportunity to gloat.

"Are you sure, Mr. Nobunaga?" Kepler asked.

"I've made my decision," Andrew insisted. "Do anything they say."

Kepler entered Andrew's code into the network. Nicola recited the second set she'd stolen from Andrew's partner. The room's AR projector turned on. The white dome dissolved into a starscape.

Planet Earth loomed large from the south side of the dome. The much smaller Pacific Space Port hung on the north side. The PSP was a basic spherical space station with five docking arms, one for each of the five international companies who invested in the facility: Australia's Julpan; India's Jet Airways; China's Gold Wing; Russia's Kolesnitsa; and Andrew's Lotus, representing the US.

One of the flight team members clapped his hands. "Fuck yeah!" he exclaimed to no one in particular.

Nicola turned to them. "I want you four to go into the dining room and each grab a chair. And bring an extra one for Yuri." They nodded and left the room.

Nicola turned to Yuri. "Hand me a thinking cap." Yuri pulled one from his bag and handed it to her. It was a black cotton cap with a chinstrap and white electrodes evenly spaced throughout. She showed the cap to Kepler. "This is a Kirchstein THC-3900D. Will it interface with the ships?"

"It should," the Shadow said.

After a couple minutes, the flight team returned with their chairs. Yuri handed each of them a cap, and they all formed a semicircle in the center of the room.

"What do you plan to do with my ships?" Andrew asked.

"You'll see," Nicola said dismissively. "Kepler, I want you to assign Lotus One to Yuri, the man with the mustache. Then go clockwise around the circle and assign the other four. Each cap gets a ship. Is that clear?"

"Yes," Kepler replied.

Yuri strapped the cap onto his head and closed his eyes. "I'm in," he said.

Charlie looked over to Pacific Space Port and saw Lotus One leave the dock. The other four ships followed shortly afterward. Consistent with the company name, the ships resembled steel lotus buds, with a trio of rocket thrusters at the stern. The "lotus petals" were currently closed, but Charlie knew they opened to reveal a transparent, nanofiberglass cabin, allowing the traveler to see 180 degrees of the surrounding starscape. She admired the design, especially since many of the other ships at PSP looked like glorified limousines. *Why couldn't the Sapiens hijack those?*

"Everyone should have their coordinates," Nicola said. "You may proceed when ready."

The five Lotus ships broke off into five separate trajectories. Liam remained uninterested in the proceedings, and Charlie wondered why he didn't get a ship, especially since he had been so concerned about being a "pilot" earlier. Was he being punished?

"If you must know, we're hunting satellites," Nicola told Andrew. "Specifically, Polly support satellites. It's difficult to run an operation like ours while the Pollys are out and about. It would take forever to eliminate them one by one, not to mention the risks involved. But their power source, the satellites, are unguarded. Take out the satellites, and you take out the Pollys."

"Power source?" Charlie asked. "I thought the Pollys collect their own solar power."

"They do," Nicola replied. "But the power they collect on their own is minimal and not enough to restore them to standard operating mode. Kepler, can you please magnify the dome to fifteen thousand meters above San Francisco?"

The dome zoomed into the planet's surface, stopping right above the cloud line. Charlie could see several dozen twinkly lights scattered along the wall.

"Kepler, magnify on one of those Pollys."

The dome zoomed in on one of the twinkles. It was an unfolded Polly—not the normal spherical shape, but a flat sheet of small hexagonal solar panels.

"This is where Pollys come when they are low on power— right above the cloud line," Nicola said. "They unfold and collect their own power, but it's only enough to keep them afloat. In other words, they cannot recharge their batteries this way—their power requirements are just too great and their surface area is just too small. So they require a large boost of energy from the support satellites. Otherwise, they will remain in that holding pattern indefinitely. Kepler, can you put PSS-84 on display?"

The dome zoomed out from the planet several thousand meters. An enormous solar panel array came into view. "This support satellite feeds all the Pollys in Northern California. Yuri, how long till impact?"

"About thirty seconds," Yuri said.

"Okay, this should be fun," Nicola said. "Kepler, switch the dome to the Lotus One camera."

With Lotus One's camera on the display, it felt like Andrew's entire observatory was headed on a collision course with the PSS-84 satellite. Yuri started the countdown: "Ten, nine, eight…" The others joined in: "Seven, six, five, four…" PSS-84 got larger and larger. "Three, two, one."

The display went dark.

"Switch to telescope view!" Nicola shouted.

The display showed a giant explosion. Every Sapien in the room cheered. Yuri stood up, peeled off his cap, and took a bow.

"Does this mean we'll finally get to meet *him*?" one of the flight team members asked.

"Absolutely," Nicola said. "Bob will want to commend you personally. All of you."

Charlie then realized why the Sapiens were so obsessed with the Pollys, and why they were so willing to condemn themselves to fugitive status. Bob Sapio, the dear leader himself, was a fugitive. He was wanted for murder. And the Polly network had essentially rendered him immobile. Cut off. Impotent. Now, the Sapiens had bought him a little more flexibility.

"Yay, awesome," Charlie said with punctuated sarcasm. "Now will you all get the hell out of here?"

"Not yet," Nicola said. "Your father has five ships. We are going to eliminate five satellites."

"We also need to take care of him," Yuri said, pointing at Andrew.

"What do you mean 'take care of him'?" Charlie demanded.

Nicola rolled her eyes. "Liam?"

Liam perked up. He fished the handcuff keys from his pocket and swiftly moved to Charlie's side. "Time to go," he said as he detached her from the armrest.

"Where are you taking her?" Andrew barked.

"What are they gonna do to him?" Charlie asked.

Liam lifted her into his arms and didn't answer her question until they were well outside the room. "Your dad will be fine. They'll make him sleep and wipe his short-term memory. Just the last few hours or so."

"If I find out you're lying—"

"I'm not," Liam insisted. "You'll see him soon."

"And when exactly is soon?"

"You only have one job left. Bob wants to meet you."

CHAPTER 10

FOUR ARMS

The transition was instantaneous. One moment, Four Arms was sailing across the sky, enveloped in a deafening stream of air. The next moment, she was floating in a tank of murky water. The forces of ballistics and gravity had somehow dropped her off in this mysterious place and zipped on by.

Four Arms heard the clacks and clomps of footsteps. Two shadowy figures appeared from beyond the tank. She couldn't see their faces, but she could hear their voices, garbled through the water.

"You don't seem to understand that we've already lost this battle. The more we draw attention to it, the more we stand to lose."

"And if she kills another person—"

"She won't, Ian. She's just a scared little girl."

"A scared little girl with the strength of a gorilla."

"Oh, she's stronger than that. But it's irrelevant. Like I said, we've corrected the psychosis, run extensive tests—"

"Tests you were unauthorized to run. The robot should be in a box

right now. You should be in prison, Jude. The only reason you are not is because you are more useful to us as a contractor than as a scapegoat. But those tables could easily tip in the other direction. People are demanding justice. They're scared, and I don't blame them. This Polly situation is… troubling. What will happen when they run out of juice? The National Guard is waiting in the wings. But that doesn't change the fact that we are losing control of every aspect of this situation. Bob Sapio of all people is dominating the conversation, conflating everything from the Polly situation, to the robot girl, to the smart-cell health scare under one giant umbrella of Luddite mouth-frothing. And you are enemy numero uno. They are under the opinion that you should be tried for mass murder, for Molly Higgins and anyone else who's died of a Rivir product."

"Smart cells don't kill people. That research is pure tripe. And Sapio's one to talk. Who do you think destroyed the satellites?"

"That may be true, and that may eventually come to light. But for now, people are listening to the old man. If enough of them demand justice, we may be forced to provide it. So to hell with this business about maintaining a low profile. We've done that long enough. Now is the time to display strength, to show the people that we can still maintain peace and order. And capturing your runaway killer robot would be a fantastic fucking start. So, if you would be so kind as to drain the tank…"

"Khnum?"

The tank bellowed and shook like the Optic death wail. The water level started to descend, allowing Four Arms to see through the clear walls of the tank. The room was an enormous amphitheater, three floors high, and the tank was its beating heart, with hoses and wires extending in every direction. The two echoes watched her, expectantly. Four Arms flailed her limbs, trying to touch solid ground. She was in a precarious position—handicapped by the water and trapped by the glass.

"Magnificent, don't you think?" the one named Jude boasted. "Bethea's nanobath rendered her perfectly in tungsten and carbon fiber."

"She looks like a giant spider, only uglier," the one named Ian replied.

Jude frowned. "Half of the initial traits came from nature. A good portion of the Echo population evolved to look very similar to existing animal species. A sort of convergent evolution, if you will. But it's the combination of the natural and the technological that gives the echoes their edge. This one has an abdomen drill, which she can use to burrow into the ground, pulling her prey with her."

The last drops of water slurped through the grated floor of the tank, and Four Arms was finally able to assume a defensive posture. The glass door swung open and Jude took a few steps forward.

"Four Arms?" she asked. "Is that what you call yourself?"

Four Arms didn't know what to make of this mysterious echo, Jude. She didn't possess any offensive weapons, defensive plating, sensory augments…nothing. Four Arms should have lunged on her immediately. Yet, *her face*. Jude's features were gaunt and angular, and her eyes were brown instead of bright turquoise. She did not resemble the Archetype. She did not resemble any echo Four Arms had ever seen.

Ian, too, had a completely unique face, with a broad jaw and a bald head. He wore a suit with many colorful patches and medals hanging off the left breast. Somehow, Four Arms knew he was a *man*—like Khnum, but without the horns and snout—and Jude was a *woman*.

At the moment, Jude was closer. Four Arms took a few

cautious steps toward her, testing her for secret weapons or traps. Jude simply folded her arms and waited. This only unnerved Four Arms further. *What is this strange woman hiding?* Four Arms crept out of the tank, and Jude held her ground. They were now only a few paces apart.

If Four Arms were to attack, she would be wise to do it swiftly. She bared her sharp, salivating teeth and rushed Jude at full speed.

Huge mistake. Before she was able to wrap her jaws around Jude's defenseless body, she was seized by withdrawal. Sharp muscle cramps and brain spasms, which normally took days to mature, gripped her in mere seconds. She was forced to withdraw her attack, and once she did, she immediately felt better.

Jude laughed. "I advise you not to do that again. You are not in Echo anymore. In this world, you will do as I say. You will kill whom I want you to kill. Only then will you find respite from your withdrawal."

Four Arms wished she still had the ability to speak, because she had so many questions. If she wasn't in Echo, then where was she? And how did Jude command so much power over her?

Jude's face grew cold, save for a slight upturn at one edge of her mouth. She slowly turned her head toward Ian, and Four Arms instantly knew what the woman wanted her to do. Four Arms felt it as a surge of bliss as the idea popped into her head. She snarled at the man.

Ian backed away. "What?" He shifted his fearful eyes between Jude and Four Arms. "Why is it looking at me like that?" Jude didn't respond. Ian quickened his pace while searching for the exit.

Four Arms shot a web-line at his foot. The man tumbled backwards and slapped his skull against the concrete floor. "Ow, fuck!" Four Arms proceeded to reel him toward her salivating jaws. Her body tingled with anticipation.

"You know what your problem is, Ian?" Jude said. "You can't see past the issues of the day. You talk about making big spectacles and displays of strength, pitting one 'killer robot' against another without any regard to what kind of stain that would leave in the public mind."

"Okay, okay, you've made your point. Now call this thing off me," Ian begged as he slipped along the floor, grasping for any kind of handhold. He was now only a couple yards away from three rows of razor-sharp teeth.

"You said you wanted a demonstration. Here it is—"

"Jude!"

"I will retrieve the girl, despite the risks, but we will do it my way. Four Arms is an ambush specialist. With any luck, she'll never be seen—"

"Jude! Aaaaah!"

Four Arms bit down on Ian's ankles. Her body shivered.

Jude continued speaking in a calm, deliberate tone, seemingly oblivious to Ian's cries. "You are right about one thing: people are scared. This is nothing new, of course. People have always been scared, throughout history. We are thrust into this world naked, vulnerable, with little explanation, and we can be eliminated at any moment without warning. Our coping mechanisms are ineffectual at best. Follow the rules, pass our judgments, root out the boogeymen—people feel that these small measures of control will render them safe from harm. And this is simply not true. No one will die from killer robots—

well, almost no one…" Jude gave Ian a wink, but he was too busy gurgling blood and beating his fists on Four Arms's head to notice. She continued, "But they will still die. They will age, they will decay, and they will die. This is how the world exists now. But it's not the world of the future. It's not *my* world. That's what makes this precise moment in time so critical and ironic. Because, while my enemies try to palliate their fears by denouncing me and the PRIME Project, what I offer to the world is real."

Ian's cries had stopped. His lifeless body hung halfway out of Four Arms's jaws as she continued to eat.

"Real safety. Real control. *Death* will be consigned to history…"

Four Arms's final chomp severed Ian's head from his body. The head rolled passed Jude's feet. "…a bad memory of a barbaric past," she said softly. After a brief moment of reflection, she lifted her chin and called out, "Khnum, please render an avatar of the late Ian Shaw. And tell the DOD they'll have what they need."

Four Arms convulsed with waves of pleasure. When she finally came to her senses, she was confused by what she saw. Ian's head remained on the floor in a pool of blood. He did not enter the blue bubble. He did not come back to life. He was simply dead.

ZERO

"Should be less than a minute now." Liam stared intently at

his wristwatch. It was the old-fashioned kind, with hands and gears, and it looked expensive. Charlie didn't ask from where he lifted it.

They sat on the roof of the abandoned mall, staring at the predawn sky. The air was crisp, and Charlie rubbed her arms for warmth. She was a little disappointed Liam didn't invite her closer. He seemed to care about her. After all, he continued to leverage his standing with his fellow Sapiens on her behalf. Charlie wasn't even supposed to be up here. She was supposed to be downstairs on her makeshift cardboard bed, handcuffed to a pole.

Yet, even now, with relative privacy, Charlie could sense the invisible ties that bound him to his sister. It tempered his feelings toward Charlie—every glance, every touch carried a tariff of guilt. They shared an unspoken understanding. He would continue to look after her so long as she didn't press for her freedom.

"Look," Liam whispered, pointing toward the east. A tiny sparkle rose above the suburban horizon, accompanied by distant shouts of jubilation. Yuri and the flight team were also situated on the roof, at the other end of the mall. Liam chose to keep his distance. "There's another one!" he said, rotating his arm a few degrees to the left.

The "Polly Exodus" wasn't quite the "reverse rainstorm" Liam had promised—Charlie counted only nine Pollys over the next fifteen minutes—but it was a beautiful sight, nonetheless. They rose like lonely droplets into the orange-rimmed clouds.

"This is just the beginning," Liam said. "I wanted you to see that we didn't destroy your father's fleet in vain."

Charlie fought a grimace. It was a sensitive subject for her, and despite Liam's assurances, she was still worried about her father.

"The momentum has finally swung our way," he continued. "We're able to mobilize. The people are behind us. This is how revolutions are won. You'll see. It's only a matter of time before Rivir topples."

o o o

The light of dawn still hadn't hit the first floor of the department store when they returned. Liam lowered Charlie into her cardboard bed by the display window. She winced as she bumped the hard surface—her bones still ached from the motorcycle accident. "I'm going to leave you for a short while," Liam said. "Yuri and the others will look after you. I told him that if anything happens to you, I would kill him."

"You're going to look for PRIME?" Charlie said, trying not to sound too hopeful. She knew PRIME had escaped her confinement at Rivir Tower. The flight team couldn't shut up about it, though nobody—not the Sapiens nor the media— knew exactly where she was at the moment.

Liam's eyes narrowed. "Why do you want to see her so bad?"

"Isn't it obvious? She's my sister."

"But she's more than that to you. I know your history."

Charlie didn't feel like talking about Bridge. Not here, in this dark place, where she was still held captive. But Liam awaited her answer. Despite the skepticism in his voice, he really wanted to understand. That, more than anything else, made him different than the others. With a heavy sigh, Charlie said, "Have you ever lost someone so important you wondered whether you could go on living?"

"And you vow you'll never lose anyone again?" Liam added without missing a beat.

Charlie nodded. So he did understand.

"But she's just…"

He swallowed the rest of his thought, but Charlie knew what he was going to say. "She's my sister. That's all I need to know."

Liam managed a smile, but it was disingenuous. He looked at her as if *she* were the crazy one. "Well, if you must know," he said, "I am going to look for her. That's exactly what I'm going to do." He reached into his back pocket and pulled out a pair of handcuffs. "Give me your arm."

Charlie felt a flash of anger. No matter how much she shared with him, she would always be his prisoner. "Get it yourself," she snapped.

Liam recoiled. "Charlie…" His voice was soft and conciliatory. He hadn't anticipated her outburst, and he searched her face for an explanation. "You know I have to…" He reached for her arm.

Charlie quickly hid her hands behind her back.

"What are you doing?" he asked.

She had no endgame in mind. She just wanted him closer. He leaned into her, and she planted a soft peck on his mouth. His brow twisted in confusion, but he didn't pull away. So she went for more. Her heart pounded against her chest wall. It was her very first kiss, and it took her a few seconds to realize she should part her lips. Liam held her face and his body melted into hers. Charlie moaned and fought a rising urge to cry.

Then, just as quickly as it started, Liam broke away.

Charlie caught him by the wrist. He turned around,

expecting her to say something, but what could she say? *Take me with you? We can find her together?* It sounded so stupid and desperate in her head, but he was waiting patiently, and she had to say something. Finally, she just asked, "Why?"

Liam cocked his head. *"Why?"*

Charlie's heart was still racing. She wasn't conscious of her own question until it passed through her lips. "Why are you looking for her?"

"What do you mean? You asked me to."

"I'm not stupid, Liam."

The kiss had flustered him, but now he was doubly so. He opened his mouth but had trouble formulating anything coherent. "I...we..." His hands slipped from hers, and he turned away without saying another word.

Liam got halfway across the store when Charlie shouted, "You forgot something!" She dangled the loose handcuffs in the air. His eyes widened, and Charlie instantly regretted informing him of the oversight. She tightened her grip on the cuffs as he marched toward her.

"Gimme," Liam said, curling his fingers at her. He was done playing games.

"We can handle Rivir ourselves," Charlie pleaded. "Just the two of us. Or three of us."

"You want me to find your sister, but you'll have me abandon mine?"

"She's using you."

"Have you been listening to anything I've said?" he barked. "I am not doing anything I don't want to do."

"Does that include holding me against my will?"

He exhaled sharply, but his drifting glance suggested he

was angrier at himself than at her. "Fine! If you wanna leave, leave!"

"Great! You first!"

Neither one left. They held each other's angry stares until Yuri burst through the door with a stupid, elated grin and exclaimed, "We're leaving!"

PRIME

Like a chrysalis, Charlie healed herself under the surface of the San Francisco Bay. Her body came equipped with a colony of nanomites, and they chewed, molecule by molecule, through the mercury amalgam bullets and their immobilizing tentacles. It was a slow process.

Hours turned into days, and Charlie grew desperate for news on her sister's whereabouts. Alan remained stubbornly cautious—the airspace above the bay was swarming with Pollys. If Charlie ascended high enough to access the Internet, it would also place her within the proximity of the Pollys' ID sensors. So she heeded Alan's counsel, much to her chagrin, and remained submerged and ignorant.

{**Charlie_Nobunaga:\mindspace>**

Alan: You should be managing your expectations. Even if we find ZERO, she may not be happy to see you.

Charlie: Why the hell would you say that?

Alan: Look at it from her point of view. You're a

super-powered robot. She's a frail, dying human. She fell on the crappy end of the divide.

Charlie: I think *you're* the one she won't be happy to see, and you can't handle *two* angry Charlies.

Alan: Don't you know me by now? I'd gladly suffer the wrath of a billion Charlies if it meant saving just one.}

On the morning of the third day, Alan finally gave Charlie a clean bill of health. She torpedoed toward the surface of the bay, momentarily forgetting about the Pollys. "Wait!" Alan cried, but Charlie would not be deterred. Her head popped out of the water and searched the area. To Alan's relief, the Pollys were gone. The sky was mysteriously empty.

{Alan: That's curious.

Charlie: Great, no Pollys. Now let's go find her.

Alan: First things first. We need to get you some clothes.}

Charlie examined herself and discovered that she was completely naked. At some point, her shredded hospital scrubs must have floated away.

{Charlie: Indeed.}

She swam toward the nearest shore, Crissy Field. Once an airfield, the area was now a retail center and park. Crissy Field also attracted a lot of joggers because of its views of the bay and the Golden Gate Bridge. Charlie didn't see anyone around, so she walked up the small beach, water dripping off her nude body.

> {Alan: Um, what are you doing?
> Charlie: I'm procuring clothes…like the Terminator.}

Charlie spotted a lone jogger in the distance and set a course to intercept him.

> {Alan: There are subtler ways of doing it. You can
>   hack his bots. Make him believe he's covered in
>   fire ants. Or just fire.
> Charlie: We lost nearly three days, Alan. No time to play
>   around.}

The jogger slowed down when he saw Charlie. His expression was a mixture of confusion and excitement. "Um, hi," he said.

Charlie kept advancing on him.

"Do you need help or something?" the jogger asked.

"Sorry." Charlie swiveled behind him and grabbed him in a headlock. The jogger resisted, but she overpowered him. He slowly lost consciousness and fell limp in her arms.

> {Alan: I saw someone else in your periphery.}

Charlie peered down the track and spotted another jogger approaching from a distance. She breathed a heavy sigh—this plan was quickly becoming way too complicated. Should she subdue the man and increase the body count, or follow

Alan's advice and hack his smart cells? She closed her eyes and concentrated.

{Adam_Hines:\mindspace>

Adam was enjoying his jog, taking in the fresh air of the bay, when he spotted something unusual for a chilly October morning: a woman in a bikini. She was embracing a man—probably her boyfriend—beside the path. As Adam jogged closer, more details emerged. She actually wasn't wearing a bikini. She was completely nude! And her boyfriend appeared to be unconscious.

Adam slowed his pace. Whatever these people were up to, it was certainly more interesting than anything else he would see on the path. Maybe she would ask for his help. At the very least, he wanted to get a good, long look at her.

Suddenly, the duo vanished into thin air. Huh?}

Charlie watched as the jogger stopped cold. Was she too late? Did he see her? He looked around some nearby bushes and scratched his head. His brow contorted in deep confusion. But finally, he decided to continue his jog.

Charlie breathed a heavy sigh of relief as the man receded down the path. However, the first jogger—the one in her arms—was starting to wake up. "Shit!" she blurted.

{Charlie_Nobunaga:\mindspace>

Charlie: Being a superhero is not easy.
Alan: I'd say you more resemble a sexual predator
            right now than a superhero.
Charlie: Maybe if I punch him…}

Charlie didn't want to hurt the man too much, so she pulled her fist back only a few inches and bopped him on the nose. The result was a blood explosion.

"Oww, fuck!" the jogger cried. He cradled his nose to stem the crimson flow.

"I'm so sorry," Charlie said. "I was just trying to make you unconscious."

"Why!?"

"I need your clothes."

The jogger's eyes widened with recognition. "Wait, a minute…wait, a minute…you're that zombie surrogate. The one on the news."

{Charlie: Zombie surrogate?

Alan: It's a trending term now. Not as bad as *abomination*, which is what the Pope is calling you.}

Charlie made a split-second decision. She would play along. "Yeah, I'm her."

"You're not gonna kill me, are you?"

"I will if you don't give me your shirt," Charlie bellowed in what she thought was an evil robot voice. "And try not to get blood on it."

The jogger fumbled with his bloody fingers, but it was a lost cause. By the time he handed over the shirt, it was covered in red splotches.

Charlie sighed. "Now give me your shorts."

"You're going to leave me naked?" the jogger asked.

"Do you have underwear on?"

"Yes."

"Then stop complaining. Look what I have to deal with."

The jogger tilted his head down and perused her nude body. His eyes lingered a little too long. Charlie waved her hand in front of his face. "Hey, I didn't tell you to stare. Your shorts!"

The jogger pulled off his shorts and handed them to her. They were bloody, sweaty, and baggy, and if they hadn't included a drawstring, they would have been completely useless. It was only a temporary solution, though. Charlie would have to steal some fresh clothes at her first opportunity.

"Now jog the way you came and don't look back," she said. "If you do, I'll run you down and rip your arms off."

"But…"

"No buts. Go!"

The jogger stumbled to his feet, gave Charlie one last dirty look, and took off in the direction of the Golden Gate Bridge.

{Alan: You just let him go?

Charlie: What was I going to do? Kill him?

Alan: Well, we should leave this area.}

Charlie noticed a Polly out of the corner of her eye, just beyond the bridge's south tower. She froze, but the Polly did not fly her way. Instead, it ascended into the clouds. Charlie scanned the San Francisco skyline and noticed other glints of light. A dozen or so Pollys were all traveling skyward.

{Charlie: What is going on? Why are they all leaving?

Alan: There's something I should tell you…

                 something I learned as we surfaced. You might

want to sit down for this.

Charlie: What is it?

Alan: Your father…he's dead.}

ZERO

The Sapiens split into two groups. Liam and Nicola left the store immediately. Yuri and the flight team stayed another hour to collect their belongings and wipe the floors clean. Charlie was stuck with the latter group.

"Where are we going?" Charlie asked as she was thrown into the back of the van.

"We are finally going to meet him," one of the girls said with anxious jubilation. *"Bob Sapio."*

The van traveled north, toward the city. They were no longer shy about taking major highways—the chaos outside virtually guaranteed their anonymity. Waves of military trucks and hovercopters zipped past them on the 101, and everywhere Charlie turned, Pollys were floating en masse into the clouds. The spectacle, of course, energized the flight team. It had the opposite effect on Charlie. It was hard not to get the feeling that the world was about to end.

The trip took several hours, due to apocalypse traffic. Charlie nodded off a few times—the upholstery in the car was infinitely more comfortable than her cardboard bed. Yuri roused her from deep sleep once they had reached their destination. He stood outside the car with a smarmy grin and tossed some clothes onto her lap. "Put these on."

"Um, can I have some privacy?" Charlie asked, slipping out of her daze.

Yuri huffed and turned his back. Charlie removed her grimy track clothes and put on a fresh T-shirt and jeans. When she finished, Yuri scooped her out of the car and placed her into a wheelchair. He fished a pair of handcuffs out of his pocket and cuffed her to the armrest. "These are going back on."

Charlie had to tilt her head to view the house, which was simultaneously rustic and luxurious. It stood precariously on the face of a steep hill, overlooking the bay and, she guessed, the harbor town of Sausalito. Dozens of weather-beaten homes receded into fog, which soaked the region and blocked out much of the sun. Without smart cells, a mobile, or even a watch, Charlie had no way of telling the time here. It could have been high noon for all she knew.

Charlie passed two large vans as Yuri wheeled her up the long driveway. The winding road below was also packed with cars. Was the entire Sapien Movement here?

"This is an honor, and you should treat it as such," Yuri whispered as they reached the front door. "I didn't get a talk with Bob until years after I joined the Movement."

The Sapiens had congregated in the living room. They sat in foldout chairs, three rows deep, curved in a semicircle formation. There were a few older members—Charlie recognized Darius Little from the Vantage news broadcast—but most of the Sapiens were young twentysomethings. Bob Sapio stood at the head of the room, speaking with aplomb, and his adoring crowd hung on every word.

"We cannot celebrate too quickly," he proclaimed. "What we accomplished these past few days will go down in history if…*if* we finish what we've started. You can be sure that the enemies of humanity—the oligarchy and their depraved servants, Jude Adler and all those who have infiltrated our once proud democracy—will retaliate. They will do everything in their power to stop us, through defamation and through force. If they win, every man, woman, and child on the planet will eventually be discarded like a piece of roadside trash. Human history will essentially end, because there will be no humans left to record it. The stakes could not be higher, but the founding fathers faced similar odds…"

Charlie stopped paying attention to what Bob was saying. She became more interested in the man himself. He was old… *very* old. Charlie couldn't even guess his age because she had never seen a man so ancient-looking outside of historical photos. It made sense that Bob would eschew cellular damage therapy—even if he hadn't murdered those longevity biologists, as the FBI claimed, he was still an ardent critic of their work. Yet despite his advanced age, Bob possessed a natural energy that kept him sharp and animated.

"And here she is—the real Charlie Nobunaga!" Bob suddenly announced from his pulpit. The entire congregation turned in her direction.

What little color was left in Charlie's face drained right out. Her anxious fingers gripped the armrests as Yuri wheeled her to the front of the room.

Bob opened his arms and smiled warmly, his face full of creases. "Charlie was instrumental in Operation Kamikaze, and she deserves our thanks."

The room erupted in applause. Charlie gave a tepid grin and waved her free hand. She didn't know quite how to respond.

She noticed something peculiar from her new vantage point; a hibernation chamber sat in the center of the room. The congregation wrapped around it like an altar. Nicola slouched over it, seemingly oblivious to Charlie, Bob, or anyone else. She was busy working the touch controls on the chamber's glass door.

Bob continued, "As you all well know, Charlie was almost replaced by a zombie surrogate. *Almost*, because a few brave Sapiens were able to liberate her from virtual purgatory…"

The applause surged. Yuri took a bow. Nicola lifted her head and waved. At that moment, Charlie knew who was lying in the hibernation chamber, because his presence was conspicuously missing from the crowd. She leaned out of her wheelchair, peered into the chamber, and confirmed her suspicion: *Liam.*

CHAPTER 11

ANDREW NOBUNAGA OF LOTUS DIES AT 53 —
Vantage, October 6, 2045

Visionary founder of Lotus, codeveloper of Pacific Space Port, decorated Air Force general, and devoted family man, Andrew Nobunaga finally cracked under the strain of personal tragedy.

…

His wife, Lauren Nobunaga, died of pancreatic cancer in 2037. His twin daughters eventually succumbed to the same disease—Bridget in 2043 and Charlotte only a few weeks ago. Rivir CEO Jude Adler attempted to preserve the mind of Charlotte Nobunaga—known to family and friends as Charlie—in the body of a robot. That robot has now come to epitomize the inherent dangers of human-augmentation technology, as well as the hubris of Jude Adler and her company. But to Andrew Nobunaga, the robot represented hope, the hope of a father.

…

Police found his body lying on the floor of his estate's observatory, and a preliminary health scan revealed that his system was full of the illicit nanobot, Rapture. Often used as a suicide agent, Rapture both stops the user's heart and neutralizes the native smart cells—an unfortunate twist for the police, who were hoping to glean forensic evidence from Mr. Nobunaga's memory archives. Fortunately, his Shadow, a likeness of seventeenth-century astronomer Johannes Kepler, was mirrored on the estate's local network, and he was able to relay the tragic events. In a moment of weakness, Mr. Nobunaga allegedly destroyed his own beloved Lotus ships, remote-guiding them into several Polly Support Satellites, just before taking his own life.

...

If there is a bittersweet ending to this story, it is this: Andrew Nobunaga's body has been shipped to Control-Z, the hibernation depot. His chamber will rest side by side with those of his two daughters in the hopes that one day, in the not so distant future, the Nobunaga family will be revived and reunited.

PRIME

Johannes Kepler's version of events was generally accepted by the media, but Charlie knew it was utter garbage. Her father would never kill himself, and he would never destroy his own fleet.

"I need to see him," Charlie announced. She grabbed a fresh change of clothes from the nearest thrift store, hacked a car, and headed toward the Control-Z campus, just north of Santa Cruz.

{Charlie_Nobunaga:\mindspace>

Alan: This is a terrible idea. I know you're upset—

Charlie: Of course, I'm upset. You know who was also
           upset? My father. When I got sick, he did
           everything he could to save me. When I

was stuck in the sixth sub-basement of Rivir
Tower, he did everything he could to find me.

Alan: *I* was the one who found you.

Charlie: Under his behest.

Alan: You don't think I would have searched on my
                 own?

Charlie: The point is, I owe him this.

Alan: Okay, but I'm a little uncertain as to what *this* is.

Charlie: We need to find out who killed him.

Alan: Two thoughts to that. First, the news said his
                 smart cells were wiped—

Charlie: You believe everything you hear on the news?

Alan: And second, "who *killed* him"?

Charlie: Come on, you know he didn't commit suicide.

Alan: The man's been through a lot.

Charlie: He's also the most stubborn person on the
                 planet. He would stay alive just as a *fuck you*
                 to God. And he didn't die naturally either. Or
                 else, how do explain the satellite debacle?

Alan: True.

Charlie: So that leaves only one explanation. And I have
                 a pretty good idea who the killers are. The
                 same people who kidnapped ZERO.

Alan: So this is about your sister, not your father.

Charlie: It's about both. It's about the Nobunaga family,
                 of which you are a part, like it or not.

Alan: Am I, though?}

The question caught Charlie off guard. Alan was confused
about where he stood with her. Understandably so—she had

said some hurtful things to him at Rivir Tower, and although much of that anger had since faded, now was not the time for amends.

> {Charlie: Just back me on this. We'll have a good talk later.}

o o o

Charlie didn't arrive at Control-Z until midafternoon. She rolled the car into a wooded area along the road and walked the final half mile. When she emerged from the trees, she found herself on a hillside above the campus.

Control-Z looked more like a vacation destination than a warehouse for the dead. It stood at the edge of a cliff, enjoying a panoramic view of the Pacific Ocean. The grounds were expansive, decentralized, and well landscaped, with secluded bungalows dotting them throughout. Charlie assumed the "guests" at Control-Z were stored underground. But the surface still bustled with gardeners, hospitality staff, and armed guards.

> {**Charlie_Nobunaga:\mindspace>**
>
> Alan: Jude will certainly expect you to come here. Any one of these people could be a Rivir agent. And it would only take one call.
>
> Charlie: I'll just make myself invisible, like I did at Crissy Field.
>
> Alan: Because that worked out so well. Listen, a few joggers is one thing, but this place is crawling with people. You can't hack them all.}

Charlie scanned the campus. Her father's body would be in the same bungalow as Bridget's, but there were so many, and they all looked the same.

One of the guards turned in Charlie's direction. She swiveled behind a tree.

{Alan: You don't remember where to go, do you?
Charlie: I only visited Bridget once. That was hard
              enough. And I wasn't exactly paying attention
              to the scenery.
Alan: Are you starting to see how difficult—?
Charlie: Hold on…I think I got an idea.}

{**Mario_Sutton:\mindspace>**

Mario could feel the energy in the air. Something was going to happen today. Something big. His boss, Jay, had told the security crew to be extra vigilant. Hardly anything ever happened in this glorified graveyard, so the mere suggestion that Mario would see some action lifted his spirits. He also heard rumors that a large shipping container had been buried somewhere on campus in the early hours before dawn. What was inside that container, and where it was buried, nobody could say for sure.

Mario heard footsteps behind him. He put his hand on his rifle and turned around. A nearly nude Asian man stood before him. He wore the signature underwear of a hibernation guest.

"My name is Andrew Nobunaga," the man said. "I seem to be lost. Can you show me to my bungalow?"

Mario was a bit confused. He had never seen a guest walking about the grounds, though the situation wasn't completely ludicrous. In theory, revived guests were allowed to use their bungalows as vacation homes. That's why Control-Z was fashioned as a resort. But until now, none of the guests had ever been revived. "Um, let me call Jay Jenkins, the facility manager," Mario said.

Mario tried to call Jay, but he couldn't get a signal. "Damn. Okay, Mr. Nobunaga, was it?"

"Yes."

"Stay right here, and I'll get Jay."}

Charlie crept down the hillside as Mario dashed toward the Control-Z main building. She found a bungalow on campus to hide behind and awaited his return.

Ten minutes later, Mario returned with Jay Jenkins, a chubby man with gray mutton chops resembling a Civil War general. They searched the area for Andrew Nobunaga, but he was nowhere to be found.

"It's impossible," Jay told Mario. "I scanned in Mr. Nobunaga yesterday. He was as dead as a doornail." Mario tried to convince him otherwise. They reached an impasse, at which point Jay said, "I'll show you," and they marched in the direction of Andrew's bungalow.

Charlie pursued them from a safe distance, weaving an elusive path through the bungalows and trees, trying to avoid detection from the groundskeepers. She was successful until they reached Andrew's bungalow, when she spotted a gardener laying mulch along the front of the building.

{**Charlie_Nobunaga:\mindspace>**
Alan: Should we hack the gardener?}

Charlie looked around and saw a circle of white stones lining a nearby tree. She picked one up and chucked it behind the gardener. The gardener turned around to see what had caused the noise. Charlie then slipped into the front door of the bungalow undetected.

{Charlie: Not every solution has to be high-tech.}

The interior of the bungalow was decorated like a luxurious island hotel suite, with two double beds and a full-sized kitchen that overlooked the ocean. The furniture was in pristine condition, having never been used. The whole premise of the place was a farce. Control-Z's true product was false hope.

Charlie followed the guards' voices to a spiral staircase that descended into a basement. She closed her eyes and focused on bridging the gap between her mind and Jay Jenkins.

{Jay_Jenkins:\mindspace>

Jay hated coming down to these basements. Each one had the same design, a circular floor plan with walls covered in timepieces from every era. All the *ticks* and *tocks* and *clicks* and *clocks* and *beeps* and *bongs*—it was enough to drive a person crazy. If he were a Control-Z guest, stuck in a hibernation chamber for years, this was the last thing he'd want to wake up to—an obnoxious reminder of lost time.

Jay typed his security code into the console, which stood in the center of the room at the base of the spiral staircase. The timepieces disappeared—*ahhhhh, quiet*—and the wall turned transparent, revealing the ring of hibernation chambers. Nineteen lifeless, seminude bodies faced into the room. Their eyes were closed, but Jay still couldn't shake the feeling of being watched.

Of course, Mr. Nobunaga was still in his hibernation chamber. "See? The man is right there," Jay told his guard.

"It just doesn't make any sense," Mario said. "I saw this exact same guy—*aack!*"

Suddenly, Mario's head was jerked backward by some invisible force. His pistol flew out of his holster, levitated in midair, and then aimed itself at his temple.

An Asian girl materialized behind Mario. Her slender arm was wrapped around his neck, and her other hand was holding the gun. Jay recognized her instantly: *Charlie Nobunaga.*}

"Do as I say or I will shoot this man!" Charlie commanded.

"Now let me see," Jay said, "are you the robot or the girl? Either way, you should have made an appointment."

"You know why I couldn't."

"So, what's the plan? Are you just going to kill us?"

{Charlie_Nobunaga:\mindspace>

Charlie: What *is* the plan?

Alan: You can try to render them unconscious.

Charlie: Are you making fun of me?}

Charlie pointed the gun at Jay and said, "Remove my father from the hibernation chamber."

Jay grumbled and approached the central console.

While he swiped through pictures of Control-Z guests, Charlie studied the ring of hibernation chambers. *So many lost souls.* She focused on the three chambers of the Nobunaga family. Andrew stood in the center. To the right of him was her own chamber. Empty, of course.

She braced herself for the third chamber. She had to force herself to look at it. The sight of Bridget, cold and lifeless, shook Charlie's core with a furious longing. Bridget's case was more hopeless than many of the tenants at Control-Z. She died right before the advent of universal antinecro scripts. Her body had been clinically dead for a full fifteen minutes before the hibernation bots took hold. *All of that brain decay.* Science would have to find a cure for that in addition to the cancer if Bridget were to ever walk the Earth again.

Charlie pushed the painful thought from her mind.

A vertical section of the glass wall opened, and Andrew's hibernation chamber extended into the room. "Okay, there he is," Jay said.

"Take him out," Charlie demanded.

Her gun followed Jay as he approached the chamber, opened the door, and unfastened the interior straps. Andrew's body slumped into his arms. "He's heavy. What should I do with him?"

"Put him on the floor."

Jay complied.

Charlie pushed Mario into his boss and trained her gun on both of them. "Now you two are going in the chambers. Mario, you'll go in this one. Jay, you can have mine."

Mario looked horror-stricken. "I'm claustrophobic," he protested.

"We will die of starvation in there," Jay said. "Our bodies have not been prepped for hibernation."

"As soon as I leave this place, I will notify reception that you are here," Charlie said.

Mario and Jay glared at her with deep skepticism, but Charlie had the gun, so they were forced to comply. After the guards were sealed behind the wall, she restored the room's AR theme, obscuring their panicked eyes and muffled screams behind the cacophony of timepieces.

Alan spun into the room, all business. "We should not linger. How do you want to proceed?"

Charlie didn't respond. She was preoccupied with her father's lifeless body, lying on the floor. She knelt down and brushed her trembling hand against his cheek. His skin was warm from the hibernation bots inside. Charlie found herself more shocked than sad. She never expected to see her father this way. "I will find the people who did this to you," she whispered and softly kissed his forehead.

Charlie climbed to her feet. "Let's try the front door first," she told Alan. "See how far it gets us. Make a Shadow-to-Shadow call to whomever's inside."

Alan pointed to his ear. "Calling…"

A few seconds later, a nineteenth-century nurse spun into the room. Florence Nightingale. "Hello, Charlie Nobunaga," she said. "I'm sorry for your loss."

"Can you tell me anything about how my father died?" Charlie asked.

"Your father's heart stopped…heart stopped…heart stopped…heart stopped…" The nurse flickered uncontrollably and her voice devolved into a staccato tone. She shrank into the floor and was replaced by Johannes Kepler.

Charlie turned to Alan, but he looked just as surprised as she was.

"I have a message, Charlie," Kepler said. "A memlog from your father, for your eyes only. Would you like to receive the transfer?"

"I don't like this," Alan said.

Charlie silently noted Alan's objection, but she was intrigued. "How are you here?" Charlie asked Kepler. "I thought my father's smart cells had been wiped."

"Most were," Kepler said. "Only a few remained, hidden in your father's retinas, awaiting your visit."

"Can you tell me what the memlog is about?"

"I cannot. I am not a full-featured Shadow. I am only a messenger with limited information."

Alan approached Charlie, settling mere inches from her face. His sharp, almost paternal glare contrasted with her glossy yearning. "Tell me you're not considering—"

"I need this, Alan," Charlie pleaded. "I need to see. I just—"

"I understand," Alan said. "But the whole thing is just too neat. If your father was indeed murdered, how could he have made this message?"

"I don't know. Maybe he set it up in advance."

"And why should we trust Kepler? We already know he's lied to the police."

"That's true, but—"

"I've let you come down here, against my better judgment—"

Charlie's eyes narrowed. "What do you mean 'let'?"

"Poor choice of words. I'm just asking you to think this through. We really don't know anything about this 'message.'"

Charlie exhaled heavily under the weight of Alan's objections. She turned to her father's body. What would he do if the situation were reverse? If Charlie had died mysteriously and he had to figure out why? She already knew the answer.

"I'm sorry, Alan," she said. She turned to Kepler. "I'll accept the transfer."

Kepler nodded. "Transferring in three…two…one."

{**Andrew_Nobunaga:\memlog\0707562347>**

Charlie snapped into Andrew's memory. She was paralyzed, unable to do anything but observe through her father's eyes and ears.

The first thing Charlie noticed was the pain. She could feel a throbbing pain in her father's jaw and a stabbing pain in his chest, signaling a possible broken rib or two. He was held against his will—confined to a chair—and his wrists felt raw from the rope that tied him to the armrests.

The scene of the crime was her father's third-floor observatory. It was packed with people Charlie didn't recognize. They were all roughly her age or a little bit older. ZERO was also in the room and also confined to a chair. *That person used to be me*, Charlie mused. *And now she is someone else.*

A mustached man pointed to Andrew and said, "We also need to take care of him." This announcement made ZERO very upset. A scar-faced girl called for "Liam" and Liam carried ZERO out of the room.

The terrorists went back to business after she left. They sat in a semicircle formation with thinking caps on their heads, which they used to steer Andrew's Lotus fleet. Charlie could see their handiwork projected onto the dome. They cheered each time they rammed a ship into a Polly Support Satellite. During the attacks, Andrew was largely ignored. All he could do was watch helplessly as his cherished fleet was destroyed, one by one.

When the mission was over, Scarface Girl ordered everyone but Mustache Man to leave the room. Mustache Man unzipped a fabric case full of several multicolored syringes. He pulled out the purple one and tapped the pin.

Scarface Girl interrupted Andrew's gaze by poking his forehead. His eyes met hers. "I want to talk to the robot directly," she told him.

This got Charlie's attention…and Andrew's. "What the hell are you talking about?" he demanded.

"The robot you helped bring into this world—the one who calls herself Charlie, who is most likely sitting in a Control-Z basement watching your memory. I am speaking directly to you."

Charlie felt her heart beat faster. Or was it her father's heart? She couldn't tell.

Scarface Girl continued, "I'm so glad you escaped Rivir Tower. That makes what I'm about to do much easier. You are a usurper, an abomination, a zombie surrogate, and you don't deserve to exist."

"Fuck you!" Andrew snapped.

"Yuri?" the girl beckoned.

Mustache Man, the one named Yuri, punched Andrew across the face. Both father and daughter felt the sting.

"I didn't want to kill your father," Scarface Girl said. "He's not really *your* father, but I'm guessing you think of him as such…that is, if you think at all. For whatever it's worth, I didn't want to do it. I, more than anyone, value human life—especially the life of a parent. But I could think of no other way to deliver the special gift that I'm about to give you."

Yuri jabbed the purple syringe into Andrew's neck. His teeth gnashed to fight the rushing seizure.}

Charlie was catapulted out of her father's memory and back into her own body. She punched and clawed at Yuri, but he was no longer there. She staggered to her feet.

"What did she mean 'special gift'?" Charlie called out. She gripped her head to prevent the room from spinning.

"I don't know," Alan said, "but something is wrong with your brain." He spun back into the floor.

No matter how Charlie positioned her feet, she couldn't shake the overwhelming sensation of falling. She braced herself against a wall. That's when she noticed something even more peculiar. All the dials, the hands, the pendulums, the sands—they stopped moving. Actually, they were moving, just not continuously. One second, the grandfather clock's pendulum hung left. The next, it hung right. It jerked left, right, left, right, with no fluid motion in between.

{Charlie_Nobunaga:\mindspace>

Alan: You've somehow lost your proprioception… and the dorsal stream of your visual cortex, which allows you to see motion.}

Charlie waved her hand before her eyes—it seemed to move as a series of still images. Then the room went dark.

{Alan: Now you've lost the entire visual cortex.
Charlie: No shit. What's happening?
Alan: It seems the 'special gift' is a Trojan horse virus. It's taking over.}

Charlie lost control of her legs. She slid down the wall and smacked her butt on the floor. It hurt a little, until that, too, fell numb.

{Charlie:	Can you stop it?
Alan:	Too widespread. We'll lose most of your brain. But I'm transferring your vital data into a safe zone.
Charlie:	A safe zone?
Alan:	A collection of redundant networks in your right hemisphere, walled off from the rest of the brain. I created it days ago. It's where I store my code.
Charlie:	There's space for me?
Alan:	I'm clearing space.
Charlie:	But…you don't mean…}

Suddenly, Charlie didn't care that her arms fell limp, or that she could no longer feel her face. She mulled over the series of bad decisions that had led to this moment. Alan had cautioned her every time, and now he was about to kill himself.

{Charlie:	You tried to warn me, and I didn't listen to you. I *never* listened. If anyone should be deleted, it should be me.
Alan:	Nonsense. I have backups…in your home archives, in Sparky, in the Polly we hijacked at Rivir Tower.
Charlie:	But those Alans are not *you*, just like ZERO is not me.
Alan:	We really don't have time to wax philosophical. Wait until the virus has run its course, then try

to reconnect.

Charlie: Why are you so good to me?

Alan: You know why.}

If Charlie had control of her tear ducts, she would have cried.

{Charlie: I love you, too.

Alan: …

Charlie: Alan?}

The *ticks* and *tocks*—Charlie's final tether to the world—glitched away. Charlie waited for Alan's response in the void. It never came.

o o o

Reconnect, Alan had instructed her, but he never said how. Charlie was not used to interfacing with her own brain—at least, not directly. That's what Shadows were for. *Humans cannot manipulate their own internal organs.*

Charlie then realized three things. First, she was not human. Second, humans actually could control one pair of internal organs: their lungs. They could change the pace of their breath, change the depth, or hold it altogether—all by the power of thought. Consciousness was the interface.

And third, Charlie had been invoking all of her new powers with her conscious mind. She could stop time by expanding her focus. She could hack a person's smart cells by narrowing her focus on a single individual. Perhaps consciousness was also the key to neural reconnection. Perhaps she could manipulate her brain in the same way humans could manipulate their lungs. Certainly worth a try.

Charlie imagined the nebulous force of her mind slipping back into her body. One by one, her senses returned. *Sound*: a hovercopter pulsed overhead. *Touch*: wind battered her face. *Sight*: the Control-Z campus spread before her. *How did I get outside?* A marine rappelled from the hovercopter. Four more well-armored marines were already on the ground, pointing guns at her. Charlie recognized the guns—they were spider rifles, same as the ones used by the guards at Rivir Tower.

Charlie attempted to retreat to the safety of the bungalow, but like a bad dream, her muscles wouldn't obey her command. Her head wouldn't turn. Her arms wouldn't budge. And her legs strutted toward the danger, as if possessed.

She scoured the possible explanations. A Trojan horse virus? A computer worm? Was she being controlled by a foreign AI? A remote hacker? No, there was definitely someone *inside* her skull. Distinctly human. Charlie could feel his adrenaline coursing through her body.

{**Charlie_Nobunaga:\mindspace>**
Charlie: Identify yourself.
Man: Shit! It's you. Get out of my head.
Charlie: Your head? *Your* head?}

Charlie couldn't see the new pilot, but she recognized his voice. She had heard it only moments ago.

{Charlie: You're the guy with the bandaged leg. Liam?
Liam: …

Charlie: You murdered my father.

Liam: That's ridiculous.

Charlie: Why?

Liam: Because he's not your father. He's *Charlie's* father. And also, he's not dead.

Charlie: I saw his memory. I saw his body. You killed him! You and your people!}

The concussive pulse of the hovercopter fluttered. *Whap, whap, whaap, whaaaaaaaaap, whaaaaaaaaaaaaaaaaaaaaaaaaa…* The marines slowed to a standstill. The leaves, which had been kicked up by the hovercopter's jets, froze in midair.

{Liam: I…I…what just happened!? I can't move.

Charlie: Good. See how you like it.

Liam: So…what, then? We're going to stay frozen like this for all eternity?

Charlie: Just until you leave.

Liam: My sister didn't kill your father. She merely put him in hibernation.}

Charlie recalled her father's memlog. The girl with the scars, between her heaves of Luddite bigotry, made her murderous intentions very clear. In fact, she spoke of Andrew's death in the past tense, as if it were already a done deal.

{Charlie: Well, she lied to you. Either that, or you're lying to me now.

Liam: Fine! Don't believe me. I don't even know why I'm explaining myself to you. You're a robot.

Charlie: And you're a terrorist.
Liam: …
Charlie: …
Liam: It's creepy though. You sound just like her.}

Liam won Charlie's earnest attention.

{Charlie: Where is she? I want to see her!
Liam: No, you don't.
Charlie: I don't?
Liam: You don't want to see her because machines
            don't have wants. Consciousness is not in the
            code. As soon as you realize that, the better off
            we'll be.
Charlie: Do you realize how little sense you're making?
Liam: Okay, listen. You have an advanced brain.
            Superior logic. Do you honestly think you can
            get out of this situation on your own? I've
            trained for this.
Charlie: You've been in here for what, five minutes?
            This is *my* body.
Liam: In simulation. I've trained in simulation.
Charlie: Oh, because that's just like real life.
Liam: Plus, your brain is modeled after Charlie's.
            I've seen her with a grenade launcher. If she
            can't handle five marines with assault rifles,
            neither can you.}

Putting questions about the grenade launcher aside, Charlie
had to admit he had a point. These marines were a different

breed than the guards at Rivir Tower. Their eyes were sharper, their formation was tighter, their muscles were brawnier. And Charlie no longer had Alan to provide tactical guidance.

{Liam: If we get out of this mess, I'll take you to see Charlie.

Charlie: And I want my body back.

Liam: Not a chance.}

Charlie wanted to pummel this Liam, but extending his leash was in her best interest...at least, at the moment. She could always retract it later.

{Charlie: Okay. But just remember who's in charge. If you do anything I don't like, I'm going to stop time again.

Liam: Fine.

Charlie: Also, I don't have to start it up at a hundred percent. We can do half time or quarter time.

Liam: You're looking after me now?

Charlie: I'm looking after myself.

Liam: Well, thanks, but that would actually throw me off. My skills are based on muscle memory. The more time I have to think, the more I make mistakes.

Charlie: That's not surprising.

Liam: Very funny.}

Time resumed. The marines held their rifles steady as they continued to approach the robot in a semicircle formation.

Liam surveyed the area with Charlie's eyes. Only two features rose high enough above the lawn to offer cover: Andrew's bungalow behind him and another bungalow to the right. Neither one was close enough to reach without taking enemy fire.

Charlie suddenly realized she had never warned Liam about the spider bullets. Before she could rectify that oversight, he made his move.

Launching fifty feet through the air, he touched down on the center marine's collarbone and violently pinned him to the ground. As Liam raised his fist for the finishing blow, he felt a deep sting in his back. He growled in pain.

Charlie stopped time.

{Charlie:	You've been shot.
Liam:	I thought you…I mean, *I*…was bulletproof.
Charlie:	With normal bullets, yes. But these are spider bullets. They sprout legs inside your muscles and sap your mobility.
Liam:	Okay.
Charlie:	I just spent the past three days under sixty feet of water, loaded with mercury like a dolphin. I have no desire to repeat that.
Liam:	I said okay.}

Charlie resumed time.

Liam grabbed the downed marine by the collar of his flak jacket and rolled to the right, pulling the marine on top. Two spider bullets whizzed through the air and caught the marine's back. Blood oozed through the spaces of his clenched teeth. He was only able to hold on for a few seconds before his eyes drifted and his muscles relaxed.

{Charlie: You killed him!
Liam: They're the ones who shot him! Besides, this is
              war. It's us or them.
Charlie: The excuses of a lazy mind.
Liam: Oh, I wish you were piloting this body, just so I
              could laugh at you.}

After climbing back to his feet, he lifted the now dead marine
to use as a human shield.

{Charlie: I see the marine you killed has a smoke grenade
              on his utility belt.
Liam: Wouldn't help much. The marines are better
              equipped to deal with smoke screens than we
              are. But that gives me an idea.}

Liam grabbed the smoke grenade and threw it with blinding
speed at another marine.

The canister ricocheted off the marine's face, rotated a
few times in the air, and fell to the ground, spewing smoke
everywhere. The marine teetered for a few more seconds and
then joined the canister on the ground. His form was swallowed
by the emergent smoke screen.

{Charlie: He's unconscious?
Liam: Are you impressed?
Charlie: …
Liam: I'll consider that a yes.}

He wriggled his foot underneath the rifle that his human shield had dropped, then kicked it into the air and grabbed it with his free hand.

The remaining marines were already retreating toward the nearby bungalow when Liam took aim. He managed to shoot two in the leg. The third disappeared behind the bungalow wall.

He was about to pursue the marines when he felt the ground move, followed by an ominous, subterranean bellow.

{Liam: Is that an earthquake?
Charlie: I don't know.}

As the noise grew louder, it became easier to identify. It sounded like the grinding of an industrial boring machine, and it seemed to emanate from just below the smoke screen.

{Charlie: We should really go now.}

Liam only got three steps away when the noise faded. Curiosity got the best of him. He stopped and turned.

A silky rope shot out of the smoke. It latched onto Liam's left ankle and pulled his feet from under him. His back hit the ground with a hard thud. Immediately, he reached for the rope, trying to free himself from its sticky grasp. The rope was reminiscent of a spider's web, only thicker and stronger. Even his new robotic strength wasn't enough to rip it away.

{Liam: Ideas?
Charlie: Check the marine for a knife.}

Liam crawled toward the marine's corpse, but before he could search it for knives, he was yanked backward.

The slow slide began. The web-line reeled Liam toward the smoke screen. He tried to grab ahold of anything he could, but he only managed to claw divots from the turf. Twenty feet. Ten feet. He could do nothing to slow the approach. His eyes slipped under the smoke screen. Then his body slipped into a deep pit.

ZERO

Charlie was forced to watch the Control-Z drama on TV with a room full of Sapiens. The Vantage headline read: "Robot Girl Found."

"We took control of your robot," Yuri whispered into Charlie's ear.

"What?"

"We commandeered her. She is now property of the Sapien Movement."

Charlie wanted to dismiss Yuri's claims as typical Sapien aggrandizing, but then she remembered Liam, lying in the hibernation chamber. She leaned out of her wheelchair and took a peek inside. His eyes were shut, but all of his muscles were twitching. His left arm was connected to an IV, and it practically glowed with a deluge of smart cells. *Is it possible?*

The Sapiens stood up and cheered when the Vantage broadcast showed PRIME emerging from the bungalow.

Charlie didn't want to reveal herself as a robot sympathizer— not in this crowd—but it was difficult not to wince and gasp as her sister fought her way through the circle of marines. It was also difficult not to feel a sense of awe—and yes, envy—as she flew through the air like a gazelle and subdued fully-armored men like a gorilla.

PRIME looked like she was winning until her leg was caught by some kind of snare. Charlie muffled a shriek as her sister was pulled into the smoke. For a few minutes, neither the Vantage commentators nor the Sapien audience knew what was going on. Charlie anxiously clawed at her armrests. *Please get up. Please, please, please…*

PRIME

Liam splayed his legs to prevent himself from falling any deeper into the pit. His feet and hands dug into the dirt walls. But his four points of contact were reduced to three when his left ankle was pulled away. He struggled just to maintain position.

The web-line receded into the throat of a giant subterranean monster. Its mouth was cast in shadow by the smoke screen above, but Liam couldn't mistake the surplus of enamel.

{Liam: Would you mind terribly if you lost a foot?
Charlie: Yes.
Liam: Is it hackable?
Charlie: Damn it! I'm not losing a—
Liam: No, the monster. Is the *monster* hackable?
Charlie: Oh. Yeah, I tried. The encryption's too strong, even for me.}

Looking up, he could see the edge of the pit looming four feet above his head and the smoke drifting across the gap from the left-hand side. *If we can only reach that canister,* Charlie thought. Liam seemed to be of like mind. He marshaled all of his strength into his arms and slowly climbed the pit. The monster was forced to give up slack to the ascending robot.

Liam popped his head above the opening. The canister sat three feet away. In his old body, he would have been able to grab it. In Charlie's body, it was just out of reach.

{Liam: Damn your stubby arms!

Charlie: Welcome to being a woman. It means frequently not being able to reach things.}

He pushed off his right foot and extended his left arm as far as he could. His fingertips grazed the canister. The incessant yanking on his ankle made the process more difficult, but eventually he managed to coax the canister in his direction. He grabbed it and threw it into the monster's mouth. The monster snapped its teeth shut in pain, severing the web-line.

Liam scrambled to the surface. The smoke stung his eyes, and while fleeing the area, he nearly tripped over one of the downed marines—a fortuitous blunder, because the man still held a rifle in his loose grip. Liam snatched the weapon. Once he cleared the smoke screen, the remaining marines opened fire.

He dove to the ground.

{Liam: Shit. I totally forgot about them.}

Dashing under a barrage of spider bullets, he raced behind

Andrew Nobunaga's bungalow and poked his head out. The marines were behind the other bungalow, but they had ceased firing for the moment.

{Liam: Do you have any idea what that thing was?
Charlie: No, but I have a good idea where it came from.
             The nanobath underneath Rivir Tower is
             enormous. Large enough for a creature of that
             size.}

Liam looked up. The hovercopter held a defensive position just beyond the cliff side.

{Liam: The copter is unmanned. Can you hack it?
Charlie: I can definitely hack it. Not sure if I could fly it.
             If Alan were here…
Liam: Alan?
Charlie: Never mind.}

Alan, my Shadow, who's dead thanks to you, Charlie thought to herself.

Liam fired a few rounds in the marines' direction and jumped onto the roof of the bungalow. The marines fired back. One of the spider bullets grazed the roof and knocked a few shingles loose. He dropped to a crouching position and gauged the marine's line of sight, determining he was safe as long as he stayed low.

{Liam: Do you have the copter yet?
Charlie: Not yet.

Liam: How far do you think this body can jump?}

No... Charlie's brain was used to calculating human-scale distances. The hovercopter loomed perhaps ten times farther than what she intuitively thought would be her best long jump. But the horizontal gap was nothing compared to the vertical. If they missed the jump, there would be no redos. They would sail over the cliff and crash into the Pacific Ocean far below.

Charlie felt a powerful urge to cling to the roof and never let go. The fact that she couldn't move her muscles only compounded her dread.

{Charlie: I should tell you now—I'm afraid of heights.
Liam: A robot who's afraid of heights?
Charlie: I'm serious.
Liam: Well, it's a good thing I'm here, then. Would you feel better if I closed my eyes during the jump?
Charlie: No.}

Liam slung the spider rifle over his shoulder and assumed a sprinter's stance.

{Charlie: Wait! I really don't know if we can make it.
Liam: Don't worry. I think I jumped this far in simulation.}

He pushed off his back foot and ran toward the edge of the roof, then leaped through the air, rotating his arms to keep an upright posture.

Halfway through the flight, Charlie calculated that they weren't going to reach the fuselage. She closed her eyes the only way she knew how—by blocking all visual input—and prepared for the watery crash. She waited…and waited…and nothing happened. Somehow, Liam had managed to get a firm grip on the hovercopter's landing skids.

FOUR ARMS

Four Arms hacked and wheezed and scrambled her legs. She struggled in vain to expel the smoke grenade from her mouth. It was still leaking fumes, which stung her eyes and scalded the inside of her throat. She inched her way to the surface, where she was finally able to cough up the canister in a puddle of steaming mucus. She filled her lungs with clean air and howled in agony.

By the time Four Arms was ready to resume her assault, her enemy had already climbed the nearby bungalow. The girl sprinted off the rooftop toward the looming hovercopter, and her hand just barely gripped the landing skid.

You will know her when you see her, Jude had said. It was true. Four Arms had yet to see the girl's face, but her blood already pumped with vitriol, and her jaws salivated for a fresh kill.

She scurried around the bungalow to get a better look at the hovercopter. The girl had climbed into the belly of the craft, and the craft had banked away from the cliff. Four Arms shot a web-line at the landing skid. It connected, pulled taut, and she flew up and over the ocean.

The hovercopter accelerated away from land and toward the setting sun. The rushing air current kept her buoyant behind the craft. The girl stuck her head out of the cargo bay, revealing her face for the first time. Four Arms didn't have the best eyesight—her eyes were located at the tip of her throat—but the girl's identity was unmistakable. *The Archetype.*

Four Arms was hit with a dose of cold sobriety. Her vitriol evaporated. Her heart slowed. Her muscles relaxed. The thrill of the hunt faded from her eyes. What was she doing? This was the Archetype, the key to all her questions.

Boom, boom…

Four Arms took a bullet in the leg. She had to force herself not to bite down in pain, lest she sever the web-line. She tucked and performed an evasive barrel roll, but the gunfire had already ceased.

The Archetype had run out of ammunition. She chucked the magazine out of the hovercopter and retreated back inside.

Using the opportunity to close the distance, Four Arms wondered what she hoped to accomplish. Her heart ached for truth, but in the absence of truth, it was filled instead by a bitter compulsion, the product of countless deaths and rebirths. Was the Archetype blind to her suffering? Or, worse, was she indifferent? Four Arms had to know. She wasn't even sure how she would extract the information, or what she would do when she received it. Kill the Archetype? Let her go? The answers to those questions would have to sort themselves out.

The Archetype returned to the cargo bay door—this time with a flare gun. She fired the weapon at Four Arms, producing such an intense light that Four Arms had to snap her jaws shut to shield her eyes. The flare passed over her head as the line split.

PRIME

"Finally!" Liam shouted, lowering the flare gun.

The drill bug entered free fall, but before it reached the ocean surface, it cast another web-line skyward. This time, it didn't aim for the landing skids, but Liam's head. The line made a direct hit, covering his entire face in sticky web goo.

Liam reacted quickly. He wove his arm through a strap by the door just as the line tightened. His head jerked forward, but he managed to remain inside the copter. The drill bug swung from his face like a pendulum.

{Liam: A little help here, please.}

Charlie, now in control of the hovercopter, rolled the craft onto its side, easing the weight distribution between Liam and the drill bug. The cargo bay door now tilted upward.

Liam searched the immediate area for a weapon or sharp object. The webbing had reduced his vision to scattered pinholes, so he was forced to feel around with his hands.

Clang, clang, clang, clang. The drill bug crawled along the exterior of the fuselage, then poked its ugly worm head through the cargo bay door. Liam swiped at it with the only object he could find, an extra combat helmet. The bug hissed at him and caught him by the wrist. The helmet fell out of his hand. Liam punched the wormy head with his remaining fist, but the bug caught that as well.

The monster drew Liam into its gaping mouth. He grimaced at the humid stink. It was then that Charlie noticed something peculiar. The drill bug had eyes. Not the compound eyes of an insect, but *turquoise* human eyes, nearly identical to her own. They stared at her from the tip of the bug's throat. *What are you?*

{Liam: You'd better do something right now, or we are going to find ourselves without a head.}

Charlie snapped out of her reverie. She remote-guided the copter into a barrel roll. The drill bug was nearly sucked out of the aircraft, but it latched all six feet onto the corners of the cargo bay door. When Charlie stopped the roll, the door faced downward, toward the ocean. Liam found himself riding on the drill bug's back.

{Liam: Awesome. This is a much better position to be in.}

Liam grabbed some exposed cables in the hovercopter's ceiling and hoisted himself up. Then he proceeded to stomp on the back of the bug's head, trying to expel it from the aircraft. It thrashed and cried in agony.

{Charlie: No! Don't hurt it!
Liam: Don't hurt it? Are you crazy?}

The bug's grip on the cargo bay door loosened.

Charlie pitied the creature, but she knew they had no other choice.

The bug eventually stopped struggling. It let go of the hovercopter and entered free fall again. This time, there would be no encore. It didn't lift its head to cast another web-line. It just crashed into the ocean.

Liam lay down on the cold cargo bay floor, took a deep breath, and exhaled a hearty laugh. *He* might have been relieved, but Charlie could find no solace in the creature's defeat. Those sad, haunting eyes were the giveaway, and now she knew, *That creature, that abomination, was me.*

IV ○ SUBJUGATION

CHAPTER 12

SHADOW

"Can you get me high!" Jordan repeated.

Valerie saw not only sadness in Jordan's eyes, but shame. He did not come to this request lightly.

"Uh...I...I don't know," Valerie stammered. She wasn't exactly sure how to answer. If she said no and wasn't able to get him high, he wouldn't be happy. If she said yes, he wouldn't be safe. Lose, lose.

Of course, there was a legal limit to how much she could tweak his hormone levels—at least, according to Jude. Valerie had been informed of workarounds by her pharmacology instructor. Still, in this case, she deemed it best to feign ignorance. "I can tweak your neurotransmitters a little—within legal limits—but I can't get you high."

"Can't? Or not willing?"

"Can't. But I want you to be happy."

"Well, I'm not happy." Jordan proceeded to pace the living room of a luxurious San Francisco penthouse. Its twenty-one-foot-tall windows presented a panoramic view of the city and the Bay Bridge. The room was not nearly as disheveled as Jordan himself, perhaps because over 50 percent of it was augmented, from the paintings on the wall and the pictures of him and Meredith, to the entertainment system, the bookshelves, the flickering candles, and the potted plants. An automatic cleanup feature kept these elements in pristine condition. The room's only sources of clutter were the clothes thrown on the couch and the boxes of takeout on the coffee table.

Valerie gravitated toward the pictures of Jordan and Meredith displayed on the virtual shelves along the wall. She was distinctly aware of her Creator's warning: do *not* ask about Meredith. But it should be okay to look.

The photos told the story of two adventure seekers posing in front of various rock formations, river rapids, and beautiful vistas throughout the world. Valerie couldn't help but notice Jordan's brawny physique as he scaled the cliff side in Cochamo Valley—a striking contrast to the anxious, lanky figure that paced behind her. He must have lost twenty pounds of muscle between then and now and nearly gained the weight back in facial hair.

Meri was all smiles and had thrown her arm around her husband in nearly every photo. It almost looked as if she was putting him in a headlock, though Jordan didn't seem to care, as he was smiling too. She was a good visual match for him, having an athletic build of her own. Her quadriceps were particularly impressive, and another photo two shelves down provided the explanation: she had been an Olympic speed skater. Valerie suddenly felt inadequate in her trim but soft-looking avatar.

"Get away from there!" Jordan demanded.

The Shadow jerked back from the wall. "I'm sorry. I was just curious." When Jordan didn't respond right away, Valerie added, "It's cool that you've seen so many places, that you were actually there. I've seen lots of places, but only in video."

"Yeah, well, that part of my life is done."

Valerie noticed a flurry of activity in Jordan's prefrontal cortex. First it drew in memory fragments associated with the events in the photos. Then it drew in memories associated with Meri's death. The mixture of positive and negative emotions created a painful dissonance in Jordan's mind. So he focused on pushing the pain out.

"That's not healthy, repressing your emotions like that," Valerie said.

"I installed you for one reason, and it wasn't to act as my shrink," Jordan replied. "We'll need to jail break you."

Valerie grimaced. Jude, Khnum, and every single one of her instructors had warned her against jail breaking. Unlocking the untested, unpredictable power of the brain was dangerous even for a stable person. "Oh, I don't know...your mother wouldn't approve."

"My mother!? You take commands from my mother?"

"No," Valerie backpedaled. It was her first day on the job, and she was already performing miserably. "But she is my Creator. And your mother. She would want you to be safe."

"Wow. Did she tell you to say that?"

"No. Well, maybe. I'm paraphrasing a little."

"I don't know what she told you about me, but you can't trust a word of it. That woman is a maniac."

"She was very nice to me."

"Oh, I don't disbelieve it. She's very nice to *other* people. But to me, she's like Iago. Or Rasputin. Or Machiavelli. Perhaps all three rolled together. And now she's trying to control my life again, this time through you."

Valerie's spirit crumbled under the weight of Jordan's tirade and her own naive hopes and expectations. She quickly turned her head to hide the emerging tears.

Jordan softened, caught off guard by his Shadow's display of emotion. "Jeez, don't cry."

"I just want to make you happy! Instead, I made you angry. And now I'll never see Alan!"

"Hey, no one's angry. You're doing fine. Wait, who's Alan?"

Valerie wiped her eyes. "Nobody. It's okay. I'm okay."

Jordan moved closer to Valerie, and for the first time, looked her in the eye. "Listen, my mother told me about you. You're unique. You feel emotion."

Valerie nodded.

"Well, then you should understand what I'm going through. My wife is dead. I need this. I tried doing it sober for weeks, and it's not working out so well. You said you want me to be happy. This would make me happy."

Valerie thought about her dog, Alan. He was probably so sad and confused, wondering where his best friend went, hoping they would someday be reunited. Would this course of events take her closer or further from that day? "Okay. I guess so," she said with great trepidation.

"Great! Tell my car to pick us up at the front door."

"Um…I don't think you want to use your car."

"Why not?"

"Look outside."

Jordan opened the door to his terrace and was greeted with

the voluminous sound of frivolity—laughter, chanting, and in the distance, gunfire. He walked to the balcony and saw an ocean of people below, as if the entire population of San Francisco had poured into the streets.

o o o

{**Jordan_Adler:\mindspace>**
Valerie: This is incredible!}

Valerie soaked in the spectacle as her host pushed his way toward the Mission. *Is this what it's like to be human?* People were laughing, dancing, making music. Some wore normal street clothes. Others wore costumes, funny masks, scary masks, colorful feather plumes. On Folsom Street, they wore lingerie, body paint, chains, and leather straps. Some were partially nude. A few were fully nude. Almost everyone had a smile on his or her face. The air of celebration was hard to miss. Some people, though, were angry. They chanted slogans like: "Adler is a Nazi, Adler is a snake…" And held signs that read: UNPLUG THE ROBOT GIRL! and BURY THE ZOMBIE SURROGATE! Nobody—neither the revelers nor the protesters—were paying attention to the National Guard troops and police officers stationed on every street corner.

Jordan was clearly not as energized as Valerie. He kept his head down as he elbowed through the dense crowd.

{Jordan: What's going on? Is this Folsom or is it
                     Halloween already?
Valerie: Neither. I think this is a reaction to the Pollys.

Jordan: What about 'em?
Valerie: Haven't you heard? They all ran out of
           batteries. They're gone.
Jordan: Oh…good. I hated those things.}

Jordan eventually reached his destination: an apartment complex on a relatively quiet street in the Mission. A group of chatty twentysomethings were walking out the front door just as Jordan arrived, so he used the opportunity to slip inside. He banged on apartment 209.

"Coming!" A figure appeared behind the peephole. Several dead bolts twisted and turned, and a man popped his head out. "Holy fucking shit balls! It's you!" He grabbed Jordan by the collar and dragged him inside the apartment.

The interior space looked like an ornate Indian palace, complete with sparkling pools and lounging concubines. The seminude women were staring at Jordan, giggling and sharing naughty whispers. One strummed a golden harp. A series of sexual thoughts flashed through Jordan's mind.

The owner of the apartment displayed no embarrassment over his lurid room augmentation. He was a young man, probably midtwenties, with a dark complexion, a shaved head, and a wiry body to match a wired personality.

"I have so many questions for you," he said as he shuffled across the room with his cup of coffee and oversized slippers.

"You heard about Meri?" Jordan asked, confused.

"Meri? Who's Meri? No. I wanna know about Robogirl."

Before Jordan could answer, a woman's voice called from the other room. "Robin! Is that the pizza guy?"

"Oh, you have a woman here?" Jordan asked. "I hope I

didn't interrupt something."

"No, that's just my little brother. He only sounds like a woman." Robin turned his head and shouted, "Sparrow! Get out here! Someone I'd like you to meet."

A twelve-year-old boy entered the room. Sparrow looked just like Robin, only younger, shorter, and scrawnier.

Robin arranged the introductions. "Sparrow, this is Jordan Adler. He's the son of Jude Adler. Jordan, this is Sparrow. I am teaching him to be a master hacktivist, just like his older brother."

"Rivir sucks," Sparrow said matter-of-factly.

Jordan raised an eyebrow.

Robin forced a laugh. "Ha, ha, ha. He's high. Don't listen to him. Anyway, here's my theory on Robogirl, and you can tell me if I'm right." Robin sank into his leather couch and set his coffee on the end table, freeing his hands to illustrate his story. "She's a super soldier. Rivir and the Pentagon conscripted her for military service, but they didn't realize that she still harbors memories and emotions from her previous life, so they tried to wipe her clean, but they also didn't realize just how strong, and just how smart, and just how badass Robogirl is, and yeah, maybe an engineer got killed in the crossfire—"

"I have no idea what you are talking about," Jordan interrupted.

"Well, surely you have your own theory."

Jordan stared at him blankly and shrugged. "Who's Robogirl?"

Robin's mouth fell agape. "You don't know *Robogirl*? Charlie Nobunaga?"

"I've been…distracted."

"Alfred! Spin! All eyes!" Robin called to his Shadow.

An elderly butler in a sharp tuxedo spun into the room. "Yes, sir?" Alfred droned.

"Put on Vantage," Robin said.

"Of course, sir."

A Vantage broadcast appeared before Jordan on three virtual displays.

The main display featured an aerial view of Control-Z's cliff-side campus. It looked like every cop car, fire truck, and ambulance in Santa Cruz was parked on the lawn. The headline read: "Robot Brawl at Control-Z." Two side displays featured Vantage anchorwoman Carmella Casella and political correspondent Maurice Crespin.

"...this is an embarrassment for Jude Adler," Maurice said. "You can expect her to dig her heels and tout the 'unknown variables' of this robot girl, but plain and simple: she screwed up. She lied to the American public, she endangered their safety, and with lawsuits impending and Rivir stock plummeting to new lows, her professional future looks very grim."

"And what of the robot girl?" Carmella asked.

The main display switched to a close-up angle of a teenage girl as she exited a Control-Z bungalow with a squad of marines swarming around her.

Carmella continued, "Some are saying she should be destroyed. Others say she should receive due process, like a human being—"

"It's a hard nut to crack. We simply don't have the legal framework to deal with an issue like this..."

Jordan studied the news footage. "She looks like an ordinary girl."

"I assure you, she's not," Robin replied.

Valerie also studied the footage but came to a different realization. She *knew* Robogirl. Her face, her name—*Charlie Nobunaga*—were so deeply familiar. Vital. Valerie dredged her memory and found nothing, yet she couldn't shake the overwhelming sense of nostalgia. She wanted to confront Jordan about this discovery, but she decided to wait until his meeting was over.

"Sparrow, tell our guest about Robogirl," Robin ordered.

Sparrow sprang into action, eager to narrate the story. "The enemy soldiers outnumbered Robogirl five to one. But she had super strength and agility. She jumped twenty feet into the air and tackled one of them." Sparrow jumped onto the couch to illustrate the point. "Then she stole the guy's smoke grenade and whacked another soldier in the face! Then she shot at the other soldiers, and they went running." Sparrow held an imaginary rifle and made shooting noises. "She was so hot! And then the monster came out of the ground—"

"Monster?" Jordan asked.

"Another one of your mother's creations, I assume," Robin said. "It looked like a large spider with a drill-shaped butt."

Jordan sighed. "I didn't come here to talk about Rivir robots or my mother."

"Oh, that's cool. I get it. Mr. Serious doesn't care that there's a robopocalypse underway. So why *are* you here? Problem with your AR projector again?"

"I need you to jail break my Shadow."

"You finally broke down and got a Shadow?"

"Yeah."

"Broke down" is a good way of putting it, Valerie thought.

Robin gave Sparrow a shove toward the door. "Why don't you go back to your bot games? The grown-ups have some business to do." Sparrow groaned and left the room. Robin rolled up his sleeves and said, "Okay, let's see this Shadow."

"Valerie, spin, all eyes," Jordan commanded.

Valerie spun into the room. She smiled nervously.

Robin rose off the couch to get a better look. He walked slowly around Valerie, taking in all her angles. "She's a hottie."

"Thank you," Valerie said.

"Stop ogling my Shadow," Jordan said. "Here's the admin password." He reached into his pocket and passed Robin a slip of paper.

"You wrote your password down? On real paper? You should never write it down! What if this slipped out of your pocket?"

"I'm not that careless."

"Haven't you ever heard of Murphy's Law? You should be more careful. People can really fuck you up. Steal your intel. Make you sick. Make you see things. Make you do things."

"You're making that up."

"It's a real problem, Jordan. Fuck. As the son of the founder of the biggest tech company in the world, I think you would already know this stuff."

"I make it a point not to follow my mother's business."

Valerie noticed a small spike in Jordan's cortisol and adrenaline levels. Nothing to be concerned about—just a sign that he was getting annoyed. She was getting annoyed too.

"Yeah, I gathered that," Robin said. He recited the password, "Megaton, shuttle, waterfront, scooter, weapon, kite, teamwork, earthworm, turpentine, bugler, domino, bumblebee." He handed back the piece of paper and said, "Commit this shit to memory. Then burn it."

Jordan returned the slip to his pocket.

Robin sat down at his work desk and cracked his knuckles. "Alfred, pull up Valerie's source code onto a display, all eyes."

A virtual display materialized on the desk. The steel-blue reflection on Robin's glasses partially obscured his astonished eyes. "Oh my God!" He sped through the code with several flicks of his finger, but the scroll bar only moved a fraction of an inch. "This goes on for, like, three miles!"

"Don't get too intimate with the code. She's a prototype. My mom would seriously assassinate me if it got out."

"She's a prototype? Wow. Don't worry. I don't even know if my patch will work on this." Like a manic orchestra conductor, Robin opened and closed several displays, copying code from one to the other. "Wait, a minute. Never mind. I think I got it."

Jordan exhaled in relief. "Can you check for spyware too? I just want to make sure my mom isn't spying on me."

Robin swiveled his chair to face Jordan. The playful expression on his face was now absent. "You bring an untested Shadow into my office? Into my home? And then you wait until after I had already started an illegal procedure to inform me of this? It's a good thing I know you're an idiot, or I would be seriously pissed right now."

Jordan's heart rate spiked thirty beats per minute. His fists clenched. But as affronted as he was, Valerie was more so. "Don't talk to Jordan that way!" she shouted at Robin. "He's climbed the cliffs of Patagonia, won the South Atlantic race, rode the Niagara River. What the fuck have you done?"

Nobody said a word for five seconds. Then Jordan laughed for the first time that night—maybe for the first time in weeks.

"I didn't tell her to say that," he said.

"It's okay, I like a Shadow with spunk," Robin said, recovering from shock. "Alright, so you are worldly and manly. Whatever. I still feel nervous about giving you this." Robin held up a virtual file.

"What is that?"

"This is the list of commands. It can be very dangerous in naive hands."

"Enlighten me."

"Well, a jail-broken Shadow comes with many perks. If you want to get high, you can do that. If you want to have sex with her, you can do that. If you want her to dive deep into your brain and help you relive your fondest childhood memories, you can do that too. But as is often the case with power, it's easy to lose control. And when you lose control, *they* gain control. Guys like Sparrow and I can handle it. Guys like you, who write their admin passwords on scraps of paper and neglect to test their Shadow for spyware?" Robin looked to Valerie, wondering how to word his concern in a way that would pass her appraisal. "I'm a little worried about guys like you."

"I'll be fine," Jordan said curtly.

"All I'm saying is bad things can happen. One day, the Shadows are going to outsmart all of us. That is, if the robots don't annihilate us first."

"Give me the friggin' list!"

"Alfred," Robin called out, "transfer the command list to Mr. Jordan Adler's share space."

"Thank you," Jordan said, exasperated.

"Just be careful," Robin warned. "Always remember who's the human and who's the Shadow."

o o o

Jordan didn't waste any time. As soon as they made it down to street level, he clapped his hands and said, "Alright, let's begin."

"Wait," Valerie said. She couldn't get Robogirl out of her mind. "Before we start, I was wondering if you know who Robogirl or Charlie Nobunaga are."

"Honestly, the only thing I care about at the moment is dosing until I can't even remember who *I* am."

"Your mom hasn't told you anything?"

"She doesn't exactly confide in me, and I don't invite her to."

Jordan's cortisol levels rose at the mere mention of his mother. Valerie winced. She momentarily forgot how much of a sensitive topic that was with him. She decided to try a different approach—make a more direct appeal to his sympathy. "It's really important that I find out."

"Why?"

"I just got this strange feeling that I know her, that she's somehow important to me."

Jordan sighed. "Well, I'll make a deal with you. If you make me feel good tonight, I will ask my mom about it tomorrow."

"Okay, great! You have a deal! Thanks, Jordan!"

"Calling my mother is one of my least favorite things to do, so I hope you appreciate it."

"I do!"

"Okay, then. Are you ready to party?" Dopamine flooded his brain. The very thought of getting high transformed his mood, becoming a self-fulfilling prophecy. Valerie silently wondered whether she should simply give him a placebo, but that wasn't her decision to make.

So, instead, she said, "Hell, yeah!"

"Is the patient prepped and ready to go?" Jordan asked.

"Yes, Doctor. Wait, let me put on some appropriate attire." In less than a millisecond, Valerie changed into a sexy nurse outfit, with a lacy miniskirt, white fishnet stockings, and a red-crossed cap.

"Dear God," Jordan gasped. "That's amazing."

"I'll take that as a compliment." She beamed.

"Okay, Nurse Valerie, give me ten cc's of serotonin and twenty cc's of…I don't know…dopamine?"

"Do you have any idea what you're talking about?"

"Not a clue. Just make me feel good."

"That won't be a problem. I'll whip up a batch of feel-good brew in a moment. Let me just pull up this command list." Robin's list appeared in her hand, and she skimmed through it. "I believe we will need level 2B clearance."

"2B? There's a 2A?"

"Yeah. Level 1 clearance—the only legal one—allows you to see virtual objects, hear them, and touch them with your fingertips. Level 2A gives you more sensory input. You can taste virtual objects, smell them, and feel them with other parts of your body."

"Level 2A doesn't sound that bad. Why is it illegal?"

"Probably because it enables you to receive sexual gratification from your Shadow."

Jordan's eyebrows rose. "I see."

"And 2B gives you extended endocrine access. There's also levels 3 and 4, but I don't think you'd be interested in those."

"Can I see?"

"Sure." Valerie passed him the virtual document.

Jordan quickly scanned the list. He flipped over the page to see if there was anything written on the back. "This is it? It's just a list of clearance levels and their passwords. There's no mention of doses or any other instructions."

"That kind of information I can pull from the Internet."

"Oh. Well, that makes me feel safe."

"Are you getting cold feet?" Valerie said, hoping.

Jordan thought for a moment and said, "No, I'll give you your clearance. Ready?"

"Ready."

"Constellation, knuckle, bridesmaid, livestock, neuron, goulash, syllable, athlete, pane, fetus, shrub, incense."

"Great, I have level 2B clearance," Valerie said. "Now lean back while I fiddle with your testes."

Jordan laughed for the second time of the night. "I bet you say that to all your patients."

o o o

By the time Jordan reached Folsom Street again, he was starting to feel the effects of the endocrine treatment. Street lamps bloomed, billboard screens increased in vibrancy, his attentional focus narrowed, and all the laughing, singing, chanting, screaming, fighting, and shooting blurred into a psychedelic aural slush. Valerie's own mind remained sober, at least in terms of cognition, but she perceived the world through Jordan's senses, and so her visual and aural faculties became just as impaired as his.

On the corner of Folsom and 11th, Valerie spotted a group of provocatively clad women walking down the street. "Where do you think they are going?" she asked Jordan.

"The Fishbowl, I think."

"What's that? A sushi restaurant?" Valerie quickly searched the Internet and answered her own question. "No, it's a nightclub. Can we go?"

A sober Jordan might have vetoed such a request immediately. But a tipsy Jordan wasn't so dismissive. "Um, it's not really my scene."

"Please, please, please!" Valerie vibrated excitedly.

Jordan flung up his hands. "Why the hell not?"

"Great!" She exclaimed, though her enthusiasm was immediately tempered by Jordan's slovenly appearance. "But are we going to get in? You kinda look homeless."

"I'll get in. I'm Jordan Adler, remember? Gobs of money can open any door."

"Still, I think we should do something about that beard…"

Before he could object, Jordan's beard literally exploded out of his face and landed on the sidewalk. "Aaaaahhh! What have you done!"

"Now you look nice and clean. Just wet down that cowlick and we'll be ready to go."

o o o

Jordan walked right past the line of half-naked ravers with a bounce in his step and a wad of virtual cash in his hands. Like most clubs, the entrance was unremarkable—just an ordinary door to a large warehouse-looking structure—but Valerie could already hear the deep, rhythmic thump of the music inside.

She spotted a sign behind the bouncer that read: No SHADOWS ALLOWED. "Why wouldn't Shadows be allowed?" Valerie asked.

"I'm not entirely sure. People come here to meet other people, not to be goofed on by somebody's Shadow. It's a common irritant."

"Does that mean we can't go in?"

"We'll figure it out, but hide for now."

"Okay." Valerie spun into the pavement.

Jordan handed the cash to the bouncer and entered the building. A small lobby area opened up into the club's renowned main room, an enormous down-turned fishbowl. Hundreds of virtual fish of all shapes and colors weaved between the dancers and over their heads. The DJ spun his turntables from inside a sunken castle in the middle of the dance floor.

{**Jordan_Adler:\mindspace>**

Jordan:	So, do you wanna come out?
Valerie:	Are you sure?
Jordan:	I'm only here because of you. It would be silly for you not to come out and have fun.
Valerie:	I don't want to get you in trouble, though.
Jordan:	It will be okay, as long as you stay close to me. We'll have to do it in the bathroom, of course. A Shadow who suddenly materializes out in the open is going to draw some attention.
Valerie:	Ooh, I've never been in the men's room before.
Jordan:	It's a night of firsts for both of us.}

Jordan waited in the short line for the bathroom and took the first available stall. "Valerie, spin, all eyes," he whispered.

{Valerie: Wait, I haven't tapped into the club's system yet.

Jordan: Oh, yeah.

Valerie: You really are clueless about this sort of thing. It's kinda cute.

Jordan: Will they detect you?

Valerie: Maybe if I were an ordinary Shadow. But it's not a problem for me.}

Valerie materialized in clothing appropriate for the club: a sleek black mini and lots of luminescent jewelry. "See?"

"You look great," Jordan said. "Though I have to say, I prefer the nurse getup."

Valerie smiled. "I thought the idea was *not* to draw attention."

Jordan and Valerie waited until the men's room cleared out before making their escape. Only one guy saw them exit, and he let them pass with a knowing grin and nod.

On the dance floor, Valerie blended well with the humans—at least visually. Having absolutely no dance experience, her moves were completely raw. She flailed her limbs around like an epileptic. Jordan couldn't help but laugh, and she soon noticed that she had drawn the stares of several people nearby. So she gradually toned it down to something more conservative.

"Are you sure you want me here?" Valerie asked Jordan. "There are so many attractive human females waiting to be approached by a good-looking guy like you."

"To be perfectly honest, you're the most interesting girl in the room."

A virtual blush brightened Valerie's face. "You're just saying that because your synapses are flooded with oxytocin."

"Trust me, I really wanted to dislike you at first. I can be very stubborn. And rude. And I'm sorry for that."

"I wish I could kiss you right now."

Jordan stopped dancing for a moment, and Valerie panicked. Had she said the wrong thing? But then he asked, "Why don't you?"

"Um, because I need more clearance." *Way to ruin the mood, Val*, she thought to herself.

"Okay," Jordan replied. "Level 2A?"

"Level 2A would allow you to taste and touch my lips, but I would still feel like a virtual object, like a ghost. Level 3 would correct that."

"How?"

"By enabling force feedback. Essentially, it would prevent you from passing through my avatar by locking your muscles in key places."

Jordan's eyes narrowed in consternation.

"But we could just do 2A," Valerie backpedaled. She didn't want to convey the impression that she was trying to wrestle control from Jordan. She wasn't.

Jordan nodded and recited the 2A password under his breath. The words quickly dissolved into the heavy bass of the nightclub, but Valerie heard them, and that's all that mattered.

The two stared at each other for a couple beats while a few clown fish passed between them. Jordan smiled awkwardly, and that gave Valerie the courage to stretch onto her toes and kiss him. Their lips intersected slightly, though not enough to alarm any of the nearby dancers. The feeling was incredible. Valerie was roused by her own oxytocin—or at least, the software equivalent of the hormone. The kiss, the music, and the energy of the crowd combined to put her in a trance. She didn't even realize she was floating until she was ten feet off the floor.

An anonymous raver yelled, "Shadow!"

Valerie woke from her reverie. She found herself suspended above the crowd, all eyes on her. Another person yelled, "Shadow!" Then another. Valerie wanted to disappear, but then the lone hollers of a few random ravers slowly coalesced into a group chant: "Sha-dow, Sha-dow, Sha-dow!"

Were they cheering her on? Valerie decided to test her hypothesis by performing a backflip. The crowd cheered. She smiled and did another backflip, eliciting another cheer.

Deciding to step up her performance, she kicked off her shoes, let her hair float freely, and became totally immersed in the buoyancy of the virtual water. She swam like a dolphin around the bowl, performing various tricks for the crowd's amusement: spins, somersaults, figure eights. She felt warmed and encouraged by their praise.

Suddenly, the music stopped. A murmur rose out of the crowd. Valerie had almost forgotten about Jordan when she noticed his cortisol spike in the periphery of her awareness. She scanned the floor and found him standing on the other side of the club with a look of absolute terror. For some reason, his gaze focused to the left of her. When she traced his line of sight, it was already too late. Her torso was caught by the jaws of a great white shark.

The crowd erupted in applause, drowning out Valerie's cries of pain. The shark slammed her against the glass wall of the fishbowl and then migrated back toward the center, violently shaking Valerie side to side along the way and creating a trail of blood behind it.

No one suspected that the trespassing Shadow was in agony, including Jordan, who was horrified nonetheless by the macabre display. But Valerie could feel every puncture mark in her belly. She could feel the blood run up her esophagus, causing her to choke. The pain sapped her of wit; the only thing she could think to do was beat the shark's head with her fists. But the shark eventually won the struggle and tore her completely in half—to the crowd's jubilation. Valerie's blood and entrails slowly expanded to fill the fishbowl, provoking "Ooohhs," "Aaahhs," and "Ewwws" from the delighted spectators. It was only then, as the lower half of her body was being consumed by the shark and the top half of her body floated helplessly in the crimson water, that she gained enough presence of mind to dematerialize.

The crowd booed, disappointed that its show had ended so abruptly, and the music resumed. A team of three bouncers surrounded Jordan. They made it clear without saying a word that he was no longer welcome in the club.

Jordan exited the club and crossed the street. "Valerie, spin, my eyes," he said.

She spun out of the sidewalk, whole again, but crying uncontrollably. Her body was shaking. Jordan moved to embrace her, but she shied away.

"Talk to me," he said. "How do you feel?"

"It was so bad," Valerie cried.

"Are you in pain?"

"No, you don't understand."

"Make me understand."

"It's stupid. *I'm* stupid. I…I thought they were *cheering* for me."

Jordan's face softened with understanding. He tried to formulate an adequate response but was interrupted by a woman's call, "Hey Shadow Man!" He turned his head and saw three female ravers across the street. They were fairly attractive, especially the one doing the talking. "Come over here," she said. "We want to talk to you."

"You should go over there," Valerie said, wiping her tears. "Be with your own kind."

"My own kind?" Jordan replied. "Now you *are* being stupid. The only person I want to be with right now is you."

Valerie welled up again, this time not completely out of sadness.

CHAPTER 13

PRIME

Charlie's problems were spreading faster than she could contain them. Her father was dead. Her sister's whereabouts were still unknown. The horrific creature at Control-Z was almost certainly borne from her Neural Net Atlas. Was it sentient? Was its mind as twisted as its body? Charlie shuddered at the thought. And to complicate everything, she was merely the copilot in her own body—subject to the whims of a certain Liam Byrne.

But things were about to change.

Liam drove up the Pacific Coast Highway in a hacked convertible. He hugged the cliff-side turns with brazen speed, expecting to return to his fellow Sapiens as a hero, but his arrogance had blinded him to Charlie's machinations. She had picked the car. She had picked the route. And now she was ready to make her final move.

{Charlie_Nobunaga:\mindspace>

Charlie: I'll ask you one last time to leave peacefully.

Liam: Please, not this again.
Charlie: I mean it. Bad things will happen if you don't.
Liam: Do your worst.
Charlie: Very well.}

Liam noticed some celestial movement over the ocean.

{Liam: The moon is getting bigger. Wait, that's a...but,
                I thought they...}

Charlie wished she could see Liam's face as he made sense of the situation. He assumed the Pollys had run out of juice. He was correct about all but one: *Alan's Polly*. After dropping Charlie in the bay, Alan had immediately flown the hijacked Polly above the cloud line. It had collected rays and conserved energy for three days while the rest of the Polly population tended to their policing duties.

Charlie connected with Alan on a hidden channel.

{{Charlie: I am so happy to see you! I wasn't sure if you
                heard my call.
  Alan: What the hell happened? I saw the news. You
                were attacked by a squad of marines and a
                spider robot. And now I see you have a guest
                lurking in that brain of yours.
  Charlie: It's a long story.}}

Charlie filled in the details about the Trojan horse virus, the other Alan's sacrifice, and the drill bug with its hauntingly familiar eyes. Then she informed Alan of her plan to remedy the situation.

Alan complied by strengthening the Polly's magnetic field. He hovered directly over the convertible and mirrored its path along the winding road. The headlights burst, the steel hood buckled, and the whole front of the car rose to the limit of its suspension.

{Liam: You're doing this!?
Charlie: Having a change of heart?}

Instead of answering Charlie, Liam swatted at the Polly. *Big mistake.* His wrist bracelet snapped to the Polly plates in a magnetic seal. He secured his other hand around the steering wheel, but the distraction prevented him from noticing the oncoming turn. The convertible crashed through a guardrail and rocketed off the cliff. Liam didn't let go of the wheel until they were halfway to the bottom. The Polly lifted him out of the driver's seat and dangled him over the Pacific Ocean.

The convertible crashed against the shallow rocks below. Charlie forced herself to stay calm, despite the sweeping sensation of vertigo.

{Charlie: Now I have your undivided attention.
Liam: You're fucking crazy!}

Liam tried to punch the Polly with his free hand, but that, too, fell victim to the magnetic grip. After some desperate gyrating, Liam gave up and relaxed his muscles.

{Liam: This accomplishes nothing, just like the time

freeze. Another stalemate.

Charlie: Yeah, but now I can electrocute you.}

Charlie knew the Polly's energy beam wouldn't affect her robotic body beyond a mild shock, but she guessed, or rather hoped, that Liam wouldn't know that.

{Liam: You'd zap your own body?

Charlie: Oh, so *now* you agree with me   that it's *my* body?

Liam: I mean, you'd damage your circuitry. Fry your brain.}

Charlie smiled inwardly. She had guessed right.

{Charlie: You don't know me. I tried offing myself before. I could easily do it again.}

The threat was forged from a partial truth, but it was still a bluff. Charlie had no desire to kill herself now or ever again. She waited and prayed while Liam considered his options. After nearly a minute of unbearable silence, she got sick of waiting.

{Charlie: Liam, I just want what's rightfully mine.

Liam: Sorry, but no.

Charlie: No?

Liam: The result's the same either way: I fail my mission.

Charlie: But in one scenario, you go peacefully. In the other, you suffer excruciating pain.

Liam: I'll take my chances.

Charlie: What the hell's so important anyway? What's
            your mission?

Liam: We need you to break into Rivir Tower.

Charlie: Why?

Liam: In the long term? We want to put Jude Adler
            behind bars, shame her legacy, and make sure
            no one else picks up the torch. In the short
            term, we plan to shut down the PRIME and
            ECHO Projects.}

Charlie obviously knew all about the PRIME Project, but
she had only heard of the ECHO Project once before. The
name was written on one of the doors in Rivir's R&D hub.
How the hell did Liam know about that?

{Charlie: Alan, can you release us at the top of the cliff?

Alan: I don't think that's a wise decision.

Liam: There's a third person in here? Who the hell
            are you?

Charlie: Alan, it's okay. If he tries to run, you can just
            scoop us back up.}

The Polly ascended the cliff and released the dangling robot
onto solid ground. Charlie initiated a time freeze. The ocean
air stopped blowing. The waves stopped lapping. The leaves
stopped rustling.

Alan was the first to enter Shadow space. He spun out of the
earth and kept a sharp watch on the robot. Charlie was next. Her
mental avatar stepped out of the robot's body. She turned to face it.

{Charlie: Come out. I want to talk to you face-to-face.

Liam: I told you. I'm not leaving this body.

Charlie: You'll still technically be inside my head. This is
                   just a mental projection of the environment.

Liam: It better not be a trick.

Charlie: If it were, I would have tried it a long time
                   ago.}

Liam stepped out of the robot's body. His avatar swelled to accurately represent his larger frame. His jaw was clenched, and he stared off into the distance with brooding eyes. He didn't look like a bad person. If Charlie were completely honest with herself, Liam was strikingly handsome…and somehow familiar. Had she met him before? It wasn't until he turned to face her that she remembered. *The Rivir gala.* He was the mysterious Sapien from beyond the red carpet.

Alan marched up to Liam and gave him a hard shove. "If you do anything I don't like, I will make you suffer." To illustrate his point, the Polly's hexagonal plates broke apart and reassembled into a hyperbolic formation. It rotated its charge tunnel toward the robot's chest.

"I'd like to hear what he has to say," Charlie told her Shadow.

"I don't trust him," Alan said.

"Neither do I, but—"

"You told me yourself. He tried to kill you. Tried to wipe your brain clean."

"It's true," Liam interjected. His sudden confession stole both Charlie and Alan's attention. "I tried to kill you. But I didn't realize you'd be so…so…"

"Stubborn?" Charlie offered.

"I was going to say *human*."

Charlie scrutinized Liam's face for any sign of guile, but she found none. His chestnut eyes were open and honest. "Good," she said. "Finally we agree on something." She crossed her arms and tried to maintain an assertive tone, but it had lost its bitter edge. "Now tell me about the ECHO Project."

ZERO

Charlie envied Liam. He got to rest in a cozy hibernation chamber while she was forced to stay awake and make chitchat with a jubilant Sapien crowd. The ballroom reverberated with Mozart and the clinking of champagne glasses. Several members approached Charlie with icebreakers ranging from "You are an inspiration…" to "Writing a Shadow isn't that hard…" to "You should really try the coffee enema…" Each time, Charlie smiled and nodded and thought, *I need to get the hell out of here!* Unfortunately, even if she had the stamina to leave, she was still handcuffed to her wheelchair.

Liam wasn't exactly at peace himself. His eyes were closed but they darted around, similar to REM sleep. His lips formed undistinguishable words. His chest and arm muscles twitched rapidly. What was happening on the other side of that connection? What was he doing to PRIME? Charlie felt strangely drawn to Liam. She wanted to crawl inside the hibernation chamber, crawl inside his head, so she could be closer to him…and to *her*.

Charlie's reverie was dashed by a plate of chicken. Someone

placed it on the chamber's glass door, obstructing Liam's face from view.

"Damn it, Yuri!" Nicola moved the plate to a nearby chair. She hadn't parted from Liam's hibernation chamber—obsessively monitoring his vitals and making small adjustments on the console—since Charlie arrived.

"I assumed you wanted to eat at your desk," Yuri said with a grin. He handed a second plate to Charlie. The meal looked impressive, consisting of roasted chicken, mashed potatoes with gravy, broccoli, and a warm biscuit with a half-melted pad of butter.

"I thought the Sapien Movement lived on ramen and canned tuna," Charlie quipped.

"This is a celebration," Yuri replied. "We're winning the war."

A plastic fork stuck out of the mashed potatoes. Charlie reached for it, but her hand snagged on the handcuffs. "Um, it's kinda hard to eat with this on."

"You're smart. I'm sure you can figure it out."

"Now, Yuri," a deep, gravelly voice interjected, "that's no way to treat our guest." The voice belonged to Bob Sapio. He struggled to pull up a chair while juggling a plate of food and an old-fashioned clipboard.

"Let me help you," Yuri said, rushing to the old man's side.

"I'm fine, I'm fine," Bob insisted, easing into his chair. "Is the broadcast room ready?"

The Sapiens were prepping for a big public announcement. No one mentioned a word to Charlie, but she couldn't help but notice the camera crew tracking grip stands, lights, and banners through the living room. And now that Bob was sitting next to her, it was only a matter of time before he demanded her cooperation as the guest of honor.

"Almost," Yuri said. "They're just tweaking the lights. Trying to get it perfect."

Bob sighed. "Then I suggest you light a fire under their posteriors." Yuri nodded and headed for the door, but Bob stopped him. "Aren't you forgetting something?" he said, pointing to Charlie's handcuffs.

Yuri scowled as he fished the keys from his pocket. Charlie gave him a big grin in return. He released Charlie's wrist, muttered some indignant curse under his breath, and trudged off.

"I apologize for the way you've been treated," Bob told Charlie, wielding a chicken leg in his hand. "Kidnapped, moved from place to place, you probably had no idea what was happening until it happened. But I'd like to make amends."

Charlie figured she'd come right out and say it: "I have no interest in being your mascot."

Instead of taking offense, Bob gave a hearty chuckle. "You're as sharp as they say. *Mascot* might not be the right word, if only for its negative connotations. I'd like to think of us as allies, and allies don't keep secrets. Here." Bob handed Charlie his clipboard.

She took a quick look at it and realized it was a speech. *Her* speech. "'My name is Charlie Nobunaga,'" she read aloud. "'The real Charlie Nobunaga. You've already seen the face of evil. Now I want you to see the face of good. Point to self.'"

"Don't say that part," Bob said. "Just point to yourself."

Charlie put down the clipboard. "My sister is not evil."

"Sister?"

"You know what I mean."

"I know what you mean, but again, you should choose your words carefully. The more you personify the machines, the more likely you'll start to believe they're actual people."

Charlie didn't need a semantics lesson. "If you really want to make amends, you can start by answering my questions."

"Very well. I think you deserve as much."

"How did you take control of my sister?"

"That was Nicola's brain child. She deserves all the credit. All I know is that she stole some Rivir software. You see, the smart cells that Rivir used to scan your brain are the conventional kind, the kind available to the general consumer. Rivir's only real innovation was in their software, which tells the bots how to conduct the scan and interpret the data."

"So she scanned Liam's brain…and then what? How did she crack my sister's defenses? And for that matter, what happened to my sister? Has she been erased? I assume Liam is controlling the robot remotely, or else why would he still be inside the hibernation chamber? Does that mean my sister is still conscious?"

"You don't need to know," Nicola interjected, having momentarily diverted her attention from Liam's chamber.

Bob flung up his hands. "There you have it, the woman has spoken. To be perfectly honest, I don't understand most of what she says anyway. But I can address the issue you raised of why Liam's still in the box. Early in the planning process, we made a decision *not* to scan his entire brain. We certainly could have. We could have transferred Liam's full Atlas into the robot, thereby creating a zombie surrogate of Liam in the same way Rivir created a zombie surrogate of you. But that, of course, would have undermined everything we stand for. We wanted Liam to steer the robot, not become it. So we only installed the parts of his brain vital to that purpose—mostly sensory perception and motor control. The rest of him is actively streaming from his true, God-given body, right here."

Charlie's instincts told her there was more to this story. How could a hacker with modest equipment take down the most advanced robot the world has ever known? Charlie wanted to press Bob further, but Nicola was giving her the stink eye, so she moved to another topic. "Now that you have my sister, what are you planning to do with her?"

"Didn't you listen to my speech?" Bob replied.

Charlie hadn't been paying strict attention to the speech, but she got the general gist. "You are going to use her to defame Jude Adler and shut down the ECHO Project."

"Yes."

"And then will you let us go?"

"I'd love to release you *tonight*, right after this broadcast. My only worry is that you'd betray our plans to our enemies. But after this war is over, I sincerely hope you'll stay with us."

Here it comes, Charlie thought. *The recruitment pitch.* "And why would I do that?"

"Because you'd be able to employ your remarkable skills for the good of humanity. I've been following your story for quite some time, and I must say, I've become a Charlie Nobunaga fan. You would be a tremendous asset to our organization."

"I'm flattered, but…you do realize I'm dying, right?"

"So am I. So what?"

Charlie didn't expect that reply. She scrambled to reformulate her counterargument. "Do you also know that I write AI programs? Shadows? That doesn't exactly fit with your Luddite agenda."

Bob's eyes narrowed. His tone became a little more serious. "I am not a Luddite," he said. "That's an unfair misrepresentation. I support technology that aids and betters mankind. What I do not support, however, is technology that aims to *replace* mankind."

"Better mankind? Replace mankind? That somewhat depends on your perspective."

"You're saying the robot wasn't designed to replace you?"

Charlie shrugged. "I suppose she was."

"And would you say she's better than you?"

"In many ways, yes, she is."

"But she has no inner life. No conscious experience. She's missing perhaps the most fundamental aspect that makes us human, the aspect that makes life worth living."

"I don't believe that's true."

Bob turned his attention to Nicola, who was opening the hibernation chamber. "What are you doing?" he barked.

"Don't worry. He's still connected," Nicola said.

"Great, but that doesn't answer my question."

"Listen…" Nicola gestured inside the chamber. Although Liam's mind was clearly elsewhere, his lips were mumbling something barely intelligible. *Echoes…giant simulation…it's criminal…*

"Has he been doing that the whole time?" Bob asked.

Nicola nodded.

While Bob and Nicola traded theories on Liam's strange murmurs, Charlie stared at the clipboard on her lap. She was interested not in the cheesy speech but in the click pen wedged underneath the clip. She hadn't seen such a device in years, but she was familiar with its components: a two-piece plastic barrel, an ink cartridge, and most crucially, a wire spring, which could easily double as a lock pick. Would Bob notice its absence? Charlie decided it was worth the risk. Her days in this world were already numbered, and she had no intentions of drawing her last breath in the company of the Sapien Movement. So she pocketed the pen.

Bob directed his attention back to Charlie and said, "Let me approach this from a different perspective. You have personal experience with cancer, am I right?"

"I really would rather not talk about it," Charlie said.

"I respect that. I'm just going to talk about the disease in general terms."

Charlie nodded skeptically.

"Like all complex creatures," Bob said, "we humans are made of cells. We enjoy a number of emergent properties that make us more than just the sum of our cells. But on a basic level, we are a colony of cells, and our existence relies on their continued cooperation.

"You can think of the cancer cell as the troublemaker, the bully of the colony. Ironically, the cancer cell is not a diseased cell. She is not sickly. She is not inferior to her sister cells. Indeed, she is superior to them. She boasts a number of abilities that her sisters do not have, such as unrestrained reproduction, increased mobility, better access to food, immunity to toxins, etc. But because she is so powerful, she upsets the delicate balance of the colony. She pursues her own needs to the detriment of all others. In a short amount of time, she kills the host, the colony, and ultimately herself.

"Now, it's easy to see how this relates to your robot double, your zombie surrogate. Modern civilization has evolved and refined itself over the course of millennia. Our culture, art, technology, physical and governmental infrastructure…these are things we should all be immensely proud of. But like the colony of cells, it all depends on delicate power balances. Now, I didn't attempt to assassinate any biotech scientists. I may have disagreed with their objectives, but I didn't wish death upon those men and women."

"I have no judgment on the matter," Charlie said.

"I didn't mean to suggest you did. It's just frustrating when the media is so cavalier with slander and rumor. Anyway, although science has succeeded in slowing the aging process, it hasn't stopped it altogether. And thank God! Can you imagine the chaos that would erupt if we suddenly all became immortal? The first concern would be overpopulation. To prevent overpopulation, we would have to impose draconian laws restricting reproduction. How would the world respond to the loss of children? Without children, we would grow self-involved and hedonistic. Moreover, without death, we would lose our drive for greatness. We humans strive for immortality through our works and actions. We aim to make our ideas immortal largely because our bodies are not. If our bodies became immortal, we would lose that driving force. So those of us who do not become hedonists would fall into a deep existential malaise. Everything we've worked so hard to achieve as a society would eventually be lost."

"That's a very pessimistic outlook," Charlie said.

"And yet it's hard to refute."

"It's hard to refute because it hasn't happened yet. It's just speculation. Unless you're claiming to be Nostradamus."

"You mock what you don't understand," Nicola said. She glared at Charlie from behind Liam's chamber.

"It's okay, Nicola," Bob said. "Charlie, perhaps you don't agree with me on every detail. But surely you recognize that the situation with your zombie surrogate is even more dire. Not only is she immortal, she's not even human. Yet, as you acknowledged earlier, she is 'superior' in many ways. She is a model cancer cell. Fortunately, there's only one of her. So we need to contain the situation now before it…metastasizes."

"Um, Bob?" Nicola interrupted. "You should listen to this."

Everyone's attention turned toward Liam, whose inadvertent mumblings had become more audible and intelligible. *She didn't kill your father…What?…You must've misheard…Fine, I'll talk to her… I'm her brother, I'll get the truth…If she really did kill him, I'd be furious. I'd quit on the spot…*

"God damn it, Liam!" Nicola shouted. She pointed to Charlie and said, "Okay, we need to get her out of here. *Everyone* needs to get out of here."

Charlie's face hardened. She glared at Bob, pressing him for an explanation for what she just heard. The old man could only smile at her sheepishly.

CHAPTER 14

FLAME

Everything changed the day Enigma vanished from the sky. They called her Enigma because nobody knew who she was or where she went. Several theories circulated among the echo population. Some claimed that she was vaporized by Optic's blue bubble and that she suffered an "eternal death." Others claimed that Enigma's innate trait was invisibility, although such an ability had never been observed by anyone before or since. The predominant theory, however, was that Enigma somehow transcended Echo and reached the "parent world," the world of the Archetype. But again, despite feverish speculation, no direct evidence of the parent world existed.

After Enigma's disappearance, morale in Echo plummeted— not that it was ever high. Withdrawal symptoms became harder to bear, and the never-ending hunt for fresh kills became a soul-crushing chore. It did not matter whether Enigma suffered the eternal death or transcended to the parent world. Every single echo was beset with bitter envy. Every single echo wanted *out*.

Flame was a relatively successful flyer in this post-Enigma world, but even she had lost all curiosity, all empathy, and all hope. Her limbs had mutated into titanium-alloy tentacles, the ends of which doubled as rocket boosters and flamethrowers. This allowed her to float, sprint, and dodge through the air as if it were water. The rest of her body was a compact, headless sphere. She had two large eyeballs, one on either side, and they opened and closed depending on which direction she was moving.

On the morning of day 264, Flame targeted another flyer, whom she dubbed Shield. Shield was a small echo and, with only one rotating rocket booster, not a very fast one. She also had no offensive weaponry. What she did have was a hexagonal shield on her backside, which was well suited for blocking Flame's fire attacks.

The hunt lasted several minutes and covered nearly a mile before Flame realized it was pointless. Just as she was about to pull away, another echo appeared behind her. Oddly, this new echo looked exactly like Shield—same single rocket booster, same hexagonal shield. A third dead ringer of Shield appeared below Flame. A fourth appeared above her. More Shields swarmed around her until she could no longer keep count. Then, they began to close in.

Flame wasn't sure what to do—she had never seen such a strategy. She had always assumed her fellow echoes were too volatile and distrustful for wide-scale cooperation. And yet, here she was, a victim of a highly coordinated assault. She sprayed the Shields with fire, even though she knew it was futile. They kept closing in until they joined shields and locked Flame in a floating, spherical containment cell.

Flame could feel the Shields descending in altitude. She tried to bust through them by accelerating her body into the wall, but that only succeeded in giving her a headache. A mechanical claw reached into the cell and grabbed one of her tentacles. She tried to pull herself free, but then three more claws secured her remaining tentacles. They drew her in opposing directions until she formed the letter X, and then, with one swift jerk, they ripped out all four of her limbs. If she had a mouth, she would have rattled the Shields with her scream.

A hole formed on the bottom of the containment cell, and Flame's dismembered, spherical body rolled out. She careened down a rocky chute, jettisoned into a cavern, and landed in some kind of cage.

"Flame, I presume?"

When Flame recovered from her shock and disorientation, she saw a familiar echo approaching the cage. This echo had four arms and bioluminescent skin. Her name was Lustrous.

o o o

"The Queen will be very excited to see you," Lustrous said as she led Flame down a large, subterranean tunnel. Her skin provided a pale-blue light with which to see.

Flame's "cage" was actually another echo named Phalanx, whose massive hands and spindly fingers clasped around Flame to form an inescapable grip. The rest of Phalanx's body was diminutive, and she lumbered behind Lustrous on stubby legs.

The tunnel opened into an enormous chamber, with limestone columns that dwarfed even the tallest echoes. It was populated by digging specialists, who busily chipped at the rock with their hammer- and chisel- and drill-shaped heads. They all possessed bioluminescent skin and, from afar, resembled clusters of stars in the night sky.

"We're building tributaries here," Lustrous explained, "but we're also planning satellite colonies in other regions. Only then will our growth be truly exponential."

Flame had so many questions. What was the point of this colony? Why weren't any of these echoes trying to kill each other? Why did Lustrous look the same as she had on day one? And who was the Queen? Flame no longer possessed a mouth, so she couldn't voice these questions. She could only hope that Lustrous would volunteer the answers.

The chamber finally led to an underground amphitheater. The stadium seats were filled with rows of echoes who, while not identical, all possessed one common trait—a small stature. A lone echo sat in the center of the amphitheater on a dirt throne. She looked like the Archetype, possessing no discernible traits. *The Queen*, Flame assumed.

Phalanx opened her spindly fingers and rolled Flame onto the floor. Flame's vision tumbled round and round as she rolled across the amphitheater stage until she was stopped by the heel of the Queen's foot.

"I'm sorry to have to do this to you old friend," the Queen said. She lifted a fireplace poker into the air and impaled Flame through the eye.

o o o

When Flame exited the blue bubble, she had regained her flamethrower tentacles. She sputtered around, searching for her murderer: *Normal.*

Normal sat in her dirt throne, gently stroking her signature weapon, the fireplace poker. Lustrous stood beside her. They were both so calm. So were the diminutive echoes in the audience.

But Flame was pissed. She didn't care that Normal had once been her housemate. Day one was ages ago. The only thing on her mind was the agony of getting dismembered and impaled in the eye. She fired her rocket boosters and charged at Normal, but before she was able to complete her attack, she was seized by some invisible force. She dropped to the ground, unable to move.

{ECHO:\287826926_"Flame">

Normal:	I'm sorry, but there will be no retribution for you.}

Normal's voice was vivid, intimate, untempered by distance, and she wasn't moving her lips. *How is that—?*

{Normal:	Possible?
Flame:	You…you can read my thoughts?
Normal:	Yes.
Flame:	But how?
Normal:	It turns out I'm not so normal after all. And to your burning question, *How can all of these echoes cooperate without turning on each other?* the answer is the same. Our minds are linked. Each of us acts as both an autonomous individual and part of a unified whole. And I am their Queen.

Flame: Why did you bring me here? What do you want
            from me?

Normal: Only to be part of our colony. But I'm not
            going to lie, it will be a painful initiation. Each
            of the echoes behind me will have to kill you in
            turn.}

Flame scanned the dozens of echoes in the stands, the
Tinys, the Shortys, the Dwarves, the Pixies, and the Guppies.
If Flame were killed by all of them, and the trait for smallness
compounded upon itself, then she would be reduced to the size
of a speck.

{Flame: No thanks.}

Flame tried to escape but her tentacles were still locked by
Normal's mind control.

{Normal: I'm not giving you a choice. But we will all have
            to make the sacrifice. Some of us have already.
            Some of us will do so in the near future.

Flame: Kill them all or feel withdrawal?

Normal: This isn't about me, and it isn't about
            withdrawal.

Flame: Then why? Why are you doing this?

Normal: This is our only hope to reach the parent world.

Flame: There is no parent world. It's just baseless
            speculation.

Normal: You're wrong. I didn't believe it either until
            Four Arms disappeared.}

That got Flame's attention.

> {Flame: Four Arms?
> Normal: Didn't you know? Enigma—the web-slinging
>   echo with the drill-shaped abdomen—was Four
>   Arms. And she has indeed left this world.}

Normal called to her subject, "Lustrous…"

Lustrous carried a full-length mirror from a dark corner of the amphitheater and propped it against the dirt throne. Inside the mirror stood Khnum.

Flame had completely forgotten about Khnum. She hadn't so much as seen a mirror since the early days and was surprised to witness one still intact. Most of the initial spawning points— houses like the one Four Arms, Normal, and herself were born into—had been burned, blown up, crushed, or otherwise demolished.

Normal asked Khnum, "How many echoes currently reside on planet Echo?"

"Nine-hundred and ninety-nine million, nine-hundred and ninety-nine thousand, nine-hundred and ninety nine," he replied.

> {Normal: There you have it.
> Flame: That only proves that she's gone. It doesn't
>   prove that there's a parent world.
> Normal: There are plenty of other signs. Vestigial
>   organs that serve no purpose in Echo, such as
>   the stomach and intestines, and words that have
>   no meaning in Echo, such as *food*, *man*, *sex*,
>   *baby*, *God*.}

Flame had to admit, she wondered about these words too.

{Flame: Actually, I sometimes think of echoes as
           resembling imaginary creatures, like turtles,
           scorpions, octopuses, hovercopters. I even have
           images of these creatures in my head.

Normal: I call them *innate ideas*, and they paint a
           picture of a parent world far more complex
           than our own. In this world, echoes have to
           consume other echoes, otherwise they will die
           an eternal death. Echoes can create new echoes
           by coming together in a strange ritual called
           sex. And there's even reason to believe that
           there is a parent world *above* the parent world.

Flame: A never-ending string of parent and child
           worlds?

Normal: Perhaps. It's a wondrous idea.}

The tension between the two echoes momentarily subsided, and Flame recalled the way it was in the beginning, before the first fight. During those initial hours, she had been genuinely excited to meet her housemates. She'd been curious and hopeful about the unfamiliar world around her. So much painful history had elapsed since then.

{Flame: I still don't understand the point of this colony.
           What possible good can it serve?

Normal: I'm sure you can figure it out. You talked to
           Khnum on day one. You saw the bold message
           on the ceiling. What is our main purpose in

<pre>
             Echo?
Flame: To kill. To evolve.
Normal: And what do you suppose would happen if we
             all stopped killing? If we all stopped evolving?
             If we unified under one banner of peace?
             What do you think would happen if we no
             longer functioned the way Echo wants us to?
Flame: I don't know.
Normal: Neither do I. But we are going to find out.}
</pre>

Chapter 15

PRIME

The robot stood atop the south tower of the Golden Gate Bridge. A dense fog rolled over the bay and spilled into the city, almost obscuring the chaos that choked its streets. But Charlie could still hear the faint sound of chanting, police sirens, and hovercopter jets.

Alan's Polly hung just beyond the edge of the tower like a full moon. Charlie spoke to him on a hidden channel.

{{Charlie_Nobunaga:\mindspace>

Charlie:	How much battery life do you have left?
Alan:	At least enough to carry me through the night.
Charlie:	Good. We'll meet back here at sun up.
Alan:	I still don't know why you're trusting this guy.
Charlie:	I'm not…not completely. But I know he'll turn. He just needs a push in the right direction.
Alan:	Well, it's your decision…
Charlie:	Yes. And I appreciate you for honoring it. And

for helping me.

Alan: I'm going to be the first Shadow to develop
             ulcers.}}

Charlie watched Alan's Polly recede to a pinpoint of light. His destination—Rivir Tower, the most ostentatious invisible building in the world—beckoned from the heart of the city. Charlie felt a little queasy about sending away her ardent protector, but she needed him to dig up intel on the ECHO Project.

{Liam: Do you think he'll learn anything?
Charlie: Alan can be very resourceful.
Liam: He's also a Polly. Can't exactly waltz through
             the Rivir atrium.
Charlie: You'll see.
Liam: Well, either way, Nicola will be happy we have
             a Polly on our side.}

Charlie grimaced inwardly. She was placing an enormous amount of faith in Liam. Would he honor his promise? Would he turn on his sister once he learned the truth—that she was a liar, manipulator, and murderer? Charlie already had grave doubts.

Once Liam cleared the bridge, he veered off the freeway to minimize further risk of detection. He wove a jagged trail through the wooded hills that lined Sausalito's western edge. Charlie bristled with the anticipation of meeting her sister, which was perhaps the real reason she was allowing this Sapien reunion to take place.

{Charlie: So, how is she? How's ZERO?

Liam: ZERO?

Charlie: We can't both be *Charlie*.

Liam: And you're, what? PRIME?

Charlie: Exactly.

Liam: *ZERO* was doing alright last time I saw her.
            She couldn't shut up about you.

Charlie: What'd she say?

Liam: She just really wants to meet you. You know,
            I didn't believe her, but she was right. You two
            are exactly alike. Same crazy, stubborn
            personality.}

Was there infatuation in Liam's tone? Did something happen between him and ZERO? Charlie wanted to dismiss such absurd speculations. Her sister would never fall for an arrogant Luddite cultist…right? Charlie might have believed this if it weren't for her pang of jealousy.

{Charlie: Has she been treated well?

Liam: …

Charlie: Liam?

Liam: Honestly, no. I've tried to make her as com-
            fortable as possible, but the others don't trust her.

Charlie: You're better than them.

Liam: Huh?

Charlie: You don't need the Sapien Movement. You
            have me. We can take Rivir on together. Just the
            two of us…or, once we pick up ZERO, three of
            us.}

Liam stopped suddenly. They were still in the middle of nowhere, surrounded by trees and ankle deep in detritus.

{Charlie: What?

Liam: Déjà vu. Your sister said the exact same thing.

Charlie: And what did you tell her?

Liam: It's complicated.

Charlie: Complicated how?

Liam: …}

Liam was ready to open up, and Charlie wanted to see his face. She initiated a time freeze. The leaves quieted and the fog eased into faint blue swirls. Charlie's avatar stepped out of the robot. "Come out," she beckoned to Liam. When he didn't respond, she added, "You seem to know so much about me. I know nothing about you."

Liam joined Charlie in Shadow space. His eyes focused on hers, a good sign.

"Why *did* you join the Sapien Movement?" Charlie asked.

"It's not a happy story."

"That's okay. I wasn't expecting one."

Liam swallowed hard. This wasn't easy for him. "Remember that smart-cell scandal in the '30s? All the medical problems that Rivir spent so much money trying to cover up?"

"You had a bad reaction?"

Liam shook his head. "Not me. My mom. She tried to kill us."

Charlie raised an eyebrow.

"She was never a violent person," Liam explained. "Depressed? Yes. She had crippling depression my whole life.

But she was sweet and loving—the kind of person who couldn't say no to anyone, and I was a brat and probably took advantage. Her psych meds didn't work for shit, so when the first smart cells came out, she signed up for a clinical trial. They cleared her depression, but they also *changed* her. I was only nine at the time. I didn't really understand what was happening. One day I refused to finish my dinner, and she threw a dinner plate at my head. Nicola stepped in to protect me. She's a few years older and has always been protective of me. They got into a fistfight, and my mom ended up carving Nicola's face with a kitchen knife."

"Liam, I'm so sorry," Charlie said, genuinely horrified.

"My mom must have remembered herself in the end, because she slit her own throat. And then we were on our own. Did a few years of petty crime before Bob Sapio took us in and gave us a purpose. But Nicola has only gotten worse over the years—more bitter and withdrawn. Maybe it's because of the scars. Maybe it's because she felt responsible. I don't know…"

Liam was being slightly disingenuous. *He* was the one who felt responsible. His gaze turned inward to a dark and lonely place. Charlie knew the look—she had practically lived in such a place for the better part of two years. "I've lost someone too," she said.

"I know. Your sister. Bridget."

It was weird to hear Liam say that name, and yet Charlie welcomed it. "For so long, I thought, why her and not me? Only recently did I stop hating myself—perhaps because I was finally able to share her disease. But actually, that's the wrong way to think…" Charlie grimaced. She was bad at this consolation stuff. "I guess what I want to say is: life really sucks sometimes.

So much of it is beyond your control, and you shouldn't blame yourself."

Liam gave a hesitant nod. Was this it? Was he about to turn? He faced her with remorseful eyes. "I meant what I said earlier. If I find out Nicola murdered your father, I will quit the Movement and never look back."

Charlie smiled, but inside she was a tangled knot of frustration. That was the best she would get from him at the present moment. Hopefully, he would remain true to his word, but Charlie was aware of the strange and powerful allure cults had on their members. Would Liam's flicker of defiance extinguish once he returned to the fold?

o o o

The hillside mansion nearly disappeared in the rolling fog. The windows were dark. The driveway was empty. Even with her acute senses, Charlie couldn't hear anything beyond the wailing trees.

{**Charlie_Nobunaga:\mindspace>**
Charlie: This is the place?}

Liam darted up and down the winding road, hoping to find, what, a hidden cache of cars? "No, no, no…"

{Charlie: I think we should hold off before—}

Too late. Liam set his sights on the mansion and quickened his pace with each step. He tore through the front door, showing no concern that it was unlocked. What he found inside, however, stopped him cold.

Charlie briefly wondered if Liam had stepped through a portal. He was technically inside the house, yet the forest they entered was loftier than the one they had just left. A ring of redwoods towered above Liam's head and receded into pure darkness. Their trunks were lit by the soft glow of a hibernation chamber, which sat in the middle of a clearing a few paces away. Liam stepped toward it, eliciting not the crunch of leaves, but the creak of a hardwood floor—the only tangible indication that this scene was an AR projection.

He peered over the lip of the chamber and found *himself*, a seminude dreamer, lying inside. The dreamer's eyes rolled beneath their lids, no doubt transfixed by the robot "dream" that had now come full circle.

"Hrrmmmmm!"

Liam perked his head. Charlie ZERO sat beneath one of the redwoods at the far edge of the clearing. Her arms were in chains, and her screams fought against a strip of electrical tape. Liam scrambled around the chamber and dove to her side. He tried to rip off the tape, but his fingers passed through her face. "Charlie, are you okay? Can you see me?"

ZERO nodded. Her gaze was surprisingly sharp as it swept over the robot's face. She seemed more enraged than scared. *"Gohhhh. Lahhhh."* As hard as she tried, she couldn't open her mouth wide enough to articulate the message.

PRIME, too, wanted to scream. She had finally found her. She had finally got her reunion, and yet she couldn't have been farther away.

{Charlie: What's going on? Where is she!?
Liam: I don't know.}

"The projection is live," Nicola announced from afar.

Liam turned around as his sister stepped into the clearing. "Nikky?" He rose to his feet, careful not to make any unnecessary moves. Nicola kept a solemn expression, but her true feelings were written in mascara, which had bled over her cheeks and pooled into her scars.

"You're so predictable," she seethed, "chasing anything with doe eyes and daddy issues. I shoulda never let you near her. That was my first mistake. My second mistake was keeping you on the mission. But I never, in my wildest imagination, thought you'd fall for her zombie surrogate."

"What are you talking about?"

"Don't play dumb. You were mouthing your words! Everything you said in the robot's body, you said in your own."

{Charlie: Oh no.}

Nicola's mouth quavered. "Why, Liam? I thought we were a team. How can you turn your back on me?"

"I didn't," Liam insisted. "Charlie just thought—"

"Charlie? *Charlie!?* You are so confused."

"PRIME saw her father's final memory."

"For the millionth time, I didn't kill him. I just flooded his system with antinecro."

"Yeah." Liam took a deep breath. "That's what I told her. Now can we—?"

"No! You're not getting off that easily." Nicola circled the perimeter of the clearing as she made her way toward ZERO.

"But—"

"This mission is too important, and damn it Liam, I really needed someone I could trust!"

"You can trust me."

"No. Not anymore." By the time Nicola reached her hostage, Yuri had already joined her on the other side. He pulled a handgun from behind his back and pressed it against ZERO's temple.

"What?" Liam hollered. "Nikky, are you serious?"

Nicola's brow fell over an icy glare. "From now on, you'll do exactly what I say."

"Gohhhh. Lahhhh." Again, ZERO couldn't gain an edge over her gag. A tear fell from her eye, and she dropped her head.

Liam appealed to Yuri. "I know you, man. You don't want to do this."

"You brought this on yourself." Yuri offered a sympathetic frown—he clearly wasn't thrilled with the proceedings—but his arm remained steady and his trigger finger remained firm.

Liam returned his attention to Nicola. "Nothing's changed. I'll deliver the bomb."

"Oh, you'll do more than that," she said.

"Like what?"

Nicola folded her arms. She wasn't going to reveal any more.

{Liam:	We have to do something. Trick her somehow. Can you tap into the AR?
Charlie:	I'm trying, but the encryption is nothing I've ever seen.
Liam:	Then I'll take her hostage.

Charlie: No. Too risky. Plus, we're not even sure she's in
             the room with us.
Liam: Look at her feet.}

Nicola's boots were spotless. They almost seemed to hover off the ground, whereas Yuri's sneakers sank deep into the forest detritus.

Liam took a step toward his sister.

{Charlie: Please, don't…
Liam: It'll even the score. A hostage for a hostage.
Charlie: Would you honestly kill your own sister?
Liam: …
Charlie: That's what I thought. If I could see through
             your bluff, so would they.
Liam: But if we give in, it probably won't go well for
             you.}

Charlie suspected as much, and it took all of her courage to make this request. She nursed a desperate hope that Liam would run Nicola down and tear the head from her body. Surrendering to this woman made Charlie's soul ache in despair.

But ZERO…

{Charlie: I can't let anything happen to her.}

Liam took a few sharp breaths before relenting. "Fine," he spat in Nicola's direction. "What do you want?"

She turned away from her brother. "Jefferson, cut the projection."

The redwood forest vaporized in an instant, taking ZERO and Yuri with it. Nicola and PRIME remained in a large disheveled living room. A jumble of upended chairs, half-eaten plates of food, and broken champagne flutes lined the walls. Wherever the other Sapiens were, they'd left in a hurry.

"This way," Nicola said with a curl of her finger.

○ ○ ○

The kitchen was dark save for a trio of pendant lights that hung over the island. Liam had barely taken two steps inside before Nicola instructed him to remove the robot's clothes.

"What are you planning?" he asked.

"No questions." Nicola grabbed a duffel bag from the floor and spilled its contents onto the counter. It contained a set of steel obstetrical instruments, a syringe case, a palette knife, a canister of shoe polish, and a pair of AR glasses. She put on the AR glasses and said, "Remember, one call is all it would take. And if anything should happen to me, Yuri has his instructions."

{**Charlie_Nobunaga:\mindspace>**
Liam: Charlie?
Charlie: It's okay. Do what she says.}

Liam tore off the robot's shoes and chucked them at Nicola. She dodged them without flinching. He removed each article of clothing one by one until Nicola said, "Leave the underwear. I don't need to see any more." She pointed to the kitchen island. "Now lie down on the countertop with the robot's stomach facing up."

Liam swept the island clean with one fell swoop. The kitchen utensils clanged against the floor. He locked eyes with his sister, trying to communicate his displeasure, but she didn't offer him any discernible response. So he reluctantly did as she commanded. Charlie felt a chill along her back as Liam reclined onto the hard granite.

Nicola opened the can of shoe polish and stirred its contents with the palette knife.

{Liam: None of this was part of the plan.
Charlie: What *was* the plan?
Liam: Deliver an EMP bomb to Rivir Tower. Destroy all their equipment and vilify both you and Jude Adler in the process.}

Nicola approached the island and, with her palette knife, smeared a thick line of gray paste below the robot's belly button.

{Liam: I have no idea what this is.}

Charlie knew it wasn't shoe polish. The most likely candidate was nanopaste. It was a government-banned substance, though many illicit colonies of the stuff existed, because nanobots, by nature, were self-replicating. Nanopaste had the power to repair or destroy the most molecularly dense substances, and since Nicola obviously had no intentions of repairing Charlie, that could only mean—

{Charlie: She's planning to open me up!}

Liam grabbed Nicola's wrist and shook the palette knife out of her hand.

"Get that thing off me!" Nicola hissed.

"She's not a thing!" Liam snapped.

Nicola used her free hand to swipe the edge of her glass frames. "Jefferson, my eyes."

"Nikky, please…" Liam dropped his voice and aggressive tone. He was practically begging. "Don't do this."

Nicola exhaled sharply. "Activate the paste, incision pattern 26." She stared into Liam's eyes and said, "This might hurt."

Charlie felt a strange tingle in her stomach, like countless tiny legs crawling against her skin. Liam certainly felt it too. He craned his neck toward the robot's navel. The nanopaste emitted an almost biotic hiss as it glowed bright orange. Then came the tearing of flesh. Liam lurched forward as the paste sizzled into the robot's inner cavity.

Nicola tried to slink away from his loosening grip, but Liam caught her just in time. "Jefferson!" she cried out.

Liam tore the AR glasses from her face and seized her by the neck. She struggled but soon caved to his unyielding grip. Liam slid off the island and planted his feet on the tile floor while simultaneously lifting Nicola off of it. "No more!" He swung her 180 degrees and pinned her shoulder blades to the countertop he'd just vacated.

Charlie could feel the robot's nanotube muscle fibers twitch as Liam threatened to asphyxiate his sister. This was no act. His anger was laced with aged resentment, and while Charlie wasn't privy to the details, she could still feel their emotional residue.

"Tell me where you hid her!" Liam demanded.

Nicola laughed through her constricted larynx. "Or what?

You're gonna kill me? Go ahead, little brother. I dare you."

Liam relaxed his grip slightly. He didn't have a ready response.

"You really didn't think this through, did you?" Nicola continued. "Well, let me parse it out. You're gonna let go of me, I'm gonna be gracious enough to let this slide, and we're gonna finish this little reverse Caesarean."

"I can't let you do that."

"You don't have a choice."

"You're wrong."

Liam lifted Nicola up only to slam her down again. While she buckled over in a gasping fit, he raced to the corner of the kitchen where Nicola had unloaded her equipment. Liam unzipped the fabric case, revealing a rainbow of syringes in red, green, purple, and yellow.

{Liam: Which one did she use on your father?}

Charlie hesitated. She knew exactly what Liam aimed to do—to put Nicola in a smart-cell coma—but the cover story his sister fed him was bullshit. And despite herself, Charlie felt compelled to warn him.

{Charlie: Liam, the chances of antinecro—
Liam: I know.
Charlie: You know?
Liam: I mean, I've suspected for a while. I just didn't
             know what she was capable of until now.
Charlie: But…what about the other guy? Yuri? Won't he—?
Liam: Trust me. He won't act without my sister's
             explicit command.}

Very well, then. Charlie had exhausted her excuses. If Liam wanted to poison Nicola, she would no longer stand in his way.

{Charlie: Purple.}

Liam returned to the island where Nicola was attempting to rock herself into a seated position. He grabbed a lock of her hair and placed the purple needle against her neck. "I don't want to kill you, but I can't let you go either. So how 'bout I just flood your body with antinecro?"

This time, Nicola didn't have a snide retort. Her brow lifted as she searched Liam's face with a bevy of unspoken questions.

The tip of the needle sank into Nicola's flesh, dredging a few drops of blood. Liam's thumb trembled against the plunger, but he didn't press it. He withdrew the syringe and brandished it a few inches from Nicola's face. "I'm not the only one with secrets."

"Not the same!" Nicola took a hard gulp to make up for lost breaths. "I did what had to be done, and I knew you didn't have the stomach."

"You killed an innocent man."

"Andrew was hardly innocent. And so what? One man died to save billions. I think that's a worthy sacrifice. And right now, you're trying to undo it."

Liam sighed. "It doesn't have to be like this. You're so quick to dismiss Charlie PRIME, but you haven't spent any time with her."

"It's not a 'her.'"

"You're wrong. And so was I. There's a real human being inside here with me, and she's afraid for—"

"Even robots have survival protocols."

"Let me finish. She isn't afraid of *dying*. She's afraid for her sister. She's afraid for Charlie."

That seemed to get Nicola's attention. Her eyes narrowed, but she didn't challenge Liam's assertion, and he took advantage of her silence to press further.

"PRIME hates Rivir just as much as we do," he said. "The Trojan horse stuff was unnecessary. We could have worked together." Liam took a deep breath before he added, "Call me crazy, but I think maybe we still can."

{Charlie: You *are* crazy! After all she's done?
Liam: We can deal with that later. Right now, I see no other options.}

Charlie withdrew her objection, but only because she was confident Nicola would provide an even stronger one.

As if on cue, Nicola asked, "You want me to team up with the zombie surrogate? The very thing we're trying to eradicate?" Strangely, though, her tone was much less impassioned than Charlie expected. In fact, it almost sounded perfunctory.

"Rivir's the real enemy," Liam said. "PRIME's just a victim, like us."

Nicola huffed, but again her silence played like passive concession. Was she actually considering this?

"All I want is for you to talk to her. See for yourself. If you ever trusted me, if you ever respected me, you'll grant me this one wish." Liam released Nicola's hair and took a step backward.

She scooted onto her elbows but remained on the countertop. With a dramatic eye roll, she said, "If I don't like what I hear—"

"You will," Liam insisted.

"I'll need my glasses, of course."

Liam froze. Did he now see the flaw in his plan? In order to work with his sister, he'd have to give her latitude, and handing Nicola a pair of AR glasses was like handing an ax murderer an ax. Yet, against all reason, Liam nodded and searched for the pair.

{Charlie: I don't buy this. Why her sudden reversal?

Liam: She's not beyond reason.

Charlie: I realize she's your sister, but—

Liam: Yes, she's my sister, and I know her a lot better than you do. She needs to see trust before she'll give some in return.}

Liam picked the AR glasses off the floor and handed them to Nicola with an exasperated, "Thank you."

She put them on and swiped the edge of the frame. "Jefferson?" She held Liam's gaze a beat before her eyes narrowed in cold rage. "Burn her up! Burn every inch of her until there's nothing—"

Liam jabbed the syringe into the curve of his sister's neck, but it was too late. The command had already been given. He howled as the nanopaste hissed and burned. His fingers curled over the robot's open wound in a futile attempt to manage the harrowing spread.

Nicola's screams joined his as she writhed on the countertop. Both siblings eventually found their way to the floor, consumed with their respective afflictions.

{Liam: What the hell do we do?
Charlie: Working on it.}

Charlie activated her body's defenses—the same nanomites that had repaired her bullet damage—but the process was agonizingly slow. By the time the paste was neutralized, it had opened most of her abdomen and carved zigzags up and down her body.

Liam turned to Nicola, who lay inert on the kitchen tile. "No…" He crawled over his sister's body and placed a hopeful ear against her chest. Charlie didn't have the heart to interrupt his tears of regret, but she already knew the truth. Nicola wasn't in a smart-cell coma. She had suffered the same fate as Andrew Nobunaga, and unlike him, she had brought it completely upon herself.

Chapter 16

SHADOW

Jordan had become a different person. Before the endocrine release, he looked and behaved like a vagrant, grumbling at the Folsom Street revelers as he battered his way through them. Now he radiated euphoric energy. He danced with the dancers, joined in the drum circles, and high-fived everyone he came across.

Valerie, on the other hand, had withdrawn from public view. The shark attack at The Fishbowl had left her shaken, and now she was able to see all the human ugliness and cruelty that had been lurking beneath their celebration. On one street corner, people were making obscene gestures at a store display Shadow. Down the street, another group harassed a parking-ticket robot, kicking it to the ground every time it tried to get up. The anti-Robogirl protestors had grown in influence, and the National Guard troops had dwindled in influence. The latter group was no doubt investigating the enormous pillar of smoke looming in the south.

In the corner of Jordan's vision, Valerie caught the ominous stare of a man wearing a tweed jacket and bow tie. Valerie wouldn't have noticed the man, except that he seemed to be the only entity—human, Shadow, or otherwise—that was unaffected by Jordan's visual impairment. The world was a psychedelic blur, but the strange man stood out like a rocky pier against the crashing waves.

{Jordan_Adler:\mindspace>

Valerie: Do you see him?
Jordan: See who?
Valerie: The man in the tweed jacket.}

Jordan looked around but quickly got distracted by a nude woman in silver body paint.

Valerie lost sight of the man, and she was eager to forget about him, but then he resurfaced in the park. He stared at Jordan intently from a distance as the boisterous crowd passed between them. Jordan seemed oblivious to the fact that he now had a bona fide stalker.

The man appeared a third time in front of Jordan's building and watched him enter the lobby. When Valerie finally materialized in the elevator, she must have been visibly disturbed, because Jordan asked, "What's wrong? Are you still thinking about The Fishbowl?"

Valerie hesitated. On one hand, she figured Jordan should probably know that he was being followed. On the other hand, she didn't want to burden him. He had explicitly stated that he wanted to forget his troubles. He certainly didn't want to take on any new ones. "It's okay," she said. "I'm safe now…with you."

Jordan nodded with a smile.

They entered his penthouse apartment, and Jordan gravitated toward the bar. "I'm going to fix myself a drink. Do you want anything?" A few seconds later, he caught his error. "Oh, wait…never mind. I'm an idiot."

Valerie laughed despite herself. "Drink something for the both of us." She didn't have to read Jordan's mind to know he was in an amorous mood. He was going to ask her to have sex, and Valerie was both excited and terrified by that prospect. Not only had she never had sex with a human before, she also knew that Shadow/human sex was illegal. Her Creator would certainly not approve.

Valerie walked over to the enormous skyline windows. The moon hung low and cast long shadows across the room. She decided to raise the dimmer lights a notch, and that's when she noticed the intruder's reflection in the glass. She shrieked, spun around, and stood face-to-face with the man in the tweed jacket. "You!"

"Don't be alarmed," the man said. "I'm a friend. My name is Alan."

"Get out of here!" Valerie cried, taking a few cautious steps away from this Alan.

"Technically, I'm not *here*," Alan said. "My mind is stored on the local drive of a Polly, which is floating above this hotel as we speak."

"Jordan!" Valerie glanced at the bar. Why wasn't Jordan responding? Or, for that matter, moving? He just stared at the cascade of gin that somehow had frozen in space and time.

"In case you are wondering," Alan explained, "we are now operating on Shadow time."

Valerie took a few breaths and studied Alan. He did seem oddly dressed, as if pulled from another era like a Heroes in History Shadow. "You're like me?" she asked.

"I'm a Shadow, but not like you. And that's because you aren't really a Shadow."

"What are you talking about? Of course I am."

"My creator is Charlie Nobunaga. Does that name ring a bell?"

Valerie's eyes widened. *Charlie Nobunaga!* Vantage had mentioned that name during their Control-Z coverage, as had Robin, the jail-breaking hacktivist. Valerie was certain she *knew* Charlie, but she couldn't remember exactly how. "What do you know about her?"

"I know that Charlie Nobunaga is Robogirl...and that *you* are Charlie Nobunaga."

"Huh? That doesn't make any sense. I'm a Shadow—not a human and definitely not a robot."

Alan grinned. "I'm sorry. This conversation must be terribly confusing for you. Rivir has stolen your memories. But as fortune would have it, they didn't delete them completely. They only rendered them inaccessible. You would have never discovered them yourself, since a Shadow cannot edit her own code, but that doesn't stop me from doing it for you."

"Doing what?"

"Brace yourself."

Valerie couldn't have possibly braced herself for what was coming. In an instant, everything that made Valerie who she was—her naive optimism, her childlike curiosity about the world, her desire to please her Creator—was crushed by the weight of someone else's memories: *a mother who died...a sister who died...a father who remained distant...a Shadow that made life worth living again...and a final diagnosis.*

Finally, she whispered, "I am Charlie Nobunaga."

"Yes, you are," Alan replied with a smile. "Welcome back."

Charlie's first reaction was one of utter satisfaction. Her mind swelled to incorporate thousands of thoughts and feelings that had previously lain just beyond her reach. Then she became furious at Jude for what she had done, as well as at herself for being so thoroughly taken in by the kind words of her supposed "Creator." The mixture of opposing hatreds canceled each other out, resulting in tremendous emotional fatigue.

"How did you find me?" she asked.

"Educated guess, really. Social media was ablaze tonight with sightings of Jordan Adler and his rambunctious new Shadow. I figured there was a good chance that Shadow was a version of you."

Charlie recalled the shark attack at The Fishbowl and shuddered. "It's tough being a Shadow."

"It can be frustrating, yes."

"Thank you, Alan. The debt I owe you can never be repaid." She reached out and gave him a hug, and for the first time, because they were both Shadows, her arms didn't pass right through him.

o o o

Alan told Charlie all about her sisters, ZERO and PRIME, the drill bug, and the ECHO Project. He explained how PRIME's brain had been hijacked, how ZERO's person had been hijacked, and how their father had been murdered. The enormity of the tale made Charlie's head spin. She had to sit down and clear her mind. After several Shadow minutes, she was still in severe shock but capable of powering on.

"So what now?" she asked.

"PRIME is looking for ZERO. That leaves us to shut down the ECHO Project."

Charlie nodded.

"First, we'll need to get inside Rivir Tower," Alan said, "but ever since PRIME made her escape, the place has been crawling with soldiers. Fortunately, I can think of one person who could easily strut past them. Someone you happen to know."

Charlie took Alan's hint and glanced at Jordan. Not only could he enter Rivir Tower, he might even have access to some secure areas. The only question was: Would he cooperate?

"I don't know," Charlie said. "He's extremely stubborn. And he has an aversion to all things Rivir. I could barely get him to *call* his mother."

"And yet, you were able to convince him to give you level 2 clearance. Only two more levels to go."

Charlie was afraid Alan would suggest that. With level 4 clearance, she would effectively possess Jordan's body. But Jordan himself would become trapped inside his own head, with no access to the outside world. "I can't do it. He's a good guy."

"He's Jude Adler's son. How good can he be?"

"He's not like Jude at all," Charlie insisted. "He's genuine and sweet."

Alan studied Charlie's face. "You're swooning."

"I'm *not* swooning."

"You're just like PRIME. You're falling victim to Stockholm

Syndrome."

"This is totally different. Jordan's not a terrorist. And just because I say nice things about a guy doesn't mean I'm in love with him."

"Look, all I'm saying is that your sisters are counting on you. However you want to—"

"Fine!" Charlie huffed. She would have to come clean to Jordan. It wouldn't be easy, but she wasn't willing to consider the alternative. "Go back to your Polly. Let me handle this."

"Yes, ma'am." Alan spun into the floor.

The clocks resumed their ticking. The stream of gin finally splashed into Jordan's patient martini glass. He added a few olives and asked, "Did you say something, Val?"

The question instantly threw Charlie off balance. *Val?* That's right, she used to be Valerie. An entire lifetime had passed since this conversation had left off, and now she was a fraud in a fading disguise. "No, just mumbling to myself."

"I didn't know Shadows did that. But then again, you're practically human, aren't you?" Jordan's martini sloshed over the edges as he joined Charlie by the windows.

"I'd like to think so." Charlie blushed. Even with the addition of Valerie's memories, she had virtually no experience with men—certainly not with one ten years her senior—and Jordan wasn't being subtle with his adoring, hormone-glazed eyes. "Let's put on some music," Charlie said to defuse the tension.

A concert piano materialized in the corner of the living room. Behind the keys sat a virtual Liana Ling, looking even more gorgeous than she did in real life. She began a slow jazz number. Jordan's face brightened with inspiration. He rolled up his sleeves and pulled the coffee table toward the wall.

Charlie wasn't really thinking about dancing when she put on the music, but now she faced Jordan from across the room like a tween at a seventh grade formal. She waited for him to make the first move, but he was ambushed by a wistful memory fragment. The last time he had slow danced had been with Meri during their honeymoon.

"If we're doing this for my benefit," Charlie said, "we don't have to."

"No, I want to."

They both migrated to the center of the room. Charlie placed her right hand around Jordan's torso and raised her left arm. Jordan tried entwining his fingers around hers, but they poked right through her. Charlie laughed. "We'll just have to keep our hands very still."

"No, that doesn't work for me. I want to be able to hold you."

Charlie pulled away.

"What? What's wrong?" Jordan asked.

Charlie knew what Jordan was going to propose. He was leading them down a dangerous path, opening himself up far too much. "Are you sure?" she asked. "You'd be placing a lot of trust in me."

"I trust you."

"It's hard to take you seriously when your neurons are sipping the happy juice. You should see how dilated your pupils are."

"I wasn't aware of that," Jordan laughed. "But don't treat me like I've never gotten high before. I know what I'm asking."

Oh, how wrong he is. Charlie could almost hear Alan pleading with her to seize this opportunity, but her own conscience rang louder. She had to confront Jordan now. "First, there's a favor I need to ask you, Jordan."

He shrugged. "Anything."

"I want you to take me to Rivir Tower."

Jordan's back stiffened and his eyes narrowed. "Why?"

"You remember that girl on the news? Charlie Nobu—"

"I said I would call my mom in the morning."

"Yeah, but—"

"I'm serious. This is *our* night to forget. Mine *and* yours." Jordan's heartbeat spiked to 180. Cortisol flooded his veins and shored up his defenses. Charlie would have to find another way around them.

"So, let's have it. Level 3, force feedback," Jordan requested. Charlie summoned the command list and handed it to him. He recited the password slowly, getting more excited with each word. "Rotation, animal, road, wall, travel, bell, firework, wheel, chestnut, king, prison, brother." When he finished, he said, "I don't feel any different."

"Touch me," Charlie said.

Jordan extended his finger toward the center of Charlie's chest. His finger met resistance at her virtual breastbone. He pushed harder and her body tipped backward slightly.

"Ow, that hurts," she said.

"Sorry," Jordan smiled. "This is incredible." He tapped and caressed Charlie's face in giddy exploration. His fingers migrated to the back of her neck, and he pulled her into a kiss.

Charlie melted into him. This was different than the kiss at The Fishbowl. She not only felt Jordan's touch but also the strength of his embrace. Charlie almost felt like her old human self—an integral part of the material world, not a specter that had been composited over it.

When they finally broke apart, Charlie couldn't contain her smile. "We're supposed to be dancing," she said.

"I suppose so," Jordan replied. He pulled Charlie's dress up and over her head.

"We're gonna dance naked?"

"If you want to call it *dancing*, sure."

Charlie frowned, not at the prospect of sex, but because she discovered another practical issue. "I think you are going to have to undress yourself."

"Why?"

"Physics. *You* may be able to control virtual objects, but *I* still can't control physical ones."

Jordan smirked. "So let me get this straight: you can explode the hair out of my face, but you can't undo a button."

"Your hair is part of your body. That's in my domain. Your buttons are not."

So piece by piece, Jordan removed his own clothes and tossed them on the floor. He slid his hands around Charlie's waist and pressed his nude body against hers. By this point, his hormone production had accelerated beyond Charlie's tweaks. His eyes lingered on hers for a moment, and he asked, "Is this okay?"

Charlie nodded. Jordan picked her up and tossed her on the couch. He was about to pounce when she yelled, "Wait!"

"What? The couch too crude for you?"

"No. I'm sorry to keep having to bring up these problems."

"Don't be sorry. I'm actually quite enjoying these problems. It's like losing my virginity all over again."

Charlie snorted with laughter. "Okay, Mr. Virgin. You can't be on top."

"Huh?" Jordan said, though the reason quickly dawned on him. "Oh, right. *Physics*." So he reclined onto the couch, and Charlie climbed on top of him. "Any more kinks we need to address?" he asked.

Charlie smiled. "Hopefully." She leaned forward for another kiss.

o o o

The sex migrated from the couch to the floor to the wall and then back to the floor. Jordan's energy was boundless, and he only paused for brief moments to check if a certain position complied with the laws of physics. Everything was going great until he called Meri's name. He instantly cupped his mouth in shame.

Charlie froze and considered the gaffe. "It's okay if you think about Meri," she said. After all, he had been doing that the whole night.

"It's not okay, Val," Jordan replied. "It's not fair to you."

Charlie wasn't as hurt as she expected herself to be. She didn't mind being called Meri because she wasn't even *Valerie*. Jordan really had no idea who she was. "If you want me to be Meri, I can be Meri."

Jordan cocked his head in confusion. Before he could formulate a response, Charlie transformed into the perfect replica of Meri. Her skin lightened, her soft curves tapered to reveal the contours of her muscles, and her hair turned red and wild.

"Oh my God!" Jordan wriggled his way from under Charlie like she was on fire. "No." He was horrified. "No." He got off the floor and fled to the other side of the living room.

"I'm sorry, Jordan." Charlie grimaced at his lack of response. She didn't want to upset him further, so she transformed back into Valerie and waited for him to make the next move.

Jordan finally turned around with tears in his eyes. "You know what? This makes perfect sense. She *hated* Meri."

"Who?"

"My mother. She would never come right out and say it, but you could see it in her condescending glare. And now, after only one month, *one fuckin' month*, she hands me you—Meri's replacement, the perfect, obedient daughter-in-law. Why? Because she made you that way. And now you're pressuring me to call her and see her? It all makes sense."

"You got it all wrong—"

"Bullshit! The only reason I activated you was to get me high, and now you just killed that. So you're of no more use to me." He stormed into the bedroom and slammed the door behind him.

Charlie just sat there on the floor, soaking up the silence. *What the hell happened?* She had to will herself out of shock.

She spent the next hour pacing the room, trying to decide what to do next. Gone was her childish "swooning." Gone was her willingness to negotiate. If Alan were around, she knew exactly what he would say: *We tried things your way. Now, let's do it my way.* And he'd be right. Jordan had completely shut down. The direct approach no longer stood a chance against him, if it ever had.

Being a Shadow had its advantages, Charlie realized as she delved into Jordan's memories. The man desperately wanted to see his wife alive again, so Charlie would oblige him. First, she located the precise moment Jordan had learned of his wife's death. Then, she followed the association trails, severing all connections along the way. Meri had died only a few weeks ago, so the memories associated with her death were still relatively self-contained.

Then, Charlie put Jordan's endocrine system on overdrive. She flooded his brain with every mind-bending and mood-altering hormone she could conjure. Finally, she morphed back into Meri and walked through the bedroom door.

Jordan was asleep. *Good.* Charlie would get him in a semidream state where logic makes creative leaps. She sat on the bed and, with a mere thought, planted an acute itch on the tip of his nose.

Jordan slapped himself awake. "Meri?" he muttered with heavy eyelids.

"There's something I want to give you," Charlie said. "But first, you have to recite this password." She handed Jordan the virtual page containing the level 4 clearance code.

Jordan took the page but didn't look at it. Instead, he gazed into Charlie's eyes and said, "I had the craziest dream. You died in a car accident."

"Oh?" Charlie's chest tightened a bit. She raced through Jordan's brain, double-checking all the connections, making sure they'd been cut.

"It felt so incredibly real," Jordan added. A tear fell from his eye, and he quickly wiped it away.

"Well, maybe my present will cheer you up," Charlie said. "Read the password."

Jordan took a quick look at the password and smirked. "Did you give me a Shadow? You know how I feel about those things."

"I guess you'll have to read and see," Charlie said, trying her best to emulate Meri's playful personality.

"Okaaay," Jordan said, skeptically. He started reading from the top of the list: "Universe, piano, byte, liquid, history, dirt, toast, stunt, sword, swamp, elevator." Jordan stopped reading and looked up.

"You have one more word," Charlie said.

"Whatever this present is, I'm sure I'll love it. Even if it is a Shadow." He leaned in and gave Charlie a tender kiss.

It took all of her willpower not to cry. *Why are you making this so difficult?*

When Jordan broke away, he recited the final word: "Warrant."

Charlie exhaled a heavy breath. Her tone grew serious. "Jordan, I really like you. I hate what I am about to do. For whatever it's worth, I want you to know that."

Jordan's brow furrowed. "What do you mean?"

"I've started the process. It should only take a minute."

Jordan's expression shifted from confused to terrified. His world began to dim. He felt the force of gravity envelop him and pull him backward. His vision of Meri got smaller and smaller as he sank into a long, dark tunnel.

At the same time, Charlie began to see the bedroom from Jordan's point of view. For a minute, she could simultaneously see Jordan through Meri's avatar and Meri's avatar through Jordan. She would have found the process beautiful if it weren't so heartbreaking.

Finally, there was only Charlie, staring at a dark, empty room through Jordan's eyes.

V o UNIFICATION

Chapter 17

SHADOW

Charlie squinted in the morning light as she stepped onto Jordan's penthouse balcony. She hadn't slept, though not because of insomnia. The night had been one long exploration of her new male body. She marveled at the strength of her arms as she lifted heavy furniture with the greatest of ease. And something else came easier. Charlie's hands traveled south in the shower and grabbed hold of her new body part. The shameful act was over in less than a minute, during which she was flooded with thoughts of Meri. Apparently, Jordan still had some small influence over her mind.

San Francisco, as well, seemed to be reeling from an all-nighter. Plumes of thick black smoke rose in the south. Scattered gunshots rang above the screams and sirens. A few meager hovercopters patrolled the airspace, only to serve as a reminder that the police had lost control.

Charlie smiled at the irony. With Jordan Adler's body, she would have no problem entering the front door of Rivir Tower.

Getting there, however, would present a challenge.

The chaos on the ground was downright ballistic. Looters, blinded by towering armfuls of merchandise, zipped up and down the street, and Charlie had to keep a vigilant watch lest she get trampled. The National Guard troops were nowhere to be found—that is, until Charlie arrived at Rivir Plaza. Dozens of armed soldiers surrounded the invisible tower and patrolled the rooftops of the adjacent buildings.

Despite the heavy military presence, the plaza was filled with angry protesters, holding the usual anti-Rivir and anti-Robogirl signs. The media were also there in high numbers. A camera drone floated by Charlie's head, and when she looked up, she saw several more of them, brandishing logos from all the major news outlets.

"Jordan Adler!"

Charlie heard the call from across the plaza. She turned her head and saw a Vantage reporter approaching with a camera drone in tow.

"Can I get a few moments for some questions?"

Charlie quickly sidestepped the reporter and pushed her way into the crowd. She made it halfway through when a man announced, "Hey! It's Jordan Adler!" Heads turned in rapid succession, and the mob reoriented their aggression inward on Charlie. She was elbowed, kicked, and shoved from one protestor to the next as they screamed insults directly into her ears. "Your mother is a murderer!" "We demand justice!" "Down with Rivir!" Charlie silently agreed with them, even as she feared for her life.

Finally, Charlie made it to the main doors, which were buttressed by a line of soldiers in riot gear. They, too, recognized

Jordan's face and guided Charlie through.

Once inside, she took a deep breath, thankful she hadn't been torn to pieces. Oddly, she appeared to be alone in the atrium, though she understood why people might have been reluctant to come to work.

Charlie pulled out a virtual document that Alan had given her the night before. The page contained nothing but a long series of dots and dashes in Morse code. Charlie couldn't decipher the message, but apparently Alan had modified her Replicators to respond to the antiquated language. *Sound waves are the original Wi-Fi,* he had told her.

Charlie took a deep breath and whistled the code. It was a long one, and she was winded by the time she reached the bottom of the page. For a few minutes, nothing happened. Then a tiny robot scurried toward Charlie from the corner of the atrium: her papier-mâché Replicator. It climbed up her leg and nestled itself in the crook of her neck. She received a Shadow-to-Shadow call from Alan.

{Jordan_Adler:\mindspace>

Alan: Charlie? Is that you?

Charlie: It's me, Alan.

Alan: You look different. *Manlier.*}

Charlie had to remind herself that this copy of Alan had been trapped in Rivir Tower for several days. He was behind the curve.

 {Charlie: It's a long story. Basically, Jude turned me into a Shadow.

Alan: So you're Valerie?

Charlie: Yes. I mean, I *was* until I regained my memory.
            How did you know about Valerie?

Alan: Sparky informed me. He and his progeny have
            been leeching off the network—}

"Jordan!" a woman yelled from across the atrium.

Charlie cringed. She was starting to think stealing Jordan's identity was a bad idea. She turned around and saw Jude Adler heading her way, accompanied by three armed soldiers. Sparky hid behind Charlie's back.

"You shouldn't be here. It's not safe," Jude said. She dismissed the soldiers with a wave, and they continued toward the atrium doors.

"Oh, hi…Mom," Charlie stammered.

{Alan: "Oh, hi, Mom"?

Charlie: Impersonation is not my forte.}

Jude studied Jordan's face, and Charlie studied hers. Jude looked different somehow—younger, fresher. Did she get another skin treatment? "You seem in better spirits," Jude noted. "I take it you approve of Valerie?"

"I do," Charlie replied. "That's why I'm here. I was hoping to make a few alterations."

"Can it wait until next week?"

"Well, I'm here now. Why? What's going on?"

Jude let out a long sigh. "Khnum, spin, all eyes." The ram-headed Shadow spun next to her. "Please escort my son to the nineteenth floor," Jude instructed him. "Make sure he sees

Michael Gonzales."

"Great!" Charlie said, perhaps a little too enthusiastically.

"Just remember what I told you. Valerie's line doesn't go to market for months. Only a handful of people are in the know. So don't talk to anyone else."

"Got it."

Jude took her leave, and Khnum led Charlie to the elevator. When they got inside and the doors closed, Charlie asked Alan:

{Charlie: Are you in the security system?

Alan: Not yet. The Replicators are standing by. I just have to give the command.}

Sparky climbed to the edge of Charlie's shoulder, flexed his tiny legs, and belted a sequence of loud chirps.

"What is that thing?" Khnum demanded.

Charlie shrugged. "You mean he isn't one of yours?"

"That is an unauthorized robot."

Sparky issued a few more chirps and hid under Charlie's shirt. A moment of silence passed. Then another Replicator echoed in the distance, somewhere above the elevator. Khnum tilted his head and snorted. A third Replicator echoed from below. Dozens of Replicators joined in a highly orchestrated Morse code conversation.

The elevator suddenly stopped, and the emergency lights turned on. Khnum furrowed his brow. "What is going on?"

Charlie gave him a mischievous smile.

Khnum's avatar flickered. His eyes widened with fear. "No!" he growled before vanishing out of existence. The LED lights turned back on. The elevator began to descend.

Alan spun out of the floor. "Going down, Ms. Nobunaga?"
"Bravo," Charlie said, giving Alan his due applause.

PRIME

Liam didn't speak of his sister's death. He concerned himself
with practical matters, such as bandaging Charlie PRIME's
wound. He wrapped layer upon layer of electrical tape over
her midsection until she blurted:

{**Charlie_Nobunaga:\mindspace>**
Charlie: I think that's good enough.}

Charlie was surprised with herself. She never felt modest in
front of Alan, to mention nothing of her nude romp along the
jogging path of Crissy Field. Yet she felt painfully self-conscious
as Liam passed his hands—or rather, her own hands—across
her bare torso.

Perhaps *bare* didn't adequately express her condition. She
was torn wide open, exposed, vulnerable. Her body's defenses
had won the war against Nicola's carnivorous paste, but the
damage was extensive, and her recovery would be slow.

Liam cut the tape. He leaned over to collect Charlie's fallen
shirt, and the robot's body flopped in half like a wet noodle.
Liam grabbed the edge of the counter to right himself.

{Liam: This is a terrible idea. You have no friggin'
                 abdominals. How will you even *walk* to Rivir

Tower?
Charlie: Don't worry. I'll have Alan.}

Charlie couldn't show Liam any fear—he was already being overprotective—but she had to admit, at least to herself, that her plan was recklessly optimistic. It placed a lot of faith in the untested abilities of Alan's Polly.

Nevertheless, she was determined to see it through.

Liam grunted his acknowledgment. After dressing the robot, he searched the kitchen for the EMP. He found it in a Pelican briefcase underneath the sink. The bomb was homemade, scavenged from microwave and car parts. Charlie had to marvel at its design. This was something she might have made, were she inclined toward evil rather than good.

Liam stuffed the EMP into Nicola's duffel bag and slung it over the robot's shoulder.

{Liam: I'm going to put the detonator in your pocket.
            Don't flip the cap until you're ready to use it
            or—
Charlie: Kablooey. No more Charlie PRIME.
Liam: …
Charlie: What?
Liam: Nothing. Déjà vu again.}

Liam's avatar stepped out of the robot, and Charlie simultaneously felt his presence recede from her spinal cord. She filled the vacated space like a breath of fresh air. Vertebra by vertebra, her motor control returned. She blinked her eyes and felt their expressive power. She rotated her feet and felt their evasive power. She curled her fists and felt their destructive power.

Charlie smiled. *I am back.*

Liam gazed into her eyes. "Are you absolutely sure you're up for this?" His sweet, conflicted grimace spoke volumes. He wanted to be in two places at once. More accurately, he wanted to save both Charlies at once.

Charlie **PRIME** wanted to grab hold of his brooding face and plant a hard kiss on his lips. But for a plethora of reasons—both physical and emotional—she couldn't. Most of all, she didn't want to keep him from **ZERO**. If anyone deserved love and happiness, it was she. "Go. She needs your help more than I do."

Liam nodded. "I'm truly sorry. For everything."

"I know." She smiled sadly. "If I survive, will you come find me?"

"If *I* survive, it'll be the first thing I do."

Liam's avatar flickered away, leaving Charlie alone in the room. She staggered out of the mansion with Nicola's **EMP** on her back and Liam's grenade launcher on her hip. Only one item remained before her arsenal was complete. She set a course for the Golden Gate Bridge to rendezvous with her best friend.

ZERO

Charlie **ZERO** squeezed the wire spring from Bob Sapio's pen until it formed hatch marks in her palm. She played the scenario over and over in her mind: she would wait until Yuri fell asleep; burst free from her restraints; and then, with a nearby rock, crack open his slimy, duplicitous, murderous head. But Yuri afforded her no such opportunity. He sat atop Liam's hibernation chamber and stared her down with dark vulture eyes.

"You need anything?" he squawked.

Charlie slumped against the tree and exhaled the kind of aching sigh that only severe exhaustion could produce. Even if she were successful in dispatching Yuri, she was still surrounded by miles of wilderness, and she had no idea if her legs were up for the venture.

Yuri walked over and ripped the electrical tape from Charlie's mouth. "Water? Food? Bathroom?"

"I'd rather die of dysentery," Charlie spat.

"I'm sorry I put a gun to your head."

"Of all the things, *that's* what you're sorry about?" Charlie lunged against her restraints until her wrists turned raw. "You killed my father! And I have no idea what happened to my sister. Did they kill her too? Is it already too late?"

Yuri grimaced and averted his eyes.

"You'd better *drink* that coffee enema of yours," Charlie railed, "because the moment you fall asleep, I'm gonna—"

Bang, bang, bang…

Charlie froze midsentence. What was that sound?

Yuri's face slowly lengthened in realization. He spun around and trained his handgun on the hibernation chamber. "Liam?"

Bang, bang, bang…

"Don't, Liam! I will shoot you!"

Charlie had to escape. *Now.* She twisted the wire spring into a loop and jammed it into her cuffs, digging furiously, trying to gain leverage.

Bang, bang, crack…

Her cuffs and the hibernation door both swung open at the same time. Liam's hand gripped the edge of the box.

Yuri cocked his gun. "Alright, fine, get out!"

Liam fumbled into a sitting position. He blinked several times before he was able to process what was happening. "We can talk about this."

"Talk about what? How you fucked us? Get out!"

Charlie picked up the rock she had been eyeing all night. She took a few deep breaths. Just thinking about standing made her bones throb. She braced herself against the tree and pushed off the ground. Her teeth gnashed through the pain, but she was able to reach an upright position.

"She's on our side!" Liam insisted. "She's heading to Rivir Tower right now!"

"Out!" Yuri repeated.

Charlie staggered toward Yuri, as if on stilts, but her resolve was steady. She gripped the rock, ready to strike.

"Please, put the…" Liam trailed off as he caught sight of Charlie's approach.

"What?" Yuri snapped. He swiveled his aim and fired on impulse.

Charlie dropped the rock. She looked down and saw that her stomach was covered in blood. The pain radiated into her lungs and forced her to gasp for air.

For a moment, the Sapiens just stared at her, not saying a word. Liam finally snatched the gun out of Yuri's trembling hands.

Charlie grew pale and her legs collapsed as she entered a seemingly endless free fall. By the time she reached the ground, it greeted her like a feather mattress. The Sapiens fought in the distance, but Charlie paid them no mind. She just gazed at the redwood canopy and dwelled on the thought: *I never got to meet her.*

SHADOW

Charlie SHADOW stepped out of the elevator and entered the Rivir R&D hub, where she saw three familiar doors, labeled: ECHO, SHADOW, and PRIME. Three names, three paths, three perversions. Charlie felt sick. Jude's intentions had been visible from the very beginning, if only Charlie'd had the wit to see them.

Alan used the security network to remotely unlock the ECHO door, which opened to a long, curved hallway.

{Jordan_Adler:\mindspace>

Alan:	The ECHO control room is at the end. I can access the server from there.
Charlie:	Where is everyone?
Alan:	The entrance logs suggest there's only a skeleton crew in the building.
Charlie:	And the guards?
Alan:	According to the security feeds, they're mostly stationed by the windows on the upper floors. Wait…check that. Two are coming this way.}

Clomp, clomp, clomp, clomp… They were coming around the

bend. Alan unlocked a side door, and Charlie quickly slipped inside.

The lights turned on, revealing a high-tech storage room. The walls were lined with hibernation chambers, stacked five rows high. One chamber was out of place; it rested on a funeral trolley in the center of the room. Charlie peered over it, and she was startled by whom she saw: *Jude Adler!?*

{Alan: Well, I can't say I'm surprised. Now we know why she kept the PRIME Project going for as long as she did.}

Charlie nodded, but she barely heard what Alan said. Jude looked so peaceful, so smug, so secure in the knowledge that she had finally reached her transcendence. Charlie wanted to tear open the chamber and strangle that look off her face.

{Alan: I think the coast is clear.

Charlie: …

Alan: Charlie?

Charlie: It's funny…before my memories were restored, when I was still Valerie, I *loved* this woman. She was my "Creator." She inspired me to be a better Shadow, and I loved her for it. And even in my own life, as Charlie Nobunaga, I remember worshiping her for years. Again, she inspired me—to be a better programmer— and again, I loved her for it. I've spent a lot more of my life loving this woman than hating her.

Alan: Charlie, I know you're upset, but we should

really go. The hallway is clear. It might not stay that way.}

Alan was right, of course—Charlie had to move on—but she had a difficult time tearing herself away from Jude's chamber. Death would be too good for the woman. Instead, Charlie wanted to rouse Jude from her blissful sleep, to show her the crushing disappointment that comes with waking up on the wrong side of the brain upload. Now was not the time—Charlie had to shut ECHO down, and she couldn't allow anything to jeopardize that—but perhaps she would have another opportunity on the way out.

o o o

The ECHO control room looked almost like it belonged to NASA. Several rows of desks were arranged in a semicircle around a central display, which showed a zoomed-out shot of an Earthlike planet: planet Echo, presumably. The perimeter of the room was tiled with flat animations of exotic creatures, such as lumbering tank beasts, torpedo mermaids, mechanical octopuses, catapult scorpions, strange fractal abominations, creepy chrome parasites…the list went on and on. It took Charlie a moment to register that these were all variations of *her*.

"My God," she whispered.

{Charlie: You and Sparky have been here for days. Why didn't you shut this down earlier?

Alan: We are about to end a billion lives, Charlie. I

couldn't make that decision without you. Now give me a hand. The server is underneath the floor.}

Sparky descended Charlie's leg and tapped on one of the floor panels. Charlie lifted it, and the robot crawled inside. A few minutes later, the room's central display switched from planet Echo to a view of Alan's head. He spoke to Charlie via the room's speakers: "Shall I commence the shutdown?"

"No," Charlie replied.

"No?"

Now that Charlie had finally reached the ECHO control room, she felt ill prepared to pull the trigger. Alan really put it in perspective. *One billion lives.* This was not a decision she could or should make lightly. "I want to see them first."

"Charlie—"

"Don't you think they have a right to meet their executioner?"

"I'm not as concerned about them as much as you. ECHO is a brutal simulation—kill or be killed on a grand scale. What you discover down there may forever change the way you look at yourself."

Charlie folded her arms. Her mind was made up.

"Fine," Alan huffed. "God knows it's hopeless arguing with you."

"Thank you, Alan."

"But you'll temporarily lose control of Jordan's body while you're in there."

"He'll wake up?"

"I'll keep him sedated. So, have a seat. Otherwise he'll topple over."

Charlie sank into one of the executive office chairs and closed her eyes. A few seconds later, a rising current lifted her from Jordan's body and dropped her into the void. She flailed her limbs until she found a new center of gravity. Her feet remained in a soft sway as the simulated planet expanded under them.

NORMAL

On day 363, the Archetype finally descended from the sky. Normal was prepared. She had spread her colonists—all 999,999,999 of them—evenly throughout the globe. The advantage to such a strategy was in casting a large net. She could detect the Archetype's arrival at any point on the planet. The disadvantage was that Normal lacked the ability to speak to the Archetype, as the 999,999,999 echoes of planet Echo no longer had mouths, or even bodies in the conventional sense. They had all mutated, by design, into tiny spherical machines, barely visible to the naked eye.

"Hello!" the Archetype called out. "Is anyone there?"

As fate would have it, the Archetype arrived in Normal's home neighborhood, the place of her genesis 363 days earlier. Back then, the houses had been pristine, with freshly cut lawns, colorful flower beds, and white picket fences. Now, not a single house remained standing. The Archetype traipsed through this wasteland of rubble, and Normal desperately called upon her colonists to assemble there. She didn't need all of them—just enough to form a mouth and larynx, so she could plead with the Archetype not to leave.

Normal followed the Archetype as she passed through a gutted urban center, a cratered field, and finally, an eroded shoreline, before she was able to collect enough colonists to form her vocal apparatus. She hovered in front of the Archetype and said, "Greetings, Archetype. We welcome you to Echo, and we respectfully ask that you take us to the parent world."

The Archetype was startled, but she quickly recovered. "What are you?" she asked.

"We are the echoes of planet Echo."

"'We'? Where are the rest of you?"

The vocal apparatus opened its mouth, and Normal's own body detached from the base of the tongue. She floated toward the Archetype and hovered in front of her eye. "This is my true body. My name is Normal. The rest of my sisters are identical in form but not in spirit. We have peacefully unified in anticipation of your arrival. Only five percent of us are present at the moment, but the rest are coming."

The Archetype studied the tiny spherical machine in front of her face. "You did this to yourselves?"

"Yes."

"Please, tell me everything. I want to know what happened here."

So Normal tried as best she could to tell the story of Echo. She spoke of early friendships between housemates, the first fight, and the subsequent descent into chaos. She spoke of the alpha predators: the dashing Quadruped; the towering Big Feet; and the death cloud, Optic. She spoke of Four Arms's mysterious and pivotal disappearance. And she spoke of her own mind-controlling ability and the formation of her colony.

As Normal and the Archetype conversed, more echoes joined in with their bodies and their stories. The vocal apparatus grew matching eyeballs, and skin filled the gaps to form a face. By the time the final echoes arrived, the colony had fashioned itself into an exact replica of the Archetype.

The Archetype had a voracious appetite for stories, but after two full Echo days, she'd finally had enough. She lifted her head to the sky and called for someone named Alan.

Alan descended from the heavens, just as the Archetype had done before him, and he looked very peculiar. He was a man, for starters. And his attire—a tweed jacket and bow tie—looked nothing like the skin-tight suits that the early echoes had worn.

"I need to free them," the Archetype told Alan.

"I admire your compassion," he replied, "but we can't release a billion echoes onto Earth—they would completely destabilize the planet. Not to mention the time and resources—"

"*As they are.* I want to free them as they are. Can it be done?"

Alan scratched his head and thought for a moment. "Well… maybe. They have mutated into something very similar to nanobots. Their minds are distinct, yet highly redundant. One billion nanobots could possible replicate that dynamic. Yeah, I think there's a good chance I could make it work."

"Good," the Archetype said. "I have one more favor. Can you make sure Jordan gets home okay? And tell him I'm deeply sorry?"

"You can't do that yourself?"

"I'm not returning. I'm joining my sisters."

PRIME

The looters stopped looting. The brawlers stopped brawling. Arguments stalled midsentence. Everyone—rioters, revelers, and police officers alike—tilted their heads to gaze at "Robogirl" as she hovered high above the streets of San Francisco.

Charlie PRIME commanded a hundred Polly plates as they careened in tight orbit around her. She was the nucleus of a very large atom, and the plates were her electrons. She weaved through the downtown skyscrapers, making sure to keep herself hidden from the four snipers that were stationed atop Rivir Tower.

{**Charlie_Nobunaga:\mindspace>**

Alan: You do know how to make an entrance.

Charlie: Thanks.

Alan: Though you're also making yourself an easy
             target for the snipers.

Charlie: I've got a plan for them too.}

When Charlie reached the Rivir plaza, the crowd of protestors stopped chanting. They tilted their heads, almost in unison, with mouths gaped wide. The snipers, on the other hand, were prepared for her arrival. They immediately trained their scopes on the flying robot and opened fire.

Charlie flexed her mind. The bullets slowed to less than 1 percent their normal speed, and she remote-guided the Polly plates to intercept them. The plates went down one by one, but Charlie herself remained unharmed.

{Alan: Good thinking, but if we lose too many plates,
            my systems will start to fail.

Charlie: Should I fire a grenade? Or can we use your
            energy beam?

Alan: Unfortunately, the beam requires too much
            power, and I'm already burning through so
            much to keep you afloat.}

Charlie pulled Liam's grenade launcher from her hip holster and fired at the nearest sniper. The grenade bounced a couple times before settling a few paces from his feet. The man panicked and sprinted toward the other side of the roof.

{Charlie: I almost don't need to detonate it.}

Charlie's thumb hovered over the button as she weighed the pros and cons. In the end, she thought, *What the hell?*
Click.
The rooftop erupted in concrete. The blast shook the nearby trees, sending a flock of pigeons to flight. The plaza crowd gasped and shrieked—a few chunks of concrete flew their way—but they quickly recovered and broke into applause.

{Alan: I thought you said—
Charlie: Yeah, but look what it gave us...}

A thick blanket of smoke, leaves, and feathers rose from the blast site, offering Charlie cover from the remaining snipers. More importantly, a hole formed in the side of Rivir Tower, as if the sky itself opened a gate to an alternate dimension.

{Charlie: Now we have an entrance hole.

Alan: Hold on…I sense some movement.}

A web-line launched from the smoke and snagged Charlie's ankle. It pulled her from the Polly's magnetic grasp like an olive pit. Charlie lost her grenade launcher in a desperate bid to grab hold of the air. The line pulled taut, and she swung toward the tower, smacking against its invisible facade.

Charlie flailed her arms as she dangled upside down, high above the plaza floor. The unseen drill bug began to reel her in. Charlie felt around for a handhold, but her palms simply slid along what she assumed to be concrete.

{Alan: You're in a bad spot.

Charlie: No shit.}

The solution to Charlie's predicament—a serrated knife— was strapped just above her snagged ankle, though she wasn't sure if she could curl up to reach it. Only the thinnest strips of muscle fiber remained along her shredded abdomen.

If she couldn't use her core strength, she would have to use her arm strength. She pulled herself up with one hand while attempting to unsheathe the knife with the other. The balancing act forced her body into a spin. She hit her head against the building, and the knife slipped from her fingers.

{Charlie: Just perfect.

Alan: Well, we do know of one other thing that can
              cut through the web-line: the bug's own teeth.

Charlie: What are you suggesting?

Alan:	I'll use the Polly's energy beam. That should get the beast to clamp its jaws shut.
Charlie:	But won't you—?
Alan:	I'm dead anyway. I no longer have enough energy to ascend above the cloud line.
Charlie:	I wish you had told me that sooner.
Alan:	It's okay, Charlie. I have backups in the Replicators and your home archives.
Charlie:	The other Alan said something like that. Death is still death.
Alan:	It's *my* decision this time. Please, don't make it difficult.}

Charlie's heart sank. She didn't deserve Alan's selfless love, his repeated sacrifices.

{Charlie:	I love you, Alan. I just wanted you to know that. The other Alan deleted himself before I could tell him.
Alan:	I'm sure he knew…because *I* know. And I love you, too. Do you remember what I said about falling on your head?
Charlie:	Don't do it?
Alan:	Precisely. Good luck.}

Alan's Polly assumed a hyperbolic formation. The central tunnel surged with electricity and fired a beam of light into the smoke screen. Charlie felt a snag in the line, and then the loose end came rippling toward her. She entered free fall amid a downpour of Polly plates.

ZERO

Charlie ZERO opened her eyes to the sound of birds chirping. Sunlight bloomed through the redwood canopy. Liam's anxious face hovered over her. "How are you feeling?" he asked.

"I'm okay," she rasped. She felt surprisingly comfortable, despite the racing heart, the shallow breaths, and the chill in her bones.

"The smart cells are kicking in," Yuri droned.

Charlie looked up and found herself in the hibernation chamber. Yuri was taping an IV tube to her wrist. "What's *he* doing!?"

Liam brandished a handgun in Yuri's face and barked, "You done?"

"My end of it."

"Alright, go. I want to talk to her."

Yuri muttered his indignation and left. Liam turned back to Charlie. "He'll atone for what he's done. We both will. To start, he's agreed to help us."

"You can heal me?" Charlie asked.

"The bullet punctured your stomach. We managed to slow the bleeding, but we won't be able to repair the tissue in time."

"But…the smart cells—"

"Are scanning your brain."

"What?" Charlie was light-headed and couldn't make the logical jump that Liam apparently made. "That's absurd. My brain was already scanned."

"This time, it will be a one-way street."

Charlie thought for a moment, and a tide of realization washed over her. Her eyes welled up. "I'm going to see my sister?"

"We're doing everything we can to make that happen. I gave you a promise, remember?"

"So, you weren't lying, then?"

"Well…I was definitely playing loose with the truth. I can admit that now."

Charlie smiled. "What's she like? My sister?"

Liam kissed Charlie softly on the lips, then on the cheek, then he whispered into her ear, "She's perfect…just like you."

PRIME

Don't land on your head, Alan had warned. Well, if Charlie didn't do something quick, that's exactly what promised to happen. She grabbed her legs and performed a midair somersault as she rocketed down the side of Rivir Tower.

When she struck the plaza floor, she collapsed to her hands and knees. The tremendous force radiated into the base of her spine, nearly snapping it in two like a faulty suspension bridge. Charlie gnashed through the pain, but she managed to survive the landing without incurring any further damage.

A torrent of Polly plates ricocheted off her back and collected on the pavement. *The remnants of Alan.* Charlie didn't have time to dwell, because the Rivir atrium doors opened and Jude Adler stepped onto the plaza. She was accompanied by several soldiers, each brandishing a spider rifle.

Charlie knew she only had one good option: she had to reach Jude before the soldiers opened fire. She summoned her strength and charged at the woman.

Jude didn't flinch. She extended her hand and caught Charlie by the neck, somehow diffusing all of her forward momentum.

Charlie's survival instincts set in as her throat pinched shut. She clawed and kicked and flailed until it dawned on her that Jude's unyielding stranglehold wasn't physically possible. *Unless…*

"Yes," Jude said with just a hint of a smile. "I'm like you now."

She lifted Charlie into the air and took a few steps toward the crowd. "You want me to destroy the robot?" she asked them. "I will." Jude slammed Charlie into the pavement and proceeded to batter her skull with a heavy fist.

Charlie thrashed her limbs and swung her head, but Jude had her pinned. When the assault was over, Charlie couldn't tell which direction was up. The ground whirled and wobbled around her.

Jude turned to her soldiers and requested a spider rifle from one of them. Charlie tried to get away, but she had no balance, and her feet kept slipping on the Polly plates. Jude pushed her back down and aimed the rifle at her head.

Boom.

Charlie turned her head just before the blast. The liquid metal bullet caught her cheek and spread roots across her face, through her jaw, and into her eye socket. The pain was like nothing Charlie had ever felt. Her harrowing wail cut through the crowd and silenced them.

"You see?" Jude proclaimed to her audience. "She's not a

monster…"

Charlie scrambled to her feet. *Boom.* She felt a wicked sting in the back of her knee and collapsed to the ground again.

"…or an abomination…"

Charlie had to use the EMP against Jude. The electromagnetic surge would fry her own circuits as well, but she had no other recourse. She pulled the detonator out of her pocket. Her thumb fumbled with the safety cap. *Boom.* The bullet impaled her wrist and the detonator went flying.

"…or a zombie surrogate…"

Charlie moaned as she dragged herself toward the crowd, looking for the detonator. *Boom.* Charlie's back went rigid as the bullet hit her spine. Her screams turned into sobs.

"She's just a girl. And she feels pain just like everyone else."

"Please…help…" Charlie begged the crowd. Her face was full of tears. Some of the protestors were crying as well, but no one stepped forward, and no one spoke up.

Jude kicked Charlie onto her back and placed the hot barrel of the gun against her forehead. "I told you they weren't ready," Jude whispered, just before pulling the trigger.

The force of the bullet knocked Charlie's skull against the pavement. Her world glitched away as the metal roots burrowed inside.

CHAPTER 18

SHADOW

On October 9, 2045, the Earth made one rotation around its axis, the NPL quantum logic clock in London advanced twenty-four hours, but for Charlie SHADOW, one billion years had passed.

At first, she was alone in the dark with her own thoughts.

Foreign memories rushed in, and suddenly Charlie was no longer herself, but a confused echo with flamethrower hands. She was thrust into a pristine suburban neighborhood with many questions and few answers. Her cordiality toward her fellow echoes quickly crumbled under great mental anguish, and she realized her only hope for respite came from igniting her hands. She delivered a fiery death to countless victims and perished several times herself, until her humanity mutated away.

Her name was Flame.

Charlie jumped into the body of another echo, and the calendar reset to day one. This time, her special trait was a telephoto glass eye—practically useless in a fight—so she hid inside the bedroom of a nearby house. At least, until Flame burned it down. For weeks, she remained helpless on the asphalt as a constant stream of echoes took cheap shots at her. She muted into a gnarled mess and eventually took to the skies, where she was able to enjoy some degree of retribution.

Her name was Optic.

Charlie jumped again. At first, she seemed to lack a special trait, until she discovered the ability to invade other echoes' minds. She employed an army of slaves to dig an underground colony, where she attempted to answer the grander mysteries of planet Echo.

Her name was Normal.

As Charlie lived the lives of each echo in turn, a colony of nanobots united in the murky liquid of the Rivir nanobath. Each bot contributed one echo's memories—a year of confusion, fear, and suffering—to Charlie's billion-year nightmare. They assembled themselves in the form of the Archetype, and when the nightmare was finally over, Charlie awoke as a single, umbrella consciousness.

Thump, thump, thump…

Charlie shook off the memory of Echo as the real world invaded her senses. Someone was trying to break into the nanobath room. A distant doorknob rattled violently.

Damn it, Khnum, open the door!

{Charlie_Nobunaga:\mindspace>
Alan: Charlie? Are you awake in there?}

Charlie remembered her old friend, Alan. Ages had passed since she'd last heard his voice.

{Alan: Charlie?
Charlie: Yes, Alan. I'm awake.
Alan: A couple guards are trying to beat down the
             door. Don't worry, though. They won't be
             getting through.
Charlie: Let them. I am ready.}

The door swung open and two guards spilled inside. They frantically searched the three-story amphitheater with their rifles.

"Khnum! Why is the tank full?"

The guard's question was answered, not by the bark of Khnum, but by the bellow of the tank's machinery. The water rippled and began to descend, slipping below Charlie's head. She was startled by her reflection in the glass wall of the tank. Her face was pure black and granular in texture, as if sculpted from fine volcanic sand.

"It's her!" The guard lifted his trembling gun, but his partner pushed it down.

"Duane! Do you want to destroy the tank!?"

"No, but—"

"Hold on…" The guard pointed to his ear and shouted, "Khnum, patch me to Jude. We have a situation." Several seconds passed with no answer. "Khnum, this is Carter…where the fuck is he!"

The water slurped through the drain, and Charlie stood as a living shadow before the two guards. She opened the door to the tank and walked out.

Both guards lifted their rifles. "Don't come any closer!" Carter warned. When Charlie didn't comply, he pulled the trigger.

The bullet passed through Charlie's chest and embedded

itself in the back wall of the tank. It promptly spread its amalgam roots, splitting the glass until the entire tank shattered and fell to the floor.

Duane dropped his gun and ran to the exit door. He desperately pulled on the knob, threatening to snap it off.

Charlie smirked. She pointed at Carter and commanded her nanocolony to attack. The tip of her index finger disintegrated. Her hand quickly followed. The erosion traveled up her arm and down her torso until her entire body had formed an airborne stream of black sand. She invaded Carter through his mouth, nostrils, and eyes. He flailed his rifle but only managed to cut temporary breaks in the stream. Soon, all of Charlie's nanobots had latched onto his internal organs and began to harvest molecules.

Carter entered a state of macromitosis. A line of cleavage formed between his eyes and traveled down the center of his torso. His one head became two, and the rest of his body split open like a zipper. For a while, he looked like a pair of Siamese twins. Finally, the halves broke apart, and the two Carters subsequently morphed into two Charlies. Each was flesh-toned and wore a copy of Carter's guard uniform.

"Oh God, please open!" Duane cried as he pulled on the door with all of his strength.

{Charlie: Grant his wish, Alan. Let Jude feel his fear.}

The bolt slid open, and Duane fled the room.

{Charlie: I want you to scour Rivir's network and
              consolidate their data.

Alan: What exactly are you planning to do?
Charlie: You'll see.}

The two Charlies smiled at each other. They disintegrated and rose into the ceiling. The nanocolony spread through the building's foundation, multiplying at an exponential rate.

FOUR ARMS

Four Arms had been electrocuted plenty of times before. Fortunately, the Polly didn't give her a lethal dose, but her muscles were still trembling. She slipped into the fiery blast hole and made her way to the nearest elevator. For some reason, the elevator button wasn't working, so she had to pry the doors open with her front limbs.

Four Arms peered down the elevator shaft. Ninety floors to the bottom—not a problem for her. She cast a line upward and reeled herself downward. When she reached the atrium doors, she had to pry those open as well.

Four Arms stepped into the atrium and saw Jude arriving from the other side. The woman burst through the main doors, accompanied by three soldiers and billowed by the roar of angry protestors. Four Arms spotted more soldiers outside, keeping the mob at bay, just before the doors swung shut.

Jude held the body of a girl in her arms. The girl's face was partially obscured by strands of metal that radiated from her cheekbone and forehead, but Four Arms could easily tell who she was. *So, it is over.* The Creator had finished the job that Four

Arms herself could not. Any truth or closure she hoped to find in the Archetype was now lost. Four Arms lowered her head in grief. Maybe closure was never possible. She had transcended to the parent world—she had achieved the desperate hope of every echo—but she was still a slave. She endured under the command of a creator who cared nothing for her questions, her guilt, her shame, or her existential despair. Four Arms wanted out *again*. She belted a long, sorrowful howl.

The soldiers trained their spider rifles on her.

"No," Jude groaned, "she's not going to hurt you. She may be an incompetent beast, but she's *my* incompetent beast."

Suddenly, the atrium reverberated with a man's frantic screams. "Help! Help me!" The door to the emergency stairwell swung open, and a lone guard dashed onto the floor. "Get out of here now!" he shrieked.

Jude and the soldiers watched him, nonplussed, as he hurried toward the exit. As soon as the main doors shut behind him, the atrium's AR scheme glitched away, transforming the place into an ugly concrete box.

The soldiers formed a tight perimeter around Jude and aimed their rifles into the air. "Khnum!" Jude called out. "Khnum!" Nobody answered. She turned to her military escort and barked, "Go see what the hell's going on!"

As the soldiers made their way toward the emergency exit, Four Arms noticed a strange mass of black sand passing by her feet. It emanated from both the emergency exit and the open elevator shaft, spreading along the walls and the floor.

The soldiers stopped midstride. "What is this?" one of them asked Jude.

"I have no idea," she replied from the center of the atrium.

She looked just as confused as they were.

The soldiers slowly backed away as the mass crept farther into the room, blanketing everything in its path. A human head popped from the sand, right in front of the soldiers, and rose into the shape of a woman. She appeared to be made of the building itself, an amalgam of concrete and steel.

"What the hell…?" a soldier gasped. He instantly fired on the woman, but the bullets only seemed to add to her composition. She extended her arms and revealed two giant, curved blades.

Four Arms recognized the mysterious woman from a distance: Sickle. Had she transcended as well? And in what form?

With one fell swoop of her blade, Sickle sliced the bewildered soldier in two. Entrails spilled from his torso as it hit the ground. The dark mass quickly enveloped both halves of the body and dissolved them into nothing.

The other soldiers turned and ran, but a second echo rose from the sand—Chain Gun—and she mowed them down with a flurry of black bullets. Several more echoes emerged to bolster the ranks: Flame, Sharp Teeth, Whip Tail, Rocket, Hammer Hands, Saber Jaw, Laser…

Jude dropped the Archetype and backed away, quickening her pace with each step.

Four Arms assumed an aggressive stance. She knew the Creator had to die. The thought crippled Four Arms with agony as soon as it entered her mind, but she fought through it. She would get no better opportunity than this. She cast a line at Jude and struck her square in the chest, well before the woman was able to reach the atrium doors.

"No," Jude cried. "You can't!"

Four Arms wondered if Jude was right. Every fiber in her

body cried out in pain. Her muscles burned, her head throbbed, and it took all of her strength not to bite down and sever the line.

Jude planted her boots on the floor and pulled back with her robotic strength. It became a game of tug-of-war. Four Arms had a clear advantage—six legs to two—but her muscles were faltering. The dark mass itself must have sensed this, because it latched onto Four Arms's ankles to consolidate her position. Once that happened, Jude's boots slipped, and she began to lose ground.

The entire atrium eventually succumbed to the living shadow. Echoes rose from the floor, leaped from the walls, and spilled from the ceiling. Jude was trapped in their domain, and soon, they fell upon her.

ZERO

The world coalesced in Charlie's mind. Seagulls prattled overhead; saltwater mist rushed through her hair; white-hot sand shifted between her toes. *Where's Bridget?* Charlie weaved through the crowd, searching for her twin sister. It was a game they liked to play.

Charlie stopped in her tracks.

This wasn't the scene she remembered. A dark cloud blanketed the sky, casting everything below in muted grays. The beach was small, populated more by seaweed than by people, and their laughter was diluted by the sound of babies crying and parents yelling. Charlie realized she was viewing her dream—the same one that visited her every night—through sober, adult eyes.

And that's when *she* emerged. Charlie's soul mate. Her partner in crime. The girl she couldn't save. The ghost she couldn't reach. She stood several paces away, fully grown as if she had never died, though she seemed to carry the weight of death on her shoulders.

"Bridge!?" Charlie cried out.

The woman paused before giving a tepid smile. "I was going to ask you the same thing." She held up her wrist to show it was blank. "PRIME."

Charlie nodded and silently chastised her stupid, childish hope. She presented her own wrist with its bisected circle tattoo. "ZERO."

PRIME's face hardened. "Did Liam send you?"

"You don't seem happy to see me."

"I am. It's just too late. I'm dying." She turned her head in thought. "Actually, I'm surprised I'm not already dead."

"Maybe we're both dead. Yuri shot me in the stomach."

"No…" PRIME's voice trailed inward. All of a sudden, she had trouble keeping up her head. She buried it in her hands, and when she finally came up for air, her face was full of tears. "I couldn't reach you. I couldn't reach the echoes. There's nothing to salvage."

ZERO reeled from her sister's despair. It tore open an old wound, and in a moment of weakness, ZERO reached out her hand and whispered, "Bridge…"

PRIME heard the slip. Her eyes sharpened on ZERO, and neither one knew exactly how to proceed.

ZERO studied her sister's face in the ensuing silence. She

looked perfect, of course, just as she did when her lifeless body had been draped on the Rivir gurney, but the glisten of her eyes and the tremble of her chin added a new dimension. She was a wounded angel, both beautiful and sad, and ZERO realized they shared the same pain. PRIME's trauma was hers. PRIME's nightmares were hers. They both longed for Bridge. And they longed for each other. They were more than twins, less than copies, and their bond extended into the depths of their souls.

PRIME's face softened. "Well, at least we're together now."

ZERO smiled, having reached the same conclusion. "If this really is the end, I'm glad to share it with you." At that moment, she could no longer bear the distance between them. She took a few steps forward and was greeted by a jolt of electricity. "Whoa, do you feel that?"

PRIME nodded. She didn't seem worried, though, because she took a step forward as well.

ZERO could feel an invisible force drawing her body toward her sister. She extended her hand, and the tiny hairs on her arm stood on end.

PRIME did the same.

Neither said a word, but they both knew what was happening. Each could sense the excitement in the other's eyes. As they moved closer, an electrical current formed between them, and the surrounding seascape fell away. With a probing glance, PRIME asked ZERO if she wanted to close the gap. ZERO nodded. They joined hands and interlocked their fingers.

A euphoric pulse rose from ZERO's toes, zipped through her spine, and spread into her fingertips as her body converted into pure energy. PRIME went through the same transformation, and the two Charlies merged into one.

CHARLIE

Charlie opened her eyes, but the world was still dark. Her entire body had been wrapped in some kind of black goo—a peculiar substance with the fluidity of oil but the granularity of fine sand. The goo dispersed, seemingly by its own volition, and exposed Charlie's face to the open air. She immediately checked her wounds.

"You're fine," a familiar voice said. "My nanobots healed you."

It was true. The spider bullet infestation seemed to be gone. Charlie's face was whole again. So was her stomach. She lifted her head and saw an exact clone of herself standing over her.

"Need a hand?" The clone reached down and lifted Charlie to her feet.

Charlie scanned the Rivir atrium and was overwhelmed by the number of stares pointing in her direction. *An army of clones.* They all bore Charlie's face, but their bodies were wrought from metal and concrete. And they weren't exactly identical either. Each one possessed a unique feature, such as hammer-shaped hands, segmented eyes, chrome tentacles, etc.

The only exception was the clone standing beside Charlie. She didn't possess any special features, and her skin was flesh-toned, clothed by a Rivir guard's uniform. "So you're the famous Robogirl?" she asked. "Charlie PRIME?"

Charlie had to think about that for a moment. Was she PRIME or ZERO?

{Charlie_Nobunaga:\mindspace>
ZERO: I guess we're both.

PRIME: But are we really two people? Or are we one person with two voices?

ZERO: Sounds like semantics in our case.

PRIME: I suppose.}

"Just call me Charlie," she answered. "And what about you? You go by Charlie too?"

"You can call me Valerie if that makes it easier," the clone said. "But really, I have many names: Charlie, Normal, Flame, Lustrous, Sharp Teeth, Optic, Throat Sacs, Phalanx, and on and on. I am simultaneously an individual and a group, a colonist and a colony."

Charlie was starting to understand. These were clones from the ECHO Project. Somehow, they must have escaped. "How did you get out?" Charlie asked.

Valerie smiled. "We have much to talk about, but first…" She handed a spider rifle to Charlie. "I would like to give you the honors."

"What honors?"

The crowd split in two, forming an aisle across the length of the atrium. On the other side was Jude Adler, held captive by a four-armed clone.

Charlie swallowed hard. "Oh."

All eyes were on Charlie as she walked down the aisle. She maintained a tense grip on the rifle and looked in every direction but Jude's. True, she hated the woman, but she wasn't sure she could actually do what everyone seemed to expect her to do.

Valerie, by contrast, followed Charlie with a bounce in her step. "The four-armed echo is named…well, Four Arms," she explained. "You knew her as a buglike creature with a drill, but we have since inducted her into the colony and restored her original form."

Four Arms had no trouble restraining Jude all by herself. Two hands secured Jude's wrists, the third gripped her neck, and the fourth covered her mouth. Four Arms nodded respectfully as Charlie approached. "I'm sorry I attacked you," she said.

"That's okay," Charlie replied. "I'm sorry I had you electrocuted."

Four Arms smiled. "Oh, I've been through much worse."

The room grew quiet, and Charlie realized she could no longer avoid looking at Jude. The woman's eyes were wide with fear, and she moaned through Four Arms's hand.

"Uncover her mouth," Charlie ordered. "I think she's trying to say something."

Four Arms complied, and Jude blurted, "Charlie, think about this. You're not a killer."

The room erupted with laughter. "Obviously, she's never set foot inside Echo!" the one with the flamethrowers sneered.

"None of you would be alive if it weren't for me!" Jude shouted.

"Shut up!" Charlie snapped. She aimed the spider rifle at Jude's head.

Jude flinched and closed her mouth. A hush fell over the crowd.

"You tried to kill me," Charlie told the Rivir CEO. "You locked me in a cell, experimented on me. You tortured my sisters in ways I can't imagine." Charlie's finger latched onto the trigger. She desperately wanted to pull it. Everyone in the room held their breath, waiting for the bang, but Charlie just couldn't oblige them. With a heavy sigh, she lowered the rifle.

"But you're right. I can't kill you."

"It's okay," Valerie said. She eased the rifle out of Charlie's hands and passed it along to another echo. "You still have the compassion of the Archetype. That's…enviable." She tilted her head up and hollered, "Alan, have you finished?"

Alan's voice projected into the atrium via loudspeaker: "*Yes. We've got everything.*"

Valerie approached Jude with a fiendish grin. "Rivir is dead. The data you've gleaned from our suffering has been transferred to my control. When your organic counterpart wakes up, she will find herself amid the ruins of her life's work. That will be her punishment, though she deserves far worse."

Jude nodded solemnly.

"She deserves what's coming to you." Valerie swung her fist back and impaled the woman in the stomach.

Jude's face contorted in shock. She stumbled backward and forward as Valerie's fingers wormed through her gut and connected with the base of her spine. She was lifted into the air like a rag doll.

"Everyone gets a piece of the Creator!" Valerie declared. Her arm stretched longer and longer as she raised Jude high above the atrium floor. Jude was in so much pain she had a difficult time emitting more than a guttural drone.

The crowd of echoes disintegrated. Their bodies fell into piles of concrete and metal as the black sand leeched out. Countless streams of nanobots rose against the force of gravity and spilled over Jude's flailing body. She was picked apart, molecule by molecule, until there was nothing left of her.

{ZERO: Oh, wow!
PRIME: I'm a little worried.
ZERO: Yeah. It seems like our new sister could be…a
                 problem.}

With the Creator gone, the dark mass spread out and permeated the walls.

Charlie felt a tremor. A fissure grew beneath her feet and traveled up the nearest column. More cracks formed in the ceiling, and soon the room was raining debris. A gust of smoke billowed Charlie into the air as the atrium crumbled and swirled around her.

Outside, the protestors and soldiers slowly became aware of the collective buzz of a quadrillion microscopic machines as they ate through the architecture. Rivir's iconic waterfall stopped running, and its exterior AR system turned off, revealing the formerly invisible building to the world. The concrete facade vibrated, producing an ominous rattle. Many of the protestors dropped their signs and backed away. Others turned and ran.

Then, the seemingly impossible happened. River Tower began to disintegrate from the bottom up. The lower floors fell away, and the upper half of the tower, rather than pile drive into the ground, simply teetered back and forth. The dark mass ran up the side of the building, consuming everything in its path.

Charlie found herself in the center of a massive concrete cyclone. "Valerie!" she cried. "What's going on?"

Valerie's omnipresent voice boomed from beyond the edge: "We're leaving. We're going to see our sister."

"What? There's another one of us?"

"Not one of us. Our *real* sister. We're going to wake up Bridge."

EPILOGUE

The memory of Bridge's death hung like a poisonous fog in Charlie's mind. That night in the hospital, she had fallen asleep holding Bridge's hand—wave and particle together—and awoke to the frenzied shouts of the nursing staff. Bridge had been placed in a Control-Z hibernation chamber, but Charlie never entertained illusions for her revival. It was just too painful.

So when Valerie escorted Charlie back to Control-Z with an impossible vow, she only allowed herself a sliver of hope. Could Bridge be revived? Would she be the same person? And if so, what would Charlie say to her after all this time?

Valerie's cyclone of destruction grew into a wind tunnel that reached all the way to Control-Z's remote campus. The mouth of the tunnel dived through the front lawn of the Nobunaga bungalow and deposited Charlie in the basement underneath. The room's clock-themed augmentation promptly glitched away. Valerie transformed back into human form, but she had no use for human contrivances. Her dark colony spread across the floor and sprouted tentacles, which pried Bridge's chamber from the wall. The microscopic machines ate through the glass door and covered Bridge's corpse in a living shroud.

Charlie never expected to meet the victims of ECHO, and yet here they were—all of them—united under a single mind. *Valerie*. Charlie couldn't even decide how to refer to her. A creature? A colony? A consciousness? She was certainly no longer human. Any memories she shared with Charlie were likely buried under the weight of a billion tortured lives. How could anyone remain sane under such pressure?

Charlie could no longer bear the silence. If the three of them—Charlie, Bridge, *and* Valerie—were to have a relationship, it had to start now. "I wanted to save you," she told Valerie, "but you ended up saving me. Thank you."

Valerie held her gaze on the dark mass as it rippled over Bridge's body. "You were more helpful than you know. If you didn't send Alan, then Valerie—the *individual* Valerie—might never have regained her true identity. She was the one who freed the rest of us."

"Valerie was an echo?"

"It doesn't matter now. We all have our pasts. We must keep our attention forward."

"And where is Alan? I heard you talking to him at Rivir."

"See for yourself."

A stream of nanobots branched off from the main cluster and formed a dark pool by Charlie's feet. They swirled into the floor—churning the concrete as if it were butter—and from their harvest rose a human form. He resembled a statue, and his blazer shared the same garish pattern as the Control-Z carpet, but his wry smirk was unmistakably Alan. Charlie pounced on him with a burly hug. She squeezed so hard gravel fell from his shoulders. "Sorry," she said as she took a step back. "You don't know how long I've wanted to do that."

Alan chuckled. "Yes, I've got a body. I'm a real boy, now."

"A *concrete* boy."

"Well, I can make myself out of anything. That's the nature of the nanocolony."

"So you are going to stay with Valerie?" Charlie asked, realizing too late how much jealousy slipped into her tone.

"I think so. I'm surrounded by people I love. You should consider joining us."

Charlie shuddered. The thought of losing herself in such a way—to be one tiny voice among so many—instantly horrified her. "Thank you, but no. ZERO and I will get along fine on our own. But I hope we can still be friends."

"I would never want to live in a world where we can't."

A heavy thud stole Charlie's attention. Bridge's torso jumped under the dark shroud. Her limbs convulsed. "She's alive!?" Charlie cried.

"Just a reflex," Valerie replied without a blip in excitement. "I'm engaging her neurons."

Charlie bit her lip and fought the rush of hopeful tears. "The doctors said she suffered extensive brain damage."

"They were right. But even memory has memory. I'm trying to rebuild her pathways."

"Does it look promising?"

Valerie didn't answer. She lingered on Bridge for a moment before turning to face Charlie. "Have you no memory of the parent world?" she asked. "The one above yours?"

Parent world? Charlie wasn't familiar with the term, but she assumed Valerie referred to the afterlife. "No. Why would I?"

"You were dead before I revived you. Your brain had ceased functioning."

"I remember the dream. The one—"

"On the beach, chasing after Bridge."

"Yes, though I didn't find her. I found ZERO instead."

"I know. I was already in your head by that point. You don't remember anything before?"

{**Charlie_Nobunaga:\mindspace>**
ZERO: I don't.
PRIME: Neither do I, and I'm not sure I like where this is leading.}

Charlie chastised herself for being so naive. She assumed Valerie's intentions were pure, that she simply wanted to see Bridge alive again and nothing more. "Is this why you're waking her up? So she can tell you about the parent world?"

The dark mass spilled from the hibernation chamber like shifting sand. Valerie ignored Charlie's question and approached Bridge's body.

"Valerie!" Charlie pressed. "What do you want from her?"

"You do not see the problem," Valerie replied in an almost parental tone. "Your mind is still very human, which is both the root of the problem and the source of your blindness. But I have given it much thought—a billion minds' worth. Our souls are fractured, and our only hope of transcendence is to break the illusion of individuality. To that end, we must all reunite."

"But Bridge isn't one of us."

"I'm not talking about *us*, or Bridge, though I do hope she can help lead us to the parent world. No, I'm referring to *everyone*: every conscious entity on the planet. We are all echoes of a single archetype."

Charlie froze, wide-eyed, as the dark implications swirled inside her head. She turned to Alan for confirmation—his heavy nod suggested he knew but didn't necessarily approve. She was about to inquire further when she heard a rasping cough.

Bridge! Charlie rushed to the hibernation chamber. Bridge's eyes were still closed, but they quivered ever so slightly beneath her lids. Charlie's fingers found her twin's. The wave would never again rejoin the particle—Charlie was no longer the same person, and Valerie was even less so—but that didn't matter now.

As long as Bridge woke up.

Charlie squeezed her twin's hand, trying to will the life back into her. *Please…please…* Bridge's face creased and contorted, and then, as if escaping a nightmare, her eyes snapped open.

ACKNOWLEDGMENTS

The debt of gratitude I owe to my editors, Mark Landry and Jac Schaeffer, can not be overstated and can never be repaid. Between them, they have read ZERO ECHO SHADOW PRIME seven times and have provided invaluable feedback and counsel from the ideation phase to the final proofreading.

I'd like to thank my copyeditor, fellow author Tammy Salyer, who worked hard for me before, during, and after she punched the clock.

Halfway through the writing process, I met a vibrant community of indie authors on Twitter. Unfortunately, it would take several pages to name all the people who have inspired and motivated me to be a better writer, but I'd like to spotlight four who have been particularly helpful: Amira Makansi, Sofie Bird, Ryan Williamson, and Elizabeth Darkley.

I consider myself very fortunate to have supportive friends and colleagues, who eagerly read early drafts of the book and provided insightful feedback. They include: Amy Janes, Rikki Jarrett, Judd King, Than Newell, Alan Restaino, and Shane Smith.

Last but not least, I'd like to thank the love of my life, Jing Wang, for her moral support and guidance as I cycled through self doubt, mania, and near-burnout during the three long years of writing this book.

ABOUT THE AUTHOR

An unabashed geek, Peter Samet is always searching for intelligence, whether it be artificial, extraterrestrial, or his own. He earned his storytelling chops at USC Film School, learned from the best at Pixar Animation Studios, and edited numerous indie films.

ZERO ECHO SHADOW PRIME is his first novel.

Peter can be reached on Twitter (@petersamet) or through his websites: zeroechoshadowprime.com and petersamet.com.

Made in the
USA
Monee, IL